continued . . .

SWORN IN STEEL

A TALE OF THE KIN

DOUGLAS HULICK

A ROC BOOK

ROC
Published by the Penguin Group
Penguin Group (USA) LLC, 375 Hudson Street,
New York, New York 10014

USA | Canada | UK | Ireland | Australia | New Zealand | India | South Africa | China
penguin.com
A Penguin Random House Company

First published by Roc, an imprint of New American Library,
a division of Penguin Group (USA) LLC

First Printing, May 2014

Copyright © Douglas Hulick, 2014

ROC REGISTERED TRADEMARK—MARCA REGISTRADA

ISBN 978-0-451-46447-7

Printed in the United States of America
10 9 8 7 6 5 4 3 2 1

For Jamie, who probably lost more sleep on this one than I did. Thanks for putting up with me above and beyond the call of matrimony. And for my editor, Anne, who was patience incarnate. May all your future sophomore novelists be less of a pain than I was.

Acknowledgments

First, a hearty thanks to my writer's group, the inestimable Wyrdsmiths: Eleanor Arnason, Naomi Kritzer, Kelly McCullough, Lyda Morehouse, Sean M. Murphy, and Adam Stemple. I don't say it nearly enough, but I honestly don't know what I'd do without you guys. Thanks for your sharp eyes and wise words.

Likewise, a deep bow of gratitude to my beta readers, Justin Landon and Haddayr Copley-Woods. If the devil is in the details, I would be hard-pressed to ask for better devils than you.

I'd also like to thank all those who were so forthcoming with their help and expertise on topics myriad and sundry, whether or not I ended up using the information you provided (writing's like that some days): Jean Hetzel, Elizabeth Kalmbach, Kellie Hultgren, Ernesto Maldonado, Patrick Bailey, Terry "That Guy" Tindill, and quite a host of others, I'm sure I've failed to remember. Thank you, one and all.

Also, thanks to my two boys, Evan and Cameron, for putting up with me during this book. It wasn't always easy, I know, but you guys were great sports.

And lastly, a profound thank-you to everyone who took the time to drop me a note, stop by the Web site, shoot me a tweet, or generally checked on the progess of things. Three years is a long time to wait between novels, and to a person, every one of you has been gracious, understanding, and encouraging. I couldn't have asked for better readers if I tried. You guys are the best.

A Brief Note on the Use of
Cant in This Book

The various forms of "cant," or thieves' argot, in this book are inspired by records of actual use from various places and times throughout history, from Elizabethan England to twentieth-century American-underworld slang, and many places in between. I have been liberal with both the meaning and forms of many of these words, changing them as I deemed necessary for the story and world. In some places, I have altered either the definition or use of a term; in others, I have left them much as they were historically used. And, not surprisingly, I have also made up certain canting terms from the whole cloth.

So, in short, you will find cant both correct and incorrect, documentable and fanciful, in the following pages. For those who know nothing of the *patter flash*, I hope it adds to the story; for those who are familiar with it, I hope any creative license on my part doesn't prove too distracting.

The following is from a playbill for the only recorded performance of the comedy, The Shadow Prince: A Djanese Adventure in Three Acts, *penned by Tobin Thespes. It opened in the courtyard of the Twin Oaks Inn on the outskirts of Ildrecca and lasted for half an act before the performers were persuaded, at knife point, to leave the stage. No known copy of the play still exists.*

Dramatis Personae

Drothe—a thief and informer of humble origins, who through some small degree of skill and a great amount of luck has been promoted to the exalted rank of Gray Prince among his thieving Kin (much to his own dismay).

Bronze Degan—a member of the storied mercenary corps known as the Order of the Degans. Formerly a friend to *Drothe*, he was recently betrayed by the Gray Prince and has fled the Empire to parts unknown.

Fowler Jess—*Drothe's* spirited and oft temperamental companion. It is her job to "stand Oak" (watch over) the Prince while he seeks his rest.

Jelem the Sly—A Djanese gambler and magician, or Mouth, living in Ildrecca. He sells his magic to the highest bidder.

Christiana Sephada, dowager Baroness of Lythos—A former courtesan, now player at the Lesser Imperial Court. It is hinted that she has contacts among the criminal underworld, and maybe—dare it be said—blood ties, but this is only a rumor at best.

Emperors Markino, Theodoi, and Lucien—The Triuvirate Eternal: the cyclically recurring incarnations of the former emperor Stephen Dorminikos, founder of the Dorminikan Empire. *Markino*, aged and infirm, sits the imperial throne.

Chapter One

I sat in the darkness, listening to the slap of the waves against the side of the boat, and watched as the outline of Ildrecca loomed toward me.

Even with my night vision, the sea wall on this side of the Imperial capital was too vast to take in. It stretched off into the distance in either direction until my magically tinged sight gave way to the night. The city was a great, hulking mass: an irregular black line drawn against the star-speckled horizon. A city I was now having to creep back into.

My city.

I brought my eyes back down to the scale of men and the forest of narrow spires that seemed to grow from the waters of the Lower Harbor. Lights flickered among those masts, swaying and bobbing like nautical will-o'-the-wisps—ships' running lights moving in the soft breeze off the sea.

"I still say you should have killed him," said Fowler Jess.

I looked back over my shoulder. The Oak Mistress was crouched amidships, scowling like an unhappy cat at the water that surrounded the narrow caïque. She had both hands out, gripping the gunwales as if she might keep the craft from capsizing by force of will. Her green flat cap was jammed down on her head, but that hadn't stopped the breeze from setting stray wisps of blond drifting and dancing about her head, giving her an amber-gold halo in my night vision. With her fine features and normally bright eyes, it would have been an enchanting image, if not for the smudges of dust and mud and old blood on her face and collar. Well, that, and the dark circles under her eyes that had come from days of hard riding and little sleep.

Not that I was doing much better, mind. My thighs and ass had stopped being able to feel anything other than pain nearly three days back.

"We've already been over this," I said, reaching down and running an absent hand over the long, canvas-wrapped bundle at my feet. Reassuring myself for the fifth time in as many minutes that it was still there.

"Yes, we have," she answered. "And you're still wrong."

I glanced past her to the figure of the boatman standing in the stern, working his long oar with slow, easy strokes. He was chanting the Nine Prayers of Imperial Ascension to himself, partly to keep time for his work, and partly to assure us he wasn't eavesdropping. Boatmen who hired out to run the Corsian Passage at night without bow or stern lights knew better than to risk overhearing things. "Fine," I said, leaning forward and dropping my voice down to a proper whisper. "Let's say I'd done what you wanted and dusted Wolf: what then? What happens when word gets out that I broke my deal with him? What happens when people learn he kept his part of the bargain and I broke mine?"

"There's a hell of a lot of difference between keeping your promise to a bandit and honoring your word to another Gray Prince."

"Is there?"

"You damn well know there is!"

"On a good day, maybe, but now?" I pointed south, across the Corsian Passage, past the lights of the tiny harbor at Kaidos and the dark smudge of the hills beyond, toward the disaster we'd fled in Barrab. "With a fellow Gray Prince lying dead three days behind us, my dagger in his eye? With me being the last person, the last Kin, to see him alive?" I shook my head and barely managed to keep the rest of me from shaking along with it. Even now, the thought of the news coming up the Imperial High Road from Barrab made my stomach queasy.

I ran my hand over the canvas-wrapped sword at my feet again. It had been worth it; it had to have been worth it.

"No one besides us has any reason to think Wolf was involved with Crook Eye's murder," I said. "All anyone on the street is going to know is that two Gray Princes met, and one walked away. Me. What kind of story does that tell?"

"But with Wolf you could've always—"

"No, I couldn't," I said. "Because if I kill him, it looks like I'm trying to cover my tracks. If the street hears I dusted the bandit who snuck me out of Barrab past Crook Eye's people, it won't matter what else I do or say, the story will be set: Drothe dusted Wolf because he knew too much. At that point, I might as well take credit for Crook Eye's death and be done with it." I settled back on my seat. "No, as much as I hate to say it, Wolf does me more good alive than dead right now."

"So he just walks?"

"He just walks."

Fowler spit her opinion of that over the side of the caïque.

I turned back around and watched as the base of Ildrecca's city wall resolved itself into the dark jumble that made up the Lower Harbor. A couple of centuries ago, it would have been alight and busy even at this hour, with wine and spices and grain weighing down the docks until they groaned, the air rich with the shouts of men and the thump of tonnage and the smell of trade. But that had been before the empire decided to expand the landings on the north and east sides of the peninsula that held Ildrecca; now the richest vessels made their way around the city's horn to Little Docks and the Pilings and the merchant pier that had been added to the Imperial naval docks, called the New Wharf. The Lower Harbor, once the hub of Ildrecca's trade, had become the haunt of timber merchants and fishermen, salvage traders and night soil barges. And, of course, the Kin.

Barely two-thirds of the docks in Lower Harbor were in regular commercial use anymore, which left the rest for us. Smugglers, spies, and the occasional small-craft pirate—along with all the people and industries that catered to them—were the stock-in-trade of the cordon that had come to be known as Dirty Waters.

I hadn't left by this route on my way to meet Crook Eye, and I certainly hadn't planned on using it to sneak back into the city I called home. Then again, I hadn't planned on being framed for his murder, either. Not after I'd sworn the Prince's Peace, promising to keep my steel sheathed and my people at bay for the meet, just as he had. The criminals of the empire didn't expect much when it came to Gray Princes and our promises, but honoring the Peace was one of them. Without it, there was no reason to expect truces to be made, territories respected, negotiations offered, or Kin wars prevented. The Prince's Peace kept the legends of the Kin from slaughtering one another on the rare occasions they met, which in turn kept the blood and the chaos from trickling down to the streets. It kept us, if not civilized, then at least careful.

But more importantly, it kept things from getting out of hand. Because if things got out of hand among the Kin, that's when the emperor took an interest in us. And no one wanted that.

Our boatman grew quiet as we approached a set of water stairs, their steps leading down into the harbor. I'd barely felt the scrape of the keel on stone before Fowler was clambering up and over me, making for the stairs even as she sent the caïque to rocking. The boatman cursed. Fowler cursed. I grabbed the bundle at my feet and made it unanimous.

A moment later, the Oak Mistress was on the steps, scrambling up toward the quay as the boat settled.

I reached into my purse and pulled out a pair of silver hawks, then thought better of it and added three more, making sure none of them were clipped. The boatman stepped forward, easy and sure in the craft, and I placed a week's worth of work in his palm. To his credit, he nodded and pocketed the windfall without comment.

I turned and considered the slime-smeared steps, the rocking of the boat, and the canvas-wrapped bundle in my hands. I bent my knees, took a breath. . . .

"You want I should throw that to you?"

I blinked and looked back over my shoulder. "What?"

"The package," said the boatman. "Steps are tricky enough as it is; figure you don't need the added trouble of your hands being full."

"I've got it," I said. I turned back to the quay. I just needed to get the timing right. . . .

"Does it float?"

I jerked back. "What?"

"Wondered if it'd sink or swim if'n you dropped it. Wonder if you'll do the same, for that matter."

"Look—" I began.

"I don't need your girl tracking me down and cutting me up 'cause I let you drown," he said. "And I don't need you doing the same if you drop your cargo gettin' off my boat. Figure it's better for us both if I toss it to you once you're ashore."

I considered the steps, the boatman, the water all around us. Considered the canvas-wrapped sword in my hands.

"I ain't stupid," he said from behind me. "Last thing I want to do is cross the likes of you."

"Last thing I want to do is be crossed," I said softly. Mostly to myself.

"Drothe!" Fowler's voice came hissing down from the quay. "What the hell. What's taking so long?"

I hefted Degan's sword, feeling more than just the weight of steel and leather and canvas in my hands. There was history here; obligation; blood. Not to mention broken promises and memories.

I'd already lost him: I couldn't lose his sword. Not after having just found it in Crook Eye's possession. Not after having almost killed for it.

I handed the wrapped blade back to the boatman. Even if he were to row off with it, I stood a better chance of finding him than I did retrieving the sword from the bottom of the harbor.

I adjusted my stance, the muscles of my back and legs protesting, and waited for the caïque to bump up against the stairs again. When it did, I half stepped, half leapt across. Only one foot ended up slipping back into the water.

When I turned, the boatman had moved his caïque up,

bringing him even with me. He hesitated a moment, bending over the blade, and then tossed the long bundle in an
easy arc over the water. The blade landed in my arms almost before I had a chance to be worried. I drew the sword
in close, then looked out at the boatman. He was already
beginning to move away.

"Hey!" I called after him.

He turned his head but didn't stop working his oar.

"I forgot to ask," I said. "Has any news worth noting
come across tonight?" Such as, I thought, word of a Gray
Prince's death?

"This a test?"

"Straight."

He seemed to consider for a moment. "Naught I heard." A
flash of teeth in the gloom. "But then, I don't hear much, yeh?"

I smiled and began to turn away.

"Heya!" he called.

I looked back.

"Check the blade." Slight pause. "Your Highness."

His chuckle was still rippling across the water as I held
up the sword, but any anxiety I felt vanished as soon as I
saw what he'd done. A worn length of rope had been tied to
Degan's sword, running from the canvas-covered crosspiece
down to a spot just above the point, forming an impromptu
sling.

The boatman was on his way to becoming an amber-
limned smudge on the water by now, but I raised my hand
in thanks anyhow. I couldn't be sure if the sound that came
back was more laughter or just the water.

I passed my left arm through the rope, ducked my head
under, and let the sword settle across my back. It felt
strange, but it also felt good. I climbed the rest of the way
up the water stairs, my left foot squelching every other step.

Fowler was waiting at the top, her travel coat thrown
back to reveal the deep green doublet and split riding skirt
beneath. Scratch was standing beside her, his heavy hands
hanging loosely at his sides, his face as expressive as a
poorly carved block of granite. He was sporting a bloody
lip. Fowler had sent him ahead to scout out the docks and

arrange for discreet passage into Ildrecca. I didn't care for the results his face predicted.

"Problems?" I asked as I reached the top.

"Misunderstanding," said Scratch.

"How big of one?"

Scratch shrugged, meaning it could be anything from broken ribs to a broken neck for the other cove.

"Is it going to get in the way of using the Gate?" I said.

"Wouldn't recommend calling on Soggy Petyr."

Fowler and I exchanged a look. Soggy Petyr was one of the local bosses down in Dirty Waters, specializing in for-hire press gangs, stolen goods, and shaking down small ship-masters. He also controlled access to the oldest and largest hidden entry point this side of Ildrecca: the Thieves' Gate.

I pointed at Scratch's lip. "Petyr's boys?" I said, hoping for the best.

"Petyr."

I pinched the bridge of my nose. "Scratch. . . ."

"Called you a cut-rate cove. Called Fowler worse. Wanted to shake us down. Backhanded me when I told him where to go."

I sighed. I should have expected this. Various bosses and Kin had been testing me ever since the street had pro-claimed me a Gray Prince three months back. Turned out having the title and keeping it weren't the same thing, espe-cially when you made the jump from street operative to criminal royalty in less than a week. People wanted to make sure my rise hadn't been a fluke, that it wasn't dumb luck that had put me on top.

Never mind that it *had* been luck—the important thing was to rise above it. A handful of hard names from the likes of Petyr weren't going to bring me down, especially if I sent some of my people to "talk" to him once I was back inside the city. But tonight, in his territory, with only two coves on my blinders, the city gates locked until dawn, and a danger-ous rumor running up behind me? This wasn't the time or place to have a thin skin.

Unfortunately, it was starting to look like Scratch hadn't seen it that way.

"And you took it, right?" I said. "When Petyr showed you his hand, you stood there and you took it, right?"

Scratch rubbed thoughtfully at the knuckles of his left hand and didn't answer.

"Right?"

"Man hits you, sometimes you don't think. Sometimes you—"

"Oh, for the Angels' sake!" I turned away, not trusting myself to keep from backhanding Scratch myself. I took two steps along the quay, paused for a breath, took two more.

I could feel the edges of the sword biting into my back through the canvas as I thought of the man who had used to own it. A bloody lip? Not fucking likely. Degan wouldn't have let Petyr touch him—wouldn't even have let him start the motion. The fight would have been over before it started. Hell, it wouldn't have started in the first place. If Degan were here . . .

No. Stop. Wishes and fishes and all that crap. Besides, I'd already poisoned that pond well and good. There was no going back.

I turned around. Fowler gave me a warning look as I came back. I nodded in response. Scratch was her man, not mine: any consequences for this would be meted out by her. Raising my hand against him would only get me a face full of Oak Mistress, and not in any way I'd like. That pond had turned sour as well.

I glared up at Scratch. "How bad was it with Petyr?"

"Don't think I broke his jaw, if that's what you mean."

"You don't think you—?" I took a deep breath, tried again. "How'd you get out of there? By all accounts, Petyr doesn't travel light."

Scratch shrugged. "Threw a table and ran."

I opened my mouth to say more, thought better of it, and turned to Fowler instead. "The Thieves' Gate is out," I said.

"You think?" She looked around the wharf. "We can't stand around here for long. Broken jaw or not, Petyr's going to have his people all over the Waters looking for us."

I nodded. Dirty Waters sat on a narrow strip of shore between Ildrecca's city wall and the Corsian Passage. It had one main thoroughfare—called either Eel Way or the Slithers, depending on who you talked to—that paralleled the city wall. Down in the Lower Harbor, it was wide enough for three wagons; here in the Waters, it was a good day when two carts could pass each other and only rub wheel hubs. People, barrels, ramshackle huts, and garbage clogged most of the road, leaving a meandering path intersected by the occasional side street or alley. The back ways were even worse.

The entire place was a warren of hidey-holes and roosting kens, but it wasn't a warren I knew well. Running would be better than hiding, if we could manage it.

"We'll need to stick to the Slithers if we want to get out of here," I said as I began to move away from the quay.

"I don't suppose you have any friends around here, do you?" said Fowler as she fell in beside me.

"No," I said, looking up the street. Had that shadow been in that doorway before? "But that's not the important question."

"It isn't?" said Fowler.

"No."

"Then what is?"

The shadow, I decided, was definitely new, as were the four that had just slipped around the corner on the opposite side of the street. All were coming our way. Fast.

"The important question," I said, drawing my rapier and my fighting dagger, "is how far is it to the end of Soggy Petyr's territory? Because unless the answer is 'pretty damn close,' we're going to have a long, hard fight ahead of us."

Chapter Two

I took the corner fast—so fast that I slipped in the small pile of fish entrails someone had dumped inside the entrance to the alley. I managed to catch myself against a crate in the process and keep running. The maneuver gained me a palmful of splinters, but it was a hell of a lot better than the alternative being offered by the pair of Petyr's Cutters running a block behind me.

I dodged past barrels and around fallen timbers, unsure whether to be grateful for the detritus or not. It could hide me and foil my trail, but it was also slowing me down. If I lost much more ground to my pursuers, all the switchbacks and trash in the world wouldn't keep them off my blinders.

I burst out of the alley and into what passed for a piazza in Dirty Waters—basically an irregular open space set off by a laundry on one side and a tavern on the other. Weak light spilled out of the tavern, illuminating a collection of ramshackle tables and benches, all set on an uneven patio made up of stray boards laid out on the ground. Men sat at the tables. Two of them looked up as I staggered past, my eyes already burning from the faint light. Neither man moved to interfere.

Small blessings.

I was most of the way across the piazza, heading for a gap in the buildings on the far side, when I heard a shout of triumph behind me.

Petyr's boys. Had to be.

I redoubled my efforts, pushing tired limbs and battered muscles as best I could. Between the trip up from Barrab and the ambush on the quay, there wasn't much left to draw on; but given the alternative was to turn and fight and—most likely—lose, I headed into the alley and prayed I wouldn't stumble over some fresh hazard.

If I could only find a handy bolt-hole, or a Rabbit Run, or maybe a Thieves' Ladder to . . .

There. I came around a turn to find a gift from the Angels themselves: a tall, sloping pile of garbage directly ahead of me. If I could get enough purchase to run up it and leap to the overhanging gutter beyond, I might be able to . . .

Pain flared along my back as I picked up my pace, reminding me I was doing good to be moving at all. I'd been striped across the back on the quay, just before we'd been forced to rabbit: now a line of fire extended from below my shoulder blade, down across my ribs, to my hip. While I still wasn't sure if it was a cut or one hell of a bruise—my hand had come back red when I'd reached around to check the wound, but there'd been no way to tell whether the blood was mine or someone else's—I did know I would have ended up in two pieces if it hadn't been for Degan's sword lying across my spine.

One piece or two, though, there was no way I was going to be making that leap.

I skirted the garbage pile, tripped over a decaying mound of fur that might have once been a dog or a cat, and fell. My knee landed on something hard and I let out a gasp. Then I was up and running again, but not for long. Thirty paces on, the alley ended in the back of a building.

I looked around. Dawn, I expect, was pushing itself toward the horizon somewhere to the east, but here in the slums of Dirty Waters, deep under the shadow of the city walls, it was still dark enough for my night vision to function.

I studied the alley in the red and gold highlights of my sight and felt my heart sink. The wooden wall before me looked weathered and worn, but that didn't mean it would give way easy. I could still be trying to kick a hole in it when my pursuers arrived. The buildings to either side were brick, tall and without doors. There was a single window high up to my right, but it was boarded over.

The sounds of voices and stumbling feet—and more ominously, of bared steel scraping up against stone—came to me from back along my path. They were getting closer.

I took a step toward the garbage. Maybe if I could bury myself in it quickly enough, I could . . .

No, wait. Even better.

To call the gap in the wall near the garbage pile an alcove would have been generous. At best, it was a space where two buildings failed to meet, just behind the stinking pile and well in the shadows of the buildings that formed it. That I had initially missed seeing the gap spoke well of its potential; that I had missed it with my night vision was even better. If I couldn't see it, it would be nearly invisible to the normally sighted Cutters on my tail.

I hoped.

I stepped over to the alcove, drew the long knife from my boot, and slipped into the small space as best I could. It was a tight fit, especially with Degan's sword strapped to my back, but I wasn't in a position to complain.

I heard smaller things shifting and scuttling away as I invaded the gap. Something hard poked me in the side, while something soft ran up my shin before deciding to jump off at the knee. My right leg and part of my hip were left sticking out into the alley.

I settled in and listened and wondered how Fowler and Scratch were faring. Whether they were even alive.

It had been an ugly fight, even by Kin standards. Scratch had dropped two of Petyr's men at the outset, and Fowler another, but the odds never shifted in our favor. By the time I'd driven one of the Cutters into the harbor, more of Petyr's people had begun to arrive. Steel and strategy quickly gave way to fists and fury, with elbows and teeth and worse coming into play in a vicious blur. When I finally managed to look up from the man who'd tried to lay my back open—I ended up pushing his eye into his head, along with four inches of my rapier's cross guard—it was to see

Fowler riding the back of another Cutter, her legs wrapped around his waist as she plunged her dagger down and into his chest. Even as I watched, another woman began to move to flank her, while a dozen yards away Scratch, his left side a study in blood, swung his sword like a scythe as he tried to fend off the three coves who were driving him backward toward a stack of barrels.

There were too many Cutters: too many on the quay, and too many more on their way. Soggy Petyr owned this corner of Dirty Waters, and he was clearly willing to empty it out to take me down. If we wanted to survive, we needed to fade.

And seeing as how they'd been sent after me in the first place . . .

I'd made noise when I left—a lot of it. I shouted, stomped my foot, banged my rapier against my dagger and yelled for Fowler and Scratch to run. Then, pausing long enough to gather a dark glare from Fowler and a handful of not nearly so intimidating looks from the Cutters, I'd bolted.

Three of Petyr's people had followed, three more had stayed behind. Not the numbers I'd been hoping for, but I wasn't in a position to be picky. At least this way, Fowler and Scratch would stand a chance of breaking free and taking to the back ways or rooftops. I hoped.

As it was, I'd heard an ominous yell and a splash as I ran up the street and ducked down an alley. The voice had sounded like Fowler's, but between the distance and the sound of my feet, it was hard to be certain. With luck, the sound had been her getting the better of her attacker and throwing them into the harbor, and not the other way around.

The crunch of brittle wood beneath shoe leather brought me back, and I drew farther into my hiding spot. A moment later, I watched as a figure came into view on the far edge of the garbage pile. A second figure followed. The third man had stumbled over an inopportune stool I'd managed to tip into the road and hit his head on the corner of a horse trough. I knew this because he'd been close enough to splash me with water—and worse—when he'd gone down. Damn, but that bastard had been fast.

Both of the remaining Cutters were moving slower now,

casting their gazes across the shadows and listening for vanished sounds of my flight. I let them pass. Darkness or no, they'd be able to make out the end of the alley in another dozen steps. Once they did, they'd come about and begin working their way back. And while my hiding spot was good, I didn't doubt their chances of finding me once they stopped worrying about the chase and instead began to search.

Which meant I needed to deal with them before they turned around.

I crouched down in my little crevice and counted their steps.

One ... three ... five ...

Far enough.

I crept forward, using my night vision to avoid any bits of garbage or debris that might give me away. In my right hand, I could feel my grip on my knife turning clammy with sweat, and was suddenly grateful for the wire wrapping on the handle. This was going to be hard enough without having to worry about the weapon slipping at the last moment.

In most instances, when you want to knife someone in an alley and aren't worried about niceties, you simply step up behind him and do your best Hasty Tailor. But in this case, there were two very good reasons I couldn't stitch the Cutter a dozen times in half as many seconds. First, because he was wearing a doublet—and not just any doublet, but one that looked to have originally been a nobleman's formal piece. Oh, the fine trim and the buttons had all been pulled off and sold ages ago, but that wasn't what I was worried about: no, even from here, I could see that his secondhand brocade was still holding its shape, which meant it was lined and stiffened with either horsehair or wool. Both of those could easily turn, if not stop, a dagger thrust. Not necessarily a problem if you had the right blade—say, a good stiletto, or even a finely tapered assassin's spike—but I had neither. Instead, I was holding a broad, leaf-shaped dagger better suited for street fights than delivering the steel cure.

And secondly, both men were Cutters. The name wasn't an accident: they made their living swinging steel. If I took too long dusting one, the other would simply turn around and carve me up before I had a chance to close the distance.

No, I needed to do this quiet, and by quiet I meant quick. A fast, definitive thrust to a place I could reach, even when the target was a good two heads taller then me. Say, the soft spot just behind and below the right ear. Nice and quiet and clean. Which was exactly where I stabbed him.

Almost.

I don't know if I made a noise or if he had a sudden premonition, but either way, he decided to turn around just as I was thrusting upward. It didn't save him—it was too late for that—but it did make for a sloppy job.

Maybe a deep-file Blade could have done it: could have stabbed, caught and lowered the body, all while moving on to the next man. I've seen professional assassins do more with less. But I was no Blade, and in any case, I was in no shape to catch a falling cove taller than I was.

So I simply I let the bastard gasp and drop.

The other Cutter was already turning by the time I had my blade free of his friend. I didn't hesitate: Screaming so as to not give myself time to think, I launched myself at him, hoping like hell that my body was faster than his sword.

We collided with a mutual grunt. I felt my dagger bite. I drew it out, brought it forward, then out, then forward. Repeat. Repeat again. And again. And again. Until I finally realized that the only thing holding him up was my arm, which I didn't remember wrapping around his back.

I dropped my free arm and stepped away. The Cutter fell to the ground. This one, at least, hadn't been wearing a doublet.

I bent over, put a bloody hand on my knee, and took a long, shaking breath. Everything hurt. Everything felt heavy.

Angels, but I was tired.

"Not bad," said a voice from behind me.

I spun around, knife up, teeth bared.

Please, I thought, *let there only be one of them. I can only handle one.*

There were two.

The bigger—and by bigger, I mean vastly wider—of the

two held up his hands. He had thick fingers and a curling black beard.

"Ho-ho. Easy, friend. We're just here to watch."

"And maybe applaud," said the other. He was a taller, slimmer version of the first, with the same hooked nose and clipped accent. No beard.

Brothers?

I ran through all the local assassin teams I knew. The only pair of siblings who worked together regularly in Ildrecca were the Knuckle Brothers, and these weren't them. Not that I'd ever met the Knuckles, but it was well known on the street that Croy Knuckle preferred farthingales and wigs when he worked, and there wasn't so much as a chemise between the two men before me.

So, not the Knuckle Brothers.

Then, who?

"A bit of applause never goes unwanted," agreed the heavier man. He eyed me up and down, then clapped his hands twice before rubbing them vigorously together. "Two less to worry about, eh, Ezak?"

"The balance grows in our favor," said the tall one.

"Only marginally, dear coz. Only marginally."

"Balance?" I said.

The first man's smile widened even farther. "Of vengeance, of course."

I stared at the two men. They were dressed well, if used— that is to say, what they wore was of good, secondhand quality. The few patches I could see were all done carefully, with fabric that had been selected to match the color or pattern of the original as closely as possible. There wasn't a weapon visible between them, which disturbed me even more.

Not Cutters, then. Or at least, not Petyr's, if the two lying on the ground were any indication.

I bent down slowly and wiped first my knife, and then my hand, on the shirt of the man at my feet. I didn't take my eyes off the pair. Both men nodded approvingly.

"See, Ezak?" said the broader of the two. "Cocksure and wary at once. Oh, how I wish Ambrose were here to see this."

"He could gain a fortnight's worth of education in just a few minutes watching this," agreed Ezak.

"And it's not as if his *Capitan* doesn't need the work."

" 'Neath dame Moon's steely light, I prowl the byways of the night,' " recited Ezak. "Aye."

Oh. Actors.

I relaxed and stood up.

"Glad I could adjust the balance for you," I said, not knowing or caring what they meant. I moved to push past them. The last thing I needed was to get distracted by a pair of Boardsmen.

A thick hand settled down on my shoulder. "Hold, now, friend," said the first man. "I think we might be able to do each other a favor here."

I stopped and stared at his hand. After a moment, it crept back from my doublet and returned to his side.

"I don't need any favors," I said. "And I'm not inclined to do any, either."

"Of course, of course. Nothing's free, after all. But I was merely thinking—"

"Don't think."

The thicker man smiled. "Yes, of course. You're a busy man. I can see that."

I was four paces along when he spoke to Ezak, his voice pitched perfectly to reach me.

"Mind you, coz," he said, "I'd give a night's share of the box to see how he makes it through the city gates looking like a slaughterhouse."

"Especially with Soggy Petyr's men scouring the streets between here and Low Harbor," returned Ezak, his voice finding me with equal ease. "Too bad we weren't the only ones to see him run past the tavern. I fear some of the others back there might sell him out."

"Aye, it's a risk. But what am I saying? Any man who can handle two such desperate coves as these can find his way across the Waters and through the Gate." He snapped his fingers. "Why, it's a good thing I didn't offer a change of drapes and a sly walk into the city: I'd like as not have insulted the fellow!"

"Never insult a Kindred cousin," advised Ezak.

"From your mouth to the Angels' ears, dear coz." I could almost hear the theatrical nod of his head.

I took two more steps before I came to a stop. I flexed my hand and felt the fingers stick against the palm from the Cutters' blood; felt the throb of the splinters in my other hand; felt my legs trembling beneath me whenever I stopped moving. I knew my pants were covered in a mixture of mud and blood, that my doublet and jerkin were stained with the same. I could strip to my shirt, but I expected there would be some of my own along the back even then.

With a cloak, at night, I might be able to make it past a patrol of Rags like this, but in broad daylight, at a port gate? Forged passport or no, my appearance would get me a seat in the rattle box—or worse. And I didn't have time to wait for night again; not if I wanted to get ahead of the news, let alone start people looking for Fowler and Scratch.

As for Petyr's men . . . that gauntlet didn't exactly appeal.

I turned around. The broad man feigned surprise; Ezak smiled outright.

"Fine," I said. "Get me clean drapes and a way into the city, and I'll consider your proposal."

"You'll agree to the proposal, sir, or get nothing. No payment, no performance."

I looked pointedly back the way I'd come. "If we stay here much longer, the only performance we'll be doing is for more of Petyr's people. Get me off the street and something in my belly, and we can talk."

"Done!" His beard split with a wide grin. "'And so away, 'neath stars' sparkling light, lest misfortune claim us in the night.'"

Actors. Angels help me.

We Kin are nothing if not a particular lot. Even before Isidore had formed us into a more-or-less cohesive body-criminal two centuries ago, the darker elements of the Empire had been naming and defining themselves for ages. Every con, every tool, every target and kind of criminal has a specific term associated with it. Just as a carpenter or a fisherman has his jargon of the trade, so we Kin have our *cant*: our gutter shorthand that lets us talk business quick and easy and on the sly. If you hear talk of a *Capper foisting* the *langrets*, know that false dice are being palmed and switched about on the board. Should a fellow be referred to as a *boman Talker*, walk the other way before you are "talked" out of every hawk you own. *Customs* are marks, *Magsmen* the cardsharps and professional nobles who prey on them, and a *cross drum*, the tavern where they meet to split their loot.

Actors, by contrast, fall somewhere between the well-lit world of the Lighters and the darker realm of the Kin. Entertainers to nobles and the mob alike, Boardsmen are nevertheless not part of proper society: they have no set address, produce nothing tangible, live and work at odd hours and in strange ways. They are never who they seem onstage, speak in a strange, almost canting tongue at times, and frequent both the highest and lowest circles at once. Most have, at one time or another, done Kindred work, be it something as simple as a bit of cardsharping or swag shifting (traveling troupes can take on stolen goods as "props" in one town and sell them off in another without notice), or as involved as playing an extended part in a local gang's "production" of Barnard's Law. But one thing is certain: Actors are not Kin proper. They can be charming and clever, demanding and egocentric, resourceful and restless, but above all, they are unreliable.

Which was what I kept reminding myself as I sat, a cup of fortified honey wine in my hand, and listened to the heavy man's story wind down.

"And that, in a nut, sir," he concluded, "is our predicament."

I looked at the circle of faces around me. There were a dozen in all: seven men and five women. Most were expectant, several were carefully neutral, and at least two seemed dubious. One—the oldest woman, who was busily mending a shirt off to one side—looked downright hostile, when she looked at me at all.

I was inclined to agree with her.

This was madness.

I turned my eyes from the rest of the troupe to the man before me. "And what do you want me to do about it?" I said.

Tobin—the broader of the two men who had met me in the alley, and who had proved to be the troupe's leader—spread his hands. We were in the hayloft of a livery stable. Tobin had rented it out as a combination sleeping ken and make-do rehearsal hall. I had, in honor of the hope I represented, been given the sole chair in the place.

None of them had figured out who or what I was, and I hadn't offered to tell. Let them think me just another Draw Latch. It made things less complicated and kept expectations low.

"I saw how you moved, the pad of your step," he said. "You're a Getter if I ever saw one. And no friend of Soggy Petyr's, from what I can fathom, either. 'A friend of my foe be mine foe as well; but let a man stand 'gainst one who stands 'gainst me, and ever after shall I—'"

"Save the soliloquy, or whatever the hell you call it," I said. "Just because I slipped the steel to a couple of Petyr's men doesn't mean I'm willing to go up against him for you."

"Told you'd he'd tell us to flog off," muttered a voice from the back of the troupe.

"Did I say I wanted our friend to challenge our tormentor?" declared Tobin to the room. He turned to Ezak. "Did I even imply such a thing?"

"You did not."

"There, you see!" he said, turning back to me. "No such thing, sir. No, I merely ask that, in return for the bounty of our aid and hospitality, you retrieve something of ours that has been wrongfully—nay, foully—taken." He smiled a smile that was likely worth three hawks on a good night. "A pittance of an exchange, I should think."

Their "bounty" so far had consisted of a basin of water to wash myself and my wound—the skin had split open from the blow to my back—some linen bandages, a cleanish shirt and coat, and the promise to help get me into the city. In return, they wanted me to lighten Soggy Petyr.

It seemed that Petyr had branched out: he was now in the business of "holding" and "insuring" certain property that came through the warehouses he owned. Tobin and his troupe had landed in Dirty Waters a week ago, fresh from a command performance in I-Hadn't-Bothered-To-Pay-Attention-opolis. Unfortunately for them, most of their property—including the chest holding all of their plays—had passed into Petyr's hands and never left.

Props could be replaced, and costumes could be remade from secondhand drapes—but plays, well, those were another matter entirely. A troupe's collection of plays was built over the course of years: unique works written, purchased, cribbed and even stolen, all for the sole use of the company. A signature piece could keep a troupe working for years, while a successful new play could open avenues of patronage and success that might have seemed unattainable just a season ago. If the actors were the scheming, turbulent, brilliant heart of the troupe, then the plays were its soul. And a company cannot survive without a soul.

The problem was, recent personal issues with Petyr aside, I didn't have the time or resources to crack the Petty Boss's ken and make off with a trunk full of paper just now. Not with news of Crook Eye galloping its way up from Barrab even as I sat here.

But it was equally clear that Tobin wasn't going to take no for an answer—not when he had something he knew I needed.

I slipped an *ahrami* seed into my mouth. I took my time, letting it settle beneath my tongue, releasing its juices and seeping into my system. It would do them good to sweat a bit, to think about what their options were if I said no. I embraced the flood of awareness and ease that came over me, listened as their feet shuffled in the straw.

Finally, I bit down. Then I stood up. The troupe shifted unconsciously, widening the circle around me. Tobin was the only one who didn't give ground.

"Breaking into a roosting ken is hardly a pittance," I said slowly. "Dirty Waters or no, Petyr's a local power. He won't leave the door standing open for someone like me; especially not me, considering what I did to his people."

"But surely—" began Tobin.

I held up my hand. "I'm not finished." I looked around the room, making sure I had their attention. "If you give me some time—a few days, maybe a week—I can get your chest for you." Along with Petyr's ass, depending on who I put on the job. "But it's not something I can do right now, not on short notice."

Toban scowled. "We weren't planning an extended engagement in the Waters."

"And I wasn't planning to wash the blood of Angels know how many coves off me, let alone buy my way into Ildrecca from a bunch of Boardsmen, but there it is. I'm playing it the best I can. I suggest you do the same."

"And how do we know you'll come back and do what you say?" This from the same doubting voice in the back of the troupe.

I didn't take my eyes off their leader. "You could have turned me over to Soggy Petyr in exchange for your property. Maybe even have gotten more than your plays back. You didn't." Tobin's eyes narrowed. He dipped his chin a fraction, telling me he'd thought of that idea and discarded it. "That would have been the easy way, but not the honorable one," I said. "I don't forget things like that. My word to you is good."

The old woman snorted. "A thief's word," she muttered, not even bothering to look up from her sewing.

It suddenly felt as if the entire room was holding its breath. I sensed more than saw every pair of eyes, save Tobin's, shift first to the old woman and then back to me.

I took a slow breath myself and forced a smile.

"Almost as bad as an actor's honor, isn't it?" I said.

The tiniest corner of her mouth turned up.

The room relaxed.

"It's settled, then!" pronounced Tobin. "In exchange for aid and succor, our good Getter here will deliver us our property within the seven-night." He extended his hand and helped me to my feet. The sudden movement made me feel light-headed, but I didn't resist. As I stood, his other hand came around and across my back—above my wound, thankfully—drawing me closer.

"But know this, thief," he muttered in my ear, his smiling lips barely moving. "I'm trusting you with the well-being of my troupe. If you fail, it's no rain off my hat—I'll get the scripts another way, if I must. But if you put any of my people in danger, or tell Petyr who sent you, I'll make sure you pay. Cousins we may be, but I've closer relation than you, and they carry long knives of their own."

I smiled as I returned the embrace. "I wouldn't have it any other way," I said. "Not any other way at all."

Chapter Three

I parted ways with Tobin and his people three blocks inside the city's walls, at the Square of the Sixteen Angels.

True to his word, the troupe's leader had gotten me through not only the city gates, but Dirty Waters and the Lower Harbor as well, all without incident. I still wasn't convinced we'd needed to lighten my hair with ash and turn my goatee into a full beard using lambswool and glue, let alone stick me on a short pair of stilts known as "giant shoes"—complete with long pants and false feet——but I hadn't been in a position to argue. And besides, as Tobin had rightly pointed out, Petyr's men would be looking for a short, dark-haired cove with sly eyes and a partial beard, not a stiff-legged old man who clearly needed help walking. Mind you, the parade of actors half a block ahead, singing and performing as they went, hadn't hurt when it came to drawing eyes away from me either.

Not that it had been easy. If you had asked me halfway up whether it it was worth it, I'd have told you that I'd rather fight my way through all of Dirty Waters and half of the Lower Harbor than take another step in those damn stilts. But now that I was standing on the ground, my own shoes on my feet and the stage makeup washed away in the fountain before me? All things being equal?

I still would have picked the fight.

"You'll not forget our deal?" said the troupe leader as I flicked wet hair away from my face.

I glanced past him, toward a small group of Rags lounging in the shade of a building, their red sashes marking them as city guardsmen. They weren't close enough to overhear, but they were handy enough to cause trouble if Tobin decided to make a scene. "You'll get your plays," I said. "Don't worry."

The corners of Tobin's mouth pulled back. Clearly, he was having second thoughts now that he'd gotten me into Ildrecca. A hawk on the wrist as opposed to a pair in the sky and all that. "Yes, of course," he said, "but I still—"

I stopped wringing out my hair and stepped closer to him. I even summoned a smile to my face. It wasn't easy, given that he'd just questioned my word. Twice. "Relax, Boardsman. I keep my promises."

Tobin's gaze went from my mouth to my eyes. He didn't seem reassured by what he saw. "Yes, well, let us hope so."

I gave him a final nod, handed him the patchwork coat they'd thrown over me to hide both of the swords I was carrying, and left.

I craned my neck as I walked, enjoying the sensation of once again taking in Ildrecca's walls from the inside. This close they loomed, extending from shadow into sunlight, the dark brick and beige stone turning to red and cream as it rose. Far up, I caught a glint—from a spear tip or helmet or bit of armor I couldn't tell—as someone made their rounds on the wall. I wondered if I'd be visible from up there, or merely a smudge against the street. Likely somewhere in between, if the hay-stuffed, flayed skins of the criminals hanging below the parapets were any indication. There were four up there today. Two looked fresh, if the number of crows circling about were any indication.

I lowered my gaze and turned away. The bodies were supposed to be a lesson in what happened if you broke imperial law, but I'd always seen them as a reminder of the cost of being careless. In this city, careless got you killed or caught, and I didn't much care for the thought of either.

Was that what the problem had been in Barrab? Had I gotten careless? I didn't think so, but then, you never think you're missing things until it's too late. And Crook Eye had certainly caught me unawares, so maybe . . .

It had been another meeting, another attempt at me trying to mollify the established lords of the Kin. Another slow dance of words and smiles and threats. As the newest Gray Prince, I was the unknown, the potential threat, and doubly so because no one had seen me coming—not even me. But kill a legend like Shadow, burn a cordon to the ground, stop a war and con an empire, and people on the street start to think you know what you're doing. They start to call you Prince. And who can argue with the street? Not me. Not a Nose who got lucky and was pushed to the top of the hill. And not, it seemed, the other Princes; or, at least, not directly, and not right away.

You learned not to challenge the street in Ildrecca when it made pronouncements. Not if you were Kin, and not if you were smart.

And Crook Eye had been smart. Smarter than I'd given him credit for. Unlike the handful of other Gray Princes I'd met, he hadn't come to our meeting full of bluff and bluster, hadn't cloaked himself in offers of mentorship, hadn't tried to warn me about my newfound peers. He'd simply approached me, one smuggler to another, to talk business. And given his web of contacts extended not only across the southern third of the empire, but deep into the lands and kingdoms beyond, I'd come. Warily, to be sure, but come I had. I needed those contacts, needed that web. Needed money if I was going to build any kind of organization, and to do that, I needed to move more of the one thing I knew how to move: holy relics.

Crook Eye had known all of that, of course. But he'd also known more: He'd known how to take hold of me. Because, like me, Crook Eye had gotten lucky.

Crook Eye, you see, had found a sword. Degan's sword.

I could still remember the shock that had ripped through me when Crook Eye held up the blackened and charred length of metal. The last time I'd seen that sword, Degan had consigned it to the flames of a burning building—leaving it, and our friendship, to be consumed on the pyre of my mistakes. He'd risked everything he believed in, everything he was, on me, and I'd repaid that trust with betrayal.

It had only seemed right to leave the sword where it lay: who was I to touch the symbol of what Degan had lost?

So to see it in another's hands, let alone Crook Eye's? To have him threaten me with it? To have him say I hadn't been alone when Shadow died? That I'd hired it done by a degan? Well, that hadn't sat well. Not his threats, and definitely not him holding Degan's sword while doing so.

Only one person got to threaten me with that blade, and Crook Eye wasn't it.

And so I'd drawn my own steel and taken Degan's blade from Crook Eye at sword's point.

And walked right into his hands.

Fowler was the first to realize it, of course. I'd been too angry to think about consequences, too focused on the sword to worry about having broken my Peace. But as Fowler had pointed out, thanks to me Crook Eye didn't need Degan's sword to shore up his story anymore: He had something better. He had me clearing steel and breaking my word and threatening his life—the exact things we'd both pledged not to do.

And I'd walked right into it. Crook Eye had set me up, and I'd repaid the bastard by making him look like a stand-up Gray Prince.

Dammit.

In the end, there hadn't been any other choice: I needed to apologize. And so, gathering up my people and tamping down on my pride, I'd stalked back across Barrab to the meeing site in hopes of finding Crook Eye so I could try to make amends.

I'd found him all right: dead, my dagger in his eye, three of his men scattered about him on the floor.

After that, it had been all about getting out of Barrab and beating the news back to Ildrecca. Wolf, the Azaari bandit and smuggler who'd served as our guide through the hills down to Barrab, had proved invaluable in this respect. Word had gotten back to the rest of Crook Eye's people in Barrab somehow, and our trip out had proved more of a challenge than anticipated. It wasn't until we were well away from town and into the hills that I'd had the luxury to wonder where Wolf had been while I was meeting with Crook Eye, to realize that he hadn't reappeared until after we'd found the bodies. To remember that he was a knife fighter, and that Crook Eye had been killed with a short blade.

By then, though, it was too late: Wolf had already disappeared.

Fowler's constant strain of "I told you so" had nearly been unbearable on the way home.

I kept to Ildrecca's thoroughfares and streets as much as possible. The back ways would have been faster, but I didn't know the twists and turns here well enough to take full advantage of them. Besides, I was familiar with the kinds of things that could happen in strange alleys, and I didn't have the time to deal with them now.

I wondered again what had happened to Fowler and Scratch, whether or not the Oak Mistress and her man had made it. Despite Tobin's hurry to be gone and Ezak's cautions, I'd done a quick nose of the blocks surrounding the actors' barn, including a stint along the Slithers. I hadn't been hoping to run into Fowler so much as to spot a specific pile of stones here, or maybe a pattern scratched into a wall or doorpost there—any of Fowler's thief's markings or signs that could tell me she was alive and on the streets. But none of the marks I saw were hers, and the few coves I risked talking to hadn't heard anything of use. The best I'd been able to manage was to sketch a few reassurances for her below some windowsills and leave a tuft of pigeon feathers stuck into the doorjamb of a tavern to let her know I was looking for her.

I passed out of Five Bells cordon and cut across a corner of Needles. It was market day, so I avoided the main square and its retired stoning-pillars. Instead, I ducked and dodged my way through the secondary streets, past carts heavy with silk and linen and wool, ignoring the calls of the fabric merchants and their barkers. Faint hints of stale piss and wood ash—trace odors left over from the dying process, not fully faded yet—were overlaid by the heavier scents of mules and men sweating in the summer heat.

It wasn't until I was almost out of the place that a new scent caught my nose: cardamom and cumin, along with a hint of citrus, all of it riding on the dark, scratchy smell of grilled meat. My stomach answered the call, and I realized that except for two boiled eggs and the fortified wine provided by the Boardsmen, I hadn't eaten since before boarding the caïque.

Mouth watering, I tracked the scent to a street vendor tending a rough metal grate set atop a fluted brazier full of coals. He was just off to the side of a narrow lane, not far from another cross-street. There was a small crowd around him, watching and waiting as he deftly drew pieces of cubed lamb from a pot of spiced yogurt marinade, threaded them on a reed skewer, and placed them on the grate. As each skewer was finished, he speared half of a young onion on the end, gave it a quick sear, and served it up with workmanlike nonchalance.

I placed an order for two, looked about me, and then changed it to four at the last moment. He put the extra meat on the grill without a thought. Since this wasn't my cordon, and I didn't want to attract attention, I waited until mine were done, rather than taking the next four that were available, which would have been the habit of most Kin.

A pair of skewers in each hand, I walked over to the nearby lane and hunkered down against the wall, shifting slightly so that Degan's sword wasn't rubbing against my bandage. Taking a small, hot onion in my mouth from one, I carefully placed two of the other skewers across the bowl of the beggar beside me.

"Care-foo," I said around the onion. "'S hop."

The beggar looked at the offerings and nodded vigorously, a ragged smile on his face. He made the sign of imperial blessing with the remaining three fingers of his bandaged right hand, then clasped both of them together in thanks. He was the picture of a pitiful, starving mendicant, grateful for the bounty that had so suddenly befallen him.

That is, until I looked him in the eye; then, for the briefest instant, I saw the cold calculation and hard-edged doubt that lived there, the tallying of costs and benefits, of risks and option, that were signified by my simple gesture. What did I want? Could he touch me for more? Was this all a setup? But it was only there for an instant, because once he realized I was looking at him—that I was actually *seeing* him—he was quick to mask his heart and avert his gaze.

But still, he knew I'd seen the real man.

I let the beggar look away and consider, as I swallowed the onion and took a piece of lamb. The char on the outside contrasted nicely with the sweet moisture the yogurt had imparted to the inner meat.

The beggar reached out and pushed at one of the skewers but didn't pick it up.

It was a feint. I saw his other hand slip into his rags. Knife? Nail-studded club? A sap of some sort? It didn't matter. I wasn't about to provoke a Master of the Black Arts in his own alley if I could help it.

I swallowed my lamb and gestured at the blisters on his leg. They were a vile, yellowish white, filled with seeping matter. "Nice work," I said. "Soap and vinegar?" It was a standard formula among those who practiced the Gimping and the Scroffing Laws: Rub a layer of soap on your skin, dribble some strong vinegar on it, and display the resulting "blisters" to best possible effect.

As for this fellow, he seemed to be a bit of an artist: It looked as if he'd added some kind of pigment beneath the soap, giving the blisters a slightly greenish tinge. It was an impressive effect.

All traces of the pitiful cripple vanished at my words. He cast me a sharp look, even as he tucked one of the skewers away in his rags and brought the other to his mouth.

"What's the dodge?" he said, using his chewing to mask his words. "You a Nose or a Whisperer or something?"

I smiled. "Or something."

"I don't know you."

"No. Just passing through."

"Then keep passing."

"I plan on it. But I've been on the fade for a bit. Taking the waters. Thought I might suss out the local talent for some mumbles."

He tore off another piece of lamb and glanced up and down the lane. Looking for support, or worried about being seen talking to someone he wasn't supposed to? If he was an Ear for a local Nose, his talking to me could raise uncomfortable questions once I'd gone.

"What's the dodge?" he asked again. "Why poke at me?"

"Old habits," I said honestly. After being away for over a week, I wanted . . . no, needed . . . to know what was happening on the street. I had my own people to check in with, of course—people who did the job I used to do—but they weren't here, and I didn't want to spend the time it would take to cross the city and find them right now. "I just want to get a sniff of what's on the wind," I said. "And you Masters are some of the best hounds I know for that."

The beggar looked at me for a long moment, then nudged his bowl. I dropped a hawk and five owls in it—a rich price for something I hadn't even gotten yet. He scooped up the coins before they had stopped rattling and nodded.

"Small or broad?" he said.

"Broad." I didn't have use for the local gossip; I needed citywide. "But I need something small first."

He eyed me warily but nodded nonetheless.

"I'm looking for word on someone named Fowler Jess," I said. "She's been out of the city but should have slipped back in last night or this morning. Short, blond. Loud when she's angry."

"She Kin?"

I nodded.

The beggar shook his head. "No whispers about a short angry woman, loud or otherwise."

"How about someone named Scratch?"

The beggar's face soured. "Is he short and loud, too?"

"Just the opposite."

"Nothing."

I considered. It was a long shot, but . . .

"There's also an Azaari named—"

"I thought you wanted broad news," said the beggar, "not a daily roster of comings and goings." He tapped the bowl again. "The gazette costs extra. Make up your mind."

"Fine," I said, letting it go. I could put people on it once I got back into friendly territory. "Broad news, then."

The beggar took another cube of lamb and worked it around in his mouth, watching me. Thinking. I pretended not to mind and nibbled at my skewer with a dry mouth.

"Crook Eye's dead," he said at last.

I didn't quite choke, but it was a close thing. I managed to cough, then swallow, before saying, *"What?"*

"Crook Eye. The Gray Prince. Heard he was killed someplace south of here."

Already? How had the word gotten here this fast? I figured I had another day at least, even after the delay caused by Soggy Petyr and the Thieves' Gate.

"When?" I said. This had to be the beginning; I had to be on the leading edge of the wave.

"Dunno. Suppose he died recently. Otherwise it wouldn't be new news, now, would it?"

"No," I said. "Not when was Crook Eye dusted: when did you first hear the news?"

"Oh." He stared off toward the street. The fingers of his right hand—even the ones bound down and hidden under the stained bandage—twitched as he walked his mind back in time, counting the hours. "Four."

I let out a slow breath. "Hours?"

"Days."

Days? That wasn't possible. Crook Eye had still been alive four days ago. I'd only talked to him three days ago, for Angels' sake!

"Are you sure?"

"That Crook Eye's dead, or that I heard it four days ago?"

"Both."

"About him being dustmans?" The beggar shrugged. "The street's been humming with it, so I believe it. As for when I first heard . . . yeah, four days ago."

Shit. This didn't make any sense. Who had called him dead before he died?

I swallowed, not wanting to ask the next question, but I didn't have a choice.

"Who dusted him?" I said.

"That new Prince, Alley Walker. Used to call himself Drothe or something. Guess he's impatient to make a name for himself." The beggar shook his head, missing the grimace I made at the latest tag the street had hung on me. Alley Walker? Really? That was almost as bad as the one I'd been hearing before I left: Shadowblade. Ugh.

"Who told you?" I said.

The beggar started at the question. "What?"

"You heard me."

"Piss off."

Not a surprising reaction. He didn't know me, which meant I was stepping beyond more boundaries than I could count. If we had a history, if I'd had him on my string for maybe six months or a year, I might have been able to ask about his sources and expect and answer. But to do it like this, after giving him little more than threats and a free lunch?

Still, I needed to know.

"Fine," I said. "How about this instead: don't tell me who, just tell me where. Give me the cordon where the news first started to spread, and I'll take it from there."

"Fuck you, Nose. You want to find the tip of the root, do your own digging."

Wrong answer.

I was crouching, he was sitting. That made it an easy thing to turn and let my knees fall across his hip and thigh, pinning him against the ground. And it was just as easy to let my elbow clip him across the side of his jaw as I did so.

His head rolled with the blow, lessening the impact, and his right hand came up. There was an expensive-looking, finely honed dagger in it. The dagger started to come up. And stopped.

The end of my skewer had found his throat first. I could feel the vein in his neck pushing gently against the tip of the wooden spike. There were still two pieces of lamb on it.

We sat there, his leg pinned beneath me, his body against the wall, my wooden skewer pressed to his neck, and glared at one another.

"Be smart," I said.

He took a breath, swallowed, and lowered his steel. I let up on the kebob but didn't remove it completely.

"All right," I said, my own breath sounding ragged. "Here's the tale: I don't want trouble with you, let alone your brothers and sisters—"

"Too late."

"—but I'll take it if it means I have to go hard to get some answers. I'm not asking for your best whisperers or looking to hunt them down. All I want to know is where you heard the mumble, and where your mumblers heard it."

"Why?"

"Because most days, I'm still called Drothe."

The beggar's eyes went wide.

"Now you know who to set your guild after if you want me," I said. "The last thing I need right now is trouble with Ildrecca's Masters of the Black Arts, but you can understand my position. I have to find out how far this has spread, and who started it."

He nodded.

"Where'd you hear it?" I said.

"Came out of Rustwater, from what I can tell. There, and maybe Stone Arch."

I scowled. I used to operate out of Stone Arch, back when it had been near the heart of Nicco's old territory. Now it was split up among a couple of bosses. One of those bosses also owned Rustwater.

Rambles.

Rambles and I had never gotten along, even when we'd both worked under Nicco, which was ironic when you considered we'd both ended up betraying the Upright Man. The last time I'd seen him, Rambles had been rolling around on the street, puking his guts up—mainly because I'd kicked him in the groin. It was only fair, though: He'd had a sword to my throat moments before.

Since then, he'd managed to carve out enough territory and get enough coves under him to become an Upright Man in his own right. True, I was even higher among the Kin now, but there comes a point where simply dusting someone because he annoys you as a person isn't a reason enough for the act. Unfortunately, Rambles had reached that point. For now.

I pulled the skewer away from the beggar's throat. He didn't raise his dagger as I leaned back and stood up—only rubbed at his leg and stared at me. I adjusted Degan's canvas-wrapped sword across my back, then dropped a gold falcon in the beggar's bowl.

"My apologies, good Master," I said. "I didn't intend to use you so roughly."

"And I didn't intend to tell a Gray Prince to fuck off," he said. "Consider us even." I noticed that the coin I'd dropped had already vanished. I hadn't even seen him move.

I was just turning away when he spoke up again.

"Did you do it?"

I stopped. "Does it matter at this point?"

"Maybe. For me. For us."

I considered his choice of words for a moment before I said, "I was there, but I didn't dust him. If anything, he was the one trying to put the cross on me."

The beggar's eyes narrowed. "You can prove this?"

"As much as Crook Eye's people can prove the opposite. But that doesn't mean I'm lying."

The beggar scratched absently at his clothing, his fingers chasing something unseen across his chest. "Crook Eye was always a bastard when it came to the students of the Begging Law," he said at last. "Tight with his ready, even when he was coming up. Had a quick boot for us, too. I'll pass your side along to my family. Can't say it'll help, but . . ." He lifted a shoulder.

I nodded my thanks and headed back into the street.

I'd known I'd been set up, but not like this. To put out word of a Gray Prince's death before it could even be confirmed? Before they could get word back from the assassin? That took more than balls. If Crook Eye had survived and come walking back into the city after he was proclaimed dead, he would have become a legend. And if I'd returned having cut a deal with him? Well, whoever had started the rumor would have had two unhappy Gray Princes to deal with. Never a wise idea.

I shook my head in disbelief. No, if even one part of this scheme had gone wrong, everything would have collapsed. That meant the people behind this hadn't just planned it; they'd been sure of it. Positive. Failure hadn't not only not been an option; it hadn't even been a consideration. No matter what happened at the meeting in Barrab—angels, had they arranged that, too?—Crook Eye had been destined to turn up dead, just as I'd been destined to be made the Cull.

It was well done. Hell, it was more than that: It was damn near perfect. Which meant it sure as hell hadn't been pulled off by Rambles.

But that didn't mean he didn't know anything about it. Not by a long shot.

Chapter Four

The sun was just beginning to flirt with the western horizon when I finally reached the top of Blackpot Street. The winding lane lay just below the crest of one of Ildrecca's five Old Hills, near what had once had been the center of the city but was now little more than a minor cordon with more history than prestige. When I first moved here after becoming a Prince, I'd thought I might enjoy the breezes that came with the elevation; now, as I paused to wipe my face and catch my breath, I remembered why I'd chosen to live down in Stone Arch cordon in the first place. My former neighborhood might have had its share of dangers and a stagnant stink, but I hadn't had to worry about climbing up a hill every time I wanted to come home—especially not after a full day of working the streets.

I'd spent the remainder of the morning and most of the afternoon making my way across Ildrecca. Normally, it wouldn't have taken this long, but it was a minor festival day—the Celebration of the Muster of the Lesser Host had fallen on the same day as the Feast of Tzemicles, angelic patron of alchemists—and the streets of the central cordons were filled with revelers and guild parades and those legionnaires lucky enough to draw a black bean and get the day off. Even the alleys had been busy. Between the Morts doing their trade up against the walls, the drunks spewing their festivities back out onto the cobbles, and the Tapsmen

ambushing and robbing the lost and unwary, it had sometimes seemed there was hardly room to move.

That had also made it harder to nose for information,
which was the other thing I'd been doing—or, at least, trying to do—on my way home. News of Fowler? None. Had
anyone heard where the news about Crook Eye had sur-
faced? Not a soul. Nothing but quick shrugs, ducked heads,
and vague mumblings that sounded like answers but told
me nothing. The street, it seemed, had little to share.

Not that it was eager in any case. I was a Gray Prince now,
and the Kin preferred to talk about their princes rather than
to them. Street wisdom held that Princes were everywhere,
that they had their hands in everything: To attract their attention was to become their unwitting tool. As reputations went,
it had its appeal: No one would bother you, and few would
cross you. But in practice? It made street life damn annoying,
especially if you were used to working on it.

Part of me had been hoping I might prove to be the exception, that my recent pre-Prince status would let me
bridge the gap between cove and crime lord. But it didn't
work that way, and most Kin weren't willing to take the
chance. I might have been of the street a few months ago,
but that history counted for naught after my rise. There
were no easy mumbles or loose whispers to be had—not by
me. Not anymore.

None of which was helping me find Fowler, dammit.

I took the next turn and headed down Scrivener's Way.
Secondhand booksellers and binders' shops ran in uneven
rows on either side of me, jumbled and jostled together like
an ill-kept bookshelf. Here was Facheltrager's, known for
his collection, variously, of Second Regency erotica and
Fourth Reform philosophy; there Falconetto's, the best
closet in town for ancient fighting manuals; off to my left,
Lazarus's Bindery, specializing in false gildings and tooled
covers. They, and the rest, were the main reason I'd moved
here: to be close to the purveyors of secondhand knowledge
and their musty wares. That I didn't get to frequent them as
much as I liked didn't detract from the allure. Their mere
presence made the climb home worth it. Most days.

I ran a finger under my rope-cum-baldric and winced. The weight of Degan's sword had been digging the cord into my shoulder all day, and now it was beginning to chafe. I swung the canvas-wrapped blade off my shoulder and sighed. Even with the rope tied north of the guard and down near the tip, it still looked more like a long bundle of cloth than a sword.

I weighed the weapon in my hands as I walked. Now what?

It wasn't as if I was going to be giving it back to Degan. He'd made his feelings clear when he tossed his sword to the floor and walked out of the burning warehouse three months ago. Nor could I ask him if he'd reconsider. In true Degan fashion, he'd vanished from the streets— disappearing like so many times in the past, only this time it wasn't for a dodge or a contract he'd taken on. This time, I knew, it was forever.

I'd wanted to go looking, of course—to track him down and find him, if only for my own peace of mind. But I hadn't. Instead, I'd respected his wishes and kept my nose to myself. Given everything I'd cost him, it seemed the least I could do.

And it had seemed to be working—right up until Crook Eye had pulled out Degan's sword and waved it under my nose, that is.

Damn that lazy-eyed bastard, anyhow.

I moved Degan's legacy to my left hand and picked up the pace. Five more blocks to home. Five more blocks until I could catch my breath and sleep and, maybe, think.

I'd gone all of two of those blocks when I felt a hand land on the back of my neck, take hold, and steer me into a doorway. It wouldn't have been so bad, except the door was closed.

"Wha—?" I said, but was interrupted by my head rebounding off the wood before me. I staggered back, then was shoved up against the door again. This time, the hand on my neck held me in place while its partner grabbed my right arm and pinned it behind my back. My shoulder turned to fire. Degan's sword fell to the ground with a thump.

"Who is it?" yelled someone on the other side of the door.

"Hello, Drothe," said a voice close to my ear. A woman's voice. "Not as hard to find as you thought you were, eh, Nose?"

I was still trying to figure out what the hell was going on when the hands yanked me back and spun me around. I half expected a blade at my throat, but felt myself pushed up against the stone wall beside the door.

I had my wrist knife in my hand in an instant.

It got slapped out just as quickly.

"Ah, ah," said the woman as she took a step back. "No steel."

From the other side of the door, the sounds of movement and cursing. "Dammit, Cyril," called the voice, "is that you?" Neither the woman nor I answered.

I blinked, my vision still recovering from my encounter with the door. The figure before me was an uneven shadow, silhouetted against the daylit street behind her. One of Crook Eye's people? A cove from Shadow's old organization who hadn't heard the vendetta was over? Someone else entirely?

Did it really matter?

I lunged forward.

The woman before me shifted, causing the light to glint off the copper-chased sword guard at her side.

I knew that sword—had one of its sisters lying on the ground, wrapped in canvas, not four feet away. A degan's sword.

Crap. This was going to hurt.

Copper Degan slipped my attack with almost casual ease, stepping aside as the flat of her dark hand connected with the side of my head. I staggered, flailed my arms, and went down.

Behind me, I heard the door open.

"By the reborn Emperor, Cyril, I told you to . . . oh."

"Go away," said Copper Degan. "Now."

The door slammed shut, followed almost immediately by the sound of a bolt being thrown. I wished I was on the other side of that bolt.

I climbed to my feet and turned around. Copper Degan was standing above me, arms folded, a look of mild disdain on her face. Or maybe it was boredom. I didn't know her well enough to distinguish between the two.

Street traffic was already rerouting itself, giving us a wide, cautious berth.

"Not a social call, then?" I said as I wiped my nose. No blood. I ran the back of my hand across my forehead. Blood, but not much. Still.

"Come with me."

Copper turned and headed down the street, not bothering to see if I followed, not worrying about showing me her back. And why should she? She was a member of one of the best mercenary Orders in the empire: My trying for her would only result in more blood being spilled—all of it mine. As for running, well, it would end the same way, only with more sweat thrown into the mix.

I retrieved my knife, made sure Degan's sword was still hidden within its wrapping, and hurried after her.

Copper turned down a nearby side street. Five doors along, she stepped into a gap between an ink seller's shop and a salve maker. I joined her.

"Just so you know," I said, wiping at my forehead again and holding out the bloody palm for her to see. "This doesn't come free. Not even for a degan."

"If you think you can collect, you're welcome to try."

I ran my gaze up and down her, more for show than anything else. I knew I couldn't take her. Taller than me but not tall, with a narrower build than you might expect and dark, tightly braided hair, Copper didn't look like a swordswoman. Aside from the heavily basketed sword at her side—chased in copper, of course, with the guard looking like a cascade of carved fish scales protecting the handle—the only thing that hinted at her skill was the slight broadening at her shoulders. That, and her eyes. They were good eyes for someone in her trade: cold and hard and distant—the kind of eyes you needed if your business was swinging steel for other people's causes. The kind that said their owner didn't give a damn about much, especially not you.

I met those eyes, then looked away. Damn degans.

"Another time," I said.

"Mm-hmm." She didn't sound worried. "We need to talk."

"About?"

"What do you think?"

I sighed. "Look, I already told your Order—"

"I'm not here on behalf of the Order. I'm here on my own." She leaned forward and dropped her voice. "Because you lied."

I snapped my gaze back to her and held my ground. "Lied?" I said. "I was the only non-degan in a room filled with degans, answering questions about a dead degan and a missing degan. I can't think of many worse places to lie than that. How stupid do you think I am?"

"Just as much as you need to be." Her finger found my chest and poked it. Hard. "We both know the tale you spun to the Order was garbage. A member of the Kin killing a degan?" She shook her head. "How stupid do you think *I* am?"

"I don't know you well enough to say. Care to give me a hint?"

Her finger thrust again, with less give than if she'd used her sword. I winced and took a step back.

"What happened to Iron, Kin?"

"I told you," I said, shoving her hand away. "Shadow killed Iron Degan. How else do you explain finding Iron's sword on Shadow's body down in Ten Ways? He dusted Iron and then he came after me. I saw the damn sword in his hands."

"And you managed to kill the man you say killed my sword brother?" She ran her eyes over me again. "You?"

I shrugged. "I got lucky."

"No one's that lucky."

She was right, of course: I'd lied. Through my teeth. The only reason I'd survived my encounter with Shadow was that Degan had distracted the Gray Prince at the last minute, allowing me to kill him. Except I wasn't about to tell her that story because I needed to keep Bronze Degan out of it; needed to keep the rest of the degans from knowing that Degan had run Iron through with a single, precise thrust; needed to shore up the lie so they wouldn't know I was the one who'd planted Iron's sword on Shadow's remains. Degan had saved my life more times than I could count: I'd be damned if I was going to give him up to Copper and the rest by telling the truth—not when I knew it meant they'd hunt him down for Iron's death.

"Look," I said, "believe me or don't believe me, I don't care. The story isn't changing no matter how many times you shove me into a door. I would have thought you figured that one out already."

Copper took a step back and folded her arms, the picture of a dangerous woman having a dangerous debate with herself.

She was the one who'd come to ask me about Degan the first time around, and later the one who had dragged me to meet with five other members of the Order of the Degans. They hadn't liked what I told them, hadn't liked not having anyone alive to pin Degan's disappearance on, let alone Iron's death. Hadn't liked it enough that I'd spent the next week pissing blood after they were done "talking" to me. But while Copper had never laid a hand on me during that entire time, she'd also clearly not reached the same conclusion as her fellows.

And that was what had me worried. It's the calm ones you have to watch out for. Always.

Finally, she let out a sigh and dropped her arms. "All right, Kin," she said, sounding tired. "We've gone over this as much as we're going to here."

I let myself relax. "Good, because I—"

"But," she added, placing her hand on my shoulder—the shoulder that had the rope riding across it. I winced. "That doesn't change the fact that Bronze is still missing, and that I still don't believe you. And that means we're going to spend some more time together." She squeezed. I grunted. "So what we're going to do is—"

"What you're going to do," said a voice behind Copper as the degan froze, her eyes going wide, "is let go of my boss and keep your hands out in front of you."

I knew that voice. I smiled.

I shook off Copper's hand and peered around the degan. Behind her, long knife prodding the space just to the left of the degan's spine, stood Fowler. The Oak Mistress's hair was a near tangle, her clothing wrinkled and stiff from having dried on her body, her eyes ringed by dark smudges of fatigue. But none of that mattered. What mattered was the spark that shone within the hollows of her eyes and the thrust of her lower lip above her dirty chin. What mattered was she was breathing. That, and the fact that she had a pair of her Oaks behind her.

If Copper hadn't been standing between us, I would have kissed Fowler then and there, consequences be damned.

Copper looked over her shoulder. I saw her grin in profile.

"Three?" she said. "You think I can't handle three of you, little bird?"

Fowler tilted her head and met the degan grin for grin. "I know you can. Which is why I made sure to send word to Blue Cloak Rhys and his boys before I came to interrupt." She looked past Copper to me for the first time. "Sorry for the delay."

I shrugged. "These things happen."

It might seem strange, but I didn't control Blackpot Street or any of the surrounding cordon, collectively known as Paper Hill. Gray Princes didn't operate that way. We didn't control territory; we controlled people. We influenced them, manipulated them, bought and sold them, steered and guided them—all without most of them being any the wiser. The threat of the Gray Prince was not that he would send his people after you—it was that he would get your people to do his bidding for him. With a Gray Prince, you didn't have to watch out for enemies—you had to watch out for everyone.

Or, at least, that was the theory. I hadn't quite figured out the finer points of pulling all of the marionette strings yet, and so had to rely on other tools, one of which was Blue Cloak Rhys. Fortunately for me, Rhys was the local Upright Man. He was also mine. And while I might not have controlled the surrounding streets, he most certainly did.

Copper knew all this, of course, just as she knew that when Rhys showed up, it wouldn't be alone. A degan she might be, but I suspected an alley full of heavily armed muscle could ruin even her day.

If the degan spent any time weighing her options, she didn't show it. She merely nodded once, put both of her hands in plain sight, and stepped slowly aside. She showed me a cool smile.

"Another time, then," she said.

I smiled back. "Mm-hmm."

Copper turned and, without sparing even a glance for Fowler or her men, strolled off down the street.

Fowler watched the degan go. When Copper was half a block away, she nodded to her Oaks. They headed out after her, one melting into the crowd so expertly that I had trouble picking him out after ten paces, the other moving toward a side street where he could parallel Copper either from roof or alley. Neither of them, I knew, would stop following the degan until she was well out of Paper Hill.

"Is Blue Cloak Rhys really coming?" I said to Fowler as I watched them go.

"Are you joking?" said Fowler. She slid her long blade home. "When's the last time you saw Rhys before sunset? That bastard's eyes would shrivel up if he ever looked on daylight."

I nodded after the retreating degan. "Thanks for tha—"

"Fuck you."

"Excuse me?"

Fowler turned, slapped both of her hands against my chest, and shoved. "I said, *fuck you!*" she shouted as I stumbled back. "What the hell were you thinking back there at the landing?"

"I—"

"Shut up. I'll tell you what you were thinking. You were thinking you knew better. You were thinking you needed to do something so you could save my ass. You were thinking you were going to be clever and fast and play the hero." She stepped forward and shoved again. This time I stayed put. "You were thinking like a fucking Nose."

"I was thinking," I said, stepping forward, "that we were overmatched and needed to get the hell out of there. Or would you have rather waited for more of Soggy Petyr's people to arrive before we ran?"

"I would have rather you left it to me in the first place. If anyone's supposed to draw Cutters away from someone else, it's me. You don't get to take those kinds of risks anymore."

"It worked, didn't it?"

"That's not the point."

"It's precisely the point. If I'd stayed we might all be dead. You were busy killing one cove and holding off another, and Scratch was pinned in; I was the only one who could play the hare. So I did."

"And ended up with three Cutters on your blinders."

"Better on my blinders than in your face."

Fowler's hand flew faster than I could catch it. The crack of it connecting with my cheek practically echoed off the surrounding buildings.

"Don't you dare," she said. "Don't you *dare* pretend that my life is more valuable than yours, that I don't get to make that choice. I'm your Oak Mistress, dammit—it's my job to watch out for you."

"Watching over me doesn't mean—"

"Doesn't mean what? Doesn't mean I get to put my ass on the line? Doesn't mean I get to care? To hell with that. I get to decide what my life is worth, not you."

"Not when it comes to trading it for mine, you don't."

"That's precisely when I get to decide: When you're busy being a stubborn, shortsighted, selfish ass."

"In other words, most days."

"Damn straight, most da—oh, you bastard." Fowler turned away, trying to stifle a grin. "You son of a bitch. That's not fair, making me laugh."

I smiled in turn and forced myself to release some of the tension that had been gathering in my shoulders. "Fair has nothing to do with it. Or didn't you realize that, now that I'm a Gray Prince?" I made the last two words sound comically ominous.

Fowler snickered, then took a deep breath. When she turned back to me, her fires were, if not out, then at least banked. "You're right," she said. "Fair has nothing to do with it. But that's my point. You're a Gray Prince now, Drothe—you don't get to take stupid risks. Drawing three swordsmen away in a street fight is our job—we're the ones who're supposed to face the steel while you fade. It's not just about you being smart enough to stay ahead of the rest of the Kin; it's about you staying alive. About letting the rest of us handle the street-level shit so you can focus on the bigger picture."

I shook my head. "That's not how I work and you know it."

"Maybe not, but it's how you need to start operating. Otherwise it won't matter whether it comes from another Prince or some cut-rate Eriff who gets lucky in an alley—you'll still end up dead because you couldn't let go of the street. And I'll be damned if I lose any more people just so you can keep playing the Nose instead of the Prince."

"Give me some cred—wait," I said, picking up on what she'd just said—or rather, what she hadn't said. I looked past her, scanning the street. "Where's Scratch? Is he dustmans?"

Fowler barked out something that, on any other day, might have passed for a laugh. Now it just sounded like pain. "There's no getting anything by you, is there?"

"How'd he—?"

"Does it matter? He was doing his fucking job, which is more than I can say for you." She turned her head as if to spit, then seemed to think better of it and instead pulled off her cap. She ran a hand through spiked, greasy hair. "People are dying for you, Drothe. And they're going to keep dying. My people, your people—Kin you don't even know. And you can't stop it. All you can do is be worth it." She put the cap back on and turned away. "Try to be worth it, will you? At least for me."

I stood there, watching her go, until the morning crowds swallowed her up.

Chapter Five

I woke to the sound of a late summer storm, the rain hitting like shovelfuls of gravel in the paved courtyard outside my window. For a moment, the remnants of a dream flitted at the edge of my consciousness—memories of roses and rivers, of blood and carpeted hallways—before the reality of the night came in and crowded them aside.

I shifted in my bed and listened to the noise.

I wasn't used to a courtyard yet, let alone one big enough to allow rain to fall down into it. The closest I'd ever come was a street running along the other side of my shutters, and most of them had been so narrow that rain didn't drop so much as seep into the gap between buildings. Before that, in my youth, it had been the rain coming down through the trees, which was a different thing entirely.

I sat up in darkness that wasn't darkness and looked over toward the window in question. Rain without, none within, thanks to the covered walkway that ran around three sides of the courtyard. I'd left the shutters open on purpose, to test myself. To see if I could sleep with them open. I had, but only, I suspected, out of exhaustion.

When was the last time I'd left a window open when I slept? When was the last time I'd had the trust, or the courage, to even try? I couldn't remember, and that alone told me too much.

I reached over and took an *ahrami* seed from the bowl beside my bed and placed it in my mouth. Rest wasn't an option anymore—not now. Not with the rain and the window and the nerves.

I stood up. It wasn't easy.

Everything felt sore, from the bottoms of my feet to the bruise on my forehead, and double for what lay in between. I stretched this way, twisted that, and filled the air with more curses and grunts than were likely necessary. Then I drew on a fresh shirt, pulled up blissfully clean pants, and padded my way—stiffly—out of the bedroom and down the hall. I stopped in the shadow of the doorway that led out onto the courtyard.

Out here, the rain was a curtain, the noise so loud I took a step back. Where normally I could have seen across the courtyard—seen the stone bench and the potted trees, the iron gate and the entry alcove beyond—now all I could make out was an amber blur of falling water. I, who could see in the dark, blinded by a bit of falling water.

In a way, I preferred it like this: the not seeing—or at least, not seeing the trappings of my princedom before me. It was still unnerving to wake up and find rooms and a courtyard and sky overhead. For nearly as long as I'd been in Ildrecca, it had been close walls, loud neighbors, and, maybe, a smoke-shrouded strip of blue glimpsed between buildings. Even when I'd graduated to apartments of my own, they'd been in the darker, danker, tighter portions of the capital. Narrow was good, loud was secure, smelly was reassuring. But this?

Even with Fowler's people standing Oak and making the rounds, the place didn't feel secure to me; didn't seem as if I belonged. Oh, I understood why it was easier to keep watch over a private house rather than a set of rooms above a shop or in a tenement, how it made sense for someone like me to set himself apart from the rest of the Kin and the Lighters—but that didn't mean I had to like it.

It had been Kells's idea, of course. Once my boss, now my sworn man, he was the closest thing I had to a mentor when it came to being a Gray Prince. It was Kells who had first told me about the street naming me a Prince, just as he had been the first to offer me his Clasp and help me begin forming what little organization I now had. He was a master when it came to running a crew, and I was happy to have him at my side.

Or would have been, if he wasn't also serving as a Long Nose for me in another Gray Prince's operation. It hadn't been my intention to put him to spying on Solitude, but she'd already taken him under her cloak when he'd approached me on the matter. We'd talked about him walking away from her over the last few months, but Kells was concerned that his leaving would make her suspicious of the other members of his former organization that had taken shelter with her. In some cases, the suspicions would have been justified—I had five people actively working the corners in Solitude's camp—but in most others, it wouldn't.

I'd spent seven years working as a Long Nose for Kells before our respective reversals of fortune—I knew what it meant to live neck deep in another person's organization, with only a slip of the tongue or the wrong piece of information standing between you and a very long, very painful death. I wasn't willing to put his people at risk simply for my convenience.

And so we communicated on the sly, using coded messages and blind drops and the occasional carefully orchestrated meeting. His advice was still invaluable—more so even than his information—but it came too seldom, and usually with too much delay, to make a difference most days.

No, just like the house, I was having to get used to more space around me when it came to the Kin. More room to maneuver, more space to make mistakes, more sky to bring down both disaster and opportunity upon me.

I sat down on the stoop and listened to the rain falling in the courtyard, comforted by the fact that right now, whether my eyes were open or closed, I was equally blind.

Eventually, I fell asleep.

"You wanted to see me?"

I looked up from my plate to find Betriz standing over me, an impish smile on her face. She always seemed to have

an impish smile on her face, usually for good reason. I just
never liked when it was directed at me.

It was two days after my entry back into the city and I
was sitting at an outdoor table at a tavern called the Plucked
Quill. It was three blocks from my new house, did respectable trade, and had an excellent board when it came to
food. I'd arranged to gain a small interest in the place after
my second meal there.

"Sit," I said, indicating the place across from me. She did,
swinging one long leg over the chair rather than pulling it
out. Betriz then placed an elbow on the table, put her chin
on her hand, and regarded me with bright brown eyes.

"You realize the answer is still no," she said. "Right?"

I smiled as I picked up a piece of flat bread. It was still
warm. "You haven't even heard my offer."

"Doesn't matter. I'm not about to be narrowed, not even
by the likes of the great Drothe himself."

I made a rude noise with my lips. "Please. If I were
'great,' I wouldn't be asking you to work for me, I'd be telling you."

"And I'd still be saying no."

"Which is why I keep making offers."

Betriz flashed an easy smile and helped herself to a corner of my bread. I didn't argue.

Betriz was a Nose, and a good one at that. She had a
strong reputation on the street, with a record of not falling
for bullshit and a habit of getting things done. I'd been trying to bring her into my organization for a couple of months
now, but she was happy playing the Wide Nose—a freelance
information scrounger—and had no interest in tying herself
down. I couldn't blame her, really: I'd felt much the same
way in my early days on the dodge. It hadn't been until I'd
fallen under Kells's sway that I'd even considered working
exclusively for one crime lord, and that had only been because he was, to my mind, a legend among Upright Men. I
might be a Gray Prince, but I hadn't done near enough to
warrant that kind of starry-eyed devotion—at least, not in
Betriz's opinion.

"So what's the dodge?" She leaned forward, eyes practically dancing. "Does it have anything to do with the ambush Soggy Petyr pulled on you the other day?"

I shook my head. Per Fowler's pointed suggestion, I already had some people looking into dealing with Petyr, not to mention getting the plays back for Tobin and his troupe. Between the bragging the Petty Boss was likely doing and the complaining I could expect from the actors if I didn't have something to show them, I didn't want to leave things longer than I had to. But that didn't mean I wanted to bring someone like Betriz in on either issue. The last thing I needed was outside talent getting wind of my debts.

"Don't worry about Petyr," I said. "All I need from you is a bit of cove hunting."

"And you can't use your own people because . . . ?"

"Because I don't want to risk them being tied to me."

"Meaning there's a chance of someone seeing me if I do this dodge."

"There's always a chance. We both know that."

Betriz put the corner of bread in her mouth and chewed. "Who?" she said.

I tore off a portion of bread myself and dragged it through a smear of young, runny goat cheese on my plate, then topped it off with a piece of sliced sausage. There were hints of cardamom and aniseed in the greasy meat, along with a healthy dose of black pepper, all of which worked against the sourness of the cheese. I chewed, swallowed, and then followed it with one of the fat black grapes to help cut the spices.

Betriz waited patiently during this, knowing it for the delay it was.

"Rambles," I said at last.

"Huh." She sat back in her seat, then leaned forward to take a grape off my plate. "Huh," she said again.

"What?"

"Way I hear it, he's been looking for someone to do a bit of snilching on you, too."

It didn't surprise me, especially considering what else he'd been doing lately. "And?"

Betriz made a face. "He's still figuring out he has money. Didn't offer nearly enough for me to turn on you. Boy has to learn that people expect a certain amount of ready when it comes to working for an Upright, let alone spying on a Gray Prince."

"I'm heartened by how hard you cling to your standards."

"Girl has to have 'em." The grape went into her mouth. "So, what d'you need?"

"Not much," I said. "Just a time and place where I can drop in on Rambles and knock the shit out of him."

"Oh, is that all?"

"That's all."

Betriz shook her head and helped herself to my cup of coffee. "And this is why I'll never take your Clasp, Drothe."

"Why's that?"

"Because if this is the kind of shit you have to talk me into doing, I hate to think about the jobs I'd get if we didn't have to dicker over price."

I smiled and signaled for another cup.

Chapter Six

I crouched, my body hidden by the decorative stonework that ran along the roof's edge, and peered around the nymph's carved ass in the growing dusk. Sweat trickled down my back. Even three stories up, it was humid and still.

Below, in the small courtyard in front of the whorehouse, I could hear the voices of two toughs talking to a third. The two were alternately joking and pleading, trying to talk their way into the Mort Ken across the way. The doorman was having none of it. He kept telling them over and over that the whorehouse was closed until an hour after sunset, but the two men weren't taking no for an answer.

Which was the whole idea.

"This is stupid," muttered Nijjan.

I flexed my fingers and stared at the roof across from us and stayed silent.

"I mean, really stupid."

"Shut up, Nijjan."

Nijjan Red Nails shifted behind her own nymph, her slippers scraping softly against the roof tiles. As an Upright Woman, Nijjan wasn't used to dancing roofs or playing the Crow; but neither was she used to having her Gray Prince at her door, demanding she put together a raid on another boss's territory in less than four hours. To say she hadn't been happy to see me would have been an understatement; to say part of her wouldn't have preferred to gut me and throw me out the door after hearing my plan would have been an outright lie. Especially since she was right: This was stupid. Really stupid.

Betriz had come through better—and faster—than I'd expected. A day of nosing had seen her back at my door, information in hand. It turned out that Rambles had developed a pattern for himself, at least when it came to checking his investments, and today was the day he collected his profits—and sampled the wares—at the whorehouse across from us.

"Are you sure he's in there?" said Nijjan.

"I'm sure."

"Because if I end up going to war over this bastard and he isn't even in there . . ."

I turned my eyes away from the roof and met Nijjan's gaze. "I'm sure."

Nijjan glared at me, her blue eyes standing out like lanterns in the fading light. She was wrapped in russets and tans and browns, her dark hair cropped short and spiky. Hennaed designs on her hands and cheeks turned round and round one another, like some lost language run amok on her skin. Only her fingernails remained devoid of any decoration, and that because she didn't want there to be any confusion about her name. She wasn't Red Nails because of what was at the end of her fingers; she was Red Nails because of the broad-headed copper spikes she used to hold people down—or up—when she was annoyed with them.

"Fine," she said. "He's in there. But I still don't see why we can't bring a few more Cutters with us in case—"

"Because more Cutters mean more noise," I said. "And being noticed is not what we need right now."

Nijjan grumbled and looked back out over the roof.

I couldn't blame her: We were deep in a rival Upright Man's territory, preparing to make a raid on one of his properties. If we were looking for a way to start a minor war, it didn't get much better than this. Add to that the fact we were outnumbered—possibly severely—and that any help we might call on was hiding in a basement at least two blocks away, and it was a wonder she'd agreed to come at all.

And yet here she was, all because I'd said one word: Rambles.

Ever since he'd climbed over the ruins of Nicco's organization to become an Upright Man, Rambles had been working on expanding his territory. Take over a minor racket here, twist the arm of a lesser gang there, and suddenly he was a growing concern. That kind of give-and-take wasn't uncommon among the Kin, especially in the aftermath of a major war—uncertainty could be translated into opportunity, after all—but in Rambles's case, some of the take had been at Nijjan's expense. Not enough to justify all-out war, but enough to fester and make her knife that much looser in its sheath when it came to his name.

I turned my attention back to the roof of the Mort Ken. It was a morass of shadows now, the planters and statues and ivy conspiring to cloak the place in early darkness. The only saving grace was that the statues and the roof behind us did the same thing over here.

I hooked a finger into the pouch around my neck and scooped out a pair of *ahrami* seeds. I slipped them into my mouth almost without noticing. They didn't help my nerves, but then, I hadn't expected them to. We were long past that.

"How long are your boys going to take?" I said.

"Give them time. They can't just start a fight at the drop of a hat."

"You're kidding me, right?"

I could hear the smile in her voice. "Not if you want them to be a distraction, they can't. Too soon, or too easy, and the Jiggerman at the door will catch on. Finesse, my Prince. Finesse."

I bit down on the seeds in irritation and reached for another. That's when I saw the shadow move on the opposite roof.

"There," I hissed. "There's our Crow."

"Where?"

"Third urn in, just past the statue of the woman with her hand up her—"

"I see it." Pause. "Are you sure?"

Of course I was sure. It was getting dark enough that my night vision was beginning to limn the edges of things with faint amber threads. Another five or ten minutes, and I wouldn't need to study the shadows—I'd just be able to see the lookout. Out loud, though, I said, "Just wait. If your boys do their job, you'll see that Crow twitch well enough."

A new voice had added itself to the noise from below. As planned, a third man had joined Nijjan's first two and begun egging the others on, upping the tension and the uncertainty. Things were getting louder now.

"Got him!" hissed Nijjan.

I looked over and smiled. Nearly directly across from us, a man's head had emerged from the shadows of the urn and was now looking over the edge of the roof.

Like me, Nijjan wasn't originally from Ildrecca. But where I'd come from the woods, she was a plains girl—raised to the horse and the herd and the bow. She'd first made a name for herself when she began poaching from the Imperial Game Reserve northwest of Ildrecca and hosting Kin-only feasts at a tavern just inside the city. She was long past that now, but still put on the occasional demonstration to remind people that, even from far away, you didn't want to anger Nijjan.

I heard a faint sound beside me and turned in time to see Nijjan lift her bow from the shadows of the roof, lay one of the handful of arrows she'd brought across it, draw, and let fly, all in a seamless, flowing motion.

By the time I looked back across the gap, the head was gone. I didn't insult her by asking if she'd gotten her man.

"Let's go," she said. "My men won't be able to keep those coves busy forever without someone getting bloodied. I'd prefer we have our hands on Rambles when the time comes."

I rose and padded along the roof, reaching behind me to adjust Degan's sword as I went. I'd managed to find a baldric to replace the rope the boatman had given me, but hadn't gotten around to finding a suitable scabbard yet. I'd wrapped the canvas into a rough covering, though, so while it might not have been stylish, Degan's sword was at least riding more comfortably across my back.

For her part, when Nijjan had first seen the bundle she'd merely looked at it, looked at me, and shaken her head. Ungainly or not, I wasn't about to risk losing it, even if it made it harder to run the roofs.

We followed the roofline around the piazza, hopping low walls, dancing leaded peaks, and jumping a narrow drainage alley, until we found ourselves on the Mort Ken's roof.

There had been a garden up here once. Raised beds meant for flowers and herbs had been shoved off to one side of the roof, their wood faded and rotting. A few potted fruit trees still struggled on, their roots crowding out of the soil around the top, or escaping through cracks in the ceramic that held them. A handful of weathered columns were scattered about, standing guard over a herd of forlorn chairs and dining couches. I could almost see how, at night, with the right lighting and enough fortified wine, the place could take on an air of neglected elegance—just the kind of surroundings to help set the mood and persuade a Lighter to be that much lighter in his purse come morning. Assuming, of course, they first got rid of the man sprawled on the roof with Nijjan's arrow sticking out of his head.

We could hear shouting from the street now—voices raised in challenge and argument. No hiss or ring of steel yet, which was good. We needed attention focused on the front door for as long as possible; a fight would be over too quickly, and not in our favor. So far, it sounded as if Nijjan's people were doing just what we wanted.

The sunset was little more than a smudge below the horizon now, making the shadows on the roof even thicker. As I looked around, amber-gold began to settle itself more easily across my vision.

"How the hell do we get down?" growled Nijjan. "I can't see the damn jigger for all the crap up here."

I scanned the space around us, looking for the trapdoor that would have been used not only by customers, but possibly by the whores themselves when they decided to sleep or eat under the stars.

"There." I led Nijjan over to a rectangle set in the roof behind a pair of pillars. I held back, letting her take the door, both because I was the Prince, and because I didn't need any sudden light blinding my recently awakened sight. When it creaked open, a faint glow crept out. Even then, my eyes still burned.

"Looks like it opens into a room," said Nijjan, her voice low. She set aside her bow and drew a long, curved knife. She stepped into the opening and went down into the building.

I blinked the last of the tears from my eyes and went over to the door. A set of steep, narrow stairs led down into the whorehouse. Nijjan was waiting at their base.

I half stepped, half climbed down into a sitting room. A single, weak tallow candle burned on the sideboard, illuminating a pair of worn chairs and a vase filled with the remains of dead flowers. Petals littered the sideboard and floor.

Nijjan moved over to the room's only door and opened it a crack. The hinge, thank the Angels, barely groaned.

"Hallway," she said. She turned to face me. "Now what?"

"Now we go down one floor."

"And then?"

I shrugged. "We look and listen."

Nijjan's hand caught mine as I moved to go past her. "Wait. Are you telling me you don't even know where Rambles is?"

"I know he's on the third floor."

"That's it? We just go down a flight and listen at whores' doors until we think we've found the right one?"

"More or less." I'd operated on a hell of a lot less for years. "No one else is doing any trade right now, so it shouldn't be that hard."

Nijjan stared at me. "And these kinds of plans work for you?"

"You'd be surprised."

The Upright Woman snorted as I opened the door the rest of the way. "I don't know whether to be disappointed or impressed."

I smiled. "Me either, some days."

We padded our way past a few doors, then down the main stairway at the center of the building. More noises from the ground floor drifted up to us, along with more voices. I peeked over the railing and saw any number of heads and shoulders straining out into the stairwell trying to catch a glimpse of the action below. Fortunately for us, the ladies of the house had migrated down to the second floor and below for a better view, leaving the third-floor landing deserted.

This floor was better appointed, if a frayed wicker chair, wall mirror, and faded wool floor runner constituted "better." Tapers burned in sconces along the wall, their light reflected back into the hallway by the polished brass plates mounted behind them.

Nijjan looked at me and quirked an eyebrow in question. I pointed left, mainly to seem decisive.

Just like the floor above, the doors here were close together. These were the narrows, where the whores made the majority of the Bawd's money, moving men and women in and out with impressive speed. The bigger rooms, for well-lined guests and the occasional orgy, would be down below, closer to the street and the money.

However, Betriz's information put Rambles's preferred room on this floor, which didn't make much sense until we came to a wide door at the end of the hall. Crimson damask had been tacked to the surface, turning the door into a flowery, bloodred rectangle. A single brass handle, shaped like an erection and polished to a high shine, shimmered in the candle light.

"A bit much, don't you think?" muttered Nijjan.

"For a Mort Ken?"

"Good point."

I leaned toward the door. There were voices on the other side. And laughter.

Nijjan fingered her knife. I drew my rapier. Surprise might be nice, but I've found that putting an extra three-plus feet of steel between you and the person you're bursting in on never hurts.

I wrapped my left hand around the brass cock, twisted, and shoved.

I'll admit, I'd been hoping to walk in and find Rambles ass-in-the-air over a doxy. Not only would it have been convenient from an ambush standpoint, but the humiliation would have been a nice touch as well. As it was, though, I wasn't overly surprised to find them both dressed and sitting at the table, their supper before them, wineglasses to hand. You learn not to count on breaks like that when it comes to raiding an enemy's ken.

What did surprise me, though, was to find another person sitting at the table with them. A person I knew from the trail to Barrab and beyond. A man I'd been hoping to find again, but never figured I would.

Wolf.

I'd been more right than I thought: Wolf was Rambles's man. Somehow, in some way, the Upright Man *had* been behind this. Now I just had to figure out how.

If hadn't had my sword in my hand, I would have drawn it then. As it was, I filled my left hand with my fighting dagger and stepped aside to let Nijjan through the door. No one at the table moved.

Wolf surprised me by speaking first. "Please," he said, his eyes still on his plate. "Don't insult me by waving your steel around as if you mean to use it."

I showed my teeth in an expression that could never have been mistaken for a smile. "If you think I'm not willing to use this, you're sadly mistaken."

Wolf held up a piece of roasted lamb on his fork. He was much as he'd appeared on the trail, only cleaner. With the dust of the road washed away, his black hair and beard had taken on an almost bluish sheen. By contrast, his complexion, though still dark from nature and sun, had lightened to a deep tan with the dirt removed. Gone was the sun-faded tunic and burnoose of the hills; instead, he now wore an embroidered silver-gray robe and matching pair of ankle pants. He'd put a striped robe on over all of it, the pattern no doubt declaring his tribe and clan to more knowledgeable eyes than my own.

Wolf put the lamb in his mouth and chewed. "I was not," he said, "speaking to you, O Prince."

I blinked, momentarily confused, until the implication settled in. Then I spun to put Nijjan fully in my field of vision. She was scowling at the Azaari bandit. She was also putting her knife away.

Hell. No wonder her people and Rambles's had never come to blows in the courtyard; they were in on this together.

I reevaluated the situation. Three on one, if you didn't count the doxy. I could do this, couldn't I? Of course I could. I was the one with steel in his hands, after all.

I was also in a hell of a lot of trouble.

I shifted my stance and extended my dagger slightly toward the table. They were maybe seven feet away, and still sitting. Nijjan had her blades away. If I could take her with one quick, clean lunge, that would leave the doorway free. Even if I couldn't pull it shut behind me, her body should—

"Don't," said Wolf, spearing another piece of lamb on his fork. "You won't make it out."

"You don't think so?" I said.

"I know so."

Wolf put down his fork and stood.

When I had first met Wolf, he was wearing a dagger. On the road to Barrab, in the town itself, even on the road back, it had been the short blade for him. Some people are just that way: They prefer a dagger, or a sword, or what have you. Wolf was a dagger man.

Except now he was wearing a sword. A sword with a silver-chased guard, set upon a well-used steel foundation. A sword that, when it was drawn, I knew would be of the finest Black Isle steel, with a single, faint tear etched into the metal where the blade met the guard.

I knew this because I had seen a sword like his countless times before, because I had watched its like cut down both Kin and Imperial White Sashes, and because I carried its sister strapped to my back. Wolf was a degan.

Which meant I was screwed.

*　　*　　*

I dropped my sword and dagger on the carpet without ceremony. If Wolf had wanted me dead, he could have done it countless times on the road. The threat here wasn't from his steel or mine: It was simply from my having walked into the room. "Knives, too?" I said, holding up my left arm and indicating my boot with my right.

"I don't see the need," said Wolf.

Ouch.

Neither of us mentioned the sword on my back.

"So, which is it," I said, "Wolf or Silver Degan?"

Wolf shrugged. "As you please."

I leaned back against the wall and folded my arms, trying to appear the Gray Prince, all the while using the maneuver to surreptitiously wipe my sweating palms on my doublet. I looked at Nijjan.

"How much?" I said sourly.

Nijjan shook her head. "You think I'd do this for money?" She brushed her hands together and made a casting-away motion in my direction, signifying she was done with our alliance, with our Clasp. "You aren't the Gray Prince you looked to be a couple of months ago, Drothe. Having your back is going to get too costly in very short order. I don't need that—not with him sniffing at my borders." She jerked a thumb at Rambles, who was still sitting quietly, the girl on his lap.

My gut clenched at her comment. I'd always held her in higher regard than most of the other Upright Men. Like me, she'd started out without any connections among the Kin and had managed to work her way up by means of sheer talent and determination. Nijjan was smart when it came to the street and her opinion carried weight. If she believed my star was on the decline, I didn't want to think about what that meant for me over the next several months.

To her face, though, I showed a blank expression and said, "So in exchange for my neck you get a quiet border? I would have given you a lot more for a lot less."

"Oh, I offered more," said Rambles. The slender Upright Man picked up his wine, the rings on his fingers clinking softly against the glass. "But Nijjan wouldn't take it." He sipped and gave a satisfied smile, although I suspected it didn't have anything to do with the vintage. "I offered her over half a cordon two months ago for your head on a platter, but she told me to—"

"No one here is interested in your failed attempts at corruption," said Wolf mildly, cutting off another piece of lamb. "If you wish to bark, little dog, go outside; otherwise, shut your snout."

The easy smile that had been on Rambles's face vanished, replaced by a dark scowl. As for the doxy, she discreetly slid to her feet and crossed the room to settle on the bed in the far corner.

Smart girl.

"This is *my* ken," said Rambles, leaning forward in his seat, "and *my* organization. You're in my house, Silver: Don't think for a moment that that sword at your side means you can tell me what to do, let alone what I can and can't say." Rambles thrust a finger in my direction. "If it wasn't for me, you wouldn't have been able to corner this shit so easily. I—"

"Don't tell a wolf how to hunt," said the degan. "If I hadn't used you, I would have found another hound equally as useful."

"I'm no one's 'hound,' you self-important Azaari son of a—"

Wolf's sword was out of its scabbard and at Rambles's throat in a blur. Across the room, the doxy squeaked. Rambles froze.

"My people," said Wolf coldly, "are *very* sensitive about our lineage. We don't take well to those who question it, let alone besmirch it. Especially when they are so-called civilized Ildrecci who couldn't find their way out of a box canyon with a week's worth of water and a map." Wolf shifted his hand, causing the blade's tip to dig into the skin of Rambles's neck. I couldn't help noticing that Wolf's sword was a curved horseman's saber. "You understand me?"

"I . . . understand," said Rambles.

"Then understand this as well: Until I release you from the last tatters of Iron's Oath, you're mine. The strings he

left on you before his death are mine to pull now. I've laid
claim to them, and I'll use you however, and as often, as I
see fit." Another twist of the blade. "Is this understood?"

I became very still against the wall. This changed things.

I'd walked in here thinking Rambles was the one pulling
Wolf's strings; that, while my old rival might not have been
the one who came up with the plan, he'd been the one passing the orders along. I couldn't see Rambles having the
stones to dust Crook Eye and set me up, but I could easily
see him being a step or two down on the ladder from whoever had.

But now, with Wolf invoking his degan's Oath and pulling the leash taut on Rambles, I had to adjust my assumptions. And what's more, it wasn't a matter of Wolf having
made an agreement with the Upright Man—it was Wolf
claiming the Oath Rambles had sworn to Iron Degan. The
Oath was the ultimate contract as far as the degans were
concerned. Swearing it not only got you one of the best
mercenaries in the empire—no small thing, considering
some degans spent years fulfilling their Oaths—it also
meant you likewise owed the degan a debt as well. A debt
that could be called in any time, for any one service. Ages
back, people were said to have killed friends and family
rather than break the Oath; now the biggest threat to breaking that promise was having an angry degan after you—
which, given the degans I'd met, was bad enough.

The truly daunting bit, though—and the one that had
given me pause when I'd sworn my Oath with Degan—was
the provision that said any degan could claim your Oath if
the degan you'd sworn it to died. How Wolf had found out
about the deal between Rambles and Iron I had no idea; all
I knew was that if he'd dug up the deal on Rambles, then it
was possible he could find out about the Oath between me
and Degan—the one I'd never fulfilled.

Whether Degan's change in status meant he could claim
it, I had no idea, but I wasn't in a hurry to find out.

"Of course," continued Wolf, his blade still lingering
about Rambles's neck, "you could always sever the Oath."

He flicked his wrist, drawing the barest hint of his sword's tip across Rambles's throat, only to bring the blade back to its original position before the Upright Man had time to do more than gasp. A thin red line began seeping from Rambles's skin. "Is this your desire, little dog?"

I could practically hear Rambles's teeth grinding from across the room. "No."

"Good." Wolf drew back his blade and wiped it clean with a napkin. "If it helps, you and I are almost done with our business."

"Not soon enough for me." Rambles picked up his own napkin and pressed it to his neck, then drew it away and frowned at the stain. "You could have learned a lot from your late sword brother about dealing with people. He used his words almost as well as his sword."

Wolf smiled as he finished polishing his blade. "Perhaps, but as much as I may have loved Iron, I can't help noticing that I'm alive while he's in the ground." He tossed the napkin on the table. "Now, all of you leave us. I need to speak to the Gray Prince alone."

Rambles, napkin back at his neck, glared at Wolf one last time and stormed out of the room. He didn't even look at me. The doxy paused long enough to take a last sweet biscuit from the table and followed him out.

For her part, Nijjan stepped partway through the doorway, then paused. She looked over and met my eye.

"It wasn't just because you're in trouble," she said. "I wouldn't cross you just for that."

"Then why?"

She looked over her shoulder at Wolf. "Ask him." Then she was out of the room and closing the door behind her.

I looked back at Wolf and cocked an eyebrow. "Well?"

He gestured at the table, inviting me to sit. I remained where I was, up against the wall.

"A clever woman, Nijjan," he said, smiling at my caution. "And one who knows how to drive a bargain."

"She wouldn't have survived very long as an Upright Woman if she didn't."

"Likely not." He picked up a fluted brass goblet and took a deliberate sip. "So. You want to know what I offered her, yes?"

"That's the idea."

"Then you'll first tell me what happened to Iron Degan."

I crossed my arms. "Seems like I've been asked to retell that tale a lot lately."

"Then it should come easily to your tongue."

"Like I told the Order, Shadow already had Iron's blade at his side when—"

The brass goblet crashed into the wall beside me with a hollow clang, taking a gouge out of the plaster and sending a spray of wine against the side of my face in the process. I flinched, and hated myself for doing so.

"I'm not interested in the tale you told the Order," he said, reaching across the table to pick up Rambles's goblet, along with the half-full decanter of wine. "The council has closed the matter. What I *am* interested in is what truly happened to Iron Degan, and how the sudden disappearance of our mutual friend . . ." Here Wolf paused to glance at the sword on my back. ". . . plays into that."

I didn't bat an eye at the reference. Wolf had heard me speak to Fowler about Degan's blade back in Barrab, had seen the bundle when we escaped the town—it didn't surprise me that he knew about it. What did impress me was they he'd been able to feign disinterest so well up to this point.

"What's Degan's disappearance to you?" I said.

Wolf rolled the goblet in his hand, took a sip. "I'm a degan," he said. "Bronze is my sword brother. We are, in many ways, of the same tribe. It's only natural I be worried about him."

"Bullshit. You don't kill one Gray Prince and set another up just because you haven't gotten a letter in a couple months. You want something: something I have or something I know—and it must be pretty damn important if you're willing to hold Crook Eye's death over me to get it."

"I didn't kill Crook Eye to hold him over you."

So Wolf had done it. I wasn't exactly surprised, but it was good to know nonetheless.

"Then why'd you dust him?" I said.

Wolf looked me in the eye for the first time since I'd entered the room. "To let you know that I could, of course. To assure you that even a Gray Prince isn't beyond my reach."

My blood seemed to cool and thicken in my veins. As threats went, that was a pretty damn good one.

"And all the rumors you had Rambles spread around?" I said. "Why do that if you just wanted to show me you can dust a Prince?"

Wolf shrugged. "A death can be easy to explain away, but a death laid at your door? Much harder. Not fatal," he added, "but harder. Plus, you needed to know I had resources among your tribe."

I looked at Wolf for a long moment—at his easy pose, his mocking smile, the confident gleam in his eye. I looked at him and realized he'd played me since before I'd met him. That he'd been playing me for weeks, if not more. That he thought he had me.

To hell with this.

I bent down and retrieved my weapons. "If you want answers," I said, resheathing my steel, "you can come and bend the knee or make an offer like any other thug on the street." I turned and reached for the door, noticing the handle was normal on this side. "I stopped giving answers in exchange for threats a long time ago."

"You speak like someone with options. Like someone who has a choice. The only choices here belong to me."

"You mean choosing whether to dust me or let me walk out the door?" The handle turned under my hand. The door latch clicked.

"No. I mean making your life much easier, or much harder. You think I'll stop at placing one dead Prince at your feet? At two? Three? What if I toss a trio of White Sashes in as well? Maybe attach Kells's name to their deaths while I'm at it. Or maybe Fowler's. How long, do you think, before the empire comes sniffing after you then? Before the Kin decide it's smarter to kill you than let you live?"

I laughed, though not as convincingly as I might have liked. "Multiple Gray Princes? A trio of Sashes?" I looked back over my shoulder. "Degan or no, no one's that good. Not even you."

A feral smile spread across Wolf's lips, almost lazy in its danger. "You've spent too much time around my more civilized sword brethren. Not all of us spend our nights wandering the gutters of Ildrecca." He sat up. "I am Silver Degan, and I am of the Azaar. I've left smoldering villages and salted fields in my wake, trampling entire tribes in the dust of my passing. Soldiers curse and widows weep at the sound of my name. What are the threats of back-alley princes and their dagger-wielding thugs to me?"

I bit the inside of my lip. It was a good speech; it was also, quite possibly, true. And even if Wolf didn't pile up bodies the way he claimed, the man could still make things a hell of a lot worse for me. Between what he knew and what he was, Wolf would have me at war with half the Kin in less than a month. All he'd have to do is set his mind to it.

The question wasn't whether or not I'd make it out the door: Wolf had invested too much time and effort into the setup to simply cut me down now. No, the real issue was whether I'd walk out with my old organization intact or a new target on my back.

I closed the door.

"I need to know one thing," I said.

"Yes?"

"Why?"

"Why what?"

"Why the setup? Why ask me about Iron Degan? Why the sudden interest in Bronze?"

"Why?" said Wolf, looking genuinely surprised. "I thought that would be obvious: I need to find Bronze Degan, of course. And I need you to help me do it."

Chapter Seven

The words were out of my mouth before I knew I was saying them.

"Like hell!"

I turned and yanked the door open and stormed down the hall.

"Wait!"

A chair turned over behind me, was followed by the sound of footsteps coming quickly.

I reached the head of the stairs and drew my rapier, spinning back as I did so. Wolf stopped short, my point less than a foot away from him, aiming center-left on his chest. I was pleased to see that my tip didn't waver in the slightest.

"You don't want to do this," he said. He could have been talking about my walking out or my drawing steel on him. I expected it was a little bit of both.

"Maybe not, but I'd rather end up ruined or dead than help you hunt down Degan."

Wolf raised an eyebrow. "You love him that much?"

"I owe him that much."

"Then I was right to choose you."

"To hell with your choices."

Wolf shrugged. "Perhaps." He gestured toward the stairs. "What about Rambles's and Nijjan's men? How will you get past them?"

"They're not what concern me right now." And besides, there was always the roof.

"Ah." Wolf looked at my sword's point, then back at me. The bastard didn't even seem worried. "In that case, I'd best earn my reputation, yes?"

Before I could shift my rapier's tip, his left hand was past it, sliding up and over and around the blade, his arm slithering up my sword like a snake. In an instant my weapon was enveloped, the fabric of his robes serving to both protect his arm from the edge and further entangle my steel. At the same time, he stepped forward and slammed the open palm of his right hand into my sternum.

I fell back, my hands empty, my breath lost, my sword in his grasp.

Fucking degans.

I was still gasping for air when Wolf put a hand under my armpit and helped me to my feet. He slid my rapier back into its scabbard.

"I think we may do better under an open sky," he said. "Come."

I didn't argue. For that matter, I didn't really walk until we were past the second landing and getting near the main floor. I was able to shake off Wolf's arm and move under my own power by the time we made it to the door.

As he'd said, there were a good number of Cutters loitering in the courtyard, although all of them seemed more worried about glaring at one another than watching us. Nijjan and Rambles were there, too, standing with their respective crews. Rambles growled to his men when he saw us and led them back inside; Nijjan simply nodded and turned away.

"So, what was her price?" I said, watching Nijjan go. I'd be lying if I said my voice wasn't bitter.

"Don't hold on to your judgment of her too tightly," said Wolf, following my gaze. "She gave you to me, yes, but only after she was certain I wouldn't kill you. She was very exacting on that point."

"And that's supposed to make me feel better?"

"It's supposed to tell you that she was only willing to go so far in her betrayal. Yes, Nijjan broke her agreement with you, but that's all she did. How many of your Kin would have taken Rambles's offer, or handed you over to me, no questions asked? You're not a man lightly crossed, and she showed courage in doing it to your face. You need to respect the respect she has shown you. Jackals eat whatever meat they find; Nijjan Red Nails is no jackal."

"That still doesn't tell me what she charged to cross me."

"Yes," said Wolf, turning away. "It does."

I started and looked down the street to where Nijjan and her men were slipping into an alley. At the last moment, I caught a glimpse of what might have been a woman's face, skin thick with hennaed patterns, turning back my way. Then she was gone.

Had that been the entirety of her price? Nijjan keeping her turf and me not dying?

Of a sudden, I wanted to go after her—to ask just how far she would have gone for me if I hadn't been set up for Crook Eye's death; to ask whether another month or ten between us would have made a difference. Part of me liked to think that it would have.

Wolf led me toward the center of the square. The cobbles beneath us were black with coal dust and mud from the smithies that populated Rustwater. Iron and water and soot hung thick in the air. Combined with the heat—both from the weather and the banked but never dead forges—it felt as if we were walking through a mine. I glanced upward to be sure and made out blotchy, moving pockets of stars overhead. Clouds rolling in from the steppes to the northwest, bringing heat but no rain.

Summer in Ildrecca. Bad time to be in the city. The walls of the basement taverns would be sweating, while the Kin would be sitting in the dank, drinking, honing their blades, and polishing their grudges. Men and women would die for words that wouldn't have garnered a hard look two weeks before, and the thinnest rumors would take on the heft of fact. More bodies to be found in the alleys, more reasons for the Rags to take their clubs to the Kin.

Bad time to be saving an organization; worse time to be losing one.

Wolf stopped beside a row of low wooden boxes that

had been set up in the middle of the square, each filled with earth. Flowers and leeks and Angels knew what else pushed up against the heat, trying to justify the communal garden. Wolf rested a foot on the corner of a plot.

"I would see his sword," he said.

I reached back, put my hand on the canvas. "No."

"As Bronze's sword brother, it's only proper that I—"

"As the person who's been framed, it's only proper that I tell you to fuck off. I faced down another Gray Prince for this—there's no way I'm handing it over to you."

"I only wish to see it."

"You haven't earned the privilege."

"The—?" Wolf's foot hit the ground with a *thump*. "I'm a degan! If anyone has the right to see Bronze's blade, let alone carry it, it's me."

I put my finger to Wolf's chest, my face in his. "You want to see it? You want to hold it? Tell me why you went through all of this—the charade, the setup, the blackmail— instead of just asking, and I'll *think* about it. Because unless it's a damn good reason, you have about as much chance of getting my help, and your hands on this sword, as I have of becoming emperor."

Without taking his eyes off mine, Wolf reached up and wrapped his hand around my finger. I half expected to hear a *crack*, followed by agonizing pain. Instead, he merely pushed it, and me, back.

"I didn't ask to see it," he said, "because I couldn't be certain of the answer. And because I suspected I already knew what your reply would be." He let go of my hand. I got the feeling that, under different circumstances, he'd have snapped it—and other parts of me—off without hesitation. "You hunted Degan after the fire in Ten Ways," he said. "Then you ceased. This tells me you lost his trail, or decided not to follow it. Either way, given your history with Bronze, I knew asking for your help wouldn't be enough: I needed to get your attention."

"So you dusted Crook Eye?"

"It worked, didn't it? I doubt we'd be standing here talking if I hadn't."

I couldn't argue with that.

I stepped over to the nearest raised bed and sat down on its corner. "So why do you want to find Degan?"

Wolf shook his head. "I answered your question about why I killed Crook Eye; now show me the sword. I'll answer your other questions after that."

I hesitated for a moment, then unslung the bundle and laid it across my legs. By the time I'd undone the rope and begun working at the canvas, Wolf was all but looming over me. When I folded back the last bit of cloth, he caught his breath.

"By the stars," he murmured. "What happened to it?"

I ran my fingers over the wreckage that had been Degan's sword. Soot blackened and charred, it looked worse than it was, but that was still bad enough. What had once been an elegant piece of moon-kissed steel now looked like something that had been abandoned in a back alley after a losing fight. Oh, the sword still ran straight, and the edge seemed to be true under all the grit—this was Black Isle steel, after all; it would take more than a simple fire to damage this blade—but no one would have taken this for a degan's weapon at first glance, or even a second. It hadn't been until I'd noticed the traces of bronze chasing left on the misshapen guard that I'd suspected it for what it was, wasn't until I'd rubbed away the grime at the base of the blade and saw the single tear etched into the sword that I'd known it for what it was. And even then, I'd doubted—that is, until Crook Eye had told me how he got his hands on it.

"It was in that fire you mentioned down in Ten Ways," I said. "I'd thought it had been lost or, I don't know, found and returned to the Order. Either way, I hadn't gone looking for it."

"Because?"

"Because I figured that's how he wanted it."

"Yet Crook Eye ended up with Degan's sword," said Wolf. "How?"

"By being smart and lucky and in the right place at the right time."

"And he wanted it why?"

"He didn't. He wanted this." I patted the rapier at my side. Shadow's rapier. The tapering length of Black Isle steel that Fowler had fished from of the embers, gotten remounted, and gifted to me. *A prince's sword for the newest prince*, she'd said at the time, knowing damn well what my having that blade would mean. I hadn't known whether to curse her or kiss her at the time; still didn't, to be honest. "For the Kin," I said, "this blade holds far more meaning and symbolism than Degan's sword ever could. Crook Eye wanted the rapier, but someone beat him to it. But in looking, he came across Degan's blade instead."

"And then?"

"And then, being the smart Gray Prince that he was, he thought and schemed and bided his time until he could use it against me."

"Blackmail?"

"More or less."

"I'm surprised I found him alive to kill."

I rewrapped the canvas around Degan's blade and hung it from the baldric. "Why? I would have done the same thing in his place. Leverage is leverage. Besides, he was under my Peace—there was no way I was going to dust him."

Wolf cocked an eyebrow. "Not even over the sword?"

"I don't break my word."

The words felt like stones in my mouth. Of course I broke my word—but only when it truly mattered. The proof was lying right there in my lap. But I had to say it, had to see if I got a reaction from Wolf—especially with Degan's name hanging in the air between us. If he knew about my Oath to Degan and what had happened, he couldn't not react, couldn't not call me out. All other things aside, he was still a degan.

I watched him as I slung Degan's sword over my shoulder: studied the amber-limned lines around his eyes to see if they tightened, took in the red-gold line of his jaw to see if it clenched beneath his beard, listened for an intake of furious breath.

But all Wolf did was follow the sword with his eyes and sigh.

"All right," I said. "You got to see it. Now it's your turn: Why do you want Bronze?"

"You mean aside from his having killed Iron?"

I looked up sharply at that. "Like I told your Order, Shadow was the one who—"

"And like I told you," said Wolf, "I don't care about the lies you told them or the half-truths they mouthed back. We both know Bronze killed Iron. There was no other reason for him to disappear without a word, nothing else that would have caused him to abandon his sword. A degan's blade is his identity, his soul. Bronze wouldn't have done that unless he felt he no longer had a right to carry it."

"You're that sure?" I said.

"We all are."

I shifted on my perch. "You all . . . ?"

"We know that Gray Prince didn't kill our brother. Not that cleanly. We're not fools, after all."

I'd kind of been hoping they were, actually. Most people wanted their answers simple, their mysteries solved. But then again, most people weren't the Order of the Degans.

"So is that why you want him?" I said, my voice tight. "You think he dusted your sword brother, and now you want to make him pay?"

"No. That may be true for the others, but not for me."

"How convenient, then, that I've been set up by the one degan who doesn't want Bronze dead. Lucky me."

"Believe what you wish, but know this: It's not my intent to hunt down Bronze so I can exact vengeance on him."

"Then why?"

Wolf gave me a long, thoughtful look. "Because I need him."

"For what?"

"I cannot say."

"Oh, Angels!" It was Degan and his reticence about Iron all over again. "You degans and your damn secrets. You're worse than a courtesan at court."

Wolf's voice took on a condescending tone. "It's a matter regarding the Order of the—"

"It's about the fucking emperor, isn't it?"

Wolf's eyes went wide. "What?"

"The emperor. You know, the man your order promised

to serve, only now you can't agree among yourselves whether that means preserving the empire or the man himself."

Wolf's eyes grew even wider. I could almost read his mind by his expression: This was all supposed to be deep-file degan information, internal politics meant to be kept within the Order.

"How . . . ?" he began.

"How the hell do you think?"

"Perhaps," said Wolf after a moment, "you should tell me—exactly—what Degan told you about the Order."

"And perhaps you should tell me which side of the split you stand on."

It wasn't an idle question. The whole reason I'd ended up breaking my Oath to Degan was because he'd decided we needed to turn an ancient Paragon's journal over to the emperor rather than let the information it contained fall into the wrong hands. Problem was, I'd already agreed to give the book to Solitude and help her throw down said emperor. That was no small thing, and not just because he was the emperor; it was also because killing him didn't mean he wouldn't come back.

For the past six-hundred-plus years, the Dorminikan Empire has been ruled by the same man—or rather, by three recurring incarnations of the same man: the founder of the empire, Stephen Dorminikos. Named, respectively, Lucien, Theodoi and Markino, each version of the emperor was reborn thirty years apart from the other two, always in the same order, always succeeding one another to the throne—more or less. The occasional revolt or stubborn regent had caused their fair share of gaps, but in the end, one version or another of the emperor always regained the throne. After all, it was the Angels who had chosen Stephen and shattered his soul into three pieces, so he could be perpetually reborn, wasn't it? It only seemed proper that the Chosen One of the Angelic Host sit the earthly throne that had been set aside for him, right?

Right.

Except it was all a load of shit.

Thanks to the notes in the Paragon's journal, I'd learned the truth: that Stephen Dorminikos's broken soul and unending rule had had nothing to do with the Angels. The sole reason he'd been able keep coming back was that he'd tasked his magicians—his Paragons—with finding the secret to immortality. Unable to figure it out, they'd instead come up with the best solution they could manage: cyclical regeneration.

The whole thing—the Angels, being chosen as the Perpetual Emperor, the resulting Imperial Cult—had been a con. And what was worse, it was slowly falling apart. Not in terms of the magic—that appeared to working fine, at least from the outside—but rather in terms of the man, or by now the men, being reincarnated.

It was no great secret that the various incarnations had been slipping into madness over the last century or so. As each emperor aged, they tended to become paranoid about various things, especially one another. Over time, that had translated to more and more hostility. Right now it was minor, but as Solitude had pointed out, the eventual path was easy enough to see: Sooner or later, one incarnation would challenge the other openly, and the empire would end up at war with itself. Forever, because if the emperor you believed in never died, neither would his cause. But I couldn't say the same for the empire itself, and that had bothered me. No Empire meant no Kin, and I wasn't about to see the closest thing to a family, and the only legacy I had, go down the sewer someday because of a religious con job. Hunting us down because we were criminals was one thing, but to be destroyed as an afterthought of history gone bad? No, thank you.

And that's where the problem had come in. Degan had stood with the part of his Order that believed preserving the empire meant preserving the emperor. If I'd let him follow his conscience and turn that journal over, there would have been no stopping the downward spiral towards civil war. I'd needed the information the journal held to try and topple the man Degan was sworn to preserve. Which was why I'd coldcocked my best friend the moment he'd turned

his back to me and run off with the Paragon's notes, even
though I knew it meant I was destroying his life.

But just because I'd betrayed Degan that one time didn't
mean I was willing to do it again. If Wolf stood on the opposite side of the Order from Degan, I'd be damn if I helped
him do anything.

For his part, Wolf waved the question off with a dismissive hand. "The Order's issues with the emperor aren't your
concern."

"You made it my concern when you set me up. So either
you come clean or I take a walk and see just how well me
and my people do against your lies."

He shifted his weight back on his heels, but otherwise
didn't move. "You like dramatic threats, don't you? To use
your knowledge like a blade. Very well: I concede the point.
I stand with the Order. No," he said, holding up a hand to
forestall my argument. "Don't interrupt me. By that, I mean
I wish to see the degans come together under one purpose,
like it used to be in the days after our founding. I wish to see
us do the things we are capable of, if only we didn't have
this thorn constantly worrying at our side. It festers and
drives us apart.

"You wonder how I know Bronze and Iron fought? Because it was inevitable. If not them, then it would have been
two others. I have no proof, no witnesses as you would say,
but that isn't important. One degan has spilled the blood of
another over what it means to serve the Empire. If that
deed stands unanswered, then the Order will fall upon itself.
I need Bronze to prevent this."

"How, by making an example of him?" I said. "By dragging him before your brothers for some kind of mock trial?"

"You understand nothing."

"And whose fault would that be, do you think?"

Wolf sighed. "How do you make an example of someone
who's already an exemplar? Where the rest of us have argued and debated and even changed our minds, Bronze has
stood unmoving, like a boulder in a gale. For him, it's not
about reasons or intentions—it's about conviction.

"Bronze holds a special place in the eyes of my Order.

By standing apart, he's gained a certain degree of moral authority among us. In a roomful of yelling, headstrong swordsmen, it's no small feat for everyone to fall silent when you speak. Bronze had that power among the degans before Iron fell, and I think he might have it still. That's why I need him: I need his authority to help settle this before it becomes worse. Before we fully turn on one another."

"But if they didn't listen to him before, what makes you think they'll listen now? You said yourself he did the unthinkable: He dusted another degan."

"Which is exactly why they may listen."

I reached up and ran my hands through my hair. "I'm sure that makes some kind of wonderful sense," I said, "but let's pretend I'm not a degan, that I don't think like a degan, and that I don't know an entire Flock or Oath or Misery or whatever the hell you call a bunch of degans, all right? Just explain it to me."

Wolf leaned forward, his left hand on his sword, and pointed over my shoulder at Degan's blade with his right. "Understand this: No degan has raised steel—not seriously—against another member of the Order in ages, and no degan has killed another since near the founding. Bronze's action is no small thing. For two of us to come to blows over something so fundamental strikes at the very core of our purpose. That it was someone as respected as Bronze makes it even worse." Wolf shook his head, something close to disbelief on his face. "No, if there's anyone who might be able to sway the Order, it would be him: the man who bloodied his blade on his brother, and then had the presence of mind to cast it away."

"And they're just going to let him stroll back in and change their minds?"

"Well, no, not exactly."

"How 'not exactly'?"

"I'm not sure he'll be allowed back into the Barracks Hall."

"And why is that?"

"Why do you think?"

Yeah, that's what I'd thought.

"Go to hell." I stood up.

A heavy hand fell on my shoulder. "Listen to me. This could work."

"Like hell it could. If you think I'm going to—"

"What I think," said Wolf, "is that Bronze is the best hope the Order has right now, and that I, in turn, am his. If any of my brothers or sisters find him first, it will most likely end in blood. We are not a forgiving family. But win or lose, it will be too late for him then: The Order *might* be willing to look past one degan's body if I can make a case for Bronze, but two? More?" He shook his head. "No. If you wish to save Bronze, and if I wish to save the Order, then I have to find him before the others."

"How does coming back with you help?" I said. "I thought you just said you weren't even sure they'd let him back into, what'd you call it, the Barracks Hall?"

"It's the closest thing we have to a council chamber. And you're right: Walking in on his own could be the same as falling on his sword. But I have this." Wolf slapped the hilt at his side. "And, with your and his permission, I'll have that, too." He pointed at Degan's blade. "Between the two, I can petition to speak for him. I can invoke the old traditions of the Order and try to shield him from their judgment until he's had a chance to speak."

"And what will he say?" I thought back to Copper, and the cold steel in her eyes when she'd been asking me about Degan. "What can he possibly tell them that will excuse his dusting Iron?"

Wolf shook his head. "I don't know. But I think he should be able to have the option to stand before the Order and give his side of the story. I think he should be able to ask for atonement and receive the judgment of his fellows face-to-face. I think he should know, once and for all, whether his name is to remain on our roles, of if it's to be struck through in shame. But mostly, I think he deserves the opportunity to choose to seek out his own redemption or damnation." Wolf looked down at me. "Don't you?"

My mouth was too dry to answer. To argue that Degan had left Ildrecca of his own free will, that he'd known what he was doing from the moment he'd walked out of that burning warehouse after saving my life. To yell that the one thing the man wanted was to be left alone.

I didn't say it because I couldn't be certain it was true. Because I realized that all of the reasons I'd been giving for Degan walking away had really been excuses for me not trying to find him, for not following after him. And because, dammit, Wolf was right.

Still, it wasn't quite enough.

"Why should I trust you?" I said. It wasn't the strongest argument, but it was all I had left. "How do I know that, despite everything you've said, you won't go for the steel cure the moment you see Degan?"

"You don't," said Wolf simply. "Aside from threatening to destroy you and your organization, there's nothing I can do to force you to do as I ask. Except to ask. And to offer my word that I'm not seeking Bronze out of any sense of vengeance."

"A sword in one hand and a promise in the other? The two don't exactly complement each other when it comes to putting my mind at ease."

Wolf arched an eyebrow. "You would have me combine the two, perhaps?" he said, drumming his fingers on the hilt of his saber.

I didn't have to ask what he was implying: I knew. Wolf was asking if I wanted to take the Oath on the matter—to bind him to me, and me to him, to the tune of a single service.

I shook my head, perhaps a bit too quickly. I'd seen where that could lead, and I didn't want to think about the kind of price Wolf might exact in exchange for his service. No, his bringing up the Oath was enough to show me just how serious he was about this.

"No need to go that far," I said.

A brief smile passed over his lips. "Then we have an accord?"

I felt myself nodding before I made the decision to do so. Then, because I'd started, I said the words. "Yeah, we have an accord."

Chapter Eight

I left the piazza maybe half an hour later with less of a plan, and fewer answers, than I would have liked. Despite neatly setting up two Gray Princes and their organizations, Wolf hadn't been able to offer me any information on the man he was actually looking for. Degan, it seems, had disappeared just as completely when it came to his brethren as he had for me. This wasn't terribly surprising, considering they wanted to kill him, but still, you'd think that the members of his Order would have some idea of where Degan might have rabbitted to.

No such luck. Nor, had I been informed, was Wolf willing to tap the few resources he had on the matter. His asking after Degan, he'd argued, would arouse suspicion among his fellows. He'd been carefully distant on the subject for months. To show a sudden interest now would only pique the wrong kind of curiosity. And the last thing we wanted, he assured me, was to have other degans taking a sudden interest in our business.

On that score, at least, we'd agreed. One degan breathing over my shoulder was bad enough, thank you very much — I didn't need more.

And breathing over my shoulder he was, too. Wolf had made it abundantly clear that the sooner we found Degan, the better — to the point that he expected me to start producing leads within a week, and ideally less. I had tried to explain why the odds of that happening were beyond slim —

that the trail was cold, that Degan had a knack for disappearing, that it was damn hard to find someone who didn't want to be found when they had a three-month head start—but Wolf hadn't been impressed. Time, he'd assured me, couldn't be wasted on this. As to whether that time was to be spent tracking down Degan or trying to deal with the bodies that might start piling up at my door, well, that was up to me.

Arrogant bastard.

I turned onto Boot Nail Lane and began the slow climb uphill, leaving the worst of the grit and heat from the forges behind. My instincts told me to start working the street right away, to begin digging up clues and tracking down rumors, but I knew I was both too exhausted and too twitchy to succeed at either. Better, I thought, to wear away some shoe leather and let my mind wander while I ran an errand I'd been putting off ever since returning to the city. The street, I told myself, would still be there tomorrow.

I almost even believed me.

Still, that didn't mean I had to contemplate the night on an empty stomach. I stopped at the first tea vendor I found and bought a cup of strong, peppery night tea from him. The drink wasn't exactly refreshing, but it helped settle my nerves. It also felt good going down since the vendor had been clever enough to store the tea in large clay pots, which kept the liquid cooler than the summer air around me.

I sighed and pulled out more coins and had another cup.

I'd ended up not telling Wolf about Copper. Part of me knew I should have shared what I had, especially since he was already worried about other members of the Order following our lead, but a larger part of me had decided he could go fuck himself. He'd been playing me for months, and I wasn't about to give up everything I had just because he had me over a barrel. We might have come to an "accord," but that didn't mean I trusted the bastard. If my keeping Copper's interest hush could give me even the tiniest bit of leverage down the line, it would be worth it. After all, what better weapon to use against a degan than another degan, even if tangentially?

As for the other Gray Princes and their increased interest in me, well, I'd gotten the feeling that Wolf was the one holding a bit back on that. He'd assured me that he had a plan to deal with the problem once we found Degan, but he hadn't been forthcoming on the details. This wasn't surprising, but it was damn annoying. When pressed, he'd finally admitted that he'd arranged for blame to shift away from me and onto someone else—all he had to do was give the word and leave a body or two in the street, and it would be done. He didn't say, but I got the feeling that the person who would end up taking the blame, and possibly end up lying in the street, might be Rambles.

I could live with that.

I tossed the tea seller an extra copper owl and pushed on into the night.

In the meantime, though, between Crook Eye's death and Degan's return, I was starting to think that my fading might not be a bad idea after all. I'd initially planned to fight the whispers about Crook Eye with rumors of my own, but I was far enough behind the wave—thanks to my new partner—that playing catch-up was proving nearly impossible. Any gains I made were transitory, and stories I spread ended up coming off as either excuses or blatant attempts to shift the blame. The street, I was coming to realize, had already made up its mind. If I wanted to change it, it was going to require more than I had to offer at the moment.

Which meant the best strategy was to not try at all—or, at least, to not seem to.

Leaving Ildrecca would accomplish part of that. Yes, it might look like I was running, but at this point staying could hurt my reputation just as much. Besides, the farther I was out of sight, the easier it would be for the street to become distracted by something else. What that something might be I wasn't sure yet, but I knew just who to talk to about coming up with a bit of flash that could turn heads. After all, what was the point of having a troupe of actors in my debt if I couldn't tap them for some inspiration when it came to making the Kin look stage left while I exited stage right?

I headed out of Rustwater and down into the Cloisters.

From there, I took to the roofs and arches of the cordon, skirting the edge of Lady of the Roses—there'd been a flare-up between two local street bosses of late, and I didn't want to get caught in an overeager ambush—and made my way to the night market over in Hides.

As the name implied, the market ran from sundown to sunup, catering to everything from Kin to late night drunks to early risers over the course of the evening. It covered a good dozen interconnected, but not necessarily immediately adjoining, blocks. Rather, the market was made up of a winding, twisting path that followed the side streets and alleys of Hides, with each shop and trader marked out by the green-glassed lantern he hung or placed before his shop. In some places, the merchants were packed close enough that I half expected to see fish swimming in the air, so much did it seem that I was strolling beneath the sea; in others, it was a long, dark walk from one jade pinpoint to another. In these dimmer spots, the local gang—a band of toughs called, aptly enough, the Green Shades—had patrols ranging, keeping an eye out for any freelance Prigs or Clickers that might otherwise decide to poach the local marks and undercut the Shade's thriving protection racket.

The shop I was looking for came after a particularly long stretch of dark—so much so that my night vision was on the verge of waking when I stepped into the pool of green light. A thick-armed, thin-haired leather worker was standing at the heavy pine table out front, his knives and shears and mallets ready to hand. At the moment, he was slowly drawing laces from a hide.

"Points in?" I said.

He didn't even look up. "In back, as usual."

I half walked, half climbed my way past the stacks of leather to the back of the shop. There, under the fitful glow of a tallow dip, sat Points. I tried to ignore the smell of the burning rag coming from the bowl of rendered grease and instead settled myself on the pile of leather scraps before his low workbench.

"Yes?" said Points. He was maybe thirty summers along, but too little food and too much sickness had made him look half again as old. What little hair he had left lay limp across his scalp, a dirty gray against only slightly pinker skin. His jaw hadn't seen a razor in over a week. His eyes hadn't seen anything in years.

"It's Drothe," I said, reaching out to give him my hand. He took it, squeezed, and showed me a lopsided smile.

"Ah, royalty," he said. "If you'd been properly announced, I'd have had the servants put out the Vennanti glassware." He shrugged. "Help: What're ya gonna do?"

I smiled in turn and took my hand back. "Got some trade for you," I said.

"Got a price for you."

"It's a rush job."

"Price just went up."

"One you can't tell anyone about."

"And up yet again." He rubbed fingertips against thumb. "What is it?"

I lifted Degan's sword off my back, laid the bundle across my legs, and began unrolling the canvas. "I need a scabbard," I said as I drew the sword free of its rough cocoon and ran my finger over the one clean spot on the blade—the space where the soot had been wiped away to reveal a single teardrop etched into the steel. "Something to protect the blade, and me, while I wear it."

"Well, that's generally the point of a scabbard, isn't it?" He held out his hands. "Let me feel what you've got."

I gave Degan's sword over, my hands lingering on the filthy steel a moment longer than they needed to. Points's fingers ran expertly up and down the blade, testing not only the width and length and weight, but also the edge and overall feel of the blade.

"Still straight. That's good. Don't want to put a twisted blade in a scabbard—doesn't like to come out." He tapped the steel with his fingernail, then pulled out a small copper hammer and tapped it again. "Black Isle?"

"Black Isle."

"Two in twice as many months for you. Impressive." His hands wandered up to the guard, paused, then performed a quick inventory. "Fire?"

"Yes."

"Um." Points's thumb rubbed at the base of the blade, where the tear marked the steel. I noticed his hands hesitate for a fraction of a moment, then continue on as if nothing had happened. "Pretty big fire down in Ten Ways couple of months back, from what I hear." I stayed quiet. Points read the silence as only a blind man could.

"It'd be my honor to make a new home for this blade," he said solemnly. "How soon do you need it?"

"As soon as you can manage."

Points ran his hands along the steel again. "I don't have anything setting up right now that will work, but it shouldn't take too long. I can get it back to you—"

"The sword walks with me when I go."

Diplomatic pause. "I need the sword here to make the scabbard for it."

"You're good enough to work off measurements."

A dip of the head. "Yes, but it goes faster if—"

"It also goes faster if you don't have three of my Cutters lingering about and getting in the way, not to mention inadvertently scaring off the rest of your customers."

"There is that." Points reached over and placed his hand on a small pile of thin wooden slats. They were of various widths and thicknesses, and his hands moved over their ends deftly. "I don't suppose you have time for me to make a quick mock-up of the blade, do you?" he said as he drew one of the slats out, ran his fingers along it, and shoved it back with a frown. "Even a wooden dummy would make it—ah, here we are, I think." He pulled a pale piece of mountain pine and hefted it.

"How long will it take?" I said, glancing out of the shop at the night beyond.

"Not long. An hour, maybe. Maybe a bit more."

I looked out into the darkness and considered. Even if I left now, I wouldn't be able to get everything done before first light. I had people to talk to, arrangements to make, a lost set of plays down that should have been recovered from Dirty Waters by now to check on. That all took time. But if I decided to hold off on those, if I stayed here and got the scabbard fitted, I wouldn't have time to worry about all that. Instead, I'd be able to look into the city's social calendar, maybe even find a time when the Baroness Christiana Sephada of Lythos wouldn't be at home. Much easier to search a house when the mistress isn't in, especially when you're looking for private missives that could give you an idea where your former friend, who was also the baroness's new want-to-be paramour, might be holding up. Degan and my sister had been hungering for one another ever since they'd first met. That had always bothered me—still did, for that matter. Degan being with the woman who had sent two assassins after me aside, I'd just never liked the idea of my best friend getting involved with my little sister. Degan had understood; as for Christiana, well, it gave her one more reason to resent me—not that she needed any more.

Now that Degan and I were done, though, I figured it had opened the door between them. I didn't know that for certain, mind, but it seemed a safe bet, especially since my sister had been in a good—no, not good, *gleeful*—mood the last two times I'd seen her. And considering there wasn't much I could think of besides Degan that would get her feeling *quite* that happy . . .

Yes, I definitely needed to find out when my sister wouldn't be in.

"Fine," I said, sitting down across from Points. "You have your hour."

"A wise choice," said Points as he put the sword and the wood in his lap and picked up a bone stylus. "You won't regret it, I assure you."

I smiled and didn't comment. Regret was one thing I didn't worry about when it came to annoying my sister.

The irony has never been lost on me: Because I helped set up the security at my sister's home in Ildrecca, it has always been easier for me to break in than anyone else. She knows this, mind you, and has taken precautions against it over the years, but still, there's something to be said for knowing about the broken pottery cemented not only at the top of the garden walls, but two and a half feet down on either side, set so the shards blend in with the decorative carvings while still being perfectly placed to lacerate an unwary scrambler. Or that the locks on all of the doors are Kettle-makers, which means you might as well try and carve your way through the walls as pick the locks, since the first stands a better chance of success. Or that the catch on the second-floor east-facing window, fourth in from the corner, has a trick spring I'd installed to make sure I had easy access on nights like tonight.

No, the irony has never been lost on me. Just as it was not lost on me now when, with my toes jammed onto a four-inch ledge and my fingers straining to keep their grip on the even thinner edging around the window, I discovered that Christiana had replaced the latch.

It was never easy with my sister. Never.

I stared at the pane of glass before me, my night vision illumining its details in the darkness. A bit bigger than my hand, it was high of quality: Blown and then quickly spun to draw it flat, it had less distortion to it than most of the glass you would find in the city. If I had known I was going to be drawing teeth, I would have brought putty and gloves and probes for removing the panes, not to mention choosing a window with a wider sill.

This was going to be a pain.

Of course, I could always just knock on the front door and have Josef show me to the salon to wait; but I also knew I stood a better chance of getting out of the Imperial prison at Athakon than I would leaving that room unobserved. Nor did I relish the idea of sitting through the lecture I would get from Christiana—again—about why I shouldn't come calling at the front door. She had gone to great pains to keep our relationship secret even before she'd married into the nobility, and I'd agreed with the sentiment. A baroness with a brother deep amongst the Kin didn't make for easy times at Court, either socially or politically; nor did I relish what would happen if it became known that I called a member of the Lower Imperial Court "sister." Blackmail aside (for either of us), the kind of leverage she could provide my enemies, or even the random Kin with a thing against Noses, wasn't something I cared to consider.

Which left me here on the ledge, with my calves beginning to burn and my fingertips going numb.

I studied the panes again. Nary a wrinkle in them. They must have cost a fortune.

Oh well: It was her fault for changing the latch, after all.

I slipped my wrist knife free and, hanging on with five white-tipped fingers, inserted its point into the lead glazing. After a bit of wiggling and prying, I got the tip where I wanted it and slowly began to lever the steel against the glass. A faint click rewarded me, along with a pair of long cracks running from the corner up to the opposite side of the pane.

I smiled to myself as I picked the lower corner of the lead glazing away. It wasn't fun or easy hanging here, popping teeth with a knife better suited to stabbing than prying, but the thought of my sister's reaction when she found the break kept me at it. That, and the fall looming at my back.

When the bottom third of the pane came free, I flicked it outward into the garden beneath me, cringing at the faint tinkle it made on the walkway. I heard Lazarus and Rinaldo and Acheron—the hounds that patrolled the garden at night—snuffling about below, but we were old friends ever since I had gotten them hooked on *ahrami*. A little rubbed into some choice scraps of pork, and the boys were nothing but wags and slobber when it came to me poking about the place.

The second fragment of glass slipped out easily. It was the third that gave me the most trouble. I ended up slicing open my middle finger getting it free, but once it was done, I was able to reach in and release the latch.

The window opened out. It took a bit of interesting gymnastics to get myself beneath its swing, but, aside from a few smears of red on the wall and casement, I managed to slip inside easily enough.

Where I settled myself onto the floor with a groan. I hadn't done any hard draw-latching for years, and I could tell. My thighs and calves were trembling, and I could still feel the stonework pressing into the fingers of my left hand. I closed my eyes for a moment, relishing the feeling of not clinging to something for dear life, and then remembered my finger.

I had come in through the music room window, which meant there was a fair supply of paper about to use as a compress. The first page from Paulus's's *The Enchanting of the Bridgemaker's Daughter*—something all the rage at Court, I was sure—was the easiest to hand, and did a passable job as I pulled out my herb wallet and dug through it. It wasn't nearly as well stocked as it had been when I was living above Eppyris's shop, but I managed to find a small envelope of powered woolman's weed and a long strip of clean linen. The woolman helped slow the bleeding, and the linen finished the job, giving me fairly unrestricted use of my hand.

Leaving Paulus bloodstained and crumpled on the floor, I crept to the door and cracked it open.

Dark. Quiet. Good.

I briefly considered the downstairs study, then rejected it. Christiana might keep her accounts and receipts and records of minor treacheries and betrayals down there, but what I wanted was of a more personal nature. And for a woman who had spent over half her life working as a courtesan, secrecy and privacy meant one place: her bedroom.

Still, just because Christiana was gone didn't mean the house was empty.

I crept to the head of the stairs, then partway down, and listened. Laughter from the kitchen, and light shining out from beneath the door to Josef's room off the main foyer. The mistress was away, and her butler was allowing the mice to play. It wasn't impossible that someone could come wandering up to Christiana's room while I was there— more dodges than I cared to think about have been ruined by a servant or a repentant spouse delivering a vase of freshly cut color at an inopportune time—but judging by the tone and volume of the talk, I didn't expect anyone to be tearing themselves away anytime soon.

I padded back upstairs and along the hallway. No light showed beneath the maid's door, but I kept it slow and silent as I slipped past and cracked the gold-accented cream-colored double doors farther along. Which was a good thing, since Sara, the maid, was there, curled up on the window seat in Christiana's receiving parlor, snoring softly.

I froze, and then slowly let out my breath. This was a problem.

If this were another Kin's ken, or even some other noble's pile of rocks, I would have had a knife to the maid's eye and a gag in her mouth in an instant. But this was my sister's servant, in my sister's house: If I damaged the goods, I'd never hear the end of it.

Besides, the girl had a nice smile. I'd only ever seen it once, and then mostly out of the corner of my eye, but she'd flashed it my way in the middle of one of my sister's tirades, when I'd delivered a particularly good comeback. I figured that kind of sympathy—not to mention spirit, given what would have happened if Christiana had caught the look—deserved a measure of respect.

So instead, I pulled out a vial of Budger's oil, scattered some across a strip of linen, and gently laid it down on the window seat near her face. In a strong enough dose, the distillations and herbs in the oil could drag a wakeful man into unconsciousness, but that required a well-soaked rag being clamped to the face for a good minute or more—a tactic I didn't relish just now. Used like this, though, the Budger would deepen the girl's sleep, so that only a sound shaking would rouse her, and then damn slowly.

I crouched, counting my heartbeats and trying not to pick at the fresh wound on my finger, until enough time had passed. Then I took the rag from near her face, laid it far away on the floor, and got to work.

Turning a room can take a long time, or very little—it all depends on the experience of two people: the one doing the hiding, and the one doing the looking. My sister didn't lack in training when it came to secreting away things she didn't want found—our stepfather, Sebastian, had seen to that—but all of her practice, at least early on, had been against me.

First in our cabin in the Balsturan Forest, and then later in the dives of Ildrecca, Christiana and I had made a game of hiding things from each other, both in typical places—nooks and spots that hadn't required construction or modification—and in more practiced locales. Eventually, the game turned serious, especially once Christiana had become a courtesan and had had things worth hiding. Even later, I'd still gotten plenty of practice against her while her late husband, Nestor, was alive.

Nestor had delighted in all things Kinnish, and had insisted that I both train him how to secret away the odd bit of paper as well as teach him how to discover other people's hiding places. Of course, Christiana had been the natural target for our lessons, and Nestor and I had spent many an afternoon and evening rooting through the house, poking into corners and prying back baseboards in search of his wife's hidden marginalia. She had played along well enough, even going out of her way to leave special messages and false trails for us—that is, until our search had turned up a small packet of papers from behind a loose piece of paneling in Christiana's armoire.

I was the one who had found the parcel, but Nestor was the one who had read the papers within it. I'd been politely but sternly excused after that, and hadn't quite made it out the front door before the yelling started. Christiana didn't speak to me for months after, and Nestor was dead within the year. I couldn't help but wonder if my missing that piece of molding might have resulted in him still being here.

Past and gone, Drothe. Mind on the matter at hand.

Even though it was obvious, I started with Christiana's desk. I decided to focus on finding any hidden papers first, and only worry about striking a light later, once I had things to go through. I can read with my night vision, but not well, and I don't welcome the headaches and nausea the effort brings with it.

The secretary, armoire, bookshelves, and side tables followed. Going through her closet was like diving into a cave filled with lace cobwebs and silk stalactites, assuming it's possible to find caves that smell of talc and cedar. After that, I moved on to the bedding, baseboards, decorative carvings, and pictures on the wall, not to mention the seams in the curtains.

By the end, I had a small pile of papers and a fair amount of splinters to show for my effort. I found a small firebox next to the fireplace, put a candle wick to the carefully banked coals inside, set myself on the floor at the foot of the bed, and examined my plunder.

Nothing. Or, rather, plenty of somethings if I were looking to blackmail any number of people at Court, but that wasn't what I was here for.

I considered the closed doors and the parlor beyond. Sara wouldn't be a problem if I wanted to turn the room, but was there really a point? If Christiana was going to secret something personal away, she wouldn't do it out there, where the practiced eyes of a visitor mighty notice something out of place. If it were anywhere, it would be here. And I hadn't been able to find it.

She'd gotten better; there was no doubt about it.

Damn her.

I pushed myself to my feet, walked over to the bell rope on the wall, and pulled.

If I was going to have to wait for my sister to come home, I might as well ask Josef to bring me up dinner and something to drink. Something strong.

Chapter Nine

I was just finishing off the last bits of a small plate of shredded pork done in a spiced vinegar sauce when I heard the key turn in the kitchen door. A moment later, it opened and Christiana entered the room.

"Still here, I see," she said as she closed the door behind her. I'd been locked in the kitchen since ringing for Josef, and while he'd been apologetic, he'd also been firm: I had to stay put until the mistress returned. That Christiana had brought neither footmen nor Josef in with her told me we weren't going to be pulling punches in front of the help this time. "I thought for sure you would have weaseled your way out by now."

"I didn't want to be rude and leave before I'd finished eating," I said, pointing not only at the pork, but also the salad of spinach, sweet onions, olives, and chickpeas Josef had put together for me. "Besides, you have Graybird locks on the kitchen doors. They may not be Kettlemakers like you have outside, but they're still a pain to deal with. Especially on an empty stomach."

"I had good advice when it came to the locks."

"You're welcome."

"Who said I was talking about you?"

Oh.

Christiana came the rest of the way into the room. It was a fair-sized place as kitchens went in this part of town, with a hearth I couldn't quite stand up in, a wall of shelves filled with jars and bricks of exotic spices, a flour cabinet, two small butcher's blocks, and a larger main worktable standing near the center of the space. A pair of lanterns hung overhead, and a couple of tapers had been scattered around the room to drive back the deepest shadows. I was seated on a stool at one end of the table; Christiana stayed at the other end.

She'd clearly taken the time to change since she'd come home: Baronesses simply did not appear in public in a plain linen overdress with a chemise underneath. Still, being Christiana, she made it seem fit for an imperial ball. The lines of the fabric hugged her figure ever so slightly in all the right places, accenting her every movement even as they hinted at deeper mysteries and grace beneath. Her deep brown hair was still piled atop her head, held in place by a pair of ivory and jade combs, made all the more elegant by their simplicity. A trace of deep burgundy clung to her lips, not fully wiped away, complementing the depth of her complexion.

Sebastian might have taught my sister many things, but one skill he'd never needed to school her in was the ability to present herself to the best possible advantage. That was something she'd been born with.

As for the veneer of restraint she was barely holding on to now? That was all our stepfather's doing. I recalled that it had been a long, arduous time in its crafting.

Christiana took the stool at the far end of the worktable, rested her chin in her palm, and regarded me with winter-sky eyes.

"You did a hell of a job on my room," she said. "It's going to be a day or more before Sara and Josef get it back together properly."

I dug an after-dinner *ahrami* seed from the bag around my neck and slipped it into my mouth. "You're getting better at stashing things," I said.

"Mmm." Christiana looked down and began tracing knife patterns in the wood with the first two fingers of her right hand. "You know," she said, "I was in the mood for dancing tonight. Not with words, but with people and music.

I was at the rarest of balls: one where, for once, there was nothing to be gained by maneuvering. The host is from a little city called Esterov in the provinces: poor enough and far enough out that no one at Court gives a damn about what he thinks or who attends his parties." She smiled faintly. "He's an adorable little man, with a plump, clucking wife, a pair of wide-eyed, left-footed sons, and a daughter that could bring the city to its knees if she knew the first thing about using the charms she's been blessed with. As it is, she'll probably marry some backcountry knight who doesn't know how lucky he is, and be deliriously happy for it.

"They're renting a manse for the season and invited half the Lower Court to the fete. Of course, only a couple dozen of us came, but they were thrilled all the same. And we were happy to be there. Because it didn't matter."

Christiana looked back up at me, and the smile faded from her face. "Do you know how rare that is, Drothe? For me to go to a ball and not have to give a damn about what I say or which jests I laugh at or who I do and don't spend time with? To simply just dance?"

"Ana," I said. "I didn't—"

"And do you know what it feels like to be pulled away, to have to make excuses, because your *fucking brother* has just broken into your house and rung for dinner service? Do you have any idea what it feels like to come home from that to find your window broken and your maid drugged and your bedchamber torn apart? After you've set that part of yourself aside for the night? After you've dared to hope that you might, just *might*, be able to relax and truly enjoy yourself for a couple of hours?"

I thought back to when I had lived above Eppyris's apothecary's shop; about my conversations with Cosima, his wife, and how we had talked about everything and anything other than Kin business; about how I hadn't been able to bring myself to speak to her, let alone her husband, after Nicco had crippled the apothecary in an attempt to get back at me.

I remembered how good that had felt back in the shop,

how rare and freeing it had been to just be: not Kin, not Nose . . . just Drothe. It had never occurred to me that my sister, the dowager baroness, might feel that same weight, might crave that same release, if only for a night, or even for a dance.

Yes, I knew what it was like.

I lifted my cup and took a sip of mead. It was fortified C'unnan, which meant it was sweeter than I liked.

"I didn't know," I said.

"Well, now you do." Christiana knuckled a spot on her forehead for a moment and stared off toward the embers Josef had unbanked in the hearth. "Did you even consider asking me?" she said at last. "Did it occur to you that I might have told you whatever it is you want to know, might have given you what you needed, if you'd just asked?"

"It occurred."

"And?"

"And I know better."

Christiana glared at me sidelong. "You know nothing."

I slammed the cup down on the table, making her jump. "Fine," I said. "You want to know why I didn't ask? Because I don't work that way. I hunt for information; I take information; I use information; I sell information. It's a commodity for me. If I come asking for something from someone, it means there's going to be a price involved. I've asked before, Ana, and I don't like paying what you charge."

"You think I don't understand that?" Christiana waved her hand toward the kitchen door and the house beyond. "I'm a fixture of the Lower Court, and not unknown in the Upper. Do you honestly think I don't know what it means to trade tidbits and keep score? Angels! It's politics, Drothe, and I've been doing it since before I became a baroness. It's how I live my life."

"I know your life," I said. "I've done enough baggage work and house cracking for you to understand what 'cost' means in your world. It's not the same in mine, not by half."

Her face went white. "You know nothing!" she said again, this time nearly screaming. "You know nothing about what things cost at Court, or what I've paid! The costs are different in the gutter? Cleaner? How dare you—"

But she was cut off by the kitchen door creaking open and Josef poking his head in. "Madam?" he said. His voice was both apologetic and stern at the same time: I'm here if you need me, and don't you dare send me away if you do.

Christiana stiffened for a moment, and then pulled her composure around herself like a shawl. She brushed sharply at her skirt. "We're fine, thank you, Josef."

"Madam." A sharp look at me, and the door closed.

Christiana took a deep breath. "My point, Drothe, is that I'm your sister: You could have asked."

I laughed in her face then. I couldn't help it. This, from the woman who had sent at least two assassins after me over the years; who had blackmailed me into helping her set up rivals at court; who had had me forcibly removed from the premises at her husband's funeral. Oh, yes, blood was such a strong bond between us.

Christiana's expression soured at my laughter. "Fine," she said. "Be that way. But you can't tell me you stuck around for the food and the cultured conversation." She leaned forward and put on the sisterly smirk I remembered so well from our youth. It made me want to choke her even now. "You couldn't find what you wanted in my rooms, and you needed to talk to me. You," she said, now almost singing the words, "need to *ask meeee.*"

I scowled and raised the cup to my mouth, only to discover I'd cracked the bottom and let all the mead leak out. Too bad. If I ever needed honey on my tongue, I expected it was now.

"I'm guessing the price has gone up since you walked into the room?" I said.

"You don't even want to know."

I pushed the mug and plates aside and rested my elbows on the table. I hadn't wanted to be this forthright with her— not about this.

"I need to find Degan," I said. "I know you two have been exchanging letters. I want to see them. I want to know where he is."

I don't know what I'd been expecting: laughter, disdain, dismissal, to be told to mind my own damn business—none of them would have been terribly surprising. What I got instead was Christiana going red in the face.

"You want what?" she shouted. I almost looked to the door to see if Josef would stick his face in again, but knew better than to take my eye off my sister just now. Instead, I settled myself onto my stool and leaned forward into her gale.

"You heard me," I said.

"And what makes you think I have any letters from him?"

"Please. Don't insult me."

"Then don't insult me by asking to see them."

"I have to find him, Ana."

"Why?" She took a step forward. "What's so important that you have to find him now, three months after you drove him away? Does he owe you money? Did you forget he has a secret you need?" She leaned forward. "Or is it just that you feel the sudden, burning need to betray him again?"

That's the thing about family: They know how to cast verbal knives better than almost anyone. And each one of Christiana's struck home. Deep.

I slowly levered myself to my feet. Even with the table between us, Christiana took a small step back.

"I'm going to assume that's you barking," I said, "and not Degan. He's better than that."

"You have no idea," she said, a vicious grin perching on her lips.

I ignored the jab—and the damn mental images it brought to mind—and pushed on. "I don't know what he told you, or what you dreamed up on your own, but I'm not about to explain or justify myself to you."

"You will if you want to know where he is."

"You don't want to push me on this one, Ana. Tell me and let it go."

Christiana crossed her arms and raised her chin, so that she was studying me along the line of her nose. I knew that look: She was digging in. Damn it.

"No," she said. "I don't think so. You couldn't find what you wanted on your own, and I don't think you're willing to go any further with me. Not with Josef and my footmen waiting in the hall. And besides, we both know I wouldn't tell you if it came to that, anyhow. Not that it ever has. Or will."

"You forget: I found some of your other letters," I said. "I can make trouble for you without raising more than a finger. The right words in the right ears, and your secrets will be winging their way toward Court before noon tomorrow."

A moment of alarm in her eyes, quickly covered. Christiana shrugged, rustling the fabric of her dress. "Go ahead," she said. "But making my life harder won't make yours any easier."

We stared at one another across the table for what felt like a long time after that. It was the cabin and the dirt floor and the argument over this toy or that rule all over again. Back then, our mother could have been counted on to bring the peace, or at least separate the warring parties; later, Sebastian would have foiled the fight by a judicious application of lessons and chores and practice regimens, invariably doled out in proportions that somehow punished us both worse than we each thought the other was getting.

Except now it was just us: Now there was no one else to break the stalemate. And, like it or not, I was still the big brother.

Damn you and your lessons, anyhow, Sebastian.

I'd never given Christiana the full story behind Degan's disappearance: about the argument he and I had had over the imperial Paragon's book and where it should ultimately go. Degan had wanted to return it to what he saw as its rightful owner—the emperor—mainly because he felt it was his job to do so as a degan, what with the Oath to protect the Empire and all. I'd needed the book to save my ass from Shadow, not to mention protect Christiana and Kells from the retribution the Gray Prince had threatened to dole out if I failed to deliver it. And, of course, I'd already promised it to Solitude, which had been a whole other mess.

The tricky part was that Degan had put himself on the line with his order by helping me in the first place. He'd known he would likely end up going against another degan—Iron—and still he'd exchanged the Oath with me. By the time I'd applied a piece of portable glimmer in the form of a knotted rope to the back of his head, Degan had already sealed his fate: Paragon's journal or no, he was outcast from the Order by his actions. My taking the book had only added betrayal to injury, and even then, the noble bastard had shown up at the last minute to help save me from Shadow.

Then he'd vanished. Which, when you thought about it, made sense. He was anathema to the rest of the degans, a target to be hunted down. It was why I'd concocted the whole story about Shadow and Degan's sword in the first place—a feeble attempt to make amends for what I'd done, too little too late.

But that wasn't the main reason he'd disappeared, not to my mind, anyhow. Degan had vanished because there was no reason for him not to. He'd sacrificed everything for friendship and duty, and in return his friend had stolen away his one chance to fulfill that duty. *I'd* stolen it away.

That wasn't the kind of thing I wanted to admit, especially to my sister. Especially since she and Degan had been mooning over each other for years. Especially since I needed her help to find him.

Problem was, this was Christiana, and she wouldn't settle for, or be fooled by, anything less than the truth at this point. So I told her. Oh, I explained and I justified and I shaved as many ugly edges off as I could, but in the end, I spilled like a Lighter under the knife. Hell, maybe I'd needed to all along.

Not surprisingly, it didn't go over well.

"You son of a bitch," she hissed.

I was on my third *ahrami* by then. This one went in and down almost without being chewed.

"What the hell did you want me to do?" I said. "Shadow was ready to dust you and Kells if he didn't get his hands on some imperial glimmer."

"Degan was your friend," said Christiana. She had come to my side of the table as I talked, which meant she was right in my face as she said, "Your best friend! He sacrificed what he was for you, Drothe, and you repaid him like that?"

"It was you and Kells and the future of the Empire on one side, and him on the other," I said. "I did the sums. He understood that."

"Sums?" said Christiana. "*Sums?* You ruin a man and you justify it with numbers?"

"You've justified a hell of a lot more with a hell of a lot less."

Christiana straightened as if I'd struck her. "That's Court. It's different."

"Yes, it is," I said. "It's much less personal and much more petty."

Christiana's hand came up. I caught it before it connected with my face—barely.

"Maybe," grated Christiana. She tugged at her hand, but I held on. "But which is worse: betraying someone who understands that it's part of the price for the game he plays, or abandoning someone who's put his whole trust in you?"

"When has that ever stopped you?" I said, drawing her closer. "When was the last time you lost sleep over someone you turned on? Five years ago? Eight? More? You're in no position to lecture me, little sister: We've both left blood and blame in our wakes." I let her arm go. She stepped away. "Hell, you wouldn't even be giving a damn about this if you didn't want to get into his pants so badly."

This time, her slap connected.

"Get out," she said, her voice ragged and cold—colder than I'd heard it in years. Not since Nestor's death. "I don't know why you want to find Degan, and I don't care; all I know is that if you need him, then I don't want you to find him. He's better off that way."

I stood there, my face still stinging on one side, and regarded her. I could have, I decided upon reflection, managed this better; could have told her why I was looking for Degan to begin with. But my mind didn't work that way—not when it came to my sister, not when it came to getting information from her.

Old, bitter habits.

Time for that to change.

"Ana—" I began.

"Get out."

"I don't want to find him for me."

"Let me guess," she said. "You're in danger, or your reputation is. Or maybe it's your organization, or some scum you care about on the street. But in any case, the only way you can fix it is by finding Degan. Am I right?"

"No. Well, yes, but—"

"Josef!"

The door swung open. Christiana's butler stood framed in the doorway, a look of resigned displeasure on his face. Behind him loomed a pair of pillarlike objects in doublets: my sister's "footmen."

If I had anything approaching an ally in this house, it was Josef, but any sympathy he might feel toward me was easily outweighed by his loyalty to his mistress. He wouldn't like ordering me thrown out—he'd always apologized to me after the fact in the past—but that wouldn't stop him from doing it again.

"Him," said Christiana, pointing at me. "Out."

Josef stepped aside. The footmen advanced.

The table was between me and Christiana's men, but that wouldn't help me for long. I began a slow retreat toward the larder. If I had to fight, doing it from a doorway was my best option right now.

"Ana, I need to find him to bring him back to Ildrecca."

"I just bet you do," she said. "Is the thought of him returning supposed to make me weak in the knees? Am I supposed to give in at the prospect of seeing him again? That might have been a better gambit earlier in the conversation, Drothe; now it just irritates me." She addressed her footmen. "Be as rough as you need to. No, *rougher*."

One nodded; the other smiled. I recalled having broken the second one's nose a couple of years back. This wasn't shaping up well at all.

To hell with it. I cleared my steel.

The footmen stopped. Josef frowned. Christiana swore.

"Dammit, Drothe!" she said, although not as fiercely as

she might have earlier. Hired help standing about and all that. "Just leave! Because, I swear, if you so much as—"

"I might be able to fix it, Ana!" I said as I eyed her men. They eyed me back. "Do you understand me? I might be able to get him back into the city. I might make it so Degan can come back and be what he was. I might be able to fix it." Be able to fix him.

One of the footmen picked up a cleaver, hefted it, and nodded. The other cast about for a moment and settled on a rolling pin. They began moving again.

I slid into a low guard, my sword threatening from below, my dagger extended out at eye level. I had to get them as they came in; if they got in past my sword, I'd be carved and clubbed in no time.

"Wait."

The footmen stopped at Christiana's word but didn't change stance: Their weight was still forward, their weapons still ready, their eyes still hard as granite. Prepared to move against me on a moment's notice. I returned the favor.

Christiana walked over and stood just behind the footman with the crooked nose. "How?" she said to me. "How can you 'fix' it?"

"Another degan," I said. "He says he may have a way to bring Degan back into the fold, but he needs me to find him."

"Why you?"

I snorted and rubbed pointedly at my nose with the back of my dagger hand. "You're joking, right?"

"And you believe him?"

"I don't really have a choice," I said. "But yes, I think he wants Degan back safe, as far as it goes." I wasn't sure what Wolf had planned after that—and I didn't for a moment believe he was doing this for purely altruistic reasons—but that didn't seem like something I should mention to my sister just now.

Christiana reached up and began twirling a loose ringlet of hair about her finger. She sighed, chewed on her lip, and sighed again.

When she said, "Dammit," I knew I had her.

"Don't get all cocky," she snapped when she saw the smile on my face. "Understand that I'm going to hold you personally responsible for his safety," she said. "*Personally*. As in, if he comes back missing more than a fingernail clipping, I'll send people after you."

I reined my grin back to a smirk and nodded. "Understood."

"No, I don't think you do." Christiana pushed past her men, past my rapier, past my dagger even, until she was close enough for me to smell the soap on her skin and the closet's lavender bouquet on her dress. She dropped her voice to a practiced, husky whisper that, on anyone else, in any other situation, would have been alluring but for me was merely threatening.

"When I say I'll send people," she said, "I mean I'll bankrupt myself. I'll embrace penury and whore myself in the streets if it means you get what you deserve. Assassins galore: more than you can count, and the best money can buy. Because if you set him up again and let him fall, I won't care about the blood we share or the history we have or any of the damn lessons Sebastian pounded into our heads. If you hurt Degan, I promise I will see to it that you suffer. And that you die. Do we understand each other?"

There wasn't the faintest hint of a smile on my face this time when I said, "Understood."

Christiana gave my eyes a long, searching look, then nodded.

"He's in el-Qaddice," she said.

I blinked. "The Djanese capital?"

"Do you know another?"

I slammed my dagger and rapier home in their sheaths. "What the hell is he doing in Djan?"

Christiana turned and began walking away, her skirts whispering against the scrubbed stones of the floor. "I'm sure I don't know, but I expect you can ask him when you get there."

"Djan?" I said again. The border was weeks away, and

el-Qaddice even farther. Fading from sight was one thing, but vanishing for months? That was more than enough time for things to go to hell.

"Oh, I almost forgot," said Christiana, pausing at the foot of the table. "The rumor at Court is that things have been going downhill with the Despotate lately. I wouldn't be surprised if the ambassador were recalled soon. Angels know, he's been treated shoddily enough by the despotic court. The man's a diplomat, after all; you'd think—"

"Christiana," I said.

"Yes?"

"By downhill, do you mean . . ."

"War?"

"Yes."

She shrugged. "I doubt it, but who knows? All I'm saying is that it might prove difficult for an Imperial to cross the border right now, let alone into el-Qaddice. But then, you're a clever boy: I'm sure you'll manage. Just don't do anything to make them suspicious."

"Right." Because I was never suspicious, either in nature or deed.

Christiana resumed her exit. "And, Drothe?"

"Yes?"

"Send the money to pay for the window and a new copy of *The Enchanting of the Bridgemaker's Daughter* before you leave town, would you? I don't want to be left on the hook for that."

I shared my thoughts on the matter with my sister as she walked out the door. Her only answer was a peal of laughter coming back along the hallway.

I wondered briefly whether Tobin and his people had a copy of *The Enchanting of the Bridgemaker's Daughter* in their collection, and whether they'd be willing to let me have a copy made of it. Wondered if Baldezar would consider it too below him to copy at all.

A throat cleared itself politely behind me. Josef reminding me it was time for me to walk out the door before I was thrown out.

I left by the servants' exit. Naturally.

· Chapter Ten

"No," said Jelem. "Absolutely not. It's impossible."

"Why the hell not?" I said.

Jelem took a long draw on the brass-tipped hose that led to the communal water pipe on our table and considered me. We'd started out sharing it with another pair of men, but a few words from Jelem had sent them seeking another table shortly after I'd arrived. As for the rest of the patrons in the place, they were busy listening to the house story-teller, who was sitting in his narrow alcove and banging his brass sword on the floor every few minutes for emphasis.

We were in a street-side café in the Raffa Na'Ir, the Djanese district of Ildrecca. A gray-blue haze filled the café, filtering the morning sunlight that streamed in through the arched facade. A dozen low tables were scattered around the place, each surrounded by a collection of battered floor pillows. Every table held a water pipe with three to five untipped hoses coming off it. Patrons rented a tip—or, as in Jelem's case, brought their own—and purchased their smoke of choice from the café. Wine, tea, coffee, and sekan-jabin were available in abundance, as were a collection of pastries and finger foods the Djanese were so fond of at the end of a night and beginning of a day.

Unlike me, Jelem looked fresh. His linen undertunic and pants were crisp, his felted wool vest spotless, his neck and the cheeks above his beard freshly scraped. Mind, that was no guarantee that he hadn't been up all night as well, but there was no way of knowing by just looking at him. He was the picture of Djanese complacency.

Which irked me to no end.

"Returning to Djan would be ... unadvisable for me at present," he said at last.

"Risky?" I said.

Jelem lifted the tip of the pipe to his mouth.

"Deadly?" I pushed.

Water bubbled in the pipe as Jelem drew in the smoke. The action almost hid the frown on his face, but not quite.

"Somewhere in between," he said at last.

"Maybe I could—"

"No, I don't think you could," said Jelem. "But I appreciate the offer. It's a Djanese matter: politics, family, magic—very complicated. Something I would not expect an Imperial to burden himself with, let alone understand."

"Still," I said. "If I'm going to be there anyhow, maybe you should prime me a bit." I picked up another pastry. "I mean, being a simple Imperial and all, I wouldn't want to step on the wrong toes and make things worse."

Jelem snorted. I had known him for years. To me, he'd always been a Djanese Mouth, an occasional gateway to the *Zakur,* a collector of information, and a damn good gambler. Sometimes he was even a friend. But in all that time, he had never hinted at, let alone revealed, why he was living among his country's traditional enemies. Oh, there were rumors, of course—murder, court intrigue, a secret romance with a member of the despot's harem, you name it—but none of them had ever quite fit the calm, capable, arrogant son of a bitch who sat across from me and peddled his magic to Djanese and Imperials alike. And none of his fellow countrymen had been willing to clarify matters, either.

Which all made his mention of "politics, family, and magic" an encyclopedic dissertation compared to what I already knew, and the reason I pressed for more.

Jelem exhaled a gray plume out of the corner of his mouth. "Make things worse?" he said. "No, even considering your exceptional talents, I doubt you could find and crush enough toes to make things worse for me. Where are you going in the Despotate?"

"El-Qaddice."

He coughed. "El-Qaddice? Then I take it back: You might just find enough toes after all."

"All the more reason for you to come along and make sure I avoid them." Having a native with me would be helpful; having a native Mouth of Jelem's ability could be crucial if things turned ugly.

Jelem refused to rise to the bait. "Why Djan?" he said instead. "And, more important, why now?"

I'd thought about this after I'd left my sister's and begun my nightlong hunt for Jelem: about the tales I could tell, the half-truths I could let drop, and the omissions I could get away with. And I'd decided that, if I wanted what I needed, none of those would suffice. Of the countless people in the Imperial capital, Jelem knew more about what had passed between Degan and me than any other soul, save my sister. So I simply said, "Degan's there."

The brass tip didn't quite slip from his fingers, but it was a close thing. He covered it well by setting the pipe's hose aside and taking up his own cup of sekanjabin. "Degan. Really. Interesting. Any idea why?"

"Part of the reason I'm going is to find out."

"And the other?"

"I hear good things about taking the waters."

"Yes, of course," said Jelem. "We're famous for our 'waters' in the desert."

We drank in silence for a while after that, each itching to learn what the other knew, each unwilling to show his hand for fear of losing any kind of perceived advantage. Finally, after a second round of coffee and sekanjabin, along with a fresh tray of sweets, Jelem leaned in and set his cup aside.

"I cannot go," he said. "While my family might be happy to see me, it would only be to put a dagger between my ribs. However, I still have associates there who might be persuaded to help. I will send word ahead of you. With luck, they will be able to assist you once you are inside the Old City."

"And the cost for this help?" I said.

"For my aid? Deliver a package. As for my friends in Djan, that will be between you and them."

"What kind of package?"

"A small one."

"What's in it?"

"Small things."

"What kind of small things?"

"Letters. Missives. Nothing you need concern yourself about."

I tapped my finger on the side of my cup, watching tremors form on the surface of the coffee. "I generally find that when people tell me I don't need to be concerned about something, it ends up concerning me." I looked up and met the Djanese's eye. "What's in the letters?"

Jelem smiled with all the charm of a snake. "I'm sorry, my memory must be slipping: Why did you say you were looking for Degan, again?"

I grimaced. "I just don't want any surprises when some customs patrol pulls a packet of diplomatic secrets out of my pocket and looks to me for an explanation."

"Then I suggest you hide them very well," said Jelem. "Besides, you know I don't deal with things like that."

"No, your secrets are likely much more dangerous."

Jelem shrugged. "Danger is in the eye of the beholder. But very well: I will show you the letters before I seal them. Acceptable?"

I regarded the man across from me, trying to read him, to decide whether he was playing me or not, and how badly. Problem was, he was too skilled a gambler to let me see anything, and I was too proud to pretend I hadn't.

"As long as you seal them in front of me," I finally said.

"As you wish." Jelem sipped coffee, sucked smoke. "But if you ask me, you should be worrying more about how you're going to get into el-Qaddice than what I put in a letter."

"Travel documents I can handle," I said. Crossing borders and getting into large cities required passports and travel papers, both in the Empire and Djan. The imperial and despotic bureaucracies, not to mention tax collectors, were always happier when they knew who was going where for what reason, and how much they could make off the process. The farther you went and the more borders you crossed, the more elaborate became the requirements, but I had people for that.

"Yes, I don't doubt that Baldezar could falsify papers for you," said Jelem. He'd met and worked with the master scribe I had reluctantly taken into my organization back when I'd been on the run from Shadow. "And they would suffice, if all you wanted to do was get as far as Waas or Geshara on the Bay or some other merchant town. But we're talking el-Qaddice; gaining access to one of the political and religious centers of the Despotate requires more than a forged passport with a false stamp of passage on it, especially for an unknown imperial traveling on his own."

"What do you mean?"

"You need letters of passage. And for that, you need a patron."

Djanese patronage. I'd heard about it but never had to deal with it myself. The few times I'd been to Djan, it had been to check with my contacts or pick up payment for one of the more valuable imperial relics I'd had smuggled. Those meetings had all happened in some dusty little border village that barely rated a name, or in one of the larger merchant towns where a simple passport and a couple of coins could get you through the gate without a second glance. I'd never needed to go deeper into the Despotate, and thus never needed the kind of contacts Jelem was bringing up.

"How hard is it to arrange for patronage?" I said.

"For established merchants or diplomats? A small matter: A handful of atrociously large bribes and a promise or two usually suffice. But for a Gray Prince and Nose?" He shook his head. "The purpose behind patronage is twofold: to maintain the old trade monopolies of the merchant tribes, and to discourage casual espionage. None of the merchant sheikhs have any reason to vouch for you, and I don't think you will find a prominent citizen willing to affix his name to a letter that makes him responsible for your actions. The Wandering Family knows *I* wouldn't tie my fortune to you like that."

"Yes, but you know me."

"True, but we're not talking about the misfortunes of my life right now. We're talking about yours. And the simple truth is, without the proper letters of passage, you won't be able to enter el-Qaddice. It is, in many ways, a closed city when it comes to unknown or questionable Imperials."

"Like thieves and former Noses."

"Just so."

I leaned forward and pushed my coffee cup around on the table. Between what I had drunk and the seeds I'd been slipping since finding Jelem, my hands had taken on a mild tremor. I wouldn't be coming down for a couple of hours yet, but when I did, it wouldn't be pretty. I needed to get as much done between now and then as I could.

"What about forging them?" I said, making sure my voice didn't carry.

Jelem arched an eyebrow, considering. "It's possible," he said, "but you have to understand that we Djanese do not look upon documents the same way as you Imperials. Especially not official ones."

"How so?"

"For you, it is a matter of what the paper says, what it allows you to do as defined by your laws; for us, it is more about who has affixed their name to the paper, as well as the splendor of the document. In Djan, important documents *look* important; the contents are tertiary at best. Even minor officials go out of their way to embellish their certificates and reports. As for something like a letter of passage . . . well, it's complex. There's an elaborate formulary specific to each writer's house and tribe. The ornamentation, illumination, and calligraphy that go into something like that are no small thing—and doubly so for a letter granting access to el-Qaddice. Gold leaf, elaborate seals, precious inks and dyes, even the blending of the fibers of the paper itself, are all carefully proscribed for each patron. The letters are works of art."

"And art can be hard to forge," I muttered.

"Especially on short notice."

"How long would it take?"

Jelem shrugged. "Much would depend on the patron, the style of embellishment, the cost and availability of materials . . ."

"Jelem, how long?"

"If it all came together quickly? A week, likely more."

I didn't think I had a week—not with Wolf breathing down my neck.

"There has to be a way," I said. "No city is that tightly shut, especially not one as big as el-Qaddice."

"Of course not," said Jelem. "But the *Zakur* have no reason to welcome a foreign crime prince, and you don't have the contacts to grease the other mechanisms that could get you in. Perhaps if the empire and the Despotate were not growling at each other quite so loudly right now it would be easier, but unless you have an in with a respected caravan master or suddenly learn to play the tambour and join a minstrel troupe, I can't see an easy way into the city for you."

"Shit." I turned, ready to call for a new pot of coffee, when I caught myself. "Minstrel troupe?" I said. "Why would a minstrel troupe be able to get in to el-Qaddice?"

Jelem waved a dismissive hand. "The sixth son of the despot, Padishah Yazir, considers himself a patron of the arts. He's made an arrangement with his father—more like nagged him into acquiescence, if truth be told—to extend the padishah's patronage to various musicians and sculptors and poets, so they may more easily enter the city. He has a vision about turning el-Qaddice into a haven for the New Culture, as he calls it. No one knows what this means, but my sources tell me that, at present, it consists mainly of poseurs and vagabonds using the padishah's patronage to stuff their bellies and empty his purse."

"And he just gives this patronage away?"

"So I'm told."

"To artistic poseurs and vagabonds?"

"On a good day."

"Tell me," I said, leaning forward, a smile forming on my lips, "how does Padishah Yazir feel about actors?"

"No," said Tobin. "Absolutely not."

"And why the hell not?" I said.

"Djan?" said the troupe leader, making a broad gesture toward what I expect was supposed to be Djan. I didn't bother to point out that he was gesturing west, not south. "Djan?" he said again. "Deserts, sir! Bandits! Nomads! Not to mention Djanese who speak . . . Djanese. Which, I might add, we do not."

"Pallias's troupe made a circuit of the Despotate a couple years back," observed Ezak. He was leaning up against the wall on the far end of the hayloft, calmly looking down a length of ash he'd been shaping into a staff. Judging by the pile of fine shavings at his feet, he was down to the finishing work. Between him and us, the rest of the troupe was seated on the floor or the hay, their heads moving back and forth with the conversation like spectators at a game of court hands.

"And what did they get for it?" huffed Tobin. "Lost for a month, and then relegated to hamlets and trading towns. And the bribes! Don't even get me started on the bribes Pallias had to pay to those thieves masquerading as despotic officials."

"And how is that different from some of our tours in the Empire?" said Ezak.

Mumbles among the troupe, both for and against.

"There's water in the empire," snapped Tobin. "And Imperials. They understand us well enough to pay, at least."

"Usually," amended Ezak.

"Mostly."

Ezak shrugged and ran his small knife down the staff, drawing a thin curl of wood from its surface.

"The point is," I said, "I have to travel to Djan, and I need you to come with me."

"'Need'?" said Tobin, rounding on me. "Need? And what, may I ask, is the source of this need?"

I'd been thinking about how to answer that question for most of the day. From the moment I'd left Jelem, through my conversation with Kells about leaving Ildrecca, then finding Fowler and making her aware of the developing plan, I'd been coming up with possible responses in the back of my mind. Threats, bribes, deals, blackmail, cons—all the usual tools in the Kin arsenal, and I'd discarded every one. I was going to be traveling with these people for over a month, sharing food and water and shelter, at the end of which I was going to be relying on them to get me into el-Qaddice. And while I could start out the journey easily enough with lies or threats as a motivator, the odds of them still being effective when we reached el-Qaddice were another matter entirely. A month is a long time to prop up a lie or keep an edge on fear, and I didn't want to risk things falling apart in the middle of Djan. Far better to take my risks here, at the start, before I'd invested not only time and effort, but hope. Far better to try the truth.

"I need to get into el-Qaddice," I said. "I need to . . . talk to someone there. Problem is, I need a letter of patronage to get inside, and I don't have one."

"All the way to Djan for a talk?" said one of the men in the troupe. "Angels, man: Just write a letter. She can't be that special!"

Mild laughter. I marked the man, making sure I remembered him, and why.

"Be quiet, Gauge," said Ezak, reading my look.

"And how does our going to el-Qaddice help you get into the city?" said Tobin. "If anything, I'd think it would make it harder. Rather than one letter, you'd need near a dozen."

I was opening my mouth to answer when Ezak looked up from his carving and said, "The Prince of Plays."

Tobin turned to face his cousin. "What? Of Plays? I thought that was in Assyram."

Ezak shook his head. "You're thinking of the Bey who pays for limericks with silver ingots."

Tobin put his hands on his hips. "Are you sure? I thought he was in Tirand."

"No," said a voice from among the troupe. "That's the countess who likes to hire actors to—"

"The point is," I said, raising my voice before the speculation got out of hand, "one of the sons of the despot—the Padishah Yazir—has made it his practice to offer patronage to artists who please him, and that patronage includes access to el-Qaddice."

Tobin turned to face me. There was a decidedly avaricious gleam to his eye now. "Patronage, you say?"

"And more."

"I told you: the Prince of Plays," repeated Ezak, still shaving the staff. "Son of the Despot. Pellias talked about him, remember?"

"I remember," said Tobin. "I just thought he was in . . . well, no matter." He looked me up and down. "And you think we can win this patronage, do you?"

"I'm willing to travel to Djan to find out."

"That's a large leap of faith," observed Ezak, "considering you've never seen us perform."

"I wouldn't call it so much faith as desperation at this point," I said. "But considering you were willing to have faith in me when it came to your plays, it only seems fair to return the favor."

Tobin and several members began to preen a bit at that; then the old matron, Muiress, cleared her throat in the center of the troupe and cut my legs out from beneath me.

"Plays we've yet to see," she grumbled, not looking up from her embroidery. "Thief."

The smiles that had been blooming in the hayloft faded. The old goat smirked.

"Good Muiress has a point," said Tobin. "You ask for a fresh bargain without first having fulfilled the old one. A bargain of a much more serious nature. What say you to that?"

"I say this bargain is as important to me as your plays are to you."

"And yet we are still owed those very plays," said Tobin.

"You are."

"Just out of curiosity," said Ezak, now looking up from his staff. "How do you plan to get the plays back?"

I folded my arms. "I don't."

"What?" This from Tobin. "But you—"

"I already have them."

The building protest whooshed out of Tobin like a gale, followed by a rolling laugh. Smiles bloomed all around the room.

"My people lifted them from Petyr two nights ago," I said. Not to mention some of the choicer items they'd found lying alongside the scripts in his warehouse. The trip to Djan wasn't going to come cheap, after all, and I needed to be ready to cover expenses.

As for Petyr, any complaints he might have had vanished with him into the harbor. I'd heard Fowler had tied the stones to his legs herself, had whispered Scratch's name in his ear just before he was pushed off the caïque.

None of this I shared with the troupe, though. Instead, I merely said, "We managed to get your props, too. And your wagon."

Tobin tilted his head back, chuckling with delight. "Oh, well done, sir." He put his hand on my shoulder, slapped it once, twice. Fortunately, it wasn't the shoulder that had Degan's sword riding behind it. "Well done. You had us. For a moment there, I thought—"

"What?"

"Well, that you were reneging on your deal."

"Reneging?" I said. "Never."

"Good, because I—"

"But changing it?" I leaned in. "Well, that's another matter."

The good cheer that had been filling Tobin's face drained away like water from a leaky tub. "Change it?" he said, echoing me. *"Change it?"* The actors, who had begun to laugh and chatter, left off. Voices faded as faces turned to us once more. "We had a bargain—a bargain we honored by getting you into the city. It seems only fitting that you honor your half as well."

"It does," I agreed, nodding. "And I will. But here's the thing—when my people went to lighten Petyr, they found out that he'd already started selling some of your plays. My guess is that he was figuring you weren't going to be able to pay, and that even if you did, he'd be able to up the interest enough to claim that you only had enough for whatever he hadn't sold yet. A shitty thing to do, I admit—but that was Petyr.

"That aside, though, maybe you can start to see my problem: I'd promised to get you all of your plays, but they weren't all where they were supposed to be. And as you said, you'd fulfilled your half of the deal; I wanted to do the same. But to do that, I had to track down the other plays and get them back." I shook my head. "What was I to do? I didn't want to come back with only two-thirds of a folio and be accused of breaking my word. So I sent my people after them—even went and recovered one myself. The only thing is, that required more effort, more time, and more money on my part. And some of those people who bought your plays? Well, they didn't want to give up their recent acquisitions. Some of them had to be persuaded."

"Persuaded?" said Tobin.

"Persuaded." I let the word hang there in the air, gaining weight. I cleared my throat. "But the good news is we were successful in the end. Except."

"Except what?"

"Except I had to go into debt for your plays. To my people. To other bosses." I leaned in, whispered, "And I don't like owing people things."

Tobin wiped a hand down the side of his pants. "But surely you can't blame us—"

I stepped forward, crowding him. Forcing him back.

"I can do whatever the hell I want," I said, "because I have your swag. The only reason I haven't done anything yet is that I gave you my word. And I'm going to keep it. Whatever paper I pulled from Petyr's warehouse is yours. But." And here I looked past him, to Ezak and the actors and Muiress, still busy with her sewing. "If you want the rest—the props and the wagon and the other plays—then we need to talk about Djan."

Tobin blinked once, twice, and then took a deep breath and gathered himself. I could almost see the role dropping on him as he threw his head back and stood up straight.

Oh, hell, Tobin—don't make me knock you down for being an ass.

He was just getting ready to speak, and I was just adjusting my weight, when Ezak spoke up.

"Add in your patronage," he said, "and you have a deal."

Both Tobin and I stared at him. Even Muiress turned to look. "What?" I said.

"You heard me: patronage."

"To a thief?" said Tobin. "You'll have to excuse me, coz, but that seems a bit desperate, even for us."

"Haven't you been listening to him?" said Ezak as he pushed away from the wall. I couldn't help notice he was still holding the staff; couldn't help remembering Tobin telling me his cousin was the troupe's weapons master. "'My people, my thieves.' 'Other bosses.' We're not dealing with just any thief here, coz, but a Kin of means. One with people to command." He smiled knowingly. "A—if I'm not mistaken—prince among his kind. Isn't that so, Master Drothe?"

"A Gray Prince?" said Tobin, turning back to stare at me.

I didn't bother asking how Ezak had figured it out. My slips in words aside, it wasn't as if I'd been going to great pains to hide things. And besides, Petyr had been crowing enough about going after me that I expect it was an easy rumor to pick up just about anywhere in Dirty Waters.

I shrugged and nodded. "A Gray Prince," I said.

"You always said you wanted royal patronage, coz," said Ezak. "This is the best I can do."

Tobin scowled. "True, but I meant the kind with a crown and a palace and a private cook."

"Our prospects are thin," said Ezak. "Without our papers, I haven't been able to present the proper documents to the Minister of Plays. None of the inns will sign us without one. Plus, it's getting into late summer, which means most of the taverns are already set for players through fall."

"Those prospects sound more than thin, coz."

"No thinner than going back on the road, and at least this way, we'd have patronage, not to mention prospects at the end of the road." Ezak grinned at his cousin's back.

"And besides, wouldn't you love to prove Pellias wrong about Djan?"

"Mmm," said Tobin. "I always have disliked that pompous sack of . . . wind." He glanced back over his shoulder at the rest of the troupe. Shrugs, nods, shakes of heads, fairly evenly distributed. And Muiress, staring fixedly at her needle and thread. Finally, when she was sure everyone was looking at her, she sniffed and gave a small nod.

"Well, there it is, then," said Tobin, turning back to me. "In exchange for your patronage and the return of our property—*all* of our property—we agree to travel to Djan and perform before the Prince of Plays in your name. Given the nature of the agreement, I don't think either of us can hope for much better. What say you, sir?"

What could I say? I reached out and took Tobin's hand in my own, shifting the grip into the Clasp. "Looks like I've bought myself an acting company," I said.

They all cheered.

Oh, Wolf was just going to love them.

Actors. Angels help me.

river Qadd, and not one of the many canals that were said to stem from it.

The river valley was a place of plenty, bursting with near-forgotten colors after what felt like an age spent among graceless browns and dirty grays. Even the blue of the sky seemed richer here, although I knew that was more me than any effect of the land on the heavens. A place that promised rich scents, damp earth, and cool water after a long journey.

It was also a place I knew I wasn't going to be going.

I turned my attention to the other spur of the road below and followed it until it reached our true destination: the walls of el-Qaddice.

El-Qaddice was really two cities: one set above the other, separated by both geography and time. The upper city—the Old City—sat atop a narrow plateau that looked as if it had been dropped into the valley from the sky. Sheer white city walls rose from rust-colored cliffs, the faces of which had been shaped by generations of stone carvers to form the elaborate geometric patterns that signified the various Djanese gods. Behind the walls, towers and domes glittered in the late daylight, their surfaces set off by metal and glass and, in some cases, I was told, gems. I suspected it was a hell of a sight when the sun hit it in the morning.

Down at the base of the plateau, things weren't nearly as resplendent. Even from here, I could see that the Lower City was a sprawling collection of whitewashed, mud brick buildings set behind a stout stone wall. A haze of smoke and dust hung over the place, and the only colors I could see came from laundry drying on the roofs. There was plenty of traffic in and out of the gates, though, and the sheep and goats wandering the pastures outside looked fat enough, so I didn't expect to be waking into abject misery. I suppose in any other setting, the Lower City would have looked normal, possibly even prosperous, but with a prince's ransom in gems perched on the shingles of the town above it? Well, maybe I was asking too much.

Regardless of how it was spilt up, el-Qaddice served as not only one of the summer capitals of the Despotate, but also a key pilgrimage and religious site. Even from the hill where our caravan had set its final camp, I could see saffron-clad dots—pilgrims—making their way up the twisting road that led from the Lower City to the Old; imagined I could almost hear the tinkling of the seven tin bells on their staffs. The thought made me shudder.

Four weeks on the road, and it had seemed as if every oasis, every caravansary, every damn well we'd stopped at had been festooned by at least one group of bell-jangling pilgrims. And each group had been happy—no, eager—to explain, at length, how the bells represented their trespasses, and how each bell would be replaced with a brass one for every pilgrimage they completed. And, of course, they'd rung their bells. A lot.

It wasn't until two weeks into the trip I'd discovered that late summer was pilgrimage season in Djan, and that we were at its peak. I had refrained from making any fresh martyrs on the road, but it had been a near thing.

"What are you brooding about?" said Fowler as she came over and settled down on the rug beside me.

"Ritual sacrifice."

She laughed. Fowler had taken to the local dress on the road, with a long tunic, short vest, head scarf, and hooded burnoose—all in greens, save for the pale wheat of the vest—while I'd stayed in a shirt and breeches. I'd finally traded out my doublet and jerkin for a sand-shaded coat and a striped kaffiyeh, more out of deference to necessity than style. Fowler wore her drapes well, though, with the sash drawing the tunic in just enough to hint at the form beneath. The hang of the rest of the clothes only added to the effect.

She gestured across the expanse of low, rocky hills that separated us from the city. "Considering your assault?"

"Something like that." I pointed at the Lower City. "We're going in there," I said, indicating a wide, arched gate, "and we need to get up there." My finger rose to indicate the Old City. "That's where the Imperial Quarter is." Most of the Lower City was open to foreigners, with only a few districts requiring an escort to enter; the Old City, though, required patronage to get through the gate.

"And you think that's where Degan will be?"

I shrugged, then reached back to adjust his sword against my back. After a month, I'd gotten used to the feel of it against my ribs and spine. It was comforting—when it didn't chafe, that is.

"Being Imperial," I said, "the Quarter seems like the best place for us to start."

Fowler nodded and stared out at the city. The sun had lightened her hair, making it almost white. It had also dusted her nose with freckles. I wasn't sure when I'd decided I liked the freckles, but I did. Not that I'd said anything about it.

I allowed myself one last appreciative glance at her and then turned my attention back to the valley. Fowler sighed, clearly getting ready to speak. I wondered whether her thoughts had been running on the same line as mine.

They hadn't.

"I need to talk to you about the troupe," she said, not turning to face me.

I rolled my eyes. "Angels, not again."

"Drothe—"

"No," I said. "If Tobin wants to complain, he can do it to my face. Emperor knows he's had enough practice. I won't have him sending you—"

"No one sent me." Fowler turned to face me. Her eyes were sharp and hard. "I'm here on my own. We need to talk about how you treat them."

"I treat them just fine."

"You almost stabbed Tobin yesterday. How is that fine?"

"I didn't stab him," I said. "I threatened to stab him. Big difference."

"And you think that's how you ought to act toward the leader of your troupe? What the hell kind of etiquette is that?"

"Knives don't have etiquette."

Fowler threw her hands up. "That's my point! You're treating them like a gang of Prigs to your Upright Man. They're actors, Drothe, not Kin. And you're their patron; that makes them your responsibility."

"You think I don't know what it means to be responsible for them? Why the hell do you think I've been paying their way and listening to them prattle and complain and boast? It's certainly not for the pleasure of their company." I started counting off on my fingers. "I've kept them fed; I've kept them safe; when Ezak told me they needed new wood for prop spears to practice with—in the middle of a fucking desert, I might add—I found him some. I've—"

"You've been doing it for yourself, and you know it."

"Excuse me?"

"You've been doing it because you need them to get into el-Qaddice so you can find Degan. That's all. If it weren't for that, you wouldn't even have them here."

"I thought that was obvious," I said. "I've never made any allusions about actually liking being their patron."

"No, you haven't," said Fowler, her opinion thick on her tongue.

At some point while growing up on the street, I knew, Fowler had done a stint as a Kinchin: the younger half of a Palliard gang. Her job had been to beg and bawl and draw people's attention while the embarrassed "mother" used the opportunity to lift purses, or whatever else was handy, off sympathetic observers. It hadn't been true acting by any stretch of the imagination, but in Fowler's head the time on the dodge had somehow made her a kindred spirit to the Boardsmen in the troupe. Nor had the actors dissuaded her; if anything, Tobin had welcomed her with open arms, no doubt sensing a potential champion in the Oak Mistress. Nor had he been wrong, much to my annoyance.

"Listen," I said. "As long as they do as they're told—"

"They're not pets, Drothe," she said. "They're actors. And what's more, they're *your* actors. They don't see this as a dodge or a deal or a convenience—it's an agreement. A pact. You give a damn about them, they'll give a damn about you. Hell, maybe they'll even write a play in your honor."

I thought about that for a moment—about a play performed in my name, by my actors, and the rumors and misunderstandings and pure chaos even the smallest comedic line could stir up among the Kin—and shuddered. "I don't need that kind of honor, thanks."

Fowler looked at me for a long moment. "For a person who's made a living off his wits for most of his life, you can be incredibly stupid sometimes."

"I certainly hope not," said a deep, easy voice behind us. I didn't bother to turn around as Wolf sauntered up and settled himself beside me, on the opposite side from Fowler. He'd been at the caravan encampment outside Ildrecca as well, where we'd gathered before leaving—though not with Fowler. "I'd be more than a bit distressed to learn that I'd worked this hard, and traveled this far, only to end up with an idiot in my employ."

"Don't worry," said Fowler, gathering her knees beneath herself and standing. "He may be an idiot about some things, but he's a genius when it comes to saving his own ass. As long as his life's on the line, you won't be disappointed."

"Ah. Good to know." Wolf looked over at me. "Clearly, I must threaten you more often."

I glanced up at Fowler. "Thanks a lot."

"Do you some good to be on the receiving end for a bit," she said, and she stalked away.

Wolf watched her go. "Among the Azaar, such a woman—"

"Would kick half your tribe's ass," I said. "Drop it."

"As if it were a scorpion." Wolf produced a wine skin from within his robe and took a long draw. He then proffered it to me, and shook his head when he saw my expression of distaste. "Not wine," he said. "Sekanjabin."

"Oh." I took the skin and pulled a long draw. The liquid was warm, but even with that, short of leaping into an oasis's pool, the well-diluted syrup of mint, sugar, and vinegar was one of the best ways to cool off I'd found on the trail.

I handed the skin back and waited.

"You have a plan for getting into the Old City?" he said after he had taken another pull and set the skin aside.

I jerked a thumb over my shoulder toward the sounds of the actors. Someone was yelling at someone else again. "You've been riding with it for a month."

"And you think they will be enough to get you in?"

"That's the plan."

"And if your plan fails?"

I thought of the doublet lying in my tent and the thin packet stitched into its lining. Jelem had been adamant about not contacting his people until I was inside the Old City itself, insisting they couldn't help me get in, and that seeking them out would only put them at risk politically. I suspected there was also some concern on his part about his contacts charging him for any favors they might do me, but his debts weren't my problem.

"Then I'm going to see about leveraging a . . ." I stopped and turned to Wolf. He was watching me carefully. "Wait. You just said 'in case *you* can't get it,' not 'we.' "

"I did."

"Meaning you're not coming into the city with us?"

"Just so."

I waited, got nothing more. "Are you coming into el-Qaddice at all?"

Wolf sniffed and turned his head away. "Perhaps." He paused to clear a nostril. "I have business to take care of elsewhere first."

"Business?" I said. "You set me up, put my organization at risk, and drag me to the heart of the Despotate, only to tell me you won't be around when it comes time to do the dodge? When you're the one who's been pushing us to make time and miles ever since we left Ildrecca? What the hell kind of a cross is this?"

Wolf turned back and set his eyes on el-Qaddice, not looking at me. "You think I'd come this far, only to leave my Order's future in the hands of a thief and a band of players?" He pursed his lips. "You know nothing."

"You're right," I said. "I know nothing. Nothing about why an Order dedicated to the preservation of the empire sell themselves as mercenaries when they could be serving the emperor directly; nothing about why your highest form of payment isn't money or advancement, but a promise; nothing about why it's so important that you all agree on what it means to serve in the first place. And I certainly have no fucking clue why any of the emperors would let you all wander around like this, when I'm sure he can come up with better uses for you." I gestured at the city before us. "All I know is that I'm being held over a barrel, and that every time I'm pushed further in, the only answer I get is 'It's for the Order. Best you don't know.' Well, fuck not knowing. If you want me in that city, working for you, you'll tell me why it's so damn important your Order not cut itself to pieces, because except for a former friend who might get caught in the middle of it, I don't have one single reason to care."

Wolf stared straight ahead. "You have reasons," he said. "We discussed them before."

"I have threats and obligations hanging over me," I said. "Those aren't the same thing."

Wolf turned a solemn gaze my way. "I see the desert has given you time to think, time to ask questions the crowds of Ildrecca managed to keep from your mind."

"When you're on a camel twelve hours a day, you try to think about anything but."

"True." Wolf tapped a finger against his knee as he continued to watch me. "I will tell you this much," he said. "We are not like the Sashes, Gold or White. We are degans, and that means we are our own men and women. Our Oath to defend the empire does not mean we bow and scrape at court. We do not answer to the generals on the field or the clerks in the hallway. Our purpose is higher than that."

"The emperor?" I said.

Wolf shook his head. "If he called, we would come, I think, but I don't expect him to. He has forgotten us over the incarnations, or at least decided he has no immediate need of us. In some ways, we're like a fine blade, left to rust in a cabinet." He turned gaze back out over the valley. "It's shameful to be a warrior of purpose with no purpose."

"So why become one in the first place?" I said. "They must have told you what it was like before you took the Oath."

"Because for some of us, the possibility of serving a higher cause is preferable to the certainty of mediocrity."

"And that's why you have the Oath? To give you some-thing to serve while you wait?"

"The Oath has been with us since the beginning; it's not something that was decided upon later to fill a void. We've always had it, have always been under the Oath, just as we've always been willing to serve certain individuals with our Oath." Wolf glanced at me without turning his head. "Bronze has told you the conditions of the Oath?"

I nodded, but stayed silent. When it came to details about the degan's Oath, I didn't trust myself to not say too much.

"Then you know we degans can be particular about who we swear to serve," he said, his eyes still lingering on me. "It's no light thing, for either party. Once, the Oaths were sworn and used to achieve specific purposes, but those days have passed." He turned his attention back to the city be-fore us. "Now some of my brothers and sisters swear for a cause or a belief, while others try to achieve an agenda, col-lecting favors like tokens to be cashed in at the end of a game. Still others choose their Oaths for personal reasons."

"And you?" I said. "What's your reason? When would Silver Degan take an Oath?"

I sat there for a while, studying his profile, waiting for an answer. Finally, Wolf cleared his throat and took another pull from the wine skin. "You asked why I'm not going to join you in the city right away," he said, sidestepping the harder question by giving me the answer to an earlier one. "El-Qaddice is one of several capitals of the Despotate, and one of four possible summer seats for the despot himself. Her sister city, el-Beyad, stands a day's ride to the north-east, near the other end of this valley." He gestured in the other city's direction with the skin. "It is also a summer cap-ital. The despot has been known to travel back and forth between the two, sometimes weekly, as the fancy suits him. Clerks and messengers and eunuchs ride the road between them day and night. If Bronze isn't here, it stands to reason that he may be there."

I followed his gesture, resigned to the fact that, for the moment, he was done telling me about the Order. "And why would he be there?" I said.

"Because to come to el-Qaddice in summer is to come within the orbit of the despot's court. If Bronze is here now, it can't be a coincidence."

"Are you saying you think he's seeking service with the despot?" I said. "That's insane! He broke his Oath and almost died defending what he thought was his duty to the empire—there's no way he'd offer his sword to the empire's enemy."

"No?" said Wolf. "A man is capable of many things when his trust has been broken . . . or when his faith has been shattered. There's no place for Bronze in the empire anymore; nothing that won't summon up memories of pain and betrayal. Where better to get away from reminders of what he's lost than in the enemy's camp? Where better to go to no longer be a degan?"

I looked back out over the vista. The pilgrims were near the top of the road now, the setting sun turning their saffron robes into red-orange points of light against the gray of the rock. Like flames climbing their way up to the fuel that fired them. I wondered how many would be snuffed out before they made it home.

"I don't see it," I said. "Degan isn't the kind to give up on something just because it didn't work out."

Wolf nodded. "I agree."

"But I thought . . ."

"You're the one who suggested his going over to the despot; I merely said I could understand the reasoning behind such an action. I never said I thought he would."

Son of a . . .

"Fine," I said. "Then why do *you* think he might be in el-Beyad?"

"Knowing Bronze, he's looking for someone or something. Not something that will exonerate him—he's not the kind to try to make excuses for his conscience—but something that will help give him a purpose, as we talked about. Or prove his point. He's stubborn that way."

"So it's not just him trying to put some distance between himself and the Order?"

"It may be as simple as that, too." Wolf shrugged. "Having never left the Order of the Degans, I can't speak to what a man does in Bronze's situation. But it's not beyond him to take work with some minor noble or man of purpose."

"And men of purpose tend to gravitate to power," I said.

"Or make it for themselves. Either way, it's best for me to ride to el-Beyad first, before attempting el-Qaddice."

Now it was my turn to look at him sidelong. I let a frown crease my mouth.

"You have history in el-Qaddice, don't you?" I said.

"I'm a degan: I have history many places."

"Yes, but this place is special, isn't it?" I said. "You said 'attempt'; that you'd attempt the city. That tells me you think you may not be able to get in, that you may not be of any use to me in there."

"I will gain entry," he said. "Do not doubt that, Kin. But it'll take some arranging, and it's better for me—and you—if I enter the city after you and your tribe of squabbling children are already inside. The less attention you draw to me, or I to you, the better."

My eyes narrowed. "What kind of attention?"

"The kind that might keep us out of the city. Or make the padishah shy away from offering his patronage. Or attract the eyes or ears of the man we're hunting." Wolf corked the wine skin. "It's the last I worry about the most: If he sees me before you find him, he may get the wrong idea. I don't need him vanishing again. I don't have the time."

"Have you considered Degan may get the wrong idea when he sees me, too?" I said.

"Yes."

"And?"

"You're not a degan; he won't assume you're there to kill him. And even if he did, you're not a threat."

"Thanks a lot."

Wolf stood and showed me his teeth. "I expect you to be in the Old City of el-Qaddice within a week," he said. "Two at the most."

"And if it takes longer? From what I hear, it's not as if the padishah is sitting outside the gates, waiting for the next troupe to roll in from Ildrecca."

"You're the Gray Prince," he said. "Figure it out. Besides, the longer we take here, the longer you're away from—and the greater the threat becomes to—your people back in Il-drecca." Wolf gestured at the sinking sun. "Time is a friend to neither of us in this."

I didn't move as Wolf sketched a brief bow and returned to camp; rather, I turned my eyes back to el-Qaddice. The pilgrims were gone from the road now, and the Lower City was already in the long shadows of evening. I sat there on the ground, watching the darkness creep up from the valley and wash over the walls and domes of the Old City, and wondered, again, just what exactly Wolf was up to.

Chapter Twelve

"Aadi el-Amah?" said the Djanese bravo, feigning igno-rance as he looked down at me. He stroked the twin braids of his beard. Neither had a brass ring at its end, which told me he was for hire, should I be so inclined. I wasn't.

We were standing off to the side of a busy side street in the Lower City, traffic jostling and passing us by in the dusty heat. I wiped at the sweat gathering below my kaffiyeh and waited for him to tell me if he knew the *Zakur* I was look-ing for. I suspected I already knew the answer I was going to get.

"I know an Aadi," said the mercenary slowly, "but his tribe name is Marud. Could that be who you mean?"

"No," I said, trying to keep my voice low. "It's Amah."

"You're sure?"

"I'm sure."

He nodded, then lifted his head and looked about the street. After a moment, he perked up. Then he yelled, "Hai, Daud!"

Across the street and several yards down, an even larger man, clothed in the short linen vest, loose breeches, yellow stockings, and low red boots of a street mercenary turned his head our way—as did half the passing traffic. I winced.

"Hai, Gilan!" Daud stopped but didn't come over.

"This little Imperial is looking for someone named Aadi el-Amah," shouted my bravo, pointing at me. "Do you know him?"

Numerous heads on the street pivoted to wait for Daud's reply.

"I know a Aadi el-Murad," shouted Daud. "Is that who he means?"

The heads pivoted back toward us.

My man, Gilan, looked down at me. "You're sure it's not Murad?"

I glared.

"It's not Murad," yelled Gilan.

"Have you tried asking Yusef ben—"

I cursed and stormed away. Roars of deep, coarse laughter followed after me.

A block later, I turned onto a twisting side street. Halfway down, I came to a teahouse. I stopped under the awning to catch my breath. And to smile.

We'd been in the Lower City for six days now, and I'd been working the streets for five of them. It had been hard. I'd forgotten how slow, frustrating, and time-consuming it could be to step into a new town without any kind of connections or weight. The last time I'd been in a remotely similar situation was when I'd first come to Ildrecca with Christiana in tow. Back then, I'd been too naive, not to mention too busy trying to survive, to know when I was doing poorly: missing a cue, getting the brush-off, being fed a line of shit. Now, though, I was able to recognize when it was happening—the only problem was, I didn't have the influence or reputation to do anything about it.

As it was, I only had Aadi's name because of my time spent with the caravan master and his drivers on the trail. Turned out that two of them were from el-Qaddice. After a week or so of sharing their fire, I'd started to learn something about the Lower City; after another several days, I'd begun to get hints and clues about its darker workings as well. I hadn't known whether I would need them or not—the goal, after all, was to pass the audition so I could have full access to the entire city and look for Degan—but I've found that learning as much as you can about how the shadows of a place work before you get there is never a bad thing.

That was the case now, especially since it looked as

though we weren't going to be getting our audition anytime soon. As it turned out, auditions for the padishah only happened once a month. The next set of auditions were in three days. Our place in line meant we wouldn't be up for two months.

I didn't have the ready, or the time, to wait two months. Which was why I was working the street, looking for the one *Zakur* whose name kept coming up again and again whenever I talked to people about making arrangements to adjust our place in line. Aadi el-Amah was the man to talk to if you wanted the fix put in.

He was also damn hard to find.

I didn't exactly think that was an accident. Local reticence aside, I was not only an Imperial in the middle of the Despotate; I was also a Kin among the *Zakur*. Just as we kept what passed for the Djanese underworld at arm's length back home, so they did the same to us here. Only, in el-Qaddice, my job was that much harder due to the lack of any kind of true Kin presence in the city. Oh, there were a few Imperial Prigs here and there, and even a couple of patchwork gangs in the Lower City, but none of them worked under any kind of higher authority. There was no one with status here, no one with any connections back home I could leverage. Here, among the Imperials, it was every cove for himself, which meant I didn't have anyone to fall back on except myself.

Naturally, Tobin and company had offered to fill in. The troupe master had suggested they play the streets or, if that failed, maybe try to pass themselves off as merchants or pilgrims or smugglers. Anything, he said, his eyebrows waggling conspiratorially, in hopes of catching a whisper or two for me.

It was all I'd been able to do to convince them to stay in the caravansary and work on their audition piece. The last thing I needed was half my ticket in to the Old City either dead or locked away for some infraction or another.

As for Fowler, she'd simply wanted to watch my blinders. And while I appreciated the offer, the idea of a tiny, angry blond woman following along in my wake in a city of dark-haired, deep-complexioned Djanese hadn't exactly shouted subtlety to me. Better, I'd persuaded her, she stay behind and keep an eye on our Boardsmen. She hadn't been pleased, but she'd agreed.

Still, even with no one on my blinders, it felt good to be out. To stalk new streets for the first time; to puzzle out how rumors flowed in a different city; to not be weighed down by history or expectations or reputation. I'd long ago learned to read the tapestries of information that made up the street in Ildrecca, but here? Here, each pattern was fresh, each rumor a new test. Was it truth? Lies? Part of a greater piece, or something that could be cast aside? And was I paying a fair price for it?

It was, in a word, exhilarating, and I ate it up.

I glanced back the way I'd come to make sure the bravos hadn't decided to follow, then took a seat at one of the low communal tables outside the tea shop. The three men who had been sitting there—two Djanese and a Rissuli horse priest—gave me an irate look, then pointedly picked up their tea bowls and moved to the next table, even though there were already two other men there. When one of the Djanese realized he'd left his plate of sweet wafers behind, he turned back, only to discover I'd already helped myself.

"Mmm, almond," I said in Djanese, holding one up before taking a bite.

He eyed the sword at my hip, then Degan's at my back, scowled some more, and turned back to his companions.

"The wafers cost six *supp*," said an uncertain voice behind me. I turned to find a nervous-looking girl at my back, her eyes purposely fixed on the table. She wore a simple shirt with embroidery fraying at both neck and sleeves, and a long underdress. Her feet were bare. She was maybe thirteen summers.

"Really?" I said.

She hesitated and glanced back over her shoulder. A dour, rotund, bearded face ducked back behind the curtain that hung across the door to the interior of the shop.

"No, not really," she admitted. Her eyes returned to the table. "My uncle said to tell you that."

"Why?"

"I think he's afraid to tell you to leave."

"Smart man. How much do you usually charge for the sweets?"

"Two."

"Did the three who were just here already pay for them?"

Pause. "Yes."

I sent a cool glance at the wavering curtain.

I reached into my pocket and drew out a silver *dharm*, along with five copper *supp*. "The silver's for you, for being brave," I said, leaning forward so I could drop the square coins into her hand without it being visible from the shop's doorway. She gasped, her eyes wide. "Hide it, then give your uncle the copper and tell him I want another plate of sweets and two pots of tea with honey. Tell him that if he tries to cheat me again, I'll show him exactly why he should be afraid of me."

The girl put her hands on her waist, bobbed an enthusiastic thanks, and hurried back into the shop.

I picked up another wafer.

"That's not a very good way to ingratiate yourself with the local *Zakur*," said a voice off to my left.

"I'm Imperial, and I'm Kin," I said, pointedly keeping my eyes on the street. "I'm not exactly popular with your people as it is."

"Yes, but there's unpopular, and then there's stupid." The man's voice sounded as if it might have once been a mellow tenor; now it rattled like a dry riverbed. "A woman called 'Act of Kindness' runs this neighborhood. She doesn't like people threatening the merchants under her protection."

I gave in and looked up at him. "'Act of Kindness'?" I said. "You've got to be joking."

The gray-haired man standing beside my table shrugged. "She's of the Sharkai," he said, naming her tribe as if that were explanation enough. "What can you do?" He sat.

Aside from his voice, he was unremarkable: shallow cheeks, sun-dark skin, a week's worth of beard that could either be left to grow or shaved off, depending on whether or not he needed to change his appearance. The small green cap he wore atop his head did little to hide his vanishing hairline, while an ankle-length thobe concealed everything else.

I pushed the plate with the last wafer over. He eyed it a moment, then nodded once and picked it up. A Djanese sharing my hospitality: No one was going to be killing anyone at the moment.

"What you did with the Red Boots back there?" he said as he took a bite. "Getting them to start yelling my name across the street? Not bad."

"You liked that, did you?"

"Like it?" said Aadi el-Amah. "I'll have every street urchin within three districts knocking at my door, telling me there's an Imperial hunting me and hoping for a coin for the trouble. If I'm lucky, the *Zakur* sheikhs won't call me in to ask why someone was shouting my—and therefore, potentially their—business up and down the street. Any criminal of standing will be avoiding me for days, worried I'm becoming either too old to keep my business private or too well known to keep theirs secret. You've cost me at least a week's worth of work, maybe more."

"Still, it got your attention."

"Pshh!" he said, a fine spray of wafer crumbs flying over the table. He wiped his mouth and took another bite. "Boy, you've had my attention ever since you started asking about me four days ago—"

"Five."

"Only as of sundown today, and the sun's still up. Don't interrupt. I've known you've been after me since you started."

"And you let me linger on the street because . . . ?"

"I don't know you. And you're Kin. And those actors you travel with give you too much room for you to be a simple Soft Palm or Winder. You don't carry yourself like a typical footpad or highwayman, even when you're working the streets in the Lower City." He pushed the empty plate away. "Until you got those two fools braying like mules, I was inclined to ignore you; now, though, I'm curious. And more than a bit annoyed. Were it only one or the other, I could walk away, but together?" He shrugged. "I'm the kind of man who has to scratch his itches. And you, Imperial—you itch."

I regarded him as the tea arrived. The girl filled my bowl first, then Aadi's, and proceeded to linger until I sampled it. It was good: deep and floral, with the faintest undertone of honey. Her hand might be light, but it was also deft. I nodded my approval and she fluttered away.

Aadi sipped his own tea, added more honey, and sipped again. He nodded.

"You know what I do?" he said.

"You're a Fixer," I said.

He smiled without looking up from his bowl. "An imperial term. What is one who is a Fixer?"

"You put coves . . . criminals in touch with one another," I said. "When someone's putting a dodge or a con together, and they need, say, a Talker or a Fisherman, they come to you."

"And I bring them together?"

"For a price," I said. "Or a cut. But only if you think both parties are on the straight. A good Fixer doesn't let the people he fixes cross him—or one another."

Aadi took a sip of tea and smiled. "A Fixer. Yes. Very good. So, what would you have from me? Besides information on that big Imperial you've been asking about, of course."

I'd been expecting this at some point. Just as I'd been asking about after Aadi, I had also been quietly searching for leads on Degan. Nothing as obvious as dropping his name, of course—I had no idea what he might be calling himself now that he'd walked away from the Order—but enough to see if I could develop some early leads on a tall, fair-haired, pale-skinned Imperial who was more than handy with a sword. So far, Aadi's comment was the only lead I'd had, if you wanted to even call it that. More likely, he was just repeating what he'd heard about me on the street.

Still, if he actually knew something . . .

"Do you—?" I began.

"I know nothing about him; I just wanted to see how important he is to you. 'Very' would seem to be the answer."

"I have an interest."

"Pah. My third son has an 'interest' in the baker's daughter at the end of my street. You want to find this man, maybe *need* to find him—it's writ in your shoulders and across your face." He set his tea bowl aside as more wafers arrived, took two at once. "Is he why you came looking for me?"

It was tempting to say yes, to tap in to the network this man had spread across the Lower City, to put him on Degan's trail. I knew firsthand what someone like Aadi could do in his hometown, who he could find, and how. But I also knew the price would be high: for Degan, or more likely, for me. I had too many marks against me to expect a fair offer, and even if it was, there was no guarantee that he wouldn't lead me to a dead end, of several kinds.

I looked in Aadi's eyes. No, not today. Not from this one. Not about Degan.

"I'm looking for something else right now," I said. "Information, and maybe a favor."

He nodded. "That's easier, then. Information doesn't run away and doesn't fight back. As for favors?" He shrugged. "Tell me what you have in mind, and I'll tell you if it's worth my time to help an Imperial."

"I want to know what I can do about this," I said as I pulled out the clay chit Tobin had collected when he'd put our troupe on the padishah's list of hopefuls. "About changing our place in line and maybe looking into putting in a fix."

Aadi look from the chit to me. Then he began to laugh. I ground my teeth and waited until he was done.

"Well?" I said.

"Thank you for the tea," he said. "And for these." He took the last three wafers and slipped them into his sleeve as he prepared to stand.

"Wait," I said. I reached out but stopped short of grabbing his arm. This was still his city, and I needed him.

"No," he said, returning to his knees and leaning toward

me. "No 'wait.'" He pointed at the round of fired clay in my fingers. "You don't fix the auditions for the Sixth Son of the Most High. Ever. The last *Zakur* who tried was a sheikh with three—three!—belts of merit to his name. They say on a quiet night you can still hear his screams coming from the cells beneath the palace. I may arrange many things, but my own death isn't one of them."

"I'd heard anything was possible in Djan, among the *Zakur*."

"Anything is, but fixing the result of one of the padishah's auditions isn't something either of us can afford."

"Fine," I said. I leaned forward slightly myself, using the illusion of intimacy to keep Aadi from walking away. "Then how about just adjusting our order in line? Moving the audition up a bit?"

Aadi's eyes narrowed. "That I can do."

I began to smile.

"But not for you."

The smile died. "What? Why not?"

"Because you are Kin, because you have inconvenienced me, and because, even were I inclined, I don't want to risk getting on the bad side of the factors at this time. They are the ones you should be talking to."

I grunted. The factors were the local trade monopoly that operated in the district of the Lower City known as the Coop. All aspiring acts were required to lodge there and charged accordingly, with a corresponding percentage going to the padishah's ministers. I'd put us up in a caravansary at a price that made blackmail look cheap. "I tried," I said.

"And?"

"They're not interested."

"Ah. So you already knew this was futile."

"I knew they said no to me. That doesn't mean they'd say no to someone who approaches them on my behalf. Someone with local weight."

The flicker of a smile crossed his lips. He inclined his head. "I appreciate your confidence in me, but the answer is still no."

"There has to be a way—"

"There isn't." Aadi sat back on his heels. "Not for you. Better to wait your turn and use the time to rehearse. The padishah's wazir had high standards, and while His Excellency may be inclined to favor players this season, the wazir is not. The extra time could end up being a boon for you."

I muttered and looked away.

Aadi grunted as he rose to his feet. "I'll ask you to refrain from seeking me out again."

"Can't promise that. Yours is the only name I have in el-Qaddice."

"Then I suggest you either learn more or forget the one you know." He salaamed a formal farewell, thanked me for my hospitality, and left.

Well, shit.

I tilted my head back and looked up at the carved cliffs and white walls of the Old City. They were visible from almost every street down here, sitting on the western skyline like a promise of splendor that would never be fulfilled, or, in my case, like a failure I couldn't afford.

Two weeks, Wolf had said. I didn't know what he would do if I didn't make it into the Old City by then, but considering what he'd done to get my attention in Ildrecca, I wasn't anxious to find out. Visions of myself being led into the Old City in chains, only to be broken out by the degan and let loose on foreign streets as a fugitive, flitted through my head. It wasn't a pleasant thought.

The thing was, I did have another name, and not just the name of a *Zakur* or a factor or some other street runner in the Lower City. I had the name of a yazani up in the Old City that Jelem had given me when he handed over his packet of letters. A name that, once I was inside, I could hopefully use to open doors and hunt for Degan—assuming people were willing and the price wasn't too high. But to contact that yazani, I needed to get into the Old City first.

"More tea or wafers?" said the girl, coming up beside me.

I blinked and looked over at her. "No, thank you."

She nodded, then looked up to where my gaze had been lingering. "Have you been?"

"No."

"You should. There's an old woman in a market in the third ring that has the most wonderful candied fruits. Lemons and apricots and, sometimes, mangoes. They're wonderful."

"They sound it."

"They are," she affirmed solemnly. "Sweet and sour and delightful. They're costly, though, and I rarely get to have them. But now ..." She glanced at me shyly and touched her tunic where she'd secreted my *dharm*. "Well, I think I'll be saying a prayer of thanks for you the next time I go up."

"I'm glad I could ... wait." I sat up straight. "You've been to the Old City?"

"Of course."

I stared at her in disbelief. "You mean you have patronage?"

"Patronage?" she said, her mouth twisting in puzzlement. "No. Why would I need—ooh!" She raised a hand to her lips and blushed furiously. "Oh, that's right: You're not of Djan. *You* need it to get in. I'm sorry. I didn't mean to make you feel—"

"No," I said quickly, throwing a smile on my lips. I could feel the beginnings of an idea, and more important, an opportunity, tugging at me. "No, it's all right: I just forgot that you don't have to have a patron to get up there. It's a holy place for Djanese, after all."

"Um, yes, it is." She tugged her tunic straight, telling me exactly how often she went to the Old City for religious reasons.

"And it has wonderful candied fruit," I added.

A quick smile. "That, too."

"Tell me," I said as I took a last drink of tea and set the bowl aside. When my hand moved away, three silver *dharm* glinted among the dregs. "Do you think you could get some of that fruit for me? Talking about it has made me hungry."

Her eyes flicked from the coins to the curtained doorway. "I don't ..."

"I could come back tomorrow if it would be easier."

She swallowed, nodded. "Tomorrow would be easier, yes."

"And even more so if I left a few *supp* for your uncle as well?"

A long, relieved breath out. "Yes."

"Good." I moved to stand, then paused, my hand at my purse. "Oh, one more thing. As long as you're up there, I was wondering if you could deliver a message for me? Just a word to a friend, really."

She shied away a bit, a willow bending in the breeze. "A friend?"

"Not to worry," I said. "He's a scholar." All right, he was a *yazani*—the one Jelem had mentioned to me—but I didn't want to scare her off. "I'd simply need to deliver a note for me. You can just take it to his door."

She looked down at the silver rectangles in the cup and pushed at the carpet with her toes. "Just a note?"

"Just a note."

More pushing, more looking. She bit her lower lip, then nodded. "All right."

"Excellent," I said. "Now, all I need is to find a scribe's stall. Is there one nearby . . . ?"

Chapter Thirteen

Three days later, as promised, I found the *yazani* squatting in the shade of a wall in the Lower City, making shadow puppets dance and perform on the street. A group of children and teens were gathered around, shouting and laughing at the spectacle. The fact that the silhouettes moved and pranced on their own, with his only input being the occasional word and gesture with a thin olive branch, didn't seem to bother anyone. As we came up, he tucked the branch under his arm, reached both hands out into the sunlight, and formed the shadow of a rooster on the dusty bricks. A few mumbled words, and the shadow-rooster hopped away from the confines of his shadow to join the dark dog, elephant, dragon, and man in their silent street performance.

The crowd hooted and applauded, and the man smiled. Then he looked up and saw Fowler and me.

"And that is all for now, my friends," he said as he stood up. The teens made nasty, sulking sounds while the younger children pleaded, but the man shook his head. "No," he said. "I've work to do. Go plague someone else for a while."

The crowd dispersed, with one or two of the older boys casting us accusatory glances. I returned the looks, making sure to keep my eyes hard but my face neutral. Pups and young wolves, yes, but they could take you down if you didn't handle them right, especially if you were unknown.

The man chuckled to himself as he brushed the dust

from his pants. He was dressed in what I was coming to think of as the "urban" style here, with bloused pants, a knee-length tunic, and a short vest. The coloring was all rust and red, with a creamy kaffiyeh wrapped turban-style around his head. Matching pale tassels hung from the bottom edges of his sleeves and vest—used, I'd been informed gravely by our caravan master on the trip here, to distract the djinn that supposedly lived throughout, and wandered in from, the desert.

As for the Mouth—or *yazani*—himself, he was smooth and wily as his shadow puppets. When he bowed to me, it was dutiful; when he bowed to Fowler, it was something more. And she blushed.

Hmm.

"Your Grace," he began in accented Imperial.

"Excuse me?" I said.

Confusion passed over his easy features. "I'm sorry," he said. "You're an emir—a prince—of your kind, yes? Is there some other honorific you'd prefer?"

Fowler snorted.

"'Drothe' is fine," I said.

"'Drothe,'" he said, playing with the sounds and accent in his mouth. I knew Jelem had mentioned me in the letter he'd sent ahead, but that didn't mean what I said matched the sounds he'd read. "Drothe. Yes. Excellent. I have the pleasure of being Rassan ibn Asim bé-Mahlak, cousin to Jelem bar-Djan, formerly named Jelem ibn Abu Jhibbar el-Tazan el-Qaddice." He paused, then added, "But you can call me Raaz."

I was opening my mouth when Fowler gave me a quick elbow to the ribs. I looked down. She arched an eyebrow at me and nodded toward Raaz.

"This is Fowler Jess," I said.

Another bow, another lingering look. "My apologies for my Imperial being too imperfect to do your ears justice, Fowler Jess."

Another blush from Fowler.

I cleared my throat. "Jelem's cousin, you say?" I said, remembering what Jelem had said about his family; about how they'd be happy to see him only if it meant seeing him dead. My left hand drifted down to hang at my side, ready to be filled with steel at the flick of a wrist. I wondered which would be faster, my hand or his mouth, if it came down to it.

"On his wife Ahnya's side," said Raaz, turning back to me. "Via her sister's husband's uncle. I am cousin, at best, by name and law, but not by blood. Unlike his own people, my tribe has had no reason to disown Jelem, even after his banishment." He glanced down at my arm. "Or want him dead."

"But you still call him family," I said. "I didn't think Djanese called anyone family after they'd been cast out."

"It's tribal," he said, waving a hand. "Very complex. Some of my own people would agree with you; others would not. Jelem helped me gain admittance to the *wajiktal* in el-Qaddice, so I had a great deal of respect for him even before he married Ahnya and became a distant relative. When his own people cast him out, I chose to continue calling him family. As for the Tazan . . ." He turned his head aside and spit casually in what I was sure was not a casual gesture. "They are petty fools. Their tribal elders have no say over what I hold in my heart."

Fowler and I exchanged a look. She lifted her shoulders, clearly saying, *Hey, you're the boss; you make the call.*

From what little I knew through my conversations with Jelem, Djanese society was a confusing tapestry of blood ties and social strictures, the two not infrequently at odds with one another. Extending vertically through society were the tribal affiliations, with each Djanese calling one group his home and family. There could be clans and other groups within a tribe, but at the end of the day, it was the loyalty to the tribe that defined which way a Djanese was supposed to jump when it came to political interests. Meanwhile, extending across those tribal lines were the various castes that existed within society. These defined the day-to-day reality of most Djanese, determining everything from how a person earned a living to where you lived and who you interacted with. A man was born into a caste, lived his whole life there, and died in the same place. The only exceptions were the two learned castes—the Path of the Pen and the Path of the Light—scribes and magicians. Anyone with enough talent and dedication could theoretically enter into these castes and improve their station through diligence and patronage. But it was a hard road according to Jelem, and one guarded by the elite against incursion from below.

If Jelem had helped Raaz get into the *wajik-tal*—the magician's academy—in el-Qaddice, I expected there was a sizable debt there. And Jelem was never one to forget, or forgive, a debt.

I crossed my arms, making sure as I did so that my hands were visibly well away from my blades. Raaz smiled.

"Now come," he said. "Your meeting is already arranged."

"Meeting?" I said. "But the message said to meet you here."

"I'm merely the messenger. I don't have the rank or status to negotiate what you desire. You will need to speak to my elders if you wish to talk of influencing an audition and its price. Now, come."

Raaz headed off into the twisting streets, and we dutifully followed. After a few turns, I said, "Tell me: How does the Despotate feel about what you were doing back there?"

"What do you mean?"

"The glimmered shadows," I said.

Raaz looked at me for a moment, then laughed. "Glimmer? You mean the magic?" He clapped his hands. "Wonderful! I must remember that: 'glimmer.' Very good." He shook his head, smiling. "I was trained in the *wajik-tals*. Like all *yazani*, my magic is pledged to the despot." He held up his left arm and pushed back his sleeve, revealing an iron shackle fixed around his wrist. "This signifies my obligation to the despot in all things. It is his patronage that makes the academies possible. By using my gifts to entertain his people, I'm doing a service for him—repaying my debt, to some small degree."

"And what does the despot get in return?" I said.

"He gets to call upon the *wajik-tals* and its students, of course."

"For anything?"

"For most things."

I nodded. It made for one hell of a power base. "And how does the despot feel about it if you use more permanent magic? Or more powerful?"

"One does what's necessary and needed. There are proscribed limits set forth by the High Magi of the Fifteen Splendid Wajiks, in consultation with the despot and his wazirs, of course, but a fair amount is left to the discretion of the practitioner; otherwise, how could we fulfill our pledge to the despot?" Raaz looked at me sidelong. "Is it not the same in your empire?"

I chuckled. "Not quite. Oh, there's street mages that mend pots and put on a bit of a show here and there, but the better-trained Mouths—the ones who know their stuff, like Jelem and you—walk a narrow path. You can speak spells just fine in Ildrecca, for a price, but crafting anything more permanent or powerful will get the empire after you." Which was why the trade in things like portable glimmer and the most potent spoken spells were the province of the Kin. The magical black market was what had made the Kin, and its first and only king, Isidore, possible.

Raaz shook his head. "But your Imperial Magi—your Paragons—are feared across Djan, and beyond. How can an empire that so closely limits magic produce such potent magi?"

"Paragons are different," I said. "They're the emperor's personal magicians. They know the spells no one else knows, have access to the kinds of knowledge that would get any normal Mouth killed." Or Nose, or Gray Prince, for that matter. "From what I understand, the kind of magic they tap is beyond what other Mouths can reach."

"Are you speaking of your Angels?" said Raaz, sounding politely dubious. "Saying they somehow help your Paragons achieve their power?"

"That's the imperial line on it," I said.

"And?"

"Do I look like a priest to you?"

We fell silent after that, but I caught Raaz studying me

from time to time as we walked. I knew the truth behind the power of the Paragons, knew the truth about Imperial magic: about how the men and women who used it used their very souls to focus and control the power, and how it scarred and ate those souls in the process. I'd read it in an ancient journal, but I wasn't about to tell a Djanese Mouth about that.

Raaz led us along the curving, twisting side streets that seemed to be the standard for most Djanese cities. Clean or dirty, crowded or empty, they were the common thread that ran through all the towns of Djan I had visited. The exceptions—the broad, straight boulevards that led from one public space to another, be they temples or parks or markets or communal ovens and more—were all the more notable because of their seeming uniqueness.

Straight and true in public, turning and subtle in private: That certainly seemed to fit the Djanese way.

We ended at a small doorway set partway below street level. An iron key and a string of muttered words gained us access. Three steps down, five forward, then four up. Another door, this one only needing a key. A large Djanese man wearing a curved sword stood there. He nodded to Raaz as he opened the door, glaring at me and Fowler. Beyond, there were spiral stairs going down.

The light coming in from the room above vanished as the guard shut the door behind us. More shone up from below, but it was faint. I could sense my night vision coming to life as we descended.

A small taper burned in a sconce at the bottom—not enough to blind me, but enough to hurt. I averted my eyes as Raaz opened another door, this time not even bothering with a key.

The room beyond was long and low, with a barrel-vaulted ceiling extending off into the darkness on either side. It felt more like a tunnel than a room. Between the columns, deep alcoves had been built into the walls, easily the height of a man and four to five times as wide. A wine vault, if I had to guess, except without the wine.

A pair of clay oil lanterns sat on the stone floor. They

were already lit. Otherwise, the space was empty. I blinked in the light and lingered in the doorway, letting my eyes burn and adjust.

"Please, come in," said Raaz, this time in Imperial.

Fowler entered, looked around the space, and nodded. I came through.

"You have to understand," said Raaz as he stepped forward, putting himself between the far wall and the lamps, casting two shadows. "Jelem is . . . not a favored person in Djan, and especially not in el-Qaddice. Since you're delivering something of his, we have to be careful. To be found in possession of messages or packages from one cast out as Jelem has been is dangerous indeed. We have to be careful."

"We?" said Fowler, placing her hand on the hilt of her long knife. I didn't discourage her. "I don't see any 'we' here beyond us."

"I say this so that you understand what I do next is a precaution, and not a slight against you, O Sheikh of the Kin."

My hand went to my own blade now. "What precautions?" I said, peering into the darkness on either side. The amber of my night vision was, at best, a washed-out gold hovering on the edges of things in this light, but it was still enough to see that dark space beyond the lamps were empty. "When people start making speeches about 'precautions' and 'slights,' I get worried. For that matter, I don't much like it when the people I'm supposed to meet aren't where I'm supposed to meet them. Those kinds of things usually mean blood." I turned back to Raaz and cleared a hand-span of steel. "Where are your elders, Mouth? Where are your magi?"

Raaz's eyes narrowed in the dimness. "I said nothing of magi."

"No, but others did, and I'm not about to think for a moment that you'd go through all this just so I could talk to a couple of tribal elders."

Raaz looked from me to Fowler and back again. Then he nodded. "Jelem said you were sly. Yes, you are going to speak to members of the *Majim*—two of them. Both are sympathetic to Jelem's plight."

"And what plight is that, exactly?" This was starting to sound a hell of a lot more complex than a simple banishment.

"I cannot say. You have to understand that you're dealing with Djanese politics now, and that you're not of our tribe or clan. While Jelem spoke well of you, we cannot trust you fully in this—there is no blood or bond between us. Hence, our precautions."

"And yet, despite this . . . gap . . . between us, your masters are willing to help me get into the Old City. Isn't that just as hazardous?"

Raaz let loose a soft laugh. "There are hazards and there are hazards, O Sheikh. What others see as an obstacle, the *Majim* see as an inconvenience. But don't assume you will get what you want: My masters have only agreed to speak with you. They will hear you and they will make their decision based on many things, not just your needs. Or theirs."

I took a deep breath, let it out. The place smelled of damp and dust and mold, and at least two of those things seemed out of place in Djan. I knew exactly how they must feel.

"All right," I said, sliding my sword home. "Take you precautions and let's get on with this."

"As you wish."

Raaz turned to face the wall and spread his arms wide, causing his two shadows to look as if they were linking hands, speaking softly as he did. It wasn't Djanese, but I recognized it—if you could call having heard the same rhythms and sounds pass Jelem's lips "recognition."

As we watched, Raaz's two shadows began to shift and change. One seemed to grow shorter and broader, while the other took on a more willowy shape. The lamps flickered, making the shadows dance, adding to the sense of change. One—the leaner form on the right—was clearly a woman's silhouette, with long flowing hair and sharp shoulders. The other shadow had grown a bulge on top I recognized as a turban, as well as a thickness around the neck that could have signified a beard.

They were moving independently of the Mouth now, but still following the general flow of his movements. When his arm fell, their arms fell, but at their own pace, and each stopped in a different position: one on a hip, the other folded in at the side. When he swayed left, they moved left—only one stepped, and the other leaned.

The lamps flickered again. This time, the light's movement didn't affect the shadows at all. It was clear that someone else was casting the shadows now—someone not remotely near this room.

Fowler leaned in next to me. "Has Jelem ever . . . ?"

"Not that I've seen," I said.

"Huh," she said.

Raaz cast a dirty look over his shoulder while still murmuring the incantations. We shut up.

A minute or two later, Raaz stopped speaking. He dropped his arms, bowed to the shadows, and then turned to us.

"May I present . . . well, the people you wished to speak to, I suppose," he said, flashing the hint of a grin. "You will understand if I don't use names, O Sheikh of the Dark Paths."

"For your sake, or mine?"

"Let us say 'both' for now; it sounds more caring, yes?"

I smiled despite myself and turned to the shadows.

They were completely distinct now—two independent silhouettes on a wall where different shadows should be. One—the man—waved jauntily, while the woman's shape seemed to cross her arms and wait. She might have been only a shadow, but I could see impatience writ large in the outline of her body language.

I looked down, curious, and saw that each patch of darkness still extended from the base of Raaz's feet to the wall. He followed my gaze and nodded.

"Yes, I'm still casting them," he said. "Just as they are casting shadows of me where they are."

"Can they hear me?"

"Once you join your shadow to theirs, they will."

"What?"

"You will have to step into the light and cast your own self upon the wall," said Raaz. "After your shadow crosses theirs, you'll be able to speak."

I glanced over my shoulder at Fowler. She was staring at the two shapes on the wall, frowning. She shook her head. I could almost read her thoughts: We didn't know this Mouth well enough, didn't know what his glimmer would do to me once I stepped into its path.

I turned back around.

The man's shadow had put a hand on either side of his head and was now waggling them back and forth, his fingers extended.

Somehow it didn't feel like a trap.

I still wasn't sure how I was supposed to hand over the package like this—or even if I could—but I knew I had to at least make contact with them. Jelem had said they'd be willing to help me once I got into the Old City, but I needed more than that now: I needed them to help get us into the Old City to begin with or, barring that, then pull some strings when it came to the audition. Assuming they had the clout to do either.

I looked from the shadows to Raaz. "So I just . . . ?"

"Step into the light, yes. I would recommend you keep your arms beside you until your shadow is distinct and the same relative size as the other two."

"Better contact?" I said as I took a step forward.

"No. Because if your shadow is too large, you might rip a hole in their physical bodies."

"What?" I said, stopping.

"I jest. Yes, better communication."

Raaz chuckled as I turned back around. He was Jelem's cousin, all right.

I took a step, another. The light wavered again, the oil-fed flames dancing in the dark.

"Do they do that often?" I said as I came even with the lamps.

"Do what?" said Raaz.

"The lamps. Is the flickering going to be a problem when I try to make contact?"

"Flickering?" said Raaz in a tone that made me stop. "The lamps are still; have been kept still since . . ." His voice trailed off.

Something was wrong.

My hand was still going for my rapier when I saw the figure run out of the darkness and leap into the space between myself and the wall. He was little more than a silhouette himself, dressed in deep blue-black robes, his face covered by a closely wrapped cloth. About the only thing I could make out for certain as he sailed through the air was the short, curved blade that he extended toward the wall midleap. I heard the scrape of metal on stone, saw his shadow pass over the woman's and the man's, and then he was landing and rolling into the darkness on the other side of the pool of light.

I was moving to go after him, my own sword clear now, when I heard a scream behind me. I glanced back and froze. One of the shadows, the woman, was teetering over, her head clearly separating from her neck as she did so. The other was pulling back a hand that, while it might look like a closed fist, I knew was now missing its fingers, if not more.

As for Raaz, he was clutching at his own neck with one hand, gagging and choking, even as he reached out for the lamps with the other. The fingers of the hand he extended were black and seemed to be smoking. Or dissolving.

I leapt back and kicked at one lamp with my foot, slashed down on the other with my rapier. I connected with both, and the room went dark.

Then someone else yelled.

Fowler.

Chapter Fourteen

I dropped into a crouch, sword across my body. Best to stay low until my night vision reawakened. Damn me for getting so close to those lamps, anyhow.

"Fowler?" I said.

No answer. I could still hear Raaz gagging, but it sounded less strained now. I couldn't decide if that was good or bad. Hell, I didn't even know if putting out the lights had helped or hurt him, but there was nothing for it now. Besides, I *knew* it would help me—assuming I lasted that long.

I let my gaze flick around the space, looking for the first hints of amber, the first sign that I had my edge back. Whoever had come leaping out of the darkness had been good, a true deep file ... Blade? Arm? Nighthawk? If I had to guess, I'd go with Blade, or whatever passed for an assassin in Djan, but that was almost beside the point. No matter what he called himself, his timing had been perfect: I'd been too far from the wall to interfere, but close enough to get in the way of any glimmer Raaz might have launched. That kind of luck didn't happen by accident.

That wasn't what had me worried, though.

What had me on edge, had me holding my breath while I waited for my night vision to awaken, was the fact that I hadn't seen the Blade before he moved. I'd peered into the shadows, studied the darkness about us before stepping fully into the light, and noticed nothing. That didn't happen—not to me, not in this much darkness.

And even if I had missed him somehow, that still didn't explain the lamps and their flickering. A flickering only I had seen. Me. The one with the night vision.

I had no idea what that might mean, but I'd be damned if I was going to pretend I wasn't scared shitless by it.

The broken lamp was the first thing to pull itself out of the darkness—jagged pieces of clay, edged in reddish gold, lying in a filmy pool of oil. The other lamp came next, on its side a short ways away, followed by a section of wall. An arch followed, then Raaz—no longer gagging, but still on the floor, still breathing roughly—then the rest of the room, all overlaid by the amber sketches and highlights of my night vision.

Fowler was lying where she had stood, her long knife halfway out of its scabbard. I couldn't see any blood, couldn't spot any wound, but that didn't mean a thing. I resisted the urge to call out, to go to her and check for breath or pulse. Going to see if she lived could get me killed.

Instead, I turned my attention to the wine cellar around us.

Empty.

I let my breath out slowly. The nearest niche was a good fifteen feet away, nothing but open space between it and I. Even if the Blade was hiding there, I'd have time to react, time to see him. Whatever glimmer he'd used to help him hide from the lantern's light hadn't seemed to affect my night vision. I might not have been able to see him earlier, but now it was darker than night. Now it was my turn.

I looked around the space again to be sure, then shifted and rose slowly out of my crouch.

And almost lost my life in the process.

I caught the blur of movement out of the corner of my eye just in time to drop my head even as I brought up my rapier. Metal hissed on metal. I felt the breeze of the deflected blade skim through the air above me. Then a shoulder I couldn't see connected with my own and shoved.

I slashed the air before me as I staggered back, found nothing. I struck a guard, my body low, sword angled before me and out.

I looked around, eyes wide. Raaz, Fowler, the walls, the extinguished lamps: all there, all visible to my night vision. So where the hell was the person who'd just missed taking off the top of my head?

I took a step back, felt for and found the wall behind me in the darkness. It was usually a tactic for other people—for the ones who couldn't see what I could see. Now, though, it felt reassuring to have the stone at my back.

Another blur, this time from a bit farther away. I saw the arc of the cut, saw a hint of . . . something . . . behind it, moving toward me. It was enough to catch the blade on my own—one, two, three times—enough to keep me breathing for the moment. Not enough to counterthrust or kill, though.

I shifted left and drew my fighting dagger from the back of my sword belt. My hand, I noticed, was shaking.

Raaz coughed. Groaned.

"Raaz!" I yelled. "What the hell is—"

"No talking," he croaked, barely getting the words out. "Listen!"

Good advice, considering I heard, more than saw, the next attack coming. The double scuff of a gathering step on the gritty stone floor, an amber bluish blur, and then I was deflecting a slash that still managed to carve a long, thin line in my forearm.

No way in hell I could last, not like this.

I peered out into the midnight-veiled cellar around me, trying to do something I'd never had any trouble doing before: trying to see someone with my night vision. It was unnerving. Every wall, every stone, every person was visible—except the one that mattered.

Was my vision failing? Had the magical flare Shadow set off in front of my eyes almost five months ago done that much damage? Had the flickering flames been a sign, an indication that something was wrong, that something had been done to me?

Dammit, Sebastian—why the hell did you have to die before you were able to tell me about the gift you gave me?

I shifted my footing, heard it echoed a moment later.

Listen, Raaz had said. But what if I wasn't the only one listening?

Another step by myself, this time echoed by two. Were they closer or farther away?

A low, gasping mutter to my right interrupted by a cough. Raaz, speaking in a tongue I recognized but didn't know. Speaking magic. Shit.

"No light!" I said, even as I used my voice to cover my movement. Two sloping paces right, one step forward. In the amber-edged darkness, someone I couldn't see shifted position as well.

Right now, I realized, we were even. Whoever was out there couldn't see me: Rather, he'd been trained to fight blind, using his opponent's sounds to direct his actions. That's why the attacks were so wide, why he relied on cuts and slashes—the bigger the movement, the more area you covered. As for me, while I had never fought blind, I could at least see the terrain, could catch the movement of his blade as it came in. My guess was that he'd never faced someone like me, had never had his supposed-to-be-blind target parry and riposte and react in time to foil his plans. And I sure as hell had never faced someone I couldn't see, especially in the dark.

But if Raaz spoke up some light . . . then it would all be different. Then I would become both blind and visible at once. Then I wouldn't be able to see the Blade through the burning and flashing in my eyes, and he'd be able to stroll up and slit my throat, no matter how easy it was for everyone else in the room to see him.

So, no light—not until it was over.

Which needed to happen soon.

I took a soft step left. Someone moved with me. Shit—I couldn't be any quieter than that.

"You are unexpected," said a soft voice out of the darkness. A woman. "A challenge."

I adjusted my rapier so the point was in line with the sound of her voice.

"You can talk," she said. Djanese, but with an accent I didn't know. "I won't kill you as you speak. It would be . . . unsporting."

"But that won't stop you from figuring out where I am in the meantime," I said.

"I offer you the same advantage with my own voice." More to my left now. I adjusted. "Although," she added, "I don't think you need it."

"Maybe I'm just that good." Ha.

"And maybe you can see in the night."

I froze, almost dropping my dagger in my surprise. How . . . ?

"And yet," she continued, "you're not Djanese, which means you can't be of the despot's chosen. Can't be a Lion." A brief pause, complete silence. "So, then, what are you?"

I didn't know how to answer that. In all the years since Sebastian had taken me deep into the Balsturan Forest and performed the rite that gave me his night vision, I'd considered myself unique. No rumors or tales about a similar ability had ever reached me, no claims to have heard about anyone who could push aside the night. And I'd been listening—first as a Prig and a Draw Latch on the street, and then as a Nose, I'd been keeping my ears open and my secret close. Aside from Christiana and Degan, there was no one living who knew what I could do. Jelem might suspect—but then, he'd suspect his own mother of faking his own birth—and Fowler might have guessed that my late-night luck was too good to be coincidence, but neither had said anything outright.

No, in all my years of looking and listening, no word had ever come in, no whisper had ever gone out.

Until now.

Of a sudden, I no longer wanted to kill this woman; I wanted to catch her. To question her. To, maybe, get an answer or two.

"You're silent, I see," she said. "I will assume I've struck true."

"What I am is dangerous," I said. "Throw your steel down or get on with this. I've got friends bleeding; I don't have time for you." As much as I might want to talk, I didn't want to die even more.

"Nor I for you," she said. Closer now, and to my right.

I turned my torso in that direction without shifting my feet. Took a shallow breath. Another. Then, after I was sure I was in the guard I thought stood the best chance of keeping me alive, I tapped the pommel of my dagger lightly against the base of my rapier blade.

This time, I saw her coming; or rather, saw the indication of her coming. A hint of motion, a blur of something that seemed too slippery for my night vision to catch, but still, *there*, just as I'd hoped.

Except she'd managed to shift silently to my left and was now coming on my open side. Damn, she was good.

I pivoted as fast as I could, bringing my dagger and rapier up on my left, one above the other, both pointing forward. Degan had liked to call it the "Wall of Steel"; I called it my best chance right about now.

I adjusted my weapons to intercept the fastest part of the approaching ripple—what I assumed to be her blade. If I was lucky, I'd be able catch the cut and perform a counterthrust at the same moment, using her momentum to let her skewer herself. If not, well, at least I had a Wall of Steel, right?

Wrong. Turns out the assassin knew about steel walls since, just before she reached me, her blur dropped low and slid along on the floor, right at my legs.

I dipped my rapier's tip even as I tried to jump up and avoid what I assumed was meant to be a sweep. Neither action was wholly unsuccessful on my part, but neither were they complete failures.

I felt my sword's tip skip and then grab, biting and then sliding along flesh at the last moment. At the same time, the front of my feet were struck in midair by something solid and muscular, causing me to tumble forward. My rapier twisted itself out of my grasp, and I let it go—better to drop a weapon than break your fingers trying to keep hold of it. Besides, I needed that hand to try and break my fall.

It did. Sort of. It also managed to wrench two of my fingers back as I hit the stone floor and half rolled, half collapsed onto my right side. I made sure to keep my dagger hand, and the blade it held, far out to my left as I fell.

That last bit is what saved my life.

Metal struck on metal as I landed, assassin's blade to Prince's dagger, deflecting whatever backhand or follow-up cut she had planned. She hit hard, sending reverberations down my arm, nearly forcing the dagger from my grip, but I held on. A moment later, I felt a hand on my right calf. The grip was weak. I kicked it off, then lashed out with my foot again as I scrambled away. Fleeting contact, a gasp, the sound of metal skittering across the floor.

I shimmied back on my elbows and heels, then gathered my legs beneath me and stood up. I kept my dagger in my left hand, drew my boot knife with the working fingers and thumb of my right, and hoped like hell she didn't come after me. Close fighting is ugly enough, but in the dark, where you can't see, against an opponent who is trained to do just that? No, thank you.

I heard a deep breath come from where I had fallen, followed by a hiss of pain.

"No, not a Lion," she said, her voice tight now. I heard movement—loud for her, I expected, and soft for anyone else. "But good enough in some ways, and worse in others." A soft scuff, and my rapier skittered across the floor in my direction, stopped at my feet. Another hiss of pain.

"I give you today as a gift, *jeffer ani*," she said softly. 'Fortunate ghost.' "But I would advise you to not rest too easily. You are marked."

Then soft sounds, fading, gone. I was across the space and kneeling over Fowler before they had completely faded.

"What . . . ?" croaked Raaz in the darkness.

"She left," I said, not looking up from my examination of Fowler. There was blood on the side of her head, and she was responding weakly at best.

"Left?" His voice was still rough, still more a gasp than speech, but even that couldn't hide the genuine astonishment in it. "How did you—?"

"If I were you, I'd give more thought to answering questions than asking them right about now."

A brief silence. "Yes, of course. I . . . it's just that I didn't expect . . ." He coughed and looked back into the darkness, in the direction of the wall he'd been casting the shadows against. "To have one of them show up here, to see one of my masters killed through my magic. I—"

"Raaz," I said, my tone sharp. "I need you with me. Fowler's hurt."

I watched him bow his head, then nod. "Yes, of course. What do you need?"

"Can you speak anything over her to help?" Jelem had used magic to heal me once, but that was special, and that was Jelem. I had no idea how patching glimmer might translate to Raaz. It wasn't the kind of thing most Kin could afford, or most Mouths could pull off.

Another cough. "Perhaps. Wait." Words spoken, power gathered, and there was light in the darkness.

Thankfully it was weak, but I still found myself looking away. Amber-tinted darkness turned into a too-bright wine vault, the bricks and stone reflecting light almost as if they were mirrors, each one directed at my eyes. I blinked, squinted, and ducked my head farther into my shoulder.

Behind me, I heard Raaz crawl over to us, settle down on the opposite side of Fowler. He turned her to better face him. I realized I was holding her hand, and that doing so hurt like hell. My strained fingers didn't like the idea of trying to hold on to anything just now. Screw them: I didn't let go.

"It's a single blow to the temple," he rasped. "Very precise."

I blinked against the light, not quite ready to turn around yet. "How bad?" I said.

Sounds of movement, a gasp from Fowler. Then, "I can't tell." Raaz spoke a series of low, broken words. The words were followed by a gust of cool air that made the hairs on my arm stand up.

I risked a look over my shoulder. A small magical flame flickered over the spilled lamp oil on the floor, floating just off the surface. Raaz was on his knees next to Fowler, leaning over her. Her hair had ice crystals in it now, and there was a thin coating of frost over the blood and swelling. As I watched, he ran his right hand over the wound, his fingers skimming the air just above her skin. Vapor filled the space between his skin and hers, and when he pulled away, the frost seemed thicker.

"That's the best I can manage," he said. "If she doesn't wake up soon, I'd suggest a physician. Or even if she does. Head wounds." He made a face.

"Find someone," I said.

"There's a charity hospital not too far away, founded by the despot's twelfth son, Padishah Shar—"

"No," I said. "Find someone who can glimmer her."

"Where?" he said, looking pointedly around the room, his voice turning even more ragged. "My masters have other concerns right now, and there's no saying the *neyajin* won't return with help. We have to leave."

He was right. Of course he was right. I shook my head, trying to clear away the post-fight comedown that seemed to be settling in faster than usual.

Between us, Fowler moaned and shifted on the floor, her hand pulling weakly against mine. I almost gasped in pain and decided to let go after all. I was amused to see that, even like this, her hand tried to find its way to where her knife hung at her belt.

"Fine," I said. "Then take us to a Carver you trust."

"A . . . ?"

"A surgeon," I said. "Or a street physicker. Or even a barber. Someone who can check her over, at least."

"I told you," said Raaz. "There's a hospital over—"

"No," I said. "No Quack Shacks. I don't want some mask-wearing herb crumbler cutting at Fowler while he burns incense and packs her wound with ground dog bones that he swears came from a griffin. I've seen enough of their shows to know the only thing they cure is their own empty pockets."

"Quack Sha . . . ?" said Raaz. Then he barked a short laugh, which turned into a rough cough. Looking, I noticed a puckered grayish line running across . . . no, around . . . his neck that hadn't been there before the lights went out. That explained his sudden change in voice. I tried to catch a brief glimpse of his hand, but it was hidden by his body. I got the feeling that wasn't by accident.

"Listen," said Raaz after the coughing had subsided, "I don't know what you're used to in your empire, but there are no dogs, or even their bones, in our hospitals. They're a public duty—a requirement of the nobility to found, fund, and oversee." Raaz leaned forward. "Do you think a great sheikh, let alone one of the despot's sons, would let something he's attached his name to bring shame upon him through poor practices? Do you think the physicians working there would risk the ire of their patron by failing in their duties? Fowler will be in better hands there than I can hope to provide here."

I glowered at him for a moment. It wasn't that I'd never heard of Djanese physickers, or even their hospitals, but they were more stories than reality in Ildrecca. Back home, unless you had the ready to pay for the best, hospitals were largely for dying in. Quacks and backdoor surgeons and, if you were lucky enough to suffer from plague or leprosy, the Sisters of the Benign Fellowship, were the options for most. A little more money might get you an apothecary or maybe a Cutter, and a fistful of hawks would buy their discretion along with the treatment. But true medical help? Honest physicking? Unless you happened to know the location of one of Margalit's disciples, you were better off taking to the street than putting yourself on a cot at the local Blood Ken.

Hospitals were for either the rich or the desperate back home, and where you ended up depended on which category you fell under. Except, I had to keep reminding myself, this wasn't Ildrecca. And we were desperate.

"All right," I said. "We'll try it your way."

I stood and went to retrieve my rapier. As I bent down, a glint of silver in the shadows caught my attention. I tensed, then relaxed once I realized it was a blade lying on the floor.

It was a dagger—the assassin's—finely crafted, with a gently forward-curving blade. The crosspiece was made of twisted metal, the steel pommel and bone handle echoing the spiral design of the guard. But what gave me pause was the blade itself: While it resembled a typical piece of forged and honed steel, when I picked it up, I saw what looked like shadow lingering along the inside of the curve.

I brought the blade back into the light. The shadow resolved itself into a faintly smoking line running along the steel. Metal slowly gave way to something else—a wavering, almost insubstantial other—that lingered where the edge should be. It was if the dagger were dissolving into its own shadow ... if that shadow could somehow exist without light or substance.

I looked from the dagger to the wall where the shadows of the magi had fallen, to Raaz and his still-hidden fingers. I pulled off my kaffiyeh, wrapped the dagger in it, and slid it into my boot.

I examined the wound on my arm as I walked back to Raaz and Fowler. It burned, but didn't seem to be bleeding badly. A shallow cut. Good.

Raaz had gone back to staring at the wall and the knife groove it now sported. I left him be for the moment.

"Fowler?" I said, bending down beside her and touching her shoulder.

Her eyelids fluttered. "Whum?" she said.

"I have to get you out of here. Can you sit up?"

"Hrmn tr," she said, and began to sit up. I caught her a moment later as she fell back.

"Looks like you get to ride a prince," I said as I shifted her and slid her over my shoulder. "Too bad ... Angels! ... it isn't the way I'd like."

"Fuf yh."

She was small, but that didn't make carrying her any easier. I was surprised to find myself staggering a bit as I straightened my knees and headed for the door. After one last look at the wall, Raaz got to his feet and followed me.

"I'm going to need some help going up," I said.

"I wish I could, but. ..." He lifted his left arm slightly. Raaz had let his robe's sleeve hang down, covering most of his hand, but I still managed to catch a glimpse of what looked like gray, curled flesh. I noted that the edges of his fingers seemed to drift in the breeze of his action, just like the edge of the dagger in my boot. He hid his hand quickly again, then opened the door.

"What the hell happened, anyhow?" I said, angling myself so that Fowler wouldn't hit the doorway as I slipped through.

"A mistake," croaked Raaz's voice, already moving up the stairs. "A trap. A disaster. Take your pick."

"I pick an actual fucking answer," I said. I wrapped my left hand around the rope handrail that ran its way up the stairs, its length held in place by iron loops spaced along the wall. The trick, I knew, was going to be getting into a rhythm once I started. I held my position, waiting for Raaz to get farther along so I'd have a clear path up.

"And you deserve one," he said. Then, after a moment, added, "As do I."

"What do you mean?" I said.

"I can't . . . ah! She killed Turgay, left him lying in the doorway. She must have followed us here."

"At least we know she wasn't lying in wait," I said, "which means you don't have to worry about someone having whispered the location of the meeting."

"Small comfort, but likely true."

"What was she, anyhow?"

Dragging and grunting sounds drifted down from above. "An assassin," said Raaz between grunts. "But a special breed."

"How special?"

"*Neyajin.* It's said they walk unseen in the night. They're hard to find and harder to hire. To have one turn up here . . ."

"I get the idea." I settled Fowler more securely on my shoulder and began to half walk, half drag myself up the stairs. Unseen assassins—as if the regular kind weren't bad enough. "She mentioned something about the despot's chosen and Lions. What was she talking about?"

"Stories, mostly. Hen-tales and old fantasies best shared over sweet wine and briny olives."

"Try me."

"Very well." Raaz cleared his throat. When he spoke

again, his voice had changed timbre, resonating and rasping its way down to me with a storyteller's rhythm. I recalled his performance on the street and wondered how much he did out of obligation to the despot, and how much came from his own personal enjoyment. "It is said that long ago, when the hands of the Seven Caliphs still held sway over the lives of men and the language of the djinn had not been forgotten, there were magi who knew how to take on certain aspects of the djinn and wear them as you or I might wear a garment."

"Aspects?" I said.

"Abilities. Curses. Call them what you like. Borrowed powers, drawn from spirits of smoke and fire and brewed into mystic unguents. To apply these oils to different parts of your body was to take on a different aspect of various djinn for a day and a night: on the arms for strength, on the legs for flight, over the heart for fire or fear. Each djinni was different, meaning each use could vary. But with all of them, one thing was constant: Any who wore the aspect of a djinni gained the spirits' ability of mystic sight.

"It's said that only a handful of the greatest magi can craft the oils anymore, and that their efforts are but pale shadows of the magic that was. Where once a wearer could fly, now he can but leap a high wall; where a swordsman glistening with oil used to be able to stand off whole armies, now he is just that much faster than those he faces. Impressive, yes, but not the stuff of legend—if it ever was."

"And the djinn sight?" I said as I looked up and saw the light shining through the door at the top of the stairs. Thank the Angels. My thighs were burning, and sweat was running down the inside of my shirt. The cut the Blade—the *neyajin*—had given me was beginning to ache from all the work my left arm was doing pulling on the rope of the handrail.

"A cat's vision in the dark," said Raaz. "The ability to see at night as others would during the day. Or so I'm told. Only the despot has access to the oils anymore, and he parcels them out sparingly. Rumors are cheap currency, especially among *yazani,* and especially at the despotic court. But I do know this: Where other assassins and spies have failed to get past those anointed with the unguent, one group succeeds. Not always, and not without loss, but of the handful of thieves and agents who have broached the despot's various palaces, all have been said to be able to move unseen, even by the djinn's sight."

"The *neyajin*."

"Even so. And now you understand my concern at her presence—and my appreciation of your achievement."

"I got lucky is all," I said as my eyes drew level with the door. *Only a little farther, Drothe.*

"Luck?" said Raaz. He was sitting on the steps on the opposite side of the small chamber—the ones that led out to the street. A bloody smear covered the short flight of steps on my side, ending at the body of Turgay, who lay in the depression between us. "I'd say it takes more than simple luck to fend off a *neyajin* in the dark."

"Say whatever you want," I said as I staggered through the doorway. "All I know is I had the longer blade and managed to put it in the right place at the right time."

"Um," said Raaz. His gaze was a little too searching, his tone a little too contemplative, for my comfort. I needed to change the subject.

"So," I said, "how about you tell me what's inside Jelem's package that's so damn important?"

That got him. The Mouth sat up and made a point of looking at anything but me. "What?" he said.

"You heard me." I adjust Fowler's drape across my shoulder and considered the blood-smeared steps before me. Damn, but it was hot in here. I blinked the sweat out of my eyes and inched my foot forward, as if testing for thin ice. "If the *neyajin* are as rarified as you say, I can't imagine she was there on my account. So what's that leave us?"

"It's tribal business," said Raaz, a bit too quickly. "Or, at the least, *tal* related. Either way, to think that someone would pay the price demanded by a *neyajin* to steal a—"

"A what?" I said. "What happened here wasn't about a blood feud, and we both know it. When you go hunting for vengeance, you do it with your own people, with your own hands. You want to see and feel and taste the blood, to make sure it was done right." I'd spent enough time on Ildrecca's streets, and seen enough vengeance in the Raffa Na'ir cordon back home, to know that there were certain values the Djanese and the Kin shared when it came to getting your own. "You don't hire this kind of thing done — not if it matters. You stay in the clan." You stayed in the organization.

Raaz didn't answer.

My legs were trembling by now. I took another look at the steps, thought better of it, and bent down to ease Fowler off my shoulders.

"Ow," she murmured as she half slid, half fell onto the steps. Then, softly, "Asshole."

That was a good sign. I took a breath and sat down on the steps beside her, mindless of the blood. I turned my gaze back to Raaz.

"Listen," I said, leaning forward and putting my elbows on my knees. My head felt loose. "We both know what happened down there was about more than me getting into the Old City. Shadow magic? Assassins? I'm not nobody, but that's more of a party than I deserve, especially here. Which means it had to be something else, and the only other thing down there besides you, me, and Fowler was the package Jelem sent. So, what is it?"

He continued to look away.

"Secrets?" I said. No reaction. "Maps?" Nothing. I swallowed, now worried. "Glimmer?"

A flick of the *yazani*'s eyes, a tensing of his shoulders.

I felt my stomach go sour.

Shit!

There was only one kind of magic Jelem would be sending into Djan; one kind of swag that would warrant this much attention. In a place as steeped in magic as the Despotate, I could only think of one thing the empire had that anyone here would want when it came to glimmer. The empire's secret weapon.

Imperial magic.

Angels! What had Jelem been thinking? No, scratch that.

I knew what he'd been thinking: If anyone knew how to slip something across the border, it was me. I'd been smuggling imperial relics out of the empire for years—hell, the first time I'd met Jelem, it was when one of my early smuggling attempts had gone wrong and we'd been forced to hole up for three days while Imperial and Djanese border troops fought over who would get to kill us. He knew I knew how to move swag.

But to use me—me!—to smuggle Imperial glimmer into Djan; magic I'd given him in the first place. Magic the emperor was so jealous of he'd wiped out an entire cordon to keep it secret. Magic that, up until a few months ago, no one but the Imperial Paragons had ever studied, let alone known how to use. People had vanished over the years for thinking too hard about the damn stuff, never mind possessing it.

And here I was, walking around with some of it my pocket. Again.

Jelem, you bastard.

I raised a shaking hand and ran it through my hair.

"Are you all right?" Raaz was staring at me, a strange, blurry look on his face.

"No, I'm not all right," I said. "I just found out I got used. Plus, I'm angry. And tired. And still don't have a way to get my people into the Old City in a week's time. But mostly, I'm angry." I looked at my hand. "And tired."

"No, not that," said the *yazani*, still staring. He pointed. "I mean the cut on your forearm. How did you get it?"

"This?" I said, plucking at my bloody sleeve with my left hand. "I got it from the *neyajin*. I didn't quite catch her blade in the dark and—"

"What?" said Raaz, leaping to his feet. Funny how I hadn't noticed the stars trailing after his movements before this. "By the Wandering Family of—why didn't you tell me?"

"Why?" I said. "It's just. . . ." I stopped, looked at the cut, then thought of my own poisoned blade in my wrist sheath. Of course. No wonder Fowler had seemed so damn heavy.

"Well, hell," I slurred.

Then I passed out.

Chapter Fifteen

It was the poking that did it. A relentless, slow, rhythmic prodding to my side that finally made me claw my way back to daylight.

"Will you stop that?" I said, my voice sounding thicker and drier than I remembered.

"Finally!" said a voice. I felt a soft, warm pressure on my chest—a hand laid gently over me. "Took you fucking long enough."

I chuckled deep in my throat, coughed, and chuckled again. Fowler. That was good.

I opened my eyes to warm, slanting sunlight. I glanced toward the source of the light, and then back again when I realized it wasn't the window to my cell at the caravansary—that it wasn't an ordinary window at all. This one housed an intricate wooden screen of finely cut arabesques, done in what looked to be sandalwood. The inner shutters thrown back against the wall were just as elaborate, with a duplicate pattern set into wood with riveted wrought iron. From what I could see of the edges, the shutters were grooved to interlock, the overlap blending in with the overall pattern of the decoration.

It was gorgeous. It would also be almost impossible to crack from the outside when shut.

That last didn't reassure me.

I lifted my head and looked down to see Fowler kneeling beside me, her hand on my chest. I'd been laid out on a well-stuffed mattress of some sort, which in turn was resting on the floor. There was a mixture of anger and relief in her gaze.

"How do you feel?" she asked.

"Well enough, considering—"

"Good." And she hit me, hand to chest. Hard. "That's for being out for two and a half days, you asshole!" Another slap. "And that's for trying to carry me when you were poisoned." Her hand pulled back again.

"Enough!" I said, sitting up partway and holding my hands out.

Fowler lowered her arm and glanced back over her shoulder. There was an ugly bruise on her left temple. "Is that awake enough?" she said.

"It will do admirably, yes," said a thin voice in Imperial. His smile was obvious in his tone.

I looked past Fowler and saw a slender, well-turned-out man standing at the far end of the room. From his olive skin and sharp features, he was clearly Imperial, which stood in contrast to his crisp yet simple Djanese clothing: small turban, tightly buttoned tunic with an open, flowing overcoat, and comfortably loose pants, all in a bone and pale purple brocade. The curled-toed slippers on his feet were the color of amethysts, and even looked to have buttons of that same stuff holding them closed.

I also saw that I wasn't on the floor: rather, I was on a wide, slightly raised platform that ran along two sides of the room. The portion I was on was called the iwan—the resting and social area in most Djanese rooms. The iwan was covered in costly carpets and had damask bolsters against the walls in various spots, while the lower section was done with tile. I noticed Fowler's shoes on the tile. I also noticed that the heavy, carved door on the other side of the room stood ajar, giving me a glimpse of not only the hallway beyond, but the guard stationed just outside the door. I doubted this was a coincidence.

I returned my attention to the Imperial and met his eyes, half expecting to find either arrogance or disdain within them. What I found instead was a challenge, but not based on authority or power; rather, it almost seemed as if he were daring me to do something—to say or see something based on our shared Imperial blood. I looked the challenge back. After a moment, he nodded; then he bowed.

When he straightened, the iron was gone from his eyes. Only calm, watery competence showed in his gaze, but I knew better. That glimpse hadn't been an accident.

The man pitched his voice to carry the distance between us. It wasn't a vast room, but it wasn't small, either. "I need to apologize for Mistress Jess's treatment of you—"

"No, you don't," said Fowler.

"—but I fear it was necessary to wake you," he said. "Nothing else had been working, and it was dangerous to let you sleep longer."

"Why?"

"The poison," said the man. "It was of a type designed to put you into a progressively deeper and deeper sleep—one from which you eventually don't awake. Your dose was mild enough that, had you simply stayed put, as was likely intended, you'd have woken up within six hours' time."

"Except you decided to carry me up the stairs," said Fowler.

"Which made things worse," said the man.

I reached up and rubbed at the tender spot on my chest where Fowler had been thrusting her finger for Angels knew how long. "As opposed to poking me, which apparently helps."

"I insisted," said Fowler.

"She was very . . . determined," agreed the man. "She also refused to let any of the assistant physicians come near you."

I looked back at Fowler. She shrugged. "Easier to keep an eye on one person at a time. I figured the physicker was the best one to let in."

"Which reminds me . . . ," said the man, eyeing Fowler meaningfully.

Fowler sighed and held open her outer robe. "See, Heron? No weapons."

"And the bulge at your back when you came in?"

Fowler reached back and pulled out a curved Djanese blade in a copper scabbard. "What, this? It's more a piece of jewelry than a knife."

Now it was Heron's turn to sigh. "We agreed on no weapons after the incident with Mah'ud."

Fowler snorted. "What 'incident'? I didn't even cut him."

"Only because he ran screaming down the hall."

"What the hell did he expect, sneaking in here like that?"

"He expected to change Master Drothe's dressing, ideally without waking you."

"Well, now he knows better. Besides, this trinket's barely a blade to begin with. If you wanted to actually kill someone, you'd have to—"

"Fowler," I said, stopping her before she went down a path I knew wouldn't help. "Enough."

Fowler grumbled but returned the knife to her back. Heron, I noted, chose not to argue the point. Wise man.

I sat up farther, wincing as I put weight on my wounded arm. As promised, it was in a clean, fresh dressing. Scared or not, Mah'ud seemed to know his business.

I looked around the room and saw my clothes, looking freshly brushed and folded, sitting on a chest beside the door. Fowler followed my gaze, then looked back at me and tapped the wallet hanging at her cloth belt. Jelem's letter and package, I took it, were safe.

I turned back to Heron, who hadn't yet moved from his position across the room.

"You're the physicker, then?" I said to the man, making a show of rubbing my forearm.

"Me? Oh, no. I'm just the secretary to the wazir." He held up a leather-bound book that he'd been holding as if in proof. One finger was stuck between the covers, marking his page. "Heronestes Karkappadolis, but 'Heron' is acceptable."

I looked at Fowler.

She leaned in close and dropped her voice. "He's our leash," she whispered.

"Leash?" I said, glancing back at Heron while keeping my own voice low. He'd opened his book, apparently content to let us lean together and murmur for a moment. I wasn't in a hospital, then, or, at least, not the one Raaz had been talking about before I passed out. "Where the hell am I?"

"El-Qaddice," said Fowler. "The Old City."

I sat up farther. "You mean Tobin and his troupe pulled it off?"

"Maybe," said Fowler, "but considering how fast the audition was arranged and held, I think they could've reenacted a pair of dogs rutting in a doorway and gotten patronage."

"A fix?" I whispered. Then, "Raaz." Or his master— assuming the shadow man I'd seen lose his fingers had survived. They were the only ones I could think of with both the resources and the reasons to smooth our way into the Old City.

"Someone sure has called in some favors," said Fowler. "Not that I've been able to get anything one way or the other out of our friend over there."

I peered past Fowler's shoulder. Heron was regarding us over the binding of his tome. At my look, his turned his eyes back to the page.

Hmm.

"Any word from the mages, then?"

"Nothing."

That didn't reassure me. There should at least have been a message, if not a visit, by now. You didn't pull strings the way they had and then walk away—not unless you had a damn good reason for not wanting to be associated with the string pulling in the first place. Which told me just how dangerous the package Jelem had sent along was, even in Djan. Not that they wouldn't be wanting their bit of smuggled glimmer—they would: They'd just be very careful about when and how they asked for it.

And they'd be mindful of what they'd paid to get it, both in blood and in treasure.

It was that last bit that worried me.

I looked at the screened window, saw nothing but blue sky and the top of a palm tree. "So, where in el-Qaddice am I, precisely?" I said, my voice still low.

"Royal artist's residence. I can't pronounce the Djanese, but I'm told it means 'Sanctuary of the Muse.' All of the padishah's potential performing toys seem to be kept here." Fowler rubbed gently at her temple. "Tobin and company love it."

"I'll just bet they do. How's your head?"

"I get headaches."

I waited for more, but didn't get any. The look Fowler gave me made it clear the situation wouldn't be changing soon. I considered pushing the matter, decided I didn't have the energy just now. Instead, I looked around the room again.

"This won't do," I said, my voice still low. "We need to be able to come and go as we please if we're going to find Degan." Not to mention deal with Jelem's package. Staying in the padishah's poet reserve would let us do neither.

"I've looked into that," said Fowler.

"And?"

"We're Imperials. We can stay in the Imperial Quarter if we want. In fact, I think they kind of prefer it that way."

And the Imperial Quarter was in the Old City, which meant we'd have access to el-Qaddice without having to worry about answering to Heron.

"Well, then—" I began.

"But," said Fowler, "we can't leave until we've been given the padishah's patronage."

"Wait, I thought that's how we got in here in the first place?"

"No. We're under the wazir's eye right now. Turns out the first audition just gets you in the door. We need to perform in front of Padishah Yazir to get his royal favor."

I turned to Heron and pitched my voice to carry. "So we can't leave? We're on probation until the padishah sees us perform?"

"Not probation, no." He closed the book—no finger to mark the page this time—and came forward. Fowler's and my private time, it seemed, was at an end. "But His Highness feels, in his wisdom, that it's best to keep his new prospects as close together as possible, especially when they're new to el-Qaddice, let alone Djan." He indicated the city outside the screened window. "There are many temptations in the Old City, and not all visitors are as . . . eh . . ."

"Experienced?"

"Well schooled as yourself and Mistre—as Fowler Jess here. Until you're fully accepted by the padishah as one of his dependents, the actions of one will be seen to reflect on all, and be judged by the wazir accordingly."

"Judged how, exactly?"

"Sternly. The wazir has little use for thespians."

"And Imperials?"

"Actors are descendants of the gods by comparison."

I gave Heron a skeptical look.

"I'm the exception," he added.

"I'll bet. What if I said I wanted to relocate to the Imperial Quarter?"

"I say you're welcome to do so, as long as your entire troupe goes with you."

"Tobin isn't going to want to leave," observed Fowler.

"You mentioned that," I said. I shifted in bed and pulled my legs underneath me. They felt good. I reached out, put a hand on Fowler's shoulder. She helped me stand.

"How do you feel?" she said, her arm lingering at my elbow.

"A little light-headed," I said, "but otherwise ready to leave." I tilted my head, trying to stretch my neck. I felt a familiar ache at the base. "I don't suppose you have my *ahrami* bag anywhere around here, do you?" I asked Fowler.

"Allow me," said Heron. He tucked the book under his arm and reached into a pocket, pulling out an ivory case the size of his palm. He thumbed open a panel on one end. Inside were four distinct compartments, each holding a collection of *ahrami* seeds. He poured some into his hand. "Do you prefer the *yarenn, oto, barbaratti,* or *cho-lan* regions?"

I stared at the bounty in his palm and felt my mouth begin to water. I think my eye even twitched.

Heron smiled and counted out a dozen seeds. "A sampling, then," he said. "I suggest the *oto* to start, since you've been traveling and not had freshly roasted for a while. Then

probably the *cho-lan* after that. Let me know what you prefer and I'll arrange for more." He put the twelve seeds in my
palm and smiled. "A gift, for a fellow Imperial."

I took one of the *oto*—a lightly roasted, dryer-looking
seed—and slipped it into my mouth and then beneath my
tongue. I felt my heart quicken in anticipation, and had a
hard time preventing myself from simply biting down on
the seed immediately.

Heron, I decided, was all right.

"Tell me," I said as the clerk slipped the case back into
his pocket, my eyes tracking its every movement. "How bad
do you have to be to get your entire group thrown out of
the Old City?"

Heron stared down at the floor, looking thoughtful. "It's
a fine edge," he said. "Especially for Imperials. What might
get a Djanese poet censure could get an Imperial cast
out—or cast into prison. Social norms and customs, not to
mention affairs of honor, can get confusing fast. Caste rival-
ries get ugly, too." He looked back up at me. "If I were you,
I'd stick to what you know. Imperial—*foreign*—matters, if
you understand what I mean. Better for everyone that way."

"All right," I said. "And what if it was discovered that
some members of a troupe were involved with, say, the
Zakur? Or other criminals?"

"Such as Imperial Kin, perhaps?" said Heron.

"Sure, why not?"

Fowler knitted her brow. I shifted my chin slightly, sig-
nally her to bide.

Heron gave me an appraising look. "I'd say," he said
slowly, "that while it wasn't enough to get that troupe's audition canceled, I'd certainly feel better if they weren't in
contact with any of the padishah's other dependents, if only
for moral reasons. After all, we can't have them trafficking
with undesirables—at least, not openly."

"In that case," I said, a smile tugging at my lips, "I'm
afraid I have some terrible news to relay to you. . . ."

Chapter Sixteen

"You mean he didn't give you any explanation at all?" said Tobin as he trudged beside me on the street.

"Nothing," I said. I threw my hands wide. "All the wazir's secretary told me was that, now that I was well enough to walk, we needed to get off the padishah's grounds and into the Imperial Quarter."

Tobin shook his head. "It doesn't make sense. There are other prospects waiting to audition still living on the grounds. Why would they single us out?"

I placed a hand on the troupe leader's shoulder and leaned in a bit. "Just a guess, but were any of those other acts Imperial?"

Tobin's eyes shifted to me. "No."

"Well, then," I said, and let the point hang between us.

Tobin cast his eyes about—at the street and the traffic and the troop of guards escorting us through both—and made a thoughtful sound. Less than two hours ago, he and his troupe had been basking in the glory that was the padishah's grounds: groomed lawns, stocked lakes, trees heavy with fruit and foliage, not to mention the paved courtyards and shade-rich verandas of the artists' sanctuary. Then I'd turned up with a troop of hard-faced guards at my back and news that we had to leave. To say it hadn't gone over well would be an understatement. Still, after the initial outburst, Tobin and the rest had been smart enough to read the guards' expressions and gather their things without any undue complaints. I'd managed to avoid the troupe leader as we'd been quick-marched away from the sanctum and across the grounds, but now that we were through the royal gates and in to the city the pace had slackened enough for him to catch both his breath and me.

"And you're sure he said nothing about why?" said Tobin.

"Not a word," I lied.

"And you? Could you have . . . ?"

"Me?" I snorted. "I've been out and on my back for two days. When would I have had the chance?"

"Yes, well. You're our patron, so I thought I should at least ask." Tobin ran a hand across his cheek and down his neck, leaving a wet sheen of sweat in its wake. "Thank you for your . . . insights. Good day, Master Drothe."

I chose to ignore the tone behind his words as he lengthened his stride and stepped away.

"Thieves," muttered Muiress as she trundled along on the other side of me, sweat rolling freely down her face in the late-morning heat.

I looked up at the broad, unbroken expanse of sky that spread out above us. Not even the hint of a cloud in sight. No relief until we got where we were going, then.

I glanced over at Muiress again, then let my knife slip into the palm of my left hand. I wandered over to one of our escorts.

"How much farther?" I asked in Djanese as I sidled up next to him, matching his pace.

He gave me a glare and shoved at me with his elbow. I stumbled into him, apologized, and faded back into the troupe.

"Here," I said, handing the matron the swatch of linen I'd cut from the guard's layered fighting skirt. "You looked like you could use a handkerchief."

"Thieves," she muttered again, but this time with less vitriol. Muiress wiped her face with the fabric and then secreted it among the folds of her gown.

I gave her a wink and let myself drift back a bit toward the rear of our procession, behind the rest of the actors, but

ahead of the final rank of guards. Fowler, who was walking
and laughing and chatting with the female contingent of the
troupe, glanced back and raised an eyebrow. She'd managed
to gain a gauzy green shawl somewhere, and the fabric,
along with her expression, made her look winsome. I shook
my head in response to her query: I wanted to be alone just
now.

Thanks to the *neyajin*'s poison, I'd missed our entry into
the Old City, not to mention the last two days overall: I
wanted to eye the place and take its measure. And while
our current route might not have been leading us through
the districts and neighborhoods I expected to be frequent-
ing, the main thoroughfares of a city can still tell you a lot.

Despite what the storytellers in the Raffa Na'Ir cordon
back home liked to say, the streets and gutters of el-Qaddice
didn't look to be lined with gold and silver. Then again, I've
never found the jeweled roofs and silk-clad beggars Ildrecca was supposedly famous for, either, so I wasn't exactly disappointed by the reality.

What I did see were buildings rising four and five stories
on either side of us. Some towered over the gardens and
orchards and courtyards that lay before them, while others
stood shoulder to shoulder along the street, their whitewashed and tiled facades gleaming in the sunlight. Every
now and then the line was broken, the buildings being replaced by the elaborately carved walls that set off one of
the private compounds of the nobles and merchant sheikhs.
Palm fronds and tree branches peeked over these walls,
hinting at the lush gardens that lay beyond the solid wood
and iron gates.

Farther back, along the western horizon, I could make
out the domes of the greater temples, their bulbous sides
shining from the silver-gilt prayers that covered their surfaces. I wondered whether the local thieves were ever
tempted to pry the precious man-high letters off the temple
roofs, and if not, what the Despotate had done to discourage them from lifting the gleaming words.

Down closer to the street, color was everywhere. Cara-
vans brought dyes to el-Qaddice from the south and west,

silks from the east, resulting in the people here draping themselves with the brilliant reds and yellows and greens that would normally be reserved for only the richest in Ildrecca. Gleaming tiles covered the roofs and walls of buildings, their deep blues and greens providing at least the cooling illusion of water. And everywhere were flowers and trees and bushes, from simple planters set at the entry to a courtyard, to the sweeping irrigated public gardens we passed with surprising frequency. El-Qaddice relied on both springs that bubbled up along the escarpment and wells that extended deep below, but even with this, I was surprised at how many more public gardens this city had compared to Ildrecca, which sat on the sea.

Djanese predominated on the street, of course, both in language and numbers, but there were enough skin tones and clothing styles, enough foreign syllables and throaty clicks in the air, to speak to the cosmopolitan nature of el-Qaddice, even in the guarded Old City. Silk-robed and -capped Ulaan'ng bureaucrats, their elaborate queues draped over their shoulders and looped in their belts, shuffled past brocade-wrapped Parvans, the latter's heavy beards split and plaited, rings thick in their hair and ears. A group of midnight-skinned Rathin passed us in gray wayfarers' robes—the only color allowed their people outside their own borders—their laughter a sharp contrast to their dour clothes. Farther along, a Betten mercenary, his linen shirt open to his waist to show off his scars of merit, barely gave our procession a passing glance, although I noticed his hands kept close to the half dozen daggers he wore at his waist.

And on every corner, it seemed, stood street magicians: juggling balls of light, drawing down dragons made of vapor and dust, casting fortunes with carved ivory rods, or simply chanting out their services to passersby. Where magicians and Mouths in Ildrecca kept their magics close and their spells soft, here the casters all but shouted their power from the rooftops. I'd seen my fair share of petty glimmer hawkers and con men in the Lower City when we'd arrived, but here, seeing dust dance and steam pull itself from the dry

air at a mere gesture or word, made me wonder if the old
tales about the origins of the Djanese were true; made me
wonder whether the men and women around me had just a
hint of the same blood as the djinn that wandered the desert.

We passed through a great arched gate, flanked on either
side by stone elephants extending out from the walls, and
entered the third ring of the city. Whereas before we'd been
passing through the realm of the nobility and the well connected, now we walked the streets of the more established
common classes. The main thoroughfare still ran straight
and the trash was mostly cleared away, but paint had replaced tiles as decorations on many of the buildings around
us, and the domes of the temple we passed were decorated
with beaten copper and glazed ceramic instead of polished
silver.

We were nearly at the wall that separated the third ring
from the fourth when the guard captain turned down a
curving lane. A short distance later, we passed through what
looked to have once been a fortified gate, but was now
merely an archway between two tall tenement buildings.
Beyond, the streets narrowed considerably, with weathered
buildings made from beaten earth and clay bricks crowding
in on either side. The paving beneath our feet changed from
shaped cobbles to well-worn stone, laid ages ago and worn
smooth by centuries of traffic. Roofs were lower, the windows narrower and higher, and most doors—all brightly
painted—stood a step or more below street level.

We had clearly gone from the Old City to the "Ancient
City," and it was here, among the twisting, crowded streets
of what was clearly the foreign district, that the Imperial
Quarter had grown up.

Long ago, the Quarter had been a simple trading district,
with all of the important diplomatic functionaries taking
residence in the second ring of the city. Most of them were
still there, but as the relationship between the Empire and
the Despotate had evolved over the centuries, so had the
quarter. Now it stood as the main symbol of all things imperial within el-Qaddice, housing not only merchants, but

craftsmen, lesser diplomats, artists, bankers, trading houses, laborers, expatriates—as well as half a cohort of legionnaires.

Heron met us in the shadow of the Quarter's gate, dressed in white and gray like some great crane. A pair of lesser clerks stood behind him. Both were Djanese. Just like back in the room where I'd woken up, he had a book open in his hands, reading. This time, though, it was a thin quarto.

He lowered the book as I approached up and indicated the walls with a nod. "They're the third set, you know."

I followed his gesture. They were high, solid things covered with bas-relief figures. Most of those figures were Imperials, and most were in the process of dying, either via sickness or at spear point. Considering the reason the walls had been torn down and rebuilt, that made sense.

"I know," I said. "The last ones were torn down during the Siege of the Paragons."

Heron raised an appreciative eyebrow. "You know of that? Most of our people have tried to forget it."

"Most have," I said, keeping my eyes on the wall. "I just got lucky and came across a copy of Petrosius's *Regimes*."

He turned to face me full-on. "*You* have a copy of Petrosius? That book was banned and burned in the empire almost a century ago. How—?"

"Who said *I* had a copy?" I said. "I know someone with an extensive collection, is all." Someone who happened to be both a master scribe and a forger, as well as in my debt.

Heron cleared his throat. I watched as his fingers played over the cover of the quarto, hungry for that which he'd never thought to even taste. "Do you think he might be willing to ... perhaps ... ?"

"Loan it out?" Loaning out rare books, even across countries, wasn't an unknown thing, especially among bibliophiles. The opportunity to exchange tomes could often outweigh the risk of loss or damage represented by transit in many minds—one of which seemed to be Heron's.

"That, or allow me to pay for a copy to be made," said Heron. "If, that is, he can find someone he trusts to copy it."

I laughed despite myself. Asking Baldezar to copy something like *Regimes*, especially if there was a chance to show off his scholarly and scribal skills, let alone make a profit, was like asking a bee to make honey. "I think he can probably find someone," I said. "I'll even make sure he doesn't cheat you too badly."

"For a copy of that book?" said Heron. "Don't concern yourself about the price."

I turned my attention back to the wall. I could understand Heron's interest, being in the middle of Djan, even as I could understand why the empire had decided long ago to sweep the incident under the rug. It had been an ignominious action on the part of the emperor at the time, and any acknowledgment by the empire, even through a banned historian, would likely play well at the despotic court.

A little over one and a quarter centuries ago, Theodoi, in his fifth incarnation as emperor, had decided that it was time to go to war with the Despotate again. This time, though, he wanted to strike at the head first, rather than work his way in from the edges, as had been the tradition for ages. To that end, he ordered almost four hundred legionnaires to be smuggled into el-Qaddice over the course of six months, the troops disguised variously as traders, servants, teamsters, and whatever else would raise the least suspicion. Alone, that was bad enough, but Theodoi had sent along three Imperial Paragons as well.

Traditionally, the emperor's private mages had been held in reserve for the defense of the empire, or, on rare occasions, sent to accompany a full Dorminikan army on the march. Paragons were simply too valuable—and too dangerous, if you thought about what one could spill if he was captured—to risk on their own. To send three into el-Qaddice with only half a cohort for protection spoke to just how seriously Theodoi had taken this war, and how badly he'd wanted to strike a crippling blow to the Djanese.

And he did. The plague started a full two weeks before war was declared. Disease swept through el-Qaddice, starting in the lower city and running all the way up to the gates of the despot's inner ring. According to Petrosius, prayers, magic, and physicians filled the streets, barely stemming the tide. When the bodies of the corpses began bursting into flames three days later, though, it quickly became obvious that this was more than a simple plague. The exodus from the city was almost immediate.

Theodoi's declaration of war had arrived four days after that, accompanied by an ultimatum that all but took direct responsibility for the plague. The despot at the time—one Mehmer Ajan III—hadn't hesitated. Marshaling his personal forces and summoning the power not only of the Fifteen High Magi, but also the magi of the disparate tribes and clans under his control, the despot had returned to el-Qaddice and laid siege to the Imperial Quarter.

Petrosius numbers the dead in the thousands outside the walls of the Imperial enclave. Once the magi learned how to turn the plague back on the Imperials, though, he speaks of tens of thousands—all within the Quarter. The walls of the Quarter were torn down, and the heads of the three Paragons were sent back to Theodoi, along with the despot's own ultimatum.

The Dorminikan Empire surrendered two provinces to the Despotate of Djan that autumn, and has only ever recovered half of one in the intervening one hundred and thirty-four years. For the Djanese, that time is referred to as the Burning Days, and they've carved depictions of them into the Quarter's walls, lest they, or we, forget.

As if reading my mood, Heron cleared his throat beside me. "Dark days, long passed," he said. He shuddered for a moment in sympathy with the past, then gestured for Tobin and Ezak to join us.

"What I have to say concerns all of you," said Heron as the mismatched pair of cousins walked up. "Accommodations have been arranged for you. Even though you aren't allowed to stay in the Sanctuary of the Muse, the wazir and, through him, the padishah are still responsible for your well-being and sustenance."

"Meaning you're covering out expenses?" said Tobin, smiling for the first time since we'd left the padishah's enclave.

"Meaning you have an allowance," said Heron. "A *strict*

allowance." He turned his eyes to me. "That you, as the imperial patron, must come to me to receive every other day."

"In person?" I said. Having to walk back and forth across the Old City every other day could put a crimp in my other work.

"In person," said Heron. "At which point you will report on your troupe's progress in their preparations, as well as answer for any complaints lodged against you—of which I expect to hear none, of course."

"Of course," I said.

"When do we appear before His Eminence, the padishah?" said Ezak.

"Whenever you are ready to perform," said Heron. "Which," he added as the two men began to grin, anticipating weeks, or more, of living on the padishah's coin, "the wazir has decided will be on the twenty-fourth day of Fallwah."

The grins faltered.

"What date is today again?" said Tobin.

"The seventeenth day of Fallwah," said Heron.

Tobin and Ezak exchanged looks. "Well," began Ezak, "it's still a week. We could always—"

"And," continued Heron, as if the men hadn't spoken, "the wazir would like you to perform something different from your original audition. Something more like..." Heron extended his hand out behind him, had it filled by one of the clerks. "This," he said, bringing forward a trimmed and bound folio.

The grins vanished.

"What?" cried Tobin, even as Ezak reached out and accepted the thin book. "You want us to read, prepare, and perform a play in seven—"

"Less," said Ezak, looking up at the sun, which was already past noon.

"In less than seven days?" finished Tobin.

My stomach clenched, and not in sympathy for the troupe. A week was barely enough time to get my feet wet in the Old City, let alone stand a chance of finding Degan. I needed longer, which meant the troupe needed longer—ideally, as long as an extended engagement as the padishah's players would allow. Seven days wasn't going to get us that—not by a long shot.

"We need more time," I said.

Heron arched an eyebrow. "Don't we all?"

"Seven days for a new play?" I said, attempting to take up my role as patron. "Is the wazir setting us up to fail?"

Heron's resulting silence was eloquence itself.

"Fuck!" I said, stepping away lest I make our situation even worse by strangling the wazir's secretary.

"Four acts," muttered Ezak, paging through the script. "At least three scene changes—one at sea. No, sorry, on a lake. Six key parts, maybe another seven minor . . ." He stopped and looked up. "Is this a translation?"

Heron gave a small bow. "From one of the padishah's current favorites. A high honor for you."

"Impossible!" said Tobin. "The sensibilities will be all wrong." He stepped forward, his hands out, placating. "We have a piece ready—a wonderful piece. Heroic, passionate: It's brilliance on the boards. We've been preparing the entire journey. If the padishah wants to see what we're made of, then he needs to see us at our best. He has to let us—"

Heron took a quick step forward—so quick that, were it not for the shifting of his robes around him, I would have missed the movement entirely. "The padishah has to *do* nothing!" snapped the secretary. "And that includes let you live. You stand in el-Qaddice at the pleasure of His Highness Yavir; you can just as easily sleep in its streets, or lie under its earth, by that same pleasure. If it *pleases* him, or his wazir, to tell you to howl like gibbons and swing from the rafters of the grand reception hall, I expect the first words out of your mouth to be 'In or out of costume, if it may please His Excellence?' Am I understood?"

Tobin opened his mouth, thought better of it, and nodded once instead. When he turned away, he made no effort to hide his disgust.

"We'll need an original copy of the text in Djanese," said Ezak, his voice carefully neutral. "In case there are questions or errors." Heron held out his hand, had it filled with another book.

"And a translator," said Ezak.

Heron looked at me.

"Oh, no," I said, holding up my hands. "I speak Djanese, I don't read it." A lie, I admit, but a convenient one nonetheless. If the padishah—or rather, the wazir—wanted to be an asshole, I wasn't about to make it easier on his purse.

Ezak weighed the two books, then looked up at me. His expression said it all.

I touched Heron lightly on the sleeve and gestured off to one side. He followed me over, the scowl on his face showing me he was getting tired of the subject. One apparently didn't question the wazir—or his secretary—when a decision had been made.

Too fucking bad.

"What happened to helping out fellow Imperials?" I said, my voice low.

"There's a difference between a crate of *ahrami* and debating a decision with the wazir."

A crate?

"Besides," said Heron, "you'll notice that I don't live in the empire anymore; that I, in fact, serve the Despotate."

"And rushing an imperial acting troupe's performance so they can fail—is that serving the Despotate, or the wazir?" I said. "Or is it merely serving your own skin?"

Heron stiffened, his eyes growing hard. I found myself taking an involuntary step back.

"You dare accuse me of . . . ?" he began. His right hand twitched toward his belt, then stopped. Heron took a short, sharp breath. "It's serving whom I must," he snapped. He gestured at the wall. "You, of all people, should know the burden we carry by our blood in this city. Be happy you were allowed in at all." Then he turned and started to walk away.

I glanced over at the wall, at the depiction of a burning corpse done in bas-relief. A thought occurred.

"Who would you want besides Petrosius?" I said to Heron's retreating back.

He stopped.

"Thycles?" I said, tossing out historians. "Verin the Younger?" I took a slow step after him. "Maybe Kessalon?"

Heron looked over his shoulder. "You can get Kessalon?"

"Both volumes of his *Commentaries*—*if* you can get us more time."

Heron's eyes narrowed. "Originals?"

"Copies." Baldezar would have a fit about me promising copies of two of his most precious texts as it was; trying to get an original out of his hands would require someone to die, and he was too valuable to go dustmans.

"Get Thycles, too," said Heron, "and you have a deal."

I pretended to think, then gave a reluctant nod. Thycles would be easy—Baldezar had three copies; that's why I'd mentioned him.

"Very well," said Heron, his voice still tight. He gestured at the younger of the two clerks. "Shaheer will show you to your accommodations in the Quarter. I will speak to the wazir. Report to me at the padishah's palace tomorrow at dusk. I'll have your answer then. Oh, and before I forget . . ."

Heron held out his hand again. Shaheer put a bag in it. The bag clinked.

"You'll need these," he said, handing the bag to me. I reached inside and pulled out an oval brass lozenge the length of my thumb, on a matching brass chain. A long flute, called a *nay*, and a rolled-up scroll were depicted on the face of the lozenge; Djanese script was etched into the back.

"Those are your tokens of patronage from the wazir," said Heron. "Wear them openly, and always. If you are seen outside the Imperial Quarter without your token, any citizen of Djan may report you, or try to detain you. There is a reward for anyone who helps capture Imperials without a mark of patronage." He looked me squarely in the eye. "A large reward."

I watched as he walked away, the elder clerk and half of the guards falling in behind him. I turned back to the rest of the troupe. Tobin was already ushering his people forward, but Ezak stood off to one side, watching me watch Heron. Fowler waited a bit farther along.

"Even an extra week won't be enough," said Ezak as I

came abreast of him. "Not if we want to perform well enough to win patronage."

"All I know," I said, "is that a hell of a lot can happen in five days." I'd seen criminal organizations fall in less, and found myself promoted from Nose to Gray Prince in just a bit more. "Five days can be forever, if you're in the wrong place."

"And are we in that wrong place?" said Ezak.

I looked through the gate and into the Imperial Quarter. "I'll let you know in seven days," I said.

Chapter Seventeen

Heron had arranged for us to take rooms at an inn named the Angel's Shadow, which made me smile despite myself. The place was put together well enough, with well-aired rooms, mostly fresh linens, a common room that smelled of mutton and wood smoke and thyme, and a small courtyard that Tobin immediately appropriated for the troupe's rehearsals—a situation, it turned out, Heron had arranged for in advance.

I checked my room—small bed, small window, small hole in the wall I stuffed with candle wax and lint to defeat prying ears or eyes—dropped my bedroll and bag on the floor, and kicked the door shut. Then I undid my doublet.

I ran a questing hand first over the outside, then across the inner lining. Aside from the slightest change in stiffness, there was no hint that Fowler and I had now twice opened up the doublet and fit the three small letters and the larger envelope that had made up Jelem's packet among the garment's padding. It hadn't been an easy job the second time around—whoever had brushed the doublet had also noticed the hasty stitching Fowler had done after removing the papers and decided to repair the job proper—but we'd managed to open the seams, adjust and restuff the doublet, and sew it all back up with proper-colored thread liberated from one of the padishah's carpets, all without being walked in on.

I picked off a few lingering bits of cord, then gave the

doublet an experimental shake. No tell-tale crackle of paper, no rattle of broken seals, no sigh of documents or lining shifting underneath the cloth. Good. I'd initially been amazed that the wax on all three letters had survived the trip; now, given that I'd guessed their contents, I wasn't surprised. If you were going to send contraband like that across the border into Djan, you'd damn well want to make sure they didn't come popping open at the first bend or tap. If anything, I expected there was glimmer in the seals, holding them tight and the paper safe.

Part of me wanted to take the doublet and bury it, if not in a hole in the ground, then at least in the bottom of my travel trunk. The idea of carrying the information those letters contained, let alone whatever magic was cast on them, made my skin crawl whenever the fabric brushed up against me. But I also knew that the best way to keep the package, and therefore myself, safe was to keep it on me. Between shadow-casting yazani and darkness-draped assassins, I wanted to be as indispensable as possible. Besides, I doubted any of them would expect me to keep something that valuable on my person after what had happened in the cellar.

Which reminded me. . . .

When I walked back out of the inn, the members of the troupe were busy unloading the wagon, taking various parcels into either the inn or the stables, or setting them to one side in the courtyard. I waited until a bundle of stage swords came off the wagon, put them over my shoulder, and headed into the stables.

Two of the stalls had been set aside—at no small expense, I was sure—for the troupe's gear. I set down the blunted props, removed Degan's Black Isle blade from its hiding place among the pile of swords, and hied myself up to the hayloft.

Five minutes later, I was walking back into the courtyard, brushing dust and bits of hay from my sleeves. Degan's sword was far up in the rafters, hidden alongside a beam and behind some stray bits of thatch. Unless someone knew where to hunt, the chances of stumbling across the weapon were exceedingly low—much lower than, say, finding it under my bed or behind a loose wallboard in my room.

I'd considered putting the *neyajin's* dagger up with Degan's sword as well, but decided against it in the end. While I wasn't comfortable with the idea of carrying around an unknown piece of portable glimmer, neither was I willing to leave it behind. It struck me as the kind of magic that, if nothing else, I could use as a bargaining chip in a pinch. Besides, you never know when a smoke-edged dagger might come in handy. So, instead, I'd slipped it and the scabbard I had bought for it down my other boot.

I found Fowler standing off to one side in the yard, partaking in one of the Kin's favorite pastimes: watching other people work.

"Well?" I said as I put my backside up against the wall beside her.

"Two Ravens in the street," she said, still watching the wagon.

"Heron's men?"

"Sure as hell not local talent—they're too obvious."

"And?"

"Thought I saw someone up on the roof, to our left and across the street. There's a trellis up there, so I can't be sure. I'll take a look later. The best blind spots for us to come and go look to be to the south and east: too many overhangs and blocked lines of sight to be able to watch the inn without being obvious."

"What do you need?" I said.

"Money. If you want me to recruit some coves and set up a perimeter, I need to be able to flash them something other than my winning smile."

I took half of what I had left from our traveling money—not as much as I would have liked—and handed it to her. "See what you can do about shorting the inn's owner a bit as well," I said. "If we can skim what Heron's giving him and keep the hostler from raising any noise, it'll make things easier."

Fowler smiled. "He looks like the nervous type. If I can promise to keep the more eager members of the troupe out of his daughters'—or his sons'—bedrooms, I expect he'll be willing to go a bit lighter in the purse."

"Just make sure you aren't cutting in on anyone else's action. I don't need the local talent complaining about us coming in and taking away their whoring money; it looks petty."

"Angels forbid," said Fowler. Then, as I pushed away from the wall, "I still don't like this, you know."

"What?"

"You, out there, with no one on your blinders."

"It's just like the Lower City," I said. "I'll be fine."

"It's nothing like the Lower City and you know it. Not after what happened with Raaz and that Blade. At least give me until nightfall to—"

"You heard Heron," I said. "We have seven days. I don't have time to wait. I need to hit the street now, to start sniffing for rumors now, to start spreading money and names now. If I want to stand any chance of turning up a lead on Degan before the audition, I have to get started."

"And what if a week isn't enough?" said Fowler. "Have you thought about that? It's not the Empire out there—it isn't even Ildrecca. Weighing down a few palms and pattering up a couple local coves isn't going to get you to Degan— hell, I doubt it'll even get you a rumor of him. If you think—"

"What I think," I said, "is that we don't have a choice. Who's going to work the streets? You? You barely patter the local lingo, never mind the cant. We both know better than that. It has to be me."

"But it's Djan. Just being an Imperial around here is bad enough, but an Imperial asking questions? That isn't going to make you any friends."

"Then I'll make an effort to smile nicely when I talk to people."

"Dammit, Drothe, you know—"

"What I know," I said, "is that I'm going to need a safe, secure roosting ken I can come back to, no matter how well or poorly it goes for me. And that I need you to make this inn that ken." I took a step closer. "If I had more time, I'd go slower. But I don't. There's no time to recruit Ears, turn mumblers, make unfriendly bosses friendly. It has to be me out there and you back here. It's the only way it can possibly work, and we both know it."

Fowler grumbled and groused and kicked at the ground, but she didn't argue. She couldn't. She knew I was right.

I turned and headed for the inn's main gate.

"If you end up getting dusted," she called after me, "make sure they bring your body back. I'll be damned if I spend the next month learning the alleys and sewers of this place, just so I can wind you and shove you under the earth."

"Done!" I called over my shoulder. Then I stepped out onto the street and into el-Qaddice.

I eased in slow: wandering the main streets, stopping at a couple of coffee stalls, chatting with a rug merchant who had the right kind of look in his eye. From there, I moved into the side streets, ducking in and out of late afternoon shadows and under the reed canopies that hung over tiny local bazaars. I listened more than I spoke, browsed more than I bought, and was careful to spread some copper *supps* and silver *dharms* when my lingering seemed to arouse suspicion. If I dropped Degan's name, it was as if by chance, and I relied more on description than anything. I doubted that he was going by "Bronze" or "Degan" anyhow.

By the time I moved into the alleys near sunset, one thing was clear: The influence of Djan ran deep on the streets of the Imperial Quarter. I could see it in the loose robes and draped kaffiyehs of borrowed fashion; could taste it in the cardamom and mint and pepper that laced the local street food; could smell it in the oils laced with cinnamon or clove or sweet rush. But more important, I could see it in the manners and actions of the Dorminikans around me. Everything was done with an eye over the shoulder—a featherlight awareness that nothing could be taken for granted or done without the risk of consequence. Local legionnaires still swaggered, hawkers still called out in Imperial, and brothels still advertised their services with paper ribbons above their doors, but it didn't have the feel of a district at ease with itself. We were surrounded by a city full of people who had been the empire's enemy more than its friend over the centuries, and that weight showed.

That went doubly so among the Kin, who not only had both the Quarter's legionnaires and the despot's green jackets to worry about, but also the local *Zakur*. I quickly discovered that there were no real bosses to speak of in the Imperial Quarter—not really. Oh, they might call themselves Anglers or Rufflers or, in one case, an Upright Man, but their organizations were just shadows of the true thing. Most failed to rise above the level of a street gang, and of those who did, all were little more than a successful raid or a failed payoff away from falling.

No, very little, I found, happened in the criminal island that was the Imperial Quarter without the tacit approval of the *Zakur*. That in itself wasn't terribly surprising—I'd expected as much, more or less, given el-Qaddice's location and particular circumstance—but it was the level of control that surprised me. Even the purse cutters and drop coves were expected to offer up a cut to the Djanese bosses.

That being the case, I kept my name close and my title closer. Better to play the new cove in town than the Gray Prince come to swagger his way through the streets. The first might get you ignored, but the second will draw the kind of attention that could end with a dagger thrust in an alley.

In the end, though, it wasn't a dagger in the dark that caught up with me; it was a pair of Cutters waiting for me as I came out of a second-story bone shop well after midnight.

"Any luck with the dice?" said the taller of the two as he leaned up against the wall in the stairwell. He was smooth—of face, of manner, of voice—with a smile that reminded me of a knife. Farther down the stairs, his partner—a brick of a man—stood eating sweet rice out of a folded palm leaf. He didn't bother to look up at us.

I sighed and put away the few coins I'd acquired while talking to the gamblers inside. "Is this going to take long?" I said. "I have things to do."

The man shrugged himself away from the wall. "Who knows? I'm just the hired help. But," he said, indicating the stairs, "I will note that this is the only way out. . . ."

He showed the blade of his grin again. I walked down the stairs. The one eating rice deigned to nod as I passed.

My, but they raised them polite down here.

There was a sedan chair waiting in the street. It was respectable as these things went, with a painted door in the side and wicker screens covering the windows. The roof had a pair of folding panels, which had been pulled back to reveal more screens up top. Even this far on the thieves' side of midnight, el-Qaddice could hold on to the day's heat, radiating it back along the alleys and, I'd guess, into any enclosed boxes traveling through them.

Eight bearers crouched against the wall beside the stairs, passing a skin between them and drinking deeply. My night vision was still sleeping from the gaming den, but I didn't need it to see the sheen of sweat that covered the men's bare backs. They moved with all the crispness and energy of a wet rag, making me wonder just how used they were to their job.

Then one of the screens slid down and I understood a bit better.

To say the man inside was vast would have been like saying the sea was deep, or the desert sun was warm. He spread to fill the entirety of the seat, his silk-covered sides pressing against the arms of his chair. A leg like the mast of small schooner sat propped up on a tasseled pillow, the foot wrapped in linen and smelling of unguents and poultice. The earthy, acrid aroma called up memories of Eppyris and his apothecary shop, back before I'd caused him to become a cripple and made his wife hate me. I took a step back from the man and, for the sake of those feelings alone, decided I already disliked him.

"For someone new to el-Qaddice," he said in Djanese, not bothering to look up from the piece of paper he was folding, "you've managed to achieve a great deal in a surprisingly short amount of time. Tentative patronage? Housing at the padishah's expense? I'm impressed."

"I like to keep myself busy."

"Yes, I can see that." His thick fingers, surprising in their dexterity, never stopped moving across the paper. "I'm much the same myself, although I know I don't look it. My pastimes are more . . . sedentary."

"I never would have guessed."

A slight pursing of his lips beneath his thin mustache. "Yes, well. The hour's late. I was wondering if I could interest you in a cup of tea, so that we might discuss our business in a more comfortable setting?"

I crossed my arms. "Not thirsty."

"Then a light meal, perhaps? I understand your people are fond of stuffed grape leaves. I know a cook who can—"

"Not hungry, either."

I knew I was being rude, but I didn't care. In offering to share his salt, the *Zakur* was also offering me his protection—at least for the duration of the meal. It was an old Djanese custom, built on countless generations of life among the dunes, where simple hospitality could be the difference between life and death. By declining, I was saying I didn't trust him to keep his word. A slap in the face of his honor, I admit, but at this point I didn't know if he had enough honor for my insult to leave a mark in the first place, and I wasn't willing to risk my life to find out.

"I see." He raised one finger slightly in the process of folding the paper, and I suddenly felt cool steel at the side of the throat.

The man set the paper down on his broad lap and looked at me. "Since you insist on behaving like a barbarian," he said, "we'll proceed in the imperial manner. Abul?"

A sharp, quick punch caught me above the kidney at precisely the same instant the knife vanished from my neck. I gasped and dropped to one knee.

"There," said the man, picking up the paper again. "Now that we have the requisite violence out of the way, I can explain why I'm here." He wiped a fleck of my spit from the window edge. "I wanted to make something clear: The Imperial Quarter doesn't belong to you. It will never belong to you. There are no great sheikhs of the Kin among your people here. No Rufflers or 'Standing Men' or—"

"Upright Men," I said from my knees.

"What?"

"They're called Upright Men, you bastard. Get it right."

Another flick of the finger, another punch. I winced and didn't quite fall over.

"No *Upright* Men," he said. The chair groaned as he leaned his head out the window. Several of the bearers started to stand, ready for a collapse that didn't come. "And no Gray Princes, either," he added.

My eyes shot up to meet his.

"Yes," he said, his eyes crinkling with a smile. "I think we understand each other."

I nodded. No stirring up the local Kin. Fragmented and frustrated was how they liked them, and a Gray Prince stepping in to give a bit of order—or even worse, a sense of purpose—wouldn't sit well with the native crime bosses.

I didn't bother asking how he'd figured out who I was. This was his—the *Zakur*'s—city: If anyone could gather up enough whispers and rumors and bits of overheard conversation to piece it together, it would be them. Even if it was a guess, it was one I'd confirmed with my look.

No, I wasn't overly surprised that they'd sussed me out; I just wanted to know how they'd done it so damn quickly.

The *Zakur* . . . Angle Master? Ruffler? Upright Man? . . . turned back to his folding. "You realize that I say this merely to avoid any misunderstandings between your esteemed personage and my own people. We recognize and respect your position and your prestige."

"Of course you do," I said, looking back at the Cutters.

"Of course. Ah, there!" He made one last fold and held up what had become a paper reproduction of a desert wolf. It was damn good. "A frivolous pastime, I admit, but one that requires great precision and planning."

"Speaking of frivolous," I said as I climbed to my feet, "you could've delivered this message any of a dozen different ways: by the street, via a messenger, through a Prig or Beggar Boss . . . hell, you could have even written it on a folded fucking frog, for that matter."

He looked at me through narrowed, puffy eyelids. "True."

"Which means there's more to this than just warning me off."

Another twitch of his lips. "I can see why you're an emir of your kind. Yes, there's another reason."

"And that reason is?"

He turned to more fully face me. The sedan chair creaked in protest, and I caught a renewed whiff of the damp peat and vinegar scent coming from his foot as the air shifted about him. Gout? Worse?

"Why are you here?" he said.

I blinked. Smiled. Would have laughed in his face if I didn't think it would've gotten me killed in that moment.

Why was I here? The very question I would have likely asked if a Grand Sheikh of the *Zakur* were to show up in Ildrecca. What did he want? What were his plans? Who was he working with? Because, Angels knew, someone like that—someone like me—didn't just show up this far from home for no particular reason, and certainly not without making contact with the local powers that be if he didn't want them to be nervous.

Only I had, because instead of thinking like a Prince, I'd been acting like a Nose. Again.

Dammit.

There was no good answer. Whatever I told him would be carved up and held to the light. Lies would be assumed, duplicity expected, misdirection anticipated.

Fuck it. I decided to tell him the truth.

"I'm here looking for someone."

"And?"

"And what? That's it."

The corners of his mouth turned up, his heavy lips making the smile look like something between a smirk and a pout. "You could have searched in a dozen different ways," he said. "Through the Kin, an agent, a local boss—even by writing a note on a folded fucking frog; surely you don't expect me to believe that a Gray Prince would come all the way to Djan just to search for someone?"

"It's not my problem what you decide to believe."

"Ah, but it is." He settled back into his seat and held up

the paper figure, rotating it gently between his fingers. "Because what I believe can directly affect what you accomplish here."

"You don't want to cross me," I said. "Not in this. It doesn't concern you."

His eyes turned back to me. They were small, hard things now. "You threaten me?"

"I warn you."

He stared at me for a long time—or what felt like a long time: It was hard to tell given the rapid pounding of my heart. When it became apparent that neither of us was about to back down, he grunted and turned away. He snapped his fingers, and the bearers rushed forward to put their shoulders beneath the rails of his chair.

"It has come to my attention," he said as the chair lurched upward, "that someone has been smuggling magic from the empire into el-Qaddice over the past few months. I believe you used to smuggle relics into the Despotate not so long ago, yes?"

I kept my face blank, even as my guts rolled over inside me. *He* knew about the glimmer? Angels—just how much had Jelem sent down here? And more important, how many shipments had he moved in the last few months?

"Dealing in relics and dealing in glimmer are two different things," I said, my voice even.

"But smuggling is still smuggling, no matter what the nature of the goods. And in my city, I oversee the smuggling of all things magical." He looked down at me from his enclosed perch. "Don't think us such the fools that we can't see why you're truly here, Shadow Prince. You would do well to think about handing the magic over, as well as disbanding whatever organization you're putting together. As I said, the Old City is ours: You don't want to challenge us."

"And if I say I don't have anything to do with any smuggled glimmer?" I said. I decided not to mention anything about my not having an organization.

"I would say only a foolish man denies a truth that's obvious to all."

I crossed my arms. "You have no idea how foolish I can be when I put my mind to it."

He smiled. "Truly, this answer pleases me to no end." The screen to the chair slid up.

It wasn't until after he and his Cutters were gone that I noticed a folded bit of paper lying at my feet: the wolf. Only, I realized when I picked it up, it wasn't a wolf; rather, it was a hyena. A hyena with hunched shoulders and an open mouth and a lolling tongue: laughing. At me.

I walked away, leaving his message torn and crumpled in the street.

Chapter Eighteen

After that, I threw myself at the street for the rest of that night and the following day. Where before I'd been lingering in the backs of low taverns and roosting kens, buying drinks to loosen other people's tongues, now I took the more direct route. When steel wasn't bared, it was shown, and my silver now carried the occasional smudge of red when it changed hands. I brandished my name like a blade, cowing those who knew better, and buying off or educating those who didn't. These were Kin: Even here, under the thumb of the *Zakur*, I knew how to read them, how to talk to them—and how to scare the hell out of them when necessary.

Nothing happened in the Imperial Quarter without the *Zakur's* say-so? I couldn't find Degan without their protection? I was a Gray Prince, dammit: Fuck them.

Still, that didn't mean I had to be stupid about it. Where I dropped my name, I did it in such a way that it wasn't attached to me. I was an agent, a front man, a sounder sent ahead to prepare the ground or ask the questions. I was both interested and disinterested in el-Qaddice, solidifying my position in Ildrecca or expanding outward. I was presence and ghost, a fact and a rumor. Anything to muddy the waters for Fat Chair—yes, that was the cove in the sedan's name—and make him wonder just what the hell was going on.

Anything, in short, to gain me some time.

As for Degan, he was proving as hard to pin down as ever. Even with him being a tall, fair-haired westerner in a land of dusky, dark-eyed Djanese, few people recalled having heard of him, let alone seen him. The best I was able to collect was a handful of stale memories about a man who might have been Degan wandering into the Imperial Quarter for a few days, and then wandering back out. That had been a month ago, and from what I could gather he'd spent most of his time strolling the bazaars and sampling street food. No word about a foreign blade selling his sword; no rumors of him signing on with a local noble or steel house. No trail of bodies or coins to follow.

All of which meant I was going to have to widen my search beyond the Imperial Quarter. Not a surprise, but part of me had been hoping Degan would stick close to what he knew. Working the Old City would require more time, money, and muscle than I had. It would require me to operate low to the ground, finding informers and sorting rumors as I went. That meant a lot of dirty Mumblers and questionable Ears, more than half of whom would either feed me a crooked line of patter or sell me to the *Zakur* if they could manage it. Plus, thanks to both Heron and Wolf, I was going to be doing all of this on a tight timeline.

No, this wasn't going to be easy at all.

By the time I made it back to the Angel's Shadow, it was well past noon on the day after I'd left. My feet were dragging and my head was pounding. I only had one *ahrami* seed left from the stash Heron had given me, and I was saving that for when I woke up, hopefully sometime tomorrow morning. Late tomorrow morning.

I found Tobin and his people in the courtyard, hard at work on the new play. Those not reading lines were fitting together the framing for the backdrops.

The moment he saw me, Tobin turned and started forward, displeasure writ large on his face. Fortunately for the troupe leader, Ezak caught the look in my eye and took his cousin by the elbow, steering him to another corner of the yard. Sounds of a brief but heated discussion drifted over as the rest of the troupe—even Muiress—gave me a wide berth. I made it to the inn's door without incident and went inside.

Fowler was sitting in the window nearest the door, one leg propped up in the sunlight, watching the rehearsal. Her hair was loose and falling over her left shoulder, the light of the sun turning it to gold. I blinked, surprised to see it down. It took me a moment longer to realize she wasn't in her street clothes—or, at least, not her normal street clothes. The well-worn travel shirt and coat had been replaced by finer stuff: a high-necked linen doublet of ivy green, its front only partially laced, with the shirt underneath likewise at ease across her collarbone. Her breeches were new, and tailored noticeably more for a woman than a man, which I found . . . distracting. The lines hugged her legs closely, until, just above the knee, the pants stopped. Below were her usual hose and low shoes. Even those looked freshly brushed.

Fowler shifted slightly in the window and ran a critical eye over me. "I'm guessing you didn't sleep."

"That would have required me to stop moving."

"Well, as long as you had a good reason . . ."

I pointed at her clothes. "What's this?"

"What's what?"

"The outfit. Is it for the play?"

Fowler stared at me for a moment, then turned back toward the courtyard.

"I borrowed it from the troupe," she said. "Sent my drapes to be laundered. After this long on the road, they could use it." She sniffed meaningfully and wiped at her nose. "Wouldn't hurt you any, either."

I scratched at my chest, suddenly self-conscious. "When I have time."

"You could always ask Muiress."

"I'd prefer they come back in one piece."

"There is that."

I watched her watch the players for a moment, then turned my gaze toward the troupe.

Ever since Fowler had come back to work for me, things had been . . . different. Before, when I'd just been a Nose and she, the person who watched over my apartments, it had been easy: Easy to talk, easy to spend time with one another, easy to fall in bed together every now and again. But that had changed when she'd learned I'd spent the past seven years lying to her about who I had actually worked for—who, in some sense, I actually was. As a Long Nose, there had been no way for me to tell her that I worked for Kells and not Nicco, but that justification hadn't lessened her sense of betrayal any. Nor would I have expected it to.

So I hadn't been surprised when she'd walked away. Even when I'd been named a Gray Prince, she hadn't returned. And then, a month later, she was suddenly back. One day, Broken Daniel was covering my blinders; the next, Fowler was back on the rooftops, her people watching my home. She never explained why she'd come back, and I'd never pushed, just as I'd never asked what had passed between her and Broken Daniel. Sometimes, it's simply better not to ask.

But ever since, there had been . . . not a distance, but a guardedness to her. I still trusted Fowler with my life—more so than anyone, now that Degan was gone—and while we still slipped into old habits now and then, it was clear a line had been drawn in her head when it came to me. Some aspects of that line were obvious, others, less so.

This, it seemed, was one of the less obvious times.

"Any luck finding us some Crows?" I said as I stood beside her and scanned the nearby roofs.

Fowler let out a small laugh. "Hardly."

"Oh?" It wasn't like Fowler to be unable to find people to stand watch over a ken, even in a place like el-Qaddice. If anyone could find willing, worthy eyes, it was her. I pulled up a chair. "Tell me."

"The Kin around here don't make sense."

"How so?"

"I'm used to Kin being careful," she said. "Being cagey. Used to their standing half a step back when you talk to them, especially if they don't know you. I can understand that. But here?" She made a dismissive gesture toward the world beyond the window. "It's more than that. They're nervous. No one wants to hire on to stand watch without checking with someone else first. It's like they're all looking at their shadows, afraid that something's going to jump out at them. Everyone's so afraid of stepping wrong, no one's willing to lift up their feet."

"It's the *Zakur*," I said. "They've got a lock on the district—more so than you'd expect. More than the Kin have on the Raffa Na'Ir district back in Ildrecca, even." I leaned back against my chair. My back cracked. It felt damn good. "I just wish I knew why their pull is so damn strong."

"It's the glimmer," said Fowler.

"The what?"

"The glimmer. They control it."

"How do you mean?"

"Remember how Heron went on about those carvings on the walls when we arrived?"

"You mean the Plague of the Paragons? When the empire sent the magical sickness?"

Fowler nodded impatiently. "Right, that. Well, it turns out not only did the despot decide to wall off the Imperial Quarter from the rest of the city; he also barred any kind of magic from the empire coming into el-Qaddice. And I'm not just talking portable glimmer here—I mean Mouths, too. Anyone who can speak a spell or mumble a charm. Getting caught with even a scrap of imperial spellcraft in this city gets you an immediate, irrevocable visit to the despot's deepest dungeon."

"Which means," I said, spinning the consequences out in my head, "the Kin in this city don't have access to glimmer."

"Oh, we can get it, all right," said Fowler, "as long at it's Djanese in origin and we're willing to pay the *Zakur* for the privilege."

I collapsed back into my chair. That would do it, all right. It wasn't that we, as Kin, were used to having easy access to magic—it was still rare and pricey in the Empire as well— but it was at least an option. The Kin were central to the illegal glimmer trade back home, which meant that we could get it when we needed it. But here, in a city where they made dust cyclones dance in the street and summoned rainbows out of the air? Working a dodge without glimmer here would be like trying to take part in an alley fight without a weapon—you could still come out of it in one piece, sure, but that steel in your hand sure made the odds better.

A thought occurred.

"You can't tell me someone hasn't tried to sneak some Mouths in here over the years?" I said. "Especially Kin."

"Of course they have," said Fowler. "And from what I hear, the despot's magi have even eased up on the punishment for it. They used to keep the offender alive for a week while they let magical fires cosume their body; now they only draw it our for three days."

Shit. No wonder Fat Chair had sought me out so soon after my arrival. He wasn't worried about me smuggling in a single piece of glimmer in; he was worried I was going to try and set up permanent shop. That I was going to step in and start supplying the Imperial Quarter with mages or magic—or both—and try to take over the district. Or more.

And all because I was a Gray Prince. Because everyone knew that a Gray Prince wouldn't come to a place like el-Qaddice in person unless he a good reason. Unless he had plans.

Dammit.

"How did I not hear about this?" I said, pushing myself away from the table so I could stand. And pace. "I just spent the last day and a half working the damn street. How did I miss it?"

Fowler stayed put in the window. "What were you looking for?" she said.

"Degan, of course."

"Well, there you go, then: You had no reason to ask."

"And you did?"

"I saw what they do on the streets for fun while we were walking to the inn from the padishah's. I figured if I wanted to have any chance of sewing this ken up, I'd need to get my hands on at least a couple glimmer-mongers, if not a proper Mouth. Only I couldn't find any." Fowler tapped the knife at her side. "It wasn't until I started digging that people began to tell me the hows and whys of it."

I nodded. Kin or no, that wasn't the kind of thing you wanted to share with some brand-new cove on the street. Weaknesses are embarrassing, no matter whose fault they are.

"If that's the case with the glimmer," I said, "then we may have a bigger problem than I first thought."

"How so?"

I took a step closer, then thought better of it and moved to put the chair between me and her.

I told her about Fat Chair.

"And you told him to go to hell?" she practically shouted once I was done.

"I thought he was a local boss flexing his muscle, trying to brush me back on some smuggling," I said. "How was I supposed to know he had a lock on all the glimmer in the Imperial Quarter?"

"Fuck," said Fowler. She looked out the window, then back at me, then back out the window again. "Fuck, fuck, *fuck*! Do you know how hard it just got for me to secure this place? How hard it's going to be to recruit any kind of Crows now? Once word gets out that this bastard is after you, no one's going to want to take our coin. I'm going to have to skip over any likely Kin or *Zakur* I may have had my eye on and go straight to the street urchins and the outcasts." She kicked the chair at me. "Fucking brilliant."

I sidestepped the chair. "We still may have one angle," I said.

"Oh, and what's that?" said Fowler. She jerked her chin toward the troupe. "You going to sonnet the *Zakur* to death?"

I tapped my doublet, where Jelem's packet had been carefully restitched between layers of lining. "There's still the *yazani* from the cellar."

Fowler sat up. "You mean Raaz?" She began to pat at her own doublet. "Shit. He was here looking for you earlier. I almost forgot. Said he needed to talk to you."

"I'll bet he did." Between the shadow magics and the yazani, he and his master had to be worried about whatever it was Jelem had hidden in those papers. My guess was that it was worth more than the price of getting us into the Old City—and if it wasn't, I was going to make it so. "Where did he say I could find him?"

"He didn't."

"Well, then, how am I—?"

"Ah, here it is." Fowler pulled a thin strip of dark fabric from beneath her waistband. The cloth was roughly the length of her little finger and half as wide. She held it up between us. "He said to burn this when you were ready to talk to him."

I reached out and took it gingerly between finger and thumb. It felt tacky and stiff, as if it had been dipped in resin or tar and left to dry. "Burn it?"

Fowler nodded.

"And then what?" I said.

Fowler shrugged.

I sighed. Sleep would have to wait. "Go get me a candle, will you?"

"Hey, Flora!" yelled Fowler. "Go get us a candle, will you?"

The girl straightening the common room dipped her head and hurried off.

I glared at Fowler and rubbed my ear. She smiled beatifically back.

"Mistress," said Flora as she hurried back into the room, her hand cupped around a burning taper. She set it on the table, bobbed another half bow, and left.

"What the hell did you do to her?" I asked as the girl scuttled away, glancing over her shoulder at the Oak Mistress.

"Nothing. Just told her older brother that if he pushes her around again, I'd snap off his cock and feed it to him with a side of hummus." Fowler winked. "Think she has a crush on me now."

I sighed and took a seat at the table. The taper's flame flickered and wavered, giving off a oily, dirty smoke. I held up Raaz's scrap, hesitated, then cautiously touched fabric to flame.

If I'd been expecting an explosion or a clap of thunder, I

would have been sorely disappointed. All that happened was a hiss and a sputter as the fabric reluctantly caught fire. I held it for a moment, then set it on the table. The flame crept slowly up the length of the scrap.

I was about to ask Fowler what we were supposed to do next when I noticed the smoke from the cloth wasn't behaving the way it should. Rather than wafting upward and spreading into a wider ribbon before dissipating, the pale line instead rippled and turned back on itself, bending to and fro, in arcs and lines, before finally resuming its journey ceilingward. It wasn't until the fabric was half-gone that I was able to discern the face hanging before me in the air like an empty carnival mask, its features sketched in smoke.

The face it depicted was, not surprisingly, Raaz's.

"Ah, you got my message," said the mask. Or, rather, wrote, since each word came out its mouth as a gray bit of imperial cephta, drifting on the air between us before vanishing. "We need to speak. Can you come now?"

I waited until the last symbol drifted away and then said, "Um, yes?" There was less than a quarter of the fabric left on the table.

"Excellent. Come to the old temple to the Family in the Blessed Sky District in the third ring. Repeat it."

"Temple to the Family in Blessed Sky, third ring."

"What the hell is going on?" whispered Fowler, leaning forward until her face almost passed though Razz's. "Who are you talking—?"

"Hsst!" I said, waving her away. The breeze from my hand caused Raaz's face to shiver and distort briefly. He didn't seem to mind.

"Good. I'll be waiting," he smoke-said. Then his face broke apart and drifted away.

I looked down at the table. The piece of fabric was nothing more than a charred line on its surface.

"What happened?" said Fowler, still leaning forward. "Was it Raaz? What did he say?"

"What did you see?"

Fowler sat back and blinked. "You sitting there muttering to a stream of smoke. I couldn't even hear what you were saying, you were talking so low. Why, what did you see?"

I brushed the line of char away and stood. "Pretty much the same. Come on."

Fowler scowled at my answer but didn't argue. "Where are we going?" she said as she rose.

"To see how the other half prays, it seems."

We found the temple easy enough. Raaz, though, was another matter.

It was an impressive place, and not what I had been expecting. Back in Ildrecca, the Empire went for vast and intimidating: vaulted ceilings, vast arches, mosaics and paintings four and five times the height of a man, all designed to make the petitioner feel both pious and penitent. What with the emperor being the direct intermediary between his subjects and the Angels, religion ran part and parcel with the state. Loyalty was one of the main businesses of the churches in the empire.

By contrast, the business of the temples in Djan, or at least this one, seemed to be ... well, everything.

The place itself was a large rectangle, open to the heavens, bordered on all sides by more pillared arcades. Out in the middle, under the brilliant blue sky, a series of winding gravel paths wandered across a patchwork of trimmed lawns and small open areas. Men and women moved about on these paths, walking and talking, arguing and laughing, reading and contemplating. Almost as an afterthought, I saw people kneeling on prayer rugs as well, facing different directions as they bowed and prayed to one of the many images depicted on the back walls of the arcade.

There was more praying going on in the shade in front of the murals. Each had been painted with a likeness of one of the members of the divine family and then decorated with various symbols and precious metals associated with each god—gold and rubies for Ahreesh, jade and lavender for A'wella, black silk and ashes for The Banished One, and so on—but there were other things going on there as well. Scholars sat conducting lessons with their students while water hawkers and rug menders called out their services, and beggars silently held out bowls, hoping for a share of the alms all Djanese were expected to donate every month. Off to one side, a young man was making an elaborate show of kneeling before a young woman and reciting poetry. I could hear her laughter from here.

"It's more like a bazaar than a temple," said Fowler. She laughed. "I like it!"

"Bazaar or temple," I said, "we need to find Raaz." I looked around, then hopped up onto the plinth for one of the columns and tried to see over the crowd. "You take that side of the temple," I said to Fowler, "while I—"

I was interrupted by the sound of a single, clear, deep note ringing out over the space.

The poetry stopped, the girl became solemn, and everyone made their way to a clear patch of ground. Those without rugs or mats chose the grass, while most of the others opted for the clearings covered with raked sand. A few of the more dedicated knelt on the gravel. I noticed that those within the arcades fell silent as well, although not all of them knelt in prayer.

As before, everyone faced in a different direction, directing their prayers at the image of the god they had come to petition. A few people seemed to pray in no particular direction at all, or looked to be facing the space between two representations. Indecisive, I wondered, or hedging their bets?

The bell sounded again, and a single priest came out from an archway on the far side of the temple. He was clad in deep red-orange robes, and carried a twisted, gnarled staff in his hands. After a brief gesture to each of the four cardinal directions, he faced back the way he'd come and began a low, sonorous chant.

The prayers lasted maybe ten minutes, and I used that time to look over the heads and backs of the various suppliants. When the bell sounded for a third time, everyone rose. Those with rugs or mats rolled them up. The water sellers and the rug menders began calling out again. Some people moved to leave, others stayed, and still others came in. The girl, I noticed, walked out before the poet could prostrate himself before her again.

The temple had turned back into something like a common green.

"Any luck?" said Fowler.

I pointed. "Over there, under the arcade."

I led us out into the temple yard and along the gravel paths, angling over toward a small group of men and women who sat in the shade halfway along the wall.

As we approached, I saw a brief shimmer appear and dance along the fingertips of one of the men in the circle. A moment later, a similar shimmer, but longer in duration and with more color, appeared on another set of fingers. Then a third. When a fourth figure—a handsome, raven-haired woman—raised her hands, only to have the magical luminescence slither up the arm and along the shoulders of the man next to her, the circle erupted in polite laughter, followed by the gentle tapping of palms on the floor of the arcade.

Raaz smiled along with the rest of them and made a show of brushing off his shoulder.

"Well done, Zural," he said. "Now, tell me—ah!" He nodded as he saw me and held up one hand. We stopped maybe four paces away.

"I'm afraid the rest will have to wait for another time," said Raaz to his students. "But remember the purpose behind this exercise: If you can recognize another's magic—can understand how he shapes the fragments of power—and form it to your own use, you are one step closer to turning it against him even as he gathers it, yes?"

Murmured agreement from the circle. The students—both young and old—rose and wandered away, leaving Raaz alone, perched on a threadbare cushion on an even more threadbare rug.

"Please," said Raaz, indicating the floor before him. Fowler and I sat. "My apologies for dragging you here, but my master isn't well and someone has to carry on the lessons."

"You teach your classes here?" said Fowler.

Raaz tilted his head. "Why not?"

"Well, I'd think . . ." She gestured at the milling square of the temple. "Privacy, for one. Secrecy for another. And, well, privacy for a third."

Raaz steepled his fingers and rested his elbows on the knees. "I can see your point," he said. "And were I a member of, say, Tal Nareesh, I might agree with you. Were I Nareesh, I would happily stay back in my hall and conduct lessons in the privacy of a classroom or closed garden. But I'm of Tal al-Faj, and that means our school is no longer our own. It is, in fact, the property of Tal Nareesh—a gift from the despot for exposing the foul conspiracy of its former owners."

"Oh," said Fowler, sounding abashed. "I didn't—"

"How could you?" cut in Raaz smoothly. "And besides, the despot has been generous. Tal al-Faj still has a school to call its own. It is just smaller. And poorer. And prone to leaning to one side. So we come here." He gestured at the temple. "Where better to teach the secrets of power and control than under the eyes of the Family?" He leaned forward. "And how better to avoid suspicion than by sitting out in the open, for all to see? If my master wants privacy, dear Fowler, he will save it for the things that truly matter—not simple lessons in manipulative magics."

"Speaking of manipulative magicians," I said, "What do you want?"

Raaz grudgingly turned his attention to me. "You have to ask?"

I smiled a thin smile and looked over my shoulder, making sure no one was near. Enough of the worshippers and loiterers had cleared out by now that we weren't in any danger of being overheard. Still, I gave Fowler a look. She got up and stepped away, placing herself between us and the rest of the arcade.

I turned back, reached into my doublet, and set Jelem's packet on the polished floor tiles.

Raaz looked from the packet to me and back again. I noted that he still had a wavering gray scar around his neck, still had a glove on his left hand where the *neyajin* had cut his shadow, and still spoke with a bit of a rasp.

His right hand moved toward the folded sheaf of papers. "I'm glad to see that—"

"Not so fast," I said, leaning forward and putting my finger on the packet's nearest corner. "The price has gone up."

Raaz frowned but didn't withdraw his hand. "Up? Why?"

"I'm nobody's mule," I said. "Especially not Jelem's."

"And yet here you are, papers and all."

"I just wanted to let you know I was serious."

"If I recall, the arrangement was for us to aid you in exchange for delivering the missives. Now here you sit in the city, and yet my hand remains empty. Not only that, but you ask more to fill it." Raaz shook his head. "I was under the impression that Gray Princes honored their word."

"I keep my word just fine," I said. "When I'm not being conned or played or used."

"That's what this is, then? Your princely pride was wounded, and so you make threats and demands to assuage it? Based on what Jelem wrote, I'd hoped for more from you, but I see you're simply another red-knuckled Imperial, just like the rest of your so-called Kin."

My hand swept down and jerked Arrebah's smoke-edged dagger from my boot. Raaz's eyes went wide at the sight, and a faint rattling sound escaped from his throat. I could have almost sworn that I saw the fingers inside his gloves deflate a bit.

"This 'red-knuckled Imperial' fought a fucking assassin in the dark for you people," I said, holding the blade low while making sure he could see the shadow-stuff trailing off it. "I saved not only your life, but your master's as well. Fowler took a click to the head, and I got cut up and poisoned in the process. So, yes, your master may have spent his money and influence on my behalf, but I spilled my blood on his. If anyone's owed anything, it's me."

Raaz sat, staring at the knife as if it were a serpent ready to strike. "You're not the only one who suffered in that chamber," he said slowly. "And we weren't the only ones in danger. Your life was under threat from the *neyajin* as well."

"True," I said. "But she didn't leave because of you, now, did she?"

His stared at me a long moment, his gloved hand clenching until the leather glove creaked with the strain. "Have I told you what happened to my master?" he said. "Why he can't be here to speak with you? It's because he's dying. Whatever that *hesheh* did, it's eating away at him. There's a line of darkness . . ." Raaz traced a mark across his fist, below the knuckles and above the wrist. "A piece of shadow where his fingers used to be. He says he can still feel the digits, that they are there on the other side of the line, and that something is nibbling at them. Devouring him. Slowly."

"Devouring him?" Of a sudden, I didn't feel quite so comfortable holding that knife.

"The original cut was at the base of the fingers. The line is moving up his arm. We don't know if the pain will drive him mad before whatever it is kills him, or if we will kill him first out of pity."

"Can't you just cut off the hand? I know it's not the best solution, but given the other options . . ."

Raaz shook his head. "The other magi say the shadow is in his blood, that it's eating him from the inside, only at a slower rate. They're trying to exorcise it, but . . ." He opened his gloved hand so he could see the fingers, rubbed at the line on his neck. "It seems I was fortunate by comparison."

I swallowed. It didn't seem wise just now to point out that over half the glimmer in that tunnel had originated with Raaz and his shadow magic, nor that my own wound had been healing well, rather than growing. Neither would help just now.

"And you think this other *tal*, the Nareesh, are behind the attack in the cellar?" I said.

"It makes the most sense," he said. "They've already benefitted from our fall. Now if they were to dig the grave and fill it with our bones? One less thing to worry about."

I grunted. If anyone could find and hire an invisible, shadow-killing assassin, I expect it would be a bunch of Mouths. "You realize someone in your organization is likely talking?" I said.

He dipped his chin. "That, or the Tal Nareesh have managed to set a spirit to observing us, despite our precautions.
Either way, we're looking into the problem, trust me. Now,
if you'd please, remove that *thing* from my presence."

I drew the *neyajin's* blade back. I noticed that as I moved
to put it away, Raaz shifted slightly to one side. It took me
a moment to realize that he'd done it to make sure his
shadow was nowhere near the blade's.

I slid the blade home more gingerly than I'd taken it out
and resettled myself on the ground.

"So, with all that said, what is it you want?" said Raaz.

"For starters? Some answers."

"About?"

I tapped my finger on the papers. "Why do you want the
package?"

For perhaps the first time since I'd met him, Raaz looked
truly puzzled. "Because it's ours."

"No. That tells me why you want what Jelem sent; I want
to know why you want what's in here. I want to know why
you want Imperial magic."

Raaz didn't even bother to deny it. "Is this a jest? You
know what your Paragons can do—who wouldn't want
those secrets?"

"Not me, for one. And not a lot of other Mouths I know,
either." I pointed at the papers. "Do you know what this is?
It's death, long and slow—just to have it, just to know about
it. It's the one secret the empire never gives out, the one
thing no one besides the emperor and his magicians have
ever been able to do. Imperial Paragons have turned men's
bones to iron and heated that iron until it burned through
their flesh, just for asking questions about it. But to have
these? To have notes about how it's done, how it was discovered?" I frowned. I had no doubts about what was in
that package—not after having had Jelem go through the
ancient Paragon's journal for me four months ago; not after
letting him keep some of the notes in payment for his work.
And definitely not after Raaz having had all but confirmed
they were smuggling Imperial glimmer just now. "No," I
said. "I know plenty of people who'd want nothing to do

with that package, either to hold it or to study what was inside. Too damn dangerous."

"Then why didn't you destroy it when you figured out what it is?" said Raaz.

It was a good question, and one I'd been trying to answer myself. The easiest solution would be the fire . . . and yet I hadn't been able to bring myself to do it.

"Three reasons," I said. "First, because I gave my word that I'd deliver it. I don't like breaking promises, not even when I've been tricked into them. But I will if I have to."

"And what would make you do that?"

"The second reason." I tapped the paper. "This isn't Jelem's first shipment—can't be. Jelem's had months to send portions of this down, and I can't believe he'd wait until I suddenly had to come down here to start. That means that, even if I destroyed this, I wouldn't be accomplishing anything. The damage has already been done—sooner or later, the empire is going to find out that one of their best-kept secrets is making the rounds and they'll come looking, even if it means coming to Djan. And that means they'll trace it back to me."

"Let them. This is el-Qaddice. Their magi will not be able to enter."

"Do you really think walls and laws are going to stop them when it comes to this? This is the foundation of the fucking Dorminikan Empire—they'll tear el-Qaddice apart down to the bedrock if they get wind of what you've been smuggling down here."

"And your third concern?"

"I'm an Imperial," I said. "I may not have much use for the emperor, but that doesn't mean I want the empire falling to Djan. And the idea of giving you the key to one of the secrets that have been keeping you from our door for centuries?" I shook my head. "Collapsing empires are bad for business."

Raaz rapped his fingers on the stone tiles. "Good arguments. And I can understand your concern. But what if I was able to reassure you that what you say won't come to pass? Would that be enough?"

"It'd be a start."

"Very well, then." Raaz sat up straighter and held his left arm above the floor, pulling the sleeve back to reveal his iron magician's manacle. Its edges were rolled and etched to suggest billowing clouds—or maybe, more appropriately, shadows. With one deft motion, he reached out with his free hand, twisted a hidden hasp, and spoke a single syllable. The supposedly permanent and unremovable symbol of a yazani's duty to the despot opened and fell to the floor with a soft *clink*.

I blinked, trying to understand what I was seeing.

"In this," said Raaz, "I do not work for the despot. It is a personal matter—a *tal* and a tribal matter. Jelem was exiled for . . . let's say 'politics,' although that's not quite right. It's not for me to talk about. But the point is, there are those who think it was ill done, and wish to correct the matter. The Imperial magic you bear can help with that correction.

"The secrets Jelem possesses are nowhere near powerful enough to bring down your empire, or to draw their attention: You know this, since you were the one who portioned it out to him. But." He raised a finger. "It's powerful enough for his friends to seek vengeance in his name, and perhaps even secure his return to Djan. Believe me when I say, I have no wish to see what you carry fall into the hands of another *tal*, or even the despot—I merely want the chance to turn the bones of *my* enemies to iron and watch them burn."

In point of fact, I didn't know this—not for certain. When I'd made my original deal with Jelem, there hadn't been another Mouth on hand to consult when it came to the notes and the glimmer. All I'd had to go on was what I was able to parse out on my own, both from the papers and Jelem's reactions to my terms, and a healthy helping of bravado. To hear Raaz say what I'd passed along wasn't going to bring down the empire, or even a corner of it, was frankly a relief. But that didn't mean I had be excited about passing those secrets on to a group of *yazani* whose only character reference came from the man who'd tricked me into smuggling the magic into Djan in the first place.

Not the best testimonial, but Angels knew I'd heard worse over the years. Hell, I was worse. And it wasn't as if I was going to get any better offers. Besides, I didn't want to keep the package on me indefinitely—that could only lead to bigger risks and worse outcomes.

Still, nothing said I had to just hand it over.

"All right," I said, "I can work with that. But like I told you when I first sat down, I'm going to need something more. The price has still gone up."

Raaz ran his gloved hand over his chin. The fingers seemed fuller again. "What did you have in mind?"

"I'm not sure yet," I said as I finally slid the papers over to him. "But I figure I'll come up with something."

"I'm certain you will," said Raaz as he snatched up the packet. He began to turn it over in his hands, and then froze. "The seal on this has been broken."

"Has it?" I said. I leaned forward. "Huh. So it has."

His fingers flipped the folds back. He began to leaf through the letters. I'd looked at them earlier and hadn't been able to find a damn thing besides tedious accounts of Jelem's daily routine in Ildrecca. My guess was either some kind of code or, more likely, a hidden magical script.

I stood up and brushed at my pants while Raaz shuffled the papers, turned them over, and shuffled them some more. He glared up at me.

"Only half of the pages are here," he said.

"You got all that from that quick read through? I'm impressed."

"I know because Jelem wrote to tell me what to expect. This isn't it—or, not all of it." He waved the papers at me. "Where are the rest?"

"Safe," I said, as I resisted the urge to run my hand along my doublet's seam. "And they'll stay that way until I get the rest of my payment."

"That wasn't our deal."

"Our deal said nothing about how many pages you get, or when. And I'm not stupid. I know that if I still have what you want, you'll be quick to answer when I call. But if you already had all of Jelem's papers?" I shook my head. "No, when I need people, I tend to need them in a hurry. This way works best for me."

"And what about what works best for us?" said Raaz, standing up. "What if something happens to you before we get the rest?"

"That doesn't sound like my problem," I said as I turned away. "It sounds like yours. I suggest you think about ways to keep it from happening, yes?"

I gathered up Fowler with a look and headed for the exit, pausing long enough to direct a nod toward the vestibule of the Banished god as I went. Somehow, it seemed appropriate.

Chapter Nineteen

I woke up to a pounding, startled that I'd been asleep. Last I'd remembered, I'd sat down on the edge of my bed to unlace my shoes. They were still on.

The pounding continued.

"What?" I yelled.

"M-m-master Drothe?" said a voice halfway between boy and man—one of the hosteler's sons. At a guess, I'd say the one with the pimples—his voice had the right crack to it. "The l-lady left instructions to wake you when, that is . . ."

"Spit it out, boy."

"That you, um, should get up and, uh, keep your appointment. Sir. With the secretary?"

Shit.

I looked up at my room's small window. It was well on into dusk—likely past the time I was supposed to have called on Heron. I'd slept maybe all of four hours in the last thirty, I guessed.

"Why didn't you wake me sooner?" I shouted as I stood up. I couldn't believe Fowler would have let things run this tight.

"I tried, sir, only you wouldn't answer. And the lady was, um, very clear about why I shouldn't enter your room."

Judging by the tremor in the lad's voice, I could guess just how clear Fowler had been. Not that I'd set up any surprises for visitors, but a little healthy hesitation on their part of the help never hurt.

"And where's the lady herself?" I said, drawing on my slops. "Why didn't she wake me?"

"She's abed, sir." Pause. "She was also very specific about why I shouldn't wake her, either."

I'd just bet she was. Fowler hadn't been in much better shape than me by the time we got back from the temple.

"Have a mug ready for me downstairs," I said, slipping my last remaining *ahrami* into my mouth. "I'll take it on the way out."

I lingered in my room just long enough to put on a less-dirty shirt, pour some water into a basin, and splash it over my face and through my hair, and then ducked out the door. The local public baths would have to wait until later.

The common room was filling up as I came down the stairs—not only with the actors, but also some of the local inhabitants of the Quarter. Having people in from Ildrecca was a draw for the Angel's Shadow, and Tobin and company were making the most of their celebrity status through stories, songs, and as many free drinks as they could scare up. The locals were happy to barter liquor for gossip of home, and I noticed the hosteler didn't frown nearly so much as the day we'd arrived.

Tobin caught my eye as I came down the stairs and began to rise. I scowled and shook my head. I didn't have time for complaints cloaked in bluster just now. The troupe master scowled right back, stood, and began pushing his way across the room.

I reached the door first. A boy—the one with the pimples, ha—met me there, eyes wide, a steaming mug in his hand. I took it from him and kept going.

Behind me, I heard Tobin boom out my name. I kept going.

Ezak was still out in the courtyard, working through a combat exchange with another actor named Paollus in the dying light. Neither looked up as I came out into the yard.

That should have been my first clue.

The tip of Ezak's staff caught the front of my left ankle as I passed. He didn't strike or sweep so much as push my foot back, using the tip of his weapon to lift my leg up and behind me. Before I knew it, I was down in the dirt of the yard.

I rolled over, a curse forming on my lips, my hand already going for a blade, when I felt Ezak's staff tap me on the chest.

"Don't be hasty," he said. "No harm done."

"Hasty?" I said, pushing the length of ash aside and sitting up. "The last damn thing on my mind right now is—" I stopped when the butt of the staff appeared in the air before my face.

"No need," repeated Ezak, "to be hasty. Tobin just wants a word with you. Has since earlier today."

"Tobin can wait until I get back."

"That's where you're wrong," said Tobin as he came across the yard. "It can't wait, especially not if you're off to where I think you are."

"And where might that be?" I said.

"To see the man who controls our collective purse strings."

I sighed. "Heron." I stood up. Ezak didn't stop me, but he didn't lower the staff, either. "Fine," I said, brushing myself off. "What's so urgent that you need to knock me down in the damn yard?"

"The play," said Tobin, his voice heavy with meaning.

"What about it?"

"It's unworkable," said Ezak.

"Unworkable?" said Tobin. "Were that only the case! It's a disaster. The dialogue is wooden, the characters anemic, the story half a pace removed from a funerary march. Any company in its right might would either walk away from a monstrosity like this or rewrite it."

"So you don't like it?" I said.

"Don't . . . ?" Tobin's color rose faster than his drama. "We . . . I . . ."

"No," said Ezak. "We don't like it."

"And you want me to do what about that, exactly?"

"Petition Heron!" cried Tobin. "Tell him the state of things. That we can't perform the work. That it's not to our style." The master stepped in closer. "We're a tragedy and

comedy company, you see. Highs and lows. This is more . . .
I don't know what to call it. Ezak?"

"Atrocious?"

"Besides that."

"Mmm. Historical?"

"That's it: It's more of a historical. Well, more a commen-
tary, if truth be told. On the Despotate, of all things. Lines
and lines and lines of explanations, of exposition, of *excla-
mations* about the nature of some ancient despot and politics and—"

"It goes on," said Ezak.

"Precisely." Tobin glanced about and waved me closer.
When I didn't move, he bent his head and leaned in. The
picture of a conspirator. "Now, I was thinking," he said. "If
you were to tell Heron that it doesn't work for us—don't
mention anything I've said here: For all we know, the hack
who penned this may be a state treasure, Angels help us—
rather, say we're afraid we won't get the proper feel for the
piece since we're not Djanese. That we won't do it justice.
Or maybe that—"

I folded my arms. "You were there when he handed it
over," I said. "You heard what he said. The wazir picked the
play out himself. Do you honestly think they're going to
give a damn whether it fits your 'style'?"

Tobin straightened. "I would hope that he'd respect a
troupe's desire to present its best face before the padishah."

"He's going to understand that you're bitching and complaining and trying to get things your own way. And, if I'm
lucky, he's going to tell me to go to hell. If I'm not so lucky,
he may simply tell us to get out."

"I don't—"

"Listen," I said. "I know we're being dealt shit, all right?
And I know you aren't happy about it. I'm on my way to see
Heron right now, and the way I see it, I can do one of two
things: I can either ask for more time or ask for another
play. Considering we only have a handful of days before
we're supposed to perform, I can't think that asking for a
completely new work—one which might even be worse, or
take days to get, or both—is the better dodge."

Tobin's displeasure was truly epic in its scope. I could see why this man was on the stage. "So you're saying you won't even try?"

"I'm saying I'll get what I can, but I'm not about to ask for what I can't get."

Tobin fumed and scowled and looked ready to argue some more, when Ezak stepped neatly between us. I couldn't help noticing the move put the staff in front of Tobin's face.

"Then we'll take what we can get," said Ezak, looking directly at his cousin. "And be grateful for it."

Tobin grumbled a moment more, then turned and stomped back to the inn. Ezak faced me.

"Apologies for the trip," he said, "but Tobin was going to be impossible until he spoke with you."

I nodded. "I understand."

"Good." He looked over his shoulder at the remaining actor with the staff. "Well, I suppose I —"

"Ezak?"

"Yes?"

"My saying 'I understand' doesn't mean it's forgiven. You know that, right?"

"I —"

I held up a finger. "You get one. That was it. Try to lay wood—or anything else—on me again, and it won't be my understanding you'll be wanting at the end of the encounter. Understand?"

Ezak's mouth compressed into a thin, tight line. "I understand."

"Good. Make sure your cousin does as well. You know the arrangement: I may be your patron, but I have other business in el-Qaddice—business that's more pressing than your play. Trust me when I say you don't want your interests to get in the way of mine."

"I'll not forget."

I turned and left him standing there in the deepening dusk. As I made my way out in the Quarter, I heard the solid *thok!* of wood striking wood. It sounded harder and faster than before.

                            *   *   *

Once I got beyond the Quarter's gates, I quickly realized
that while I'd paid attention to the route coming down from
the padishah's estate, navigating in reverse in a town you
don't know, on little sleep, while periodically being looked
over—or outright stopped—to be sure you had a patronage
token, can be a different thing entirely. Fifteen minutes and
three false turns into my trek, I gave in and slipped a pair of
copper *supps* to a street urchin of maybe fourteen who
looked to be on the verge of graduating to thug.

The day's crowds had all but vanished, but I knew that the
souks and gardens and wine shops would fill up again once
the full heat of the day had left the streets. Most Djanese
were at their coffee or baths now, relaxing and gathering
themselves for the city's second wind. With the stars would
come late dinners, and even later meetings and assignations.
El-Qaddice was a city that ran—at least partly—on my time,
a trait I found both pleasing and frustrating at once.

Our path was a bit roundabout, especially since I refused
to follow the "shortcuts" the urchin kept suggesting. While
they might've gotten me where I wanted to go, they could
just as easily have ended up with me clubbed, stripped, and
abandoned in some backstreet grotto. Urchins in Ildrecca
weren't above making arrangement with various gangs
from time to time, and I doubted it was any different here.
Regardless of his motivations, my guide stopped urging de-
tours after my fourth refusal.

Still, even with the wider way and the empty streets, I
couldn't help but notice that I was gathering more dark
looks than usual. I asked the urchin about it.

"You're imperial," he said simply.

"Your people hate us that much?" I said.

"Hate?" he said, looking back at me. "It's not about hate,
it's about greed." He pointed at me. "If you weren't wearing
that, you'd be a healthy profit for anyone who managed to
bring you in or send the city guard after you."

I glanced down and realized that, rather than pointing to
my sword or knife, he was indicating the brass lozenge
hanging about my neck—the wazir's token of patronage.

"They watch for it that closely?" I said. I'd expected to be stopped at gates between the city's rings and have the occasional merchant or local Rag demand to see it just to because he could—but to have Lighters on the street looking for it? "How much is the reward for finding someone like me without a token?"

The urchin smiled. "Were you to not have one and I to lead the green jackets to your side, I could live like a prince for a month and more."

I reached up and ran a careful hand over the token, giving the chain a tug just to be sure. The urchin smiled wider and led on.

By the time we arrived outside the padishah's grounds, full night had fallen, but you couldn't tell it for all the lanterns and torches before us. Large, enameled wrought-iron gates spanned a gap wider than the whole of the Angel's Shadow—including the stables—flanked on either side by spindle-thin towers covered in elaborate carvings. An expanse of colorful glazed bricks extended into the space before the gate, forming a massive half circle on the ground, the colors of the bricks blending to depict a giant phoenix, the symbol of the padishah's household. Guards resplendent in silk arming coats and tall-plumed turbans patrolled the towers and gate, the torchlight glinting equally off their acid-etched spear heads and the jewels in their turban pins.

I dismissed the urchin with another coin and walked up to the gate. A bored-looking guard captain—or, at least I assumed he was a captain, given the cloth of silver sash around his waist and thumb-sized opal in his turban pin— wandered over and regarded me from behind a colorful iron hummingbird.

"I'm here to see Secretary Heron."

"Poet?" he said, glancing at the medallion on the matching bronze chain.

"Acting troupe."

He motioned over his shoulder with his chin. "Nonpoets shielded by the wazir have to use the Dog Gate on the west side of the estate."

We, of course, were standing on the east side of the estate.

He began to turn away.

"What if I said I was also a poet?" I said.

He turned back, a resigned look on his face. "Then I'd ask you to compose something on the spot to prove it." He looked up at the gate. "Something depicted on this, probably. Something complicated."

"And if my poem didn't meet your standards?"

"We scrub the blood off the bricks every morning."

It took me another half an hour to wend my way to the Dog Gate. I discovered it was named so on account of the padishah's kennels being located next to it; that, and because the kennel masters made a habit of throwing scraps over the wall, meaning the small, irregular square before the gate was filled with packs of street hounds, not to mention their droppings.

The guard here was more officious than those at the main gate, which made no sense. Then again, when a person's in charge of watching over dogs and their shit, I suppose one clings to whatever dignity one can.

"You're late," he said, staring down his nose at me. "I was told to expect you at dusk."

"I like to think of this time of night as dusk simply wearing a darker cloak, don't you?"

Not even the hint of a grin. Fine. I could play that way, too.

"Look," I said, shaking my right boot in an attempt to get a particularly stubborn piece of dog shit off it, "Heron wants to see me, all right? He told me to come. Explicitly. Now, if you want to be the one who tells him you turned me awa—"

"The noble secretary already sent word; you're not to be admitted."

I stopped working on my shoe. "Has he, now?"

Now the guard decided to grin. "He doesn't tolerate tardiness. Or," he said, looking down at my shoes, "poor hygiene."

I considered the guard, the gate, the height of the wall. It could be done: He was close enough for me to be able to reach through the bars, grab hold, and introduce him to my dagger. Then it would be up and over the bars. This near the kennels, any noise probably wouldn't even be remarked on. From there, I could stick to the shadows, grab a servant, and put the blade to him to locate Heron's ken.

Except I knew better. Tempting as it might be to my fatigue-edged temper to take out my frustrations on Heron and the guard, breaking into the padishah's estate, let alone dusting one of his men, wouldn't do anything other than make my life in Djan harder.

But, damn, it would feel good.

I shook my head. Angels, did I need some sleep.

"Fine," I said. "Just give me whatever he sent along and I'll fade." Late or not, I couldn't see Heron leaving us short on our account at the inn: As he had said, it was the wazir's responsibility to watch over us while we wore his tokens. Besides, he'd said he would send along some *ahrami*.

The guard frowned and shifted his feet slightly. "You come late and expect the secretary to send gifts?" He took a firmer hold on his spear. "Get out of here."

I wrapped one hand around the plain ironwork of the Dog Gate and made a show of scraping my shoe off on one of the lower bars. The guard's scowl deepened.

"My apologies to the secretary for my tardiness, then," I said. "Let him know I'll do my best to be on time tomorrow."

"I'm not your messenger," said the guard. "I'll be damned if I—"

This time my hand did reach out and grab him, pulling him close enough for my dagger to find his side—but not to enter it.

I leaned in close, the tip of my blade pushing the cotton of his uniform coat—no silk for the Dog Gate guard, I noted—into his ribs. I could smell fresh *ahrami*—*my ahrami*—on his breath. "You're whatever the fuck I say you are," I said through the bars. "Now, where's the package Heron sent along with his message for me?"

"Package?" he said, a bit too quickly. "I told you—"

"Let me explain how this works," I said. "Either you give me what's mine or I call for your captain. Your captain goes through your things. He finds the money and whatever else Heron sent. Maybe he believes you, maybe he believes me; I don't really care. Because, either way, when someone finally gets around to dragging the secretary down here—and they will, since I'll scream my damn head off and invoke the wazir's patronage until they do—you won't have to worry about me anymore; you'll have the secretary to answer to." I pushed the dagger a bit harder. "How's that sound?"

I watched as the color fled his face in the lamplight.

"I thought so," I said. I yanked on his coat once, forcing his forehead into the bars. The iron clanged dully, and the guard grunted. "Now get me what Heron sent." I looked down at my boots. "And give me your sash while you're at it—I've been told I need to take better care of my 'personal hygiene.'"

Chapter Twenty

I left the Dog Gate as the night was beginning to pick up in the Old City. Lanterns flared, torches burned, and Djanese Mouths juggled tiny rainbows and offered to sell charms to the crowds to light their way.

The displays played hell on my night vision, and I found myself drifting toward the back streets despite the greater risk. That helped a bit, but even here lights burned and revelers shouted, neither of which did much good for the budding ache at the back of my head. Part of the sensitivity, I knew, was simple fatigue; but just as much was coming from the charge the *ahrami* was giving me.

As I'd hoped, Heron had not only left our daily stipend with the guard; he'd also included a down payment on the *ahrami* he'd promised me. A letter had chastised me—mildly—for missing the appointment, but I got the impression that Heron had half expected me to get lost, or distracted, or the like. Our next meeting, he'd written, would be in two days' time, and this one I was expected to make.

As for the requested extension of the performance date, there was no mention. I chose to read the silence as a ploy to keep me hungry, rather than him avoiding bad news. Either way, though, it meant we'd have to operate on the old timetable until we heard otherwise.

Tobin wouldn't like that. Tough shit: Neither did I.

I slipped two more *ahrami* into my mouth, bringing the total up to six—or was it seven?—since I'd left the padishah's gate. I could feel my pulse surging at my temple now. Soon enough, the flush of those latest seeds would pass, and that thrumming would become a steady beat of pain.

What I needed, I knew, was sleep: What I was going to get, though, was another night full of seeds and coffee and questions. Rest would come in the morning, when both the back alleys and my night vision went to bed.

I paused on a few street corners, stopped to watch a handler and his trained fox perform, lost a handful of *supps* at a street-side mags table, and even managed to find a snake-baiting ring, but all the while, I kept working my way back toward the Imperial Quarter. It's not that I didn't want to work the street: I did. It drove me nearly to distraction to have to stick to the streets and alleys, rather than jump to the roofs or dive myself down into the connected cellars and hidden ways that ran through every city, but I was still too fresh to the Old City to slip those paths yet. Without a guide, or a name to use as my passport, the odds of me stumbling across trouble rather than answers was high. And while I might welcome the opportunities even the occasional bit of bluff and blood could lead to, I wasn't about to pursue them with Heron's ready, not to mention my stash of *ahrami*, still on me for the plucking.

I slipped back into the Imperial Quarter with a nod and a pair of small bribes for the guards at the gate—one for the Djanese patrol on the outside, and another for their imperial counterparts standing just within the sally port. I made a mental note to see if the same swads were on duty every night. If so, it would likely be cheaper to pay them for a week at a time, rather than on a nightly basis, to forget my comings and goings.

Unlike portions of el-Qaddice, the Imperial Quarter was dark and quiet. Oh, taverns still spilled light out into the darkness and late-night hawkers chanted out wares—and offers—from street corners, but the level of activity didn't compare. Just as the walls separated Imperial from Djanese, so did they lock out the differing schedules. Both peoples might share the same sky, but it was clear that, at least in the empire's case, we weren't about to bow down to it. Here in the Quarter, food and clothing and weather aside, the empire still held sway.

Or so we wanted to think. Me, I knew better, as did the two Cutters who stepped out in front of me five blocks from the Angel's Shadow.

I stopped. They smiled. They were the same coves that Fat Chair had sent to escort me to his sedan chair.

Well, shit.

It was a good place for an ambush: We were on a narrow street, well past one curve and not quite to another, meaning no one would be able to see us from farther along the way. The walls were blank on either side, with the only opening being a gated archway several feet past my ambushers. I looked over my shoulder; sure enough, there was two more figures back there, too. And I could guarantee we were outside whatever perimeter Fowler had managed to set up.

I looked back and forth, judging distances, and checked the walls again: tall, with smooth tops shining in the moonlight. That was good, in that it meant they likely didn't have broken shards of glass and pottery cemented atop them to keep people like me out, but bad in that the walls were too tall and smooth for me to do anything with. Maybe if I had some rope and a crawler's crown, but a grapnel wasn't something I'd planned on needing tonight.

Metal hissed as steel cleared leather. I turned back the way I'd been going to see the native tough holding a short, straight Djanese duelist's sword in one hand and a brass buckler in the other. The imperial Cutter beside him had a slightly longer, thinner blade. Behind me, I'd already seen a brace of small axes and a short, ball-headed mace and knife.

None were rapiers by any means, which gave me the advantage of reach, but considering the circumstances, that didn't count for much.

I cleared my sword and drew my boot knife, making sure the moonlight slid along their lengths as I did so. Where the hell was Degan, or even Wolf, for that matter, when I needed them?

"We have a message for you," said the man with the sword and buckler.

"I don't suppose it's in the form of a folded piece of paper, is it?" I said.

The man didn't even blink.

"You were warned," said the *Zakur*. "You ignored my lord's warning, refused to hand over the magic you brought into el-Qaddice, and continue to intrude on his business. You insult him with your very presence."

"If I'd known it was that easy to insult your boss, I'd have done it sooner."

The Cutter struck his buckler with the flat of his blade, sending a flat *clang* echoing up and down the street. "Now you'll learn what it means to cross the *Zakur*-Mulaad!" he snapped. He leaned forward and extended both arms forward, laying the buckler over the sword guard so they could function as one entity. He looked very comfortable doing it.

I didn't wait for the others to come on guard; didn't wait for any commands to be given; didn't wait for him to start moving forward. I simply turned and ran at the two Cutters behind me.

It stood to reason that the man delivering the message was the best hitter in the crew. That's how Cutters tend to work, and, more important, how most bosses tend to think: Give the toughest muscle the orders and let him keep the rest in line. If you needed something more complex, you sent someone besides a Cutter—say an Arm, or maybe a Bender.

So, Sword and Buckler was in charge. That meant there was no way in hell I was going to face him in a fair—or even an unfair—fight if I could help it.

The two Cutters in back didn't seem overly surprised that I'd chosen to close with them. They did, however, widen their eyes when I threw my boot knife from a handful of paces away.

I aimed at the one with the axes—specifically, at his head. I didn't expect the knife to land, didn't even throw it well enough to have much of a chance of hitting. All I wanted was for them to see a threat in the moonlight and react. They did.

Axes stepped back and pivoted, moving to let the knife

slip by, while his partner dropped down low. Unfortunately for Axes, his movement also caused him to lower his weapons in an attempt to lessen his profile. That left the opening I'd been hoping for.

I lunged toward Axes' middle with my rapier, then quickly redirected the blade in midmotion as the Cutter with the mace tried to take advantage of my attack and come in on my exposed side.

My rapier's tip slashed across Mace's shoulder and upper chest before his momentum drove the blade into the notch below his neck. There was a brief moment of resistance before cartilage gave way to my steel; then I was pulling my blade out and away, opening the side of his neck as I frantically backed away from the ax that was coming at my head.

The man with the axes was faster than I'd expected. The first blade passed so close to my face I suspect I could have seen my reflection in it if it had been daylight out. As for the second, it followed quickly after, arcing down and in from my left.

I raised my sword, but knew it wouldn't be enough: My guard was weak, my blade pointed the wrong way. Without thinking, I brought my empty left hand up. If I was lucky, I'd only lose a couple of fingers while trying to stop the ax; I wasn't feeling particularly lucky.

Then the ax jerked to a stop in midswing.

The man's expression went from elation to confusion in an instant. It was followed almost immediately by a look of pain as his arm jerked back and blood blossomed along his side in one, two, three spots.

He howled. The ax fell.

It was then that I noticed the the blotch of shadow running around his elbow, almost as if someone I couldn't see had wrapped her arm around the joint and pulled Axes off-balance so she could stab him at leisure.

I would advise you to not rest too easily, she had said in the cellar. *You are marked.*

Shit. *Neyajin.*

I leapt back as Axes' body fell away from me, my eyes

searching the street for hints of blurred, oily motion. Back
the way I had come, I could see the lead *Zakur* already
down on his knees, sword arm hanging useless at his side,
the buckler covered in blood as he held it over the gash in
his chest. His partner was halfway up the opposite wall, legs
kicking, hands grabbing at the rope that led from his neck
to the roof above. I couldn't see anyone at the other end of
the line, but that didn't stop the man from ascending the
wall, one short jerk at a time.

Not just one assassin, then. Wonderful. And here I stood,
marked—whatever the hell that meant.

I put my sword before me, paused, then spun, figuring
the best place to find an assassin is behind you. They must
have known that trick, too, because as soon as I turned, a
bag was dropped over my head from what had just been my
front.

I swung my rapier across my body, bringing it around so
the point faced behind me on my left side, and thrust. All it
found was air. I immediately pivoted to my right and swung
the elbow of my sword arm back. That met meaty resistance. I smiled as I heard a *whuff!* of surprise near my ear.

Then a steel edge found my throat, and I froze.

"I told you you were marked, *jeffer ani,*" hissed a familiar woman's voice, only slightly ragged from her encounter
with my elbow. "Drop your steel."

I opened my hand and let my sword clatter to the street.

The blade at my neck went away, and was replaced a
moment later by something hard to the back of my head. I
staggered, found the ground, and stayed there. I wasn't
about to push matters. I just hoped I didn't throw up with
the bag still over my head.

"Bind him and bring him," said a man's voice from somewhere above me. It was reedy, but also used to giving commands.

I couldn't have resisted if I wanted to; things were fuzz-
ing in and out around me. The next thing I remembered was
finding my wrists and ankles bound, and having the distinct
sensation of being carried. It felt like a short distance, but
there were enough lights flickering in my head that I

couldn't be sure whether time and I were still on speaking terms.

After a bit, the sounds became closer, telling me we were inside. A door closed. Then I was set down on the floor. Hands ran over me, drawing steel, unbuckling my sword belt, checking the pouch about my neck. I held still as I felt fingers cross over the portion of my doublet where I'd stitched Jelem's packet into the padding, but they moved on without pause. The bag smelled like apples.

My bonds were cut.

I waited for the lights in my head to fade, then reached up and pulled off the bag.

The room was dark and empty of furnishings: just me in the center and my weapons piled up in the corner. And Angels knew how many assassins I couldn't see with my night vision.

I sat up slowly and rubbed at the back of my head. My hand came away dry, which was something. I took a couple of deep breaths, let them out, looked around room again. There—the sliver of an outline of someone's foot, and there—what looked like the faint curve of . . . a scabbard? A bent leg? Hard to tell.

I looked from the foot to the scabbard and back again. Then I threw the empty bag at the foot.

A slippery flash of action, a hint of blurred amber to my eyes, and the foot was gone. More important, the bag changed direction in midair: blocked, or cut down. Either way, it told me what to expect.

I looked back over at my steel. Yes, definitely bait.

I rested my hands on my thighs.

"I'm not stupid," I said.

"I can see that," said the man's thin voice. He was behind me, where I hadn't seen anything but blank wall, where I still couldn't see anything but a blank wall when I turned. "But it's best to be certain."

"You can be certain I'm not going to go for the blades."

"I can see that, too."

Silence.

"Well?" I said. And they came at me.

Not all at once, but in quick succession. Blurs of amber, hints of motion—hands, feet, elbows, knees. I tumbled and stumbled and blocked and voided, flinching away from every movement I saw, real or imagined. Duck a hand here, avoid a body there, fall back from a sweep more by luck than planning, throw in a punch or two for good measure. One even connected, albeit fleetingly. The grunt of surprise was a reward all its own.

Through it all, I was pushing myself, pushing my night vision to *see*. It couldn't just be the motion that helped me make them out: I'd seen the foot before all this had started, had caught sight of the scabbard, or whatever the hell it was, in the stillness. There had to be some way to single them out, to pull them away from the midnight they were wearing. Didn't there?

I was still straining my eyes when a foot caught me square in the chest. For the briefest instant—the moment between when the kick landed and my body reacted—I saw the shape of the *neyajin*, leg out, body back, arm thrust toward the floor to add power to the kick. Then she disappeared, and I was falling back. I hit the floor hard, not so much rolling with the blow as crumpling from it.

"Jeffer ani," she said in the darkness, her voice cold with judgment.

"Aribah . . . ," said the man, naming my attacker. His voice was equal parts warning and exasperation.

The girl sniffed, not even trying to hide the sound of her steps as she walked away from me.

So, a test. But for me, or for them?

I took a ragged breath. Either way, I didn't know how much more I could take, but I knew how much more I was willing to accept.

I sat up and rested my hands on my knees.

"Enough," I said, forcing myself to relax, to not search out the next attack. "I'm not going to dance in the darkness for your entertainment. If you want to knock the hell out of me, have at, but I refuse to be your moving practice target."

"If this were a 'dance,' Imperial, you'd be laid out on the floor by now," said the man, off to my right now, moving around me. "I just wanted to confirm what I'd been told about you."

"And that is?"

Silence in the darkness. Then, "Light the lantern."

I closed my eyes and ducked my head. A moment later flint struck steel, lighting tinder. Shortly after that, I caught the flicker of flame through my eyelids. I opened my eyes slowly, letting the candle light work its way past my night vision until the burning ceased.

There were three of them. It had felt like more in the dark. They stood, waiting, in a tight triangle before me.

For some reason, I'd been expecting the *neyajin* to be wearing black, but instead they were covered in a deep, almost shimmering indigo. Two wore kaffiyehs, while the third—the woman, judging by the lines of her clothing—favored a tightly wrapped turban. All had the lower parts of their faces covered by the ends of their head cloths. Their feet and hands were bare, yet had the same deep, midnight purple tint as their clothing. Dye, or something else, I wondered?

The figure directly before me crouched down on his haunches. His robes were both finer and more worn that the others', and covered over by a loose outerrobe of the same material.

He reached up and pulled the tail of his kaffiyeh away, revealing an untinted mouth and jaw. Coarse white stubble covered his chin, and when he smiled, I was put in mind of a jackal baring his teeth. Shaggy white eyebrows—temporarily tinted blue—hung down over a pair of dark, red-rimmed eyes.

"I wanted to know whether or not you had the dark sight, of course," he said, his voice just as thin and raspy as it had been in the street. "And whether we could steal it from you."

Chapter Twenty-one

"Steal it?" I said, rearing back despite myself. The two *neyajin* behind the old man shifted their feet; the man himself merely widened his hunter's grin.

"Ah," he said. "So you *do* have something worth stealing, then. Good to know."

Son of a . . .

"Not that you need to worry," said the old assassin, waving a hand. "Were you Favored, or even just Djanese, I'd know where we stood, and so where to begin. For that matter, I'd know how to end this, too. But you being an Imperial?" He shook his head. "I'm not sure how this will play out."

"It's as I told you, Grandfather," said Aribah. Here, in the light, her voice was as relentless as her gaze. "Like the Lions, but not of them."

"Be silent, child," he said, not turning to look at her. "You're here on sufferance. Let the adults speak."

I looked up at her. Given what I'd seen in the tunnel — the way she moved, the way she handled a herself — and the timbre of her voice, not to mention the curves I was starting to notice beneath her robes, I had a hard time thinking of her as a "child." So, apparently, did she, if the sudden rigidity of her back was any indication. Still, she turned her eyes away after a moment and fell silent.

The elder assassin sighed and shifted his weight back onto his heels. "Still, despite her poor manners, my granddaughter is right: You have the dark sight, or something like it. I didn't think such a thing was possible outside the despot's court, but . . ." He gestured at the room around us, at the scuffs and scrapes our fight had left in the dirt floor. "I don't suppose you'd happen to be a sorcerer, would you? That would make things much easier."

"No, sorry. Just a thief."

"Ah, well."

"Have you considered the possibility that maybe my 'dark vision' isn't what you think it is?" I said. "That maybe I'm just that good?"

A snort from behind Aribah's drape. I ignored her.

"Please," said the grandfather. "I didn't save you from Fat Chair's men so you could lie to me. I know the difference between training and the dark sight, and you, Imperial," he said, tapping two fingers just below his own eyes, "have the sight."

"And you don't. But you know how to hide from it." I looked up at the woman. "It has something to do with flickering lamps in wine vaults and winds no one feels, doesn't it?"

Although her eyes grew wide, it was the grandfather who answered.

"What *did* you see?" he said.

"Depends." I turned back to him. "What was I supposed to see?"

"Since it didn't work, does it matter?"

"It seems to me this whole meeting is happening because of what didn't work; so yes, I'd say it matters."

The old man held up his hand, had it filled by a water skin that the male *neyajin* handed him. "Faysal," said the elder, "make sure we aren't disturbed."

The man bowed and left the room. Aribah and the old assassin stayed.

The old man drew the cork from the skin and took a brief pull, then held it out to me. "Drink?"

I wanted to refuse, but my thirst wouldn't let me. I took the skin and drank. The water almost burned going down, it felt so good.

I handed the skin back. The old man took another short pull, then replaced the cork.

"As far as I can tell," he said, "you were supposed to see nothing. Or almost nothing."

"What do you mean?"

A lift of one shoulder. "How can I describe what I've never seen? All we know is that the cantrip we recite helps dim both normal and dark sight, making our robes work that much better."

"Better?" I said. "Better how?"

He stared at me, then turned his head so that he could talk to Aribah without taking his eyes off me. "What think you, granddaughter: How do we answer his question?"

"I think the *neyajin* hold their secrets tight," she said—no, recited. "We walk in darkness by respecting the darkness; we possess the night by emulating the night."

"True," he said. "But I didn't ask what you've been taught; I asked what you *think*. If I wanted rules parroted back to me, I'd train a bird. Or ask Faysal."

A tense pause from his granddaughter, then, "He's Imperial. Beyond *neyajin*, beyond even Djanese. He's an outsider."

"But he has something we want, and he's not stupid. What, then?"

"We take it."

"And how do you take that which you can't touch and don't understand?"

No answer.

The old man's expression soured. "With something this rare, you don't turn to the blade or the foot, not unless you have to. Think, girl! Sometimes you have to give secrets to get them." He made a soft, *tsk*ing sound, added softly, "Your mother would have understood this without needing to be told."

I saw Aribah catch the comment, saw her eyes harden and her shoulders droop ever so slightly. An old complaint on his part—and an old wound on hers.

The old man might be a damn good assassin, I decided, but that didn't stop him from being a bastard of a grandfather.

"When we waken the power of our robes," he said, "we also dull the power of your dark sight."

I took another look at his and Aribah's drapes, as if I could somehow see the magic in them. Clothing that functioned as portable glimmer wasn't unknown—I've seen cloaks stiffen themselves against attacks and a scarf that could unravel and reknit itself into a fine rope—but drapes meant to work against night vision? That was beyond rare: That was fucking personal.

"How's that possible?" I said. "If you can't use the ... 'dark sight,' then how do you know how to foul it?"

"I don't know how a man lives and breathes and makes shit, but I know how to kill him; is it so different?"

"Yes."

The old man snorted. "Maybe you're right. But it's worked for us for generations, so who am I to argue, eh?"

"Generations," I said. "And in all that time, you've never gotten one of the ..." I waved a hand, pretending to have forgotten the name, pretending to be only mildly interested.

"Lions of Arat," said Aribah.

"One of the Lions of Arat? You've been skulking around for generations, and yet you've never managed to capture one and gotten them to tell you about the dark sight?"

"Captured? Of course. We've taken many."

"And none have talked?"

The old man looked away.

I slipped another seed into my mouth. "Tell me about them."

The old assassin regarded me for a long moment. "What do you know of the *neyajin*?" he said at last.

"I thought we were talking about the Lions."

"To speak of one, you must understand the other."

I shrugged. "Fine. I know that you're hard to see in the dark."

"And?"

"And you do a hell of a job on magi and their shadows."

The flicker of a smile on his face. "That bothered you?"

"It inconvenienced me. I had business with them. Also, one of my people got hurt."

"And you stabbed Aribah," he said. "What happened in the tunnel was business. We are both what we are."

"And what, exactly, are you?"

He pulled the cork and took a long draw on the water skin. "Long ago? We were demon hunters . . . djinn trackers. Under the Caliphates of Brass, and on into the reigns of the early despots, we were charged with bringing judgment to those magi who trafficked with darker spirits."

"'Judgment'?"

"Judgment. Death, yes, but other things as well. We brought the laws of heaven and man into the warrens of spirit and smoke. My tribe long ago learned how to write enchantments into the warp and weft of their robes. Magic couldn't see us, and because magic couldn't see us, neither could its servants."

"You mean the djinn," I said, remembering what Raaz had told me.

"I mean the spirits of the air and the sands and the heat and the night: the djinn and the ifrit and the angels of the barren places—"

"Angels?" I said, sitting up.

The assassin smiled and shook his head. "No, not the figments your people worship. I speak of the real thing: of the spirits who haunt the forgotten places, shredding the minds of men so they can use their empty husks to come back and wreak havoc among the living."

"You have different angels than we do."

"As I said, ours are real, and we hunted them and the sorcerers who brought them down from the skies and up from the earth. We are the *neyajin,* the scythe that harvested the djinn. Or at least we were, until they learned to make the bindings." He took another pull from the skin, then spit off into the shadows. "Just as the sorcerers had learned to bind the dark spirits, so the despot and his magi learned how to bind magicians."

"You mean those things on their wrists are real?" I said, thinking back to the iron shackle Raaz had shown me on the way to the disaster in the tunnel. "I thought they were just symbolic."

"They are now, mostly, but originally, the shackles were truly enchanted. The despot Inaya—"

"May her name be three times cursed, and three times again," said Aribah, clearly following some kind of formula.

"—and her High Magi—"

"Sons of three-legged dogs, all!"

"—set the *neyajin* the task of finding and binding the various sorcerers and magicians of the Despotate. And we did. It was neither easy nor pleasant, but as more magi were bound to the despot, she began to gather them into *tals*, or schools. Each received her patronage, but she never kept it constant—one year one school gained more favor; another year, a different *tal* saw its star rise. And always, as more magi took the bracelet, so they joined the *tals*."

"She used her favor to keep them off balance, to keep them plotting against one another rather than herself," I said. Oh, Christiana would have liked this despot, I could tell.

He nodded. "Yes. And, over time, as the *wajik tals* became established and the magi became used to turning to the despot for favor and advancement, the need for the shackles diminished. Shackles of iron and silver became shackles of promises and tradition—symbols that held the magi and their students stronger than any precious metals or spells. Shackles of honor."

"Honor the despots heaped upon the magi even as they stripped it from us," snapped Aribah. This didn't seem part of the recitation. "We, the *neyajin*, who had once counted our robes of merit by the roomful and been presented with turbans of the greatest size by the hands of the caliphs themselves, were reduced to prostrating ourselves for ribbons from ministers and minor chains of favor from secretaries."

Her grandfather glanced over his shoulder at her again, but this time there was a glint of pride in his eye.

"She speaks the truth," he said. "We who hunted djinn and and their summoners for the despots were cast aside. As the magi gained favor, they remembered the *neyajin* as the serpent remembers the hawk. We thought ourselves too valuable, grew too secure in our standing, but when—"

"You were kicked to the gutter," I said.

"We were hunted and driven into it," said the old man, glaring at the interruption.

I shifted my seat and grunted as circulation resumed in parts of it. Bits of me had begun to settle as the old assassin spoke, and I could feel my fatigue building like a wave on the horizon. *Ahrami* could only do so much, and between the darkness and the fight and the miles I'd covered in the last day and a half, I was starting to realize just how little I had left in me.

"Listen," I said, leaning forward onto my thighs. "I love history. Really. Especially this kind of thing. But I've had the shit knocked out of me today, and not just by you. So if you could get to the part about the Lions of Arrat and my night vision, I'd be grateful."

I watched as the old man glowered and the young woman seethed, and tried to get worked up about having pissed on the treasured tale of two assassins. I couldn't. Instead, I swallowed a yawn and rubbed my face.

"The Lions," said the old assassin, "are those who were sent to hunt the hunters. Guardsmen and agents of the despot, granted the powers and sight of the djinn so they might move through the night where we were blind. They tracked the *neyajin* for generations, using their newfound favor to hunt us down, first to break our tribes, then to scatter and slaughter our clan. When they finally stopped—when we finally became too few, and thus too much work, to track down—there was little more than a handful of families and households left to us.

"By then, we were so used to the shadows, we remained there, turning our hands to killing for hire. No more did we dream of swaggering down the streets or sitting on great councils: We knew where we were safe." He worked his jaw for a moment, chewing on his history and his anger. Then he looked up at me. "But you can change that."

"Me?" I said. "How? You're already nearly impossible to see in the dark. And you can blind-fight better than anyone I've ever heard of. Seeing is nice, sure, but—"

"Useless," snapped Aribah. "He's useless, Grandfather."

"He doesn't understand, is all."

"What's to understand? He can see, we can't."

"Yes, but he couldn't see you in the tunnel," growled the old man. "Think. What's he used to? How could we, who move unseen to his eye, be at a disadvantage? See as he would see it; think as he would think."

"I'm not—" I began.

The old man held up his hand without looking at me. "Please," he said. "Let the girl learn."

I bit back my annoyance but didn't push my luck.

"I think I see," said Aribah after a moment.

"Then explain it to the Imperial, so we can all understand."

Aribah turned dark eyes in my direction. "The Lions of Arat may not be able to see us," she said, "but we see even less. Not the uneven ground, not the overturned chair, not the pile of garbage lying in the middle of a pitch-black alley. They can see on a cloudy night in the darkest of rooms, while we're limited to starlight and the grace of the moon. We're only as good as the darkness allows us to be, while they . . ." She paused, sorting her words. "They are as good as their vision makes them."

The grandfather smiled at her and turned back to me. "When we were favored by the despot and hunting renegades, our tricks and minor magics were enough. But with the magi and their pets organized and under the protection of the Despotate? On our best days, we manage a stalemate; on the rest, we try to not cross paths with the Lions. But if we could see as the *ak'ker jinnim* see?" He smiled: It was a cold, ruthless thing. "Then we could remind the High Magi why they feared us so long ago, could stir the heart—or at least the bowels—of the despot once more. If the *neyajin* possessed the dark sight, our path toward redemption and the revival of our tribe would be that much clearer before us."

I looked back and forth between them—between the murderous gleam in his eyes and the stern, judging look in hers—and weighed my options. None of them were good. There was no way in hell I was going to fight my way out of here, and there was no way in hell I was going to be able to do what they wanted. I considered lying, but there wasn't any angle I could think of that would get me out the door, or at least not in one piece. I was the answer to a prayer they hadn't even known they could ask. But now that they'd found me?

No, reassuring—and habitual—as lying might be when it came to the subject of my night vision, I knew the only thing that was going to get me out of here in one piece was the truth. I didn't much care for the notion, mind, but what can you do?

"I can't help you," I said.

Aribah's hand slipped from her lap to linger near a curved bit of darkness on her belt. I let my own hand drift to my boot, felt the absence there. Yup, she'd taken her dagger back.

"Can't," she said, her fingers touching the handle, "or won't?"

"Can't. The price is too high for me to pass it along."

"Price? What price? Either you know how to prepare the oils of the djinn, or you know someone who does. If it's a matter of—"

"No," said the grandfather. He was regarding me now the way a thief might regard a locked strongbox. I didn't much care for the sensation. "Listen to what he said—that the price would be too high for him to *pass* it along. That means it's not a matter of teaching, but rather one of giving. Isn't that so, Imperial?"

I nodded. "If I give it, it's gone."

He ran a finger over his beard. It sounded like pumice scraping over vellum. "Your sight doesn't fade, does it? Doesn't leave you after a day and night, like with the Lions?"

"No."

"Then you don't have the dark sight—or at least, not as we've been discussing it."

"No."

More scraping, more staring. Then an abrupt nod. "You're not the answer I was expecting." He rocked back, then leaned forward and sprang to his feet. "You're of no use to me like this."

I climbed, with less grace and speed, to my own feet. "Which means?"

Grandfather drew the edge of his kaffiyeh back across his face. "Aribah, you will see to it?"

She bowed low to the ground. "I will."

Shit. I'd just become disposable.

I took a step back. The room was lit now, which made it harder for me since we were all on the same footing. Still, he was old and she was seated; if I could duck around him and manage a quick blow to Aribah's face as I ran for my weapons, I might—

"Aribah will escort you back to your inn," said the elder assassin, his jackal's smile clearly evident in his voice.

"She what?" I said, sounding nothing like what a Gray Prince ought to.

"We've shared water and secrets," said the elder assassin. "Two of the foundations of life. And you've seen my face. That leaves me one of two choices, and I think you too valuable—and resourceful—a man to waste on the edge of a blade. I would see you safely back to your fellows." I must have looked as dubious as I felt, because he bowed and extended a hand toward the door behind me. "Please, for my honor as a host."

I regard him for a long moment. "Two conditions," I said. "Seeing as how it's for your honor, and I've been the one inconvenienced."

He rose slowly from his bow. "Within reason."

I gestured at Aribah's waist. "First, I want my knife back."

"*My* knife," said Aribah, her hand going to the shadow-edged dagger.

"I plucked it straight and true during our fight," I said. "Taking it back when I was unconscious isn't the same. It's still mine."

"I will *not*—" began Aribah.

"Is what he says true?" said her grandfather.

"It doesn't matter! You know that—"

"Give it to him."

"*What?*"

"You heard me, girl. We're not thieves. Return it."

Aribah stood up straight. "I will not."

He tensed. "I am you *amma*," he said. "The head of your school. You will do as I say."

"But, Grandfather, you more than anyone knows that what he asks is—"

The old assassin turned and lashed out so fast I almost didn't see it. One moment, Aribah was standing, fists on her hips, eyes ablaze, yelling at her grandfather; the next, she was on the ground, limbs splayed, eyes still ablaze, but in a different way.

"You may be my blood and my favorite," he said, drawing his hand back, "but until you wear the braid of a *kalat*, you will not question my decisions. Am I understood?"

Aribah glared at her grandfather. After a moment, she gave a grudging nod of assent.

"Speak!" he yelled.

"I hear and obey, O my sheikh."

"May it always be so," he replied, not sounding convinced. He turned back to me. I found my hand had gone for my own steel, even though it wasn't there. He glanced down at my empty grip, then back up at me. And chuckled. The bastard.

Behind him, Aribah got to her feet and drew the dagger from her belt. A moment later, it landed at my feet.

All of sudden, I didn't much want the blade anymore, but refusing it now would only make things worse between the two of them. I bent down and picked up the weapon.

"You mentioned two conditions," he said. "What's the second?"

"Who sent you after the magi?"

Aribah gasped outright; as for her grandfather, he crossed his arms and stared at me so hard that I almost expected him to put a dagger in my throat. Not that I could blame him: not only was my question inappropriate in hired-killing circles; it also implied I thought he might be unscrupulous enough to name his employer. The only thing that could have made it more insulting would have been to offer money for the information.

"You would ask who hired us?" he said.

"I would."

"And I should tell you, why?"

"You mean besides our sudden, yet enduring, friendship?"

"Beyond that, yes."

"Three reasons," I said. "First, because I need those magi alive, and I'd like to know who's after them. Second, because I was down in that cellar, too, and I don't appreciate being a target, even tangentially. And third, because, if it's who I think it is, you don't have much to lose by telling me."

The elder assassin glanced at his granddaughter then back to me. I saw his eyes crinkle into a smile. "You could learn from this one, Aribah. Not even an hour with us and he is already reading our motives. Very well: It was Fat Chair who hired us. Is that what you thought?"

I nodded. It made sense. Fat Chair had flat out told me he thought I had an organization in place in el-Qaddice when it came to smuggling glimmer. And to believe that, he had to have reason to believe that magic had already been coming in from the empire. That meant that Jelem and his people had somehow come to Fat Chair's attention even before I'd arrived. My looking for the yazani had only confirmed his suspicions, which had resulted in they *neyajin* being hired.

Well, at least I didn't have to worry about them taking another contract from Fat Chair, considering the pile of bodies they were leaving him.

"My thanks," I said. I offered the elder assassin the best salaam of leave-taking I could manage, given my condition, and turned to Aribah. "Shall we?"

She grunted and brushed past me, knocking into my shoulder as she went. I turned back to her grandfather.

"She knows I'm supposed to make it back alive, right?"

"Oh, she knows," he said. "As to whether she's inclined to listen . . ." He shrugged.

I recovered my steel and made sure that all my blades were in place before I followed her out the door.

Chapter Twenty-two

By the time I made it back to the Angel's Shadow, the sun was turning the eastern sky a dull gray. I rubbed at my eyes and considered another *ahrami,* then thought better of it. I was beyond their help at this point — taking more would only make me awake, not alert. And awake was something I was looking forward to not being soon.

I was also looking forward to not having a surly assassin stalking at my side.

When we reached the inn, she stopped at the edge of the courtyard, in the shadow of the entryway.

"You'll be safe here?" she said, her voice at once perfunctory and smoky behind the drape of her turban.

I looked about the place. One of the innkeeper's sons was hauling tables away from the inn's wall, preparing the outside seating for the day. A handful of chickens pecked the ground, and I could see the window and side door to the kitchen standing open. Smoke rose from the chimney at the back.

There was no sign of Fowler, but that wasn't a bad thing — her job was not to be seen when she was standing Oak. I scanned the roofline, just be sure, and saw the silhouette of a head and shoulder poke up over the stables. It gave a small wave, using a hand signal I was familiar with from back in Ildrecca. A moment later, the figure vanished.

"I'll be fine," I said.

A long pause from Aribah as she considered me, the yard, and Angels knew what else.

"This isn't right," she said at last.

My hand went to my rapier as my eyes swept the street around us. "Excuse me?"

"Grandfather shouldn't have let you go."

Oh, that. I let myself relax, then thought better of it and positioned my hand closer to my dagger than my rapier. Aribah was too close for sword work should she suddenly decide to "fix" things.

"You're too potentially valuable to us," she said, turning her eyes back to me. "He doesn't see that, but I do."

Her eyes were big and deep and brown and edged with kohl, set close beside a narrow nose. There looked to be cheekbones happening under there as well. Between that and the smoke of her voice, not to mention the stray curve I'd noticed beneath those loose robes . . .

I blinked. *Focus, Drothe. Assassin. Happy to see you dead.*

I cleared my throat. "You were there," I said. "You heard: I couldn't show you how to see what I see, even if I wanted to."

"I'm not talking about want; I'm talking about need. We *need* to be able to face the Lions, to best them, to . . . restore our pride. You can help us do that."

I watched as her thumb began absently rubbing at the silver ring on her middle finger. It had been the same way in the empty room when he'd argued with her, when he'd mentioned her mother. Old wounds? Frustrations? Something else?

Either way, I'd be a fool not to pick at it.

"You and your grandfather don't agree on many things, do you?" I said.

"We agree on enough."

"But not when it comes to me."

She leaned in close. "There are *yazani*," she said, "who can keep parts of a man—a finger, an ear, a foot, a heart— alive for months using magic and alchemy. How long, do you think, they could keep a man's eye alive and intact? Long enough to draw the secrets from it, perhaps?"

"That's assuming the magic is held in my eye," I said.

"Who's to say? Like I told your grandfather, I have no idea how the magic works. Taking my eyes might be the surest way of losing it."

I saw Aribah's brow furrow. Clearly, she hadn't expected her threat to fall quite so flat. I didn't blame her, though— I've been threatened by the best.

"What interests me more," I continued, "is how long they can keep the head of an assassin alive. Because if you try to find an answer to your question using those *yazani*, I guarantee you they'll get a chance to figure out the answer to mine."

We eyed each other a long moment, her measuring me, me returning the favor while trying not to get lost in her gaze in the process. Finally, she raised an exquisite eyebrow and snorted.

"You're still too valuable to kill, Marked Man," she said, and turned away.

I watched her go until she slipped into the shadows. Then I crossed the courtyard and entered the inn.

A couple of Quarter locals were sitting at tables, finishing off their breakfasts. A few glanced up as I entered, but most kept their eyes on their bowls. None of Tobin's people were present, and neither was Fowler. The former I didn't care about—I wasn't in the mood to deal with a brood of clucking actors—but Fowler I could have done with. To have her by me, swearing and fussing and, ultimately, understanding my news held a strong appeal just now. Maybe it was just the hour and the locale, but sharing the burden suddenly sounded damn good.

Tired as I was, I couldn't help noticing that my stomach was trying to eat a hole through my spine. I made my way over to the bar and signaled for a serving of whatever they'd made for breakfast. Then I put my back to the counter, rested my elbows on its top, and gave myself permission to relax.

Djinn hunters? What the hell did a bunch of djinn hunters have to do with me, let alone my night vision? Bad enough when I'd thought they were some sort of shadow-wearing assassins, but now . . . now I had to wonder at the

connection between my night sight and that of the djinn, or
their riders, or whatever the hell the Lions of Arat were.
The old assassin's dismissal aside, I didn't believe for one
moment it was a coincidence that the *neyajin*'s glimmer
foiled both the Lion's vision and my own. In my limited
experience, those kinds of things don't just happen when it
comes to magic: If anything, unexpected glimmer usually
makes a situation worse, not better. No, as much as I disliked the notion, odds were good that, if there wasn't a direct connection between the Lions of Arat's vision and my
own, then there were some damn close similarities. Similarities that might very well point to Djanese magic and the
djinn.

Djinn.

*Damn it, Sebastian, how the hell had you gotten our night
vision, anyhow? And from where?*

The innkeeper's girl set a bowl near my elbow, practically startling me. I turned around to take it up, and smiled.
The porridge inside was done in the Ildreccan style, smelling of rice and goat's milk and honey and coriander. My
stomach grumbled at the memories of home. I took up the
bowl and the horn spoon she'd set beside it, and headed for
the stairs.

Well, one thing was for certain: If I didn't believe my
night vision was a lucky coincidence, neither did Aribah's
grandfather. His letting me go simply meant that holding on
to me right now wasn't tenable. I was under no illusions
about being done with him, or his granddaughter, or their
interest in me. You don't break a contract and then dust
four of the local Upright Man's enforcers, only to let the
man you put your people at risk or go free. No, he was playing a long game, but whether I was a target or a tool at the
moment, I couldn't tell.

I put a foot on the stairs, then another, and dipped the
spoon into the porridge. It was hot and thick and grainy, and
dropped into my gut like a stone. Despite that, it felt good—
like a piece of home, sitting in my center and giving me in-
digestion. Small comfort, but a comfort nonetheless.

I didn't want to think about anything right now: not glim-

mer, not *neyajin*, not the audition, not anything. I just
wanted to fill my stomach and crawl into bed and come
back out on the other side with enough energy to get back
out onto the streets again. That's where the answers would
be: lying on hesitant, twisting tongues in the dark places of
el-Qaddice—places that didn't welcome anyone with open
arms, let alone an Imperial. Places I had to tread carefully
because answers didn't come wandering in and sit themselves down on your doorstep in a new city. You had to fight
and pay and lie and bleed for them; had to keep one hand
in the open and the other on your knife; had to wonder
whether the Djanese across from you was smiling because
you'd offered the pay, or because he was planning to gut
you the first chance he got. You had to throw yourself at the
night over and over, hoping each time that it would be the
one that broke instead of you.

It was never easy. Never.

Which made it all the more stunning when I reached the
top of the stairs and found Bronze Degan sitting in a chair
outside my room, eating breakfast.

My porridge and bowl hit the floor with a heavy *thud*. For
the moment, my exhaustion fell away with it.

I felt a smile begin to split my face as I stepped over the
bowl and started down the hall. How had he—?

"What the hell do you think you're doing?" said Degan,
not looking up from his own repast. He'd forgone the morning's offering, and instead had a platter of what looked like
last night's leftovers from the kitchen.

I stopped where I was, the smile dying on my lips. So
much for happy reunions. Not that I'd been expecting one,
but still.

"I'm inclined to ask the same thing," I said.

"What a surprise."

Degan was still Degan: broad-brimmed hat, tailored but
comfortably loose fitting doublet and breeches, and tall
campaign boots—the last rolled down to let the air get to
his bare calves. The doublet was open as well, revealing a
worn but clean shirt, its weave loose in deference to the

Djanese climate. He was all in grays and faded yellows this morning, the dusty gold of the doublet's piping matching the pale fall of his hair.

He had a sword at his side, of course—he was Degan: he couldn't not have one. But while it was a handsome piece of steel, with the guard filed and chiseled to look like a sweeping length of fixed, heavy chain, it didn't feel right seeing it at his side. There was no bronze, no carefully etched vines, no . . . Degan to it.

I could fix that with one quick trip to the stables, but I knew better than to offer. Not now. Not yet.

"Fowler knows you're here?" I said. Above me, I could hear the rafters creak as the inn settled in for the day's heat.

"She wouldn't be much of an Oak Mistress if she didn't."

"And she didn't tell me, why?"

Degan shrugged and turned back to his plate, pausing to brush a small fall of dust from his knee. "You'd have to a—"

"Wait," I said. I looked up at the ceiling. Another creak, another fall of dust.

Dammit.

"Fowler!" I shouted. "Get your ass out of the attic and stop listening in!"

Silence.

"Angels help me," I said, "I'll start poking holes through the ceiling with my sword if you don't move."

More silence.

"Now, Fowler."

Fowler's voice came drifting down from somewhere above Degan. "You couldn't reach the ceiling if you tried."

I began to clear my steel, making sure to scrape the blade along the lip of the scabbard. "You want to risk it?"

Another pause, then, "Fine!" The ceiling creaked and rained small falls of dust as she made her way among the rafters.

I waited until the last drift of plaster had settled to the floor before I turned my attention away from the ceiling and to the hallway. "And if there's anyone else listening at doors," I yelled, "I'll find out and gut you as well!"

Doors began opening on my right and left, releasing actors in various states of dress, embarrassment, and amusement. They muttered and joked their way down the stairs, with Degan gathering at least a few winks from the female members of the troupe along the way.

When the hallway was empty, I looked back toward Degan. There was a reluctant smile on his face. "It can never be easy with you, can it?" he said.

"Why didn't Fowler tell me?" I said again.

Degan's smile left altogether. "Because I asked her not to."

I nodded: I could see that. It didn't mean I liked it, but I could understand it. Even Fowler didn't know all of what had fallen out between Degan and me, but she knew enough to respect Degan's wishes when it came to me.

"All right," I said. I walked the rest of the way down the hall and stopped beside Degan. "Congratulations, you've caught me by surprise and put me off balance: What next?"

"Normally, I'd press the advantage and thrust home as soon as I was able, but this isn't that kind of a conversation."

"What kind is it?" I said.

"It's the kind where I tell you to get the hell out of Djan and mind your own business."

"And how well do you think that's going to work?"

Degan set his plate on the floor and stood up. "Better than you seem to."

I stared up at him. "I think you may be misjudging the nature of this conversation," I said.

Degan clenched his jaw, along with his fists, and ran a hard eye over me. It was a look I'd seen before: the look of a degan weighing not just options, but his points of attack, the geometry of the conflict, the measure of his opponent. It was a cold, bloodless look, and one I wasn't used to being on the receiving end of. It scared the hell out of me.

Then he turned away and let out a sigh. I almost joined him.

"Why Djan?" he said, not looking back. "Why now?"

"Why the hell do you think?" I said.

"Well, I'm fairly certain it's not to keep your Oath," he said. "We both know better than to expect that."

I stared at his back. I'd expected as much—and, honestly, deserved as much—but it still stung. No, it did more than that: a hell of a lot more.

"I explained that," I said.

"I recall," said Degan, "although it was hard to grasp all the subtleties of your argument: You'd just clipped me in the back of the head with a glimmered rope, after all, and my hair was smoldering. That can be a bit distracting. Something about your ass and the empire, wasn't it?"

"You know why I did what I did," I said. "It wasn't just about me or you or the empire or that damn journal: It was about Christiana and Kells and the rest of the Kin. It was about keeping them all alive *despite* the emperor and Shadow, about keeping my hands on the one thing that gave me any hope of bringing them out of that mess in one piece."

"I know," said Degan.

"And?"

"And at first, I thought your argument was enough, that it could be enough to let me let it go," said Degan. He turned back to face me, and his eyes were hard: hard like a soldier's, hard like a broken promise, hard like the truth. "But I was wrong."

"Wrong?" I said, my guilt flaring, turning into anger. "Wrong how? Wrong in that you didn't leave me a good choice? Wrong in that I didn't know what the hell was going on with you and your Order until it was too late? Wrong in that I not only bent over backward to cover your involvement, but lied to your 'brothers' when they came asking questions with their fists?" I stepped forward, putting myself inches from Degan. "What part of that is so fucking 'wrong' that you can't see past what either of us—what *both* of us—did?"

"The part," said Degan, glaring down at me, "where only one of us kept his word."

I held my ground under his gaze, even though part of me wanted to throw pride and pretense aside and ask for forgiveness, to say, fuck it, we both were wrong, let's start over. But there was too much history between us to start fresh,

just as there was too much spine in either of us to bend.
Both of our trades had trained us to equate giving ground
with weakness, and neither of us was in the habit of appearing weak.

This was going to be even harder than I'd expected, for
any number of reasons.

"You could have told me about the Oath," I said. "Told
me that by taking it, you were going against the laws of your
Order. If I'd known what it meant for you—"

"Angels!" said Degan. "It's not about the Oath! Don't
you understand that? If this were only about you breaking
your word to a degan, I might be able to look past it, but it
isn't. It's about you breaking your word to *me*. I took your
Oath because of who we were, Drothe, because I didn't
want to see you cut down by Iron or Solitude or anyone
else. Even if I ended up going against the Order, I knew I'd
be doing it for two good reasons: you, and my duty to the
empire. If everything else collapsed, I'd still be able to hold
on to those things.

"But then you swung your rope, and I fell, and both
promises were broken." Degan sighed and leaned his head
back against the wall. "My failure is for me to bear, but I
won't carry yours as well: That's your concern. Nor am I
going to absolve you. You have to realize that knowing the
'why' behind something isn't always enough, especially
when it comes to things like this. Being able to talk your
way out of a dilemma doesn't mean it goes away."

He reached down to let his hand rest on his sword guard,
then hesitated, steel untouched. "I have to remind myself
what I am every day now," he said, looking down as his
fingers hovered over the chain-wrapped handle. "Every
time I buckle this on in the morning, every time I take it off
at night, every time my hand brushes against the guard, I
stop and realize I'm no longer a degan. I remember that my
word doesn't carry any more weight than a mercenary's,
that my blade doesn't serve any higher purpose than the
one it's been paid to enforce. My steel is just steel." He lowered his hand and looked at me. "All the excuses and reasons in the world aren't going to change that."

Just like all my pondering wasn't going to change my being a Gray Prince, I thought. But that was different: I'd moved up the chain, not been cast from it. I might have lost friends and my ability to work the street as I once had, but Degan had lost everything that defined him. There was no way I could make a comparison between where he'd ended up and where I was—there wasn't any, and I wasn't going to insult him by trying.

I sighed and sat down in Degan's chair, suddenly tired. I could feel the spot where Aribah had tapped me on the back of the head starting to throb again, feel the aches and fatigue of earlier fights begin to reassert themselves. At fault or no, I was still a Gray Prince, and I still had a job to do and people to protect. If I wanted to make my case with Degan, I was going to need to do it quickly, before my brain decided to follow my body's slide toward exhaustion.

I looked down at the plate of food on the floor: A leg and thigh of chicken, braised in a reduced wine sauce that smelled of rosemary and tart cherries, sat alongside a small charcoal-roasted turnip, the outside dark with ash, the inside smooth and buttery to the eye. Degan had hardly touched it, and it looked as if the inn's cockroaches hadn't found the bounty yet. My stomach rumbled. I licked my lips.

Degan sighed. "Help yourself."

I did. The chicken had cooled and the sauce congealed, but there was an undercurrent of pepper that stood out nicely against the sweet-bitterness of the liquid. The turnip was still warm in the center, touched with a hint of olive oil, and delicious.

Degan stood, watching and waiting. I knew he was going to start back in the moment I was done, so I decided to strike first.

"You know," I said, still chewing, "I could always help."

A harsh bark of a laugh. I winced. "The last thing I need—"

"How long have you been down here?" I said.

Degan frowned. "A little over two months."

I nodded, scooped the last bit of turnip into my mouth, and wiped my mustache and beard with my other hand.

"I've been here less than two weeks," I said. "And in the Old City maybe that many days. Want to know what I've found out in that time?"

"Not really, no."

"But you get my point?"

"I get it," said Degan, "and I don't care. I don't want your help. What I want is for you to leave."

"Why?"

"Because what I'm doing down here has nothing to do with you or the Kin, and I don't want it to have anything to do with you or the Kin. It's personal."

I took up the chicken's thighbone and examined it for any remaining meat. No, I'd picked it clean. Oh well. I put it down on the plate, set the plate on the floor, and stood.

"Fine," I said.

Degan took a small step back. "Fine? Just like that?"

"Just like that. All I ask is that you answer me one question."

Degan's brow furrowed. "All riiight."

"What's so damn important about a bunch of ivory and papers that you had to come all the way to el-Qaddice?" I asked.

The question was a gamble. It was one of the few consistent rumors I'd heard about Degan up to this point, but that wasn't saying much. But I needed something, anything, to catch him off guard.

Luckily for me, my play worked. Degan's eyes went wide and, after a moment, he shook his head in disgust. "Damn Noses."

I suppressed a smile and pressed forward instead, keeping up the assault.

"What are they?" I said. "Relics? Notes? Something you can use to protect yourself from the Order?" *Something that might help me talk you into going back to Ildrecca with me?*

"Something like that."

"What kind of something?"

Degan shook his head.

"Dammit, Degan, I don't have time for this!"

"No, you don't," he said. "And neither do I." And he began to turn away.

Crap. I'd been hoping to figure out what Degan was after before I told him why I was here, before I told him there was another degan in el-Qaddice. I hadn't wanted to admit I'd come down here for any reason other than our lost friendship. It was stupid, I knew—there was no way to tell him about Wolf's side of the deal without mentioning the threat to my own organization—but it made it sound more mercenary than it felt. And the last thing I wanted Degan to think was that I was using him as a means to help myself—again.

Except that I was, to a degree. And I didn't have much of a choice.

"If your being here is about the Order of the Degans and getting back in," I said, "I can help."

"Blackmail won't work on them, Drothe," he said as he walked down the hall. "And even you can't cut a deal with the Order when it comes to fixing what I did."

I took a deep breath, let it out, and steadied myself with a hand against the wall.

"I didn't come down here alone," I said.

"I don't care if you tied your sister in a sack and brought her along kicking and screaming, I'm not about to—"

"Silver Degan is here, too," I said, barely keeping myself from calling him "Wolf." "We came to el-Qaddice together."

Degan stopped in his tracks. I saw his hand go to his sword. "Silver's here?" he said, turning partway around so he could see the entire length of the hallway. He took a small step backward, putting himself up against the wall. "With you?"

"Not here in the inn, no. And not so much with me as . . . pushing me along."

Degan shot a sharp look my way. "Pushing how?"

"Blackmail may not work against degans," I said, "but it operates just fine when it comes to newer Gray Princes."

Degan lowered his hand and cocked his head. "Silver blackmailed *you*?"

"He set me up as the finger for another Gray Prince's

death, made it look like I dusted the prince when he was under the protection of my peace. It was all just whispers when I left Ildrecca, but if enough Kin start to believe it, or if Silver decides to up the stakes by laying a few more bodies at my door, all hell will break loose. Nijjan Red Nails has already brushed her hands of me, and I might've lost others in the last month. I don't know. All I do know is that, if the rumor takes hold, it's a perfect excuse for a couple of the other Gray Princes to get rid of me."

"That's a bit extreme for Silver, but I suppose I can see him doing it. Especially now." Degan considered a moment. "And he wanted to use you to find me?"

I nodded. "He says the Order's falling in on itself since Iron was dusted. From what I can tell, no one is saying directly that you did it, but it's common knowledge among the degans. I tried to convince them Shadow killed Iron instead of you, but—"

"You did?" said Degan. "How?"

"I left Iron's sword on Shadow's body and made sure the Order found it. You'd crossed swords with Shadow already, and he was on the opposite side of the fence from Iron. I didn't think it'd be too much of a stretch."

"Nice. But I'm gathering it didn't work, considering you're down here."

I shook my head. "To hear Silver tell it, no one argued with the official story, but no one's fully buying it, either. Not having you, or at least your body, around seems to be making it a hard sell."

"Sorry to complicate things for you by being alive," said Degan. "So which camp is Silver in? Does he want to give me a hearty handshake or a sword thrust through my heart?"

"He wants to get you back to Ildrecca," I said. "He says you carry enough weight with the Order that you can help keep things from getting worse, that you can prevent the two sides from coming to blows over the whole 'How do we serve the empire' thing."

"He gives me too much credit."

"He also thinks he can get you back into the degans."

"He gives himself too much credit as well." Degan smiled thinly. "But that's Silver all over."

"Is he right, though?" I said.

Degan stared down at his boots, kicking absently at a spot on the floor. "Maybe," he said at last. "It's possible that, having killed Iron, I'm now in a position to step forward—if only as an example of what can happen—and ease some of the tension. It's been a long time since one degan killed another, and it gives me a sort of grisly cachet, I suppose. Mind you, I don't believe for a moment I can heal the split, but could I put it in perspective? Maybe. But that would require the Order not cutting me down the moment I confirmed their suspicions. And to even stand a chance of doing that, I'd need to get into the Barracks Hall, and that's only slightly less likely than me not getting killed in the first place."

"But if they aren't willing to admit for certain you dusted Iron, what's keeping you out?"

"I cast my sword away," said Degan. "Turned my back on my brothers and my Oath. That's not exactly something they can overlook. If I wanted to enter the hall in anything other than chains and an iron gag, I'd need the support of at least three degans. Last I checked, Silver is only one man, no matter how big his ego."

"Which is why he wants to get you back into the Order: so he can bring you into the Barracks Hall."

"Probably," said Degan. "If I'm a degan, no one can keep me out, but that'd be one hell of an achievement, even for Silver. No one's been reinstated to the Order after leaving it. Ever. Oh, there's supposed to be rules governing that, but they were lost a long time ago."

"Lost how?"

"Someone took them."

"From a bunch of degans?"

"Being good with a sword doesn't mean you don't make mistakes."

I was about to ask what kind of mistake would allow a person to walk away with something like that, but then I caught the look in Degan's eye and stopped myself. Things were delicate enough between us as it was at the moment; the last thing I needed to do was give him another excuse to tell me to fuck myself. Given his look, this time he might just do it.

So instead, I said, "Lost rules aside, do you think Silver could get you back in the Order?"

Degan shrugged. "Silver knows more about the old laws and rituals than I ever will. I suppose it's possible."

"So then we *could* help you get back in," I said, suddenly feeling as if sunlight were shining on me for the first time in months. "Which means all we need to do is get you and Silver back to Ildrecca, maybe find at least one more degan to speak for you, and—"

"No."

"What?"

"I'm not worried about becoming a degan again, Drothe."

"But you said—"

"I said I'm trying to come to terms with it, but that doesn't mean I think I should carry a sword of the order again. I killed one of my sword brothers: I can't just walk back in like it never happened. For all that I disagreed with him, Iron's memory deserves better than that." Degan pushed himself away from the wall. "No, if I'm interested in anything, it's in saving the Order from itself. I may no longer be a degan, but that doesn't mean I can't still love what the Order represents and what my former brothers stand for.

"I appreciate your offer and your effort—you don't know how much, truly—but I don't think my going back to Ildrecca is the best way to accomplish that. I'm here for a reason, and if I'm right, it'll make more of a difference to the Order than anything Silver can pull off."

"How?" I said. "With a bunch of ivory and paper?"

Degan smiled and began to turn away. "With ivory and paper, yes."

"So the answer's no, just like that?" I said.

He stopped but didn't turn back. "You think this is easy for me? That I walk away lightly? Even after everything that happened, part of me still wants to say yes, to come back and run and fight and laugh at your side again. But the rest of me knows better. It would be too easy to fall back into old habits with you, too easy to forget what happened and why it should matter.

"So no, it's not just like that—it's a hell of a lot more than that."

I stood there and watched Degan walk down the steps and away, feeling the sunlight go out on my face and the darkness return. Suddenly, it was hard to stand, let alone think. I stumbled back to my room, turned the lock, and opened the door.

Wolf was there, lying on my bed, his hands clasped behind his head.

"Well, that could have gone better, yes?" he said.

Chapter Twenty-three

I stood there stupidly for a moment, staring at the other degan. Then I closed the door behind me.

"Get the fuck out of my bed," I said.

Wolf met me halfway and sat up, but didn't stand.

"What the hell are you doing here?" I said.

"As it appears, waiting for you."

"And Degan just *happened* to show up right outside my door while you were in here?"

"I've been waiting for a long time," he said. "We need to talk."

"You talk; I'll sleep. Feel free to make up my side of the conversation in case you get bored. I recommend throwing in the occasional 'fuck you' on my behalf, just to keep things true to life." I bent down and, after succeeding in not falling over, began undoing my shoes.

"For someone who just let the man we traveled over a month to find walk out the doo—"

"Hey," I said, looking up from the tangled knot that was my left shoelace. "I didn't exactly see you out there making the case to your sword brother. You're the one who wants him back in Ildrecca so damn bad, why didn't you come out and join us?"

Wolf shifted on the bed and looked away. "Now is not the time for me to confront Bronze."

"How convenient for you," I said, turning back to my shoes. To hell with it: I drew my dagger and sliced the offending lace away. The shoe loosened and released my foot. I sighed in relief. How many hours—no, days at this point—had I been on my feet?

I looked back over at Wolf. "How did you get in here, anyhow? I can understand Fowler looking the other way for Degan, but not you."

"What kind of a bandit would I be if I couldn't sneak into a room in an inn?"

"The kind that's a hell of a lot better than most Draw Latches and Star Glazers I know back in Ildrecca. Fowler keeps a tight watch: How'd you get past it?"

"The Azaar do not move as other men move."

"Maybe not, but they sure as hell seem to bullshit as other men bullshit," I said, taking my other shoe off. Paradise! "I don't suppose there's any chance of you telling me where you've been, let alone how you got into el-Qaddice?"

Wolf flicked a bit of dust from his caftan. "There's not much to tell: A bey of one of the smaller military districts owed me a favor. He happens to be in el-Qaddice reporting to the mogul, and so I was able to arrange entrance. Why?"

I stood up and went over to sit on my travel chest, since it was clear Wolf wasn't about to abandon the bed. "Because it would have been nice not to have to sing for our supper if you could have gotten us in," I said, settling myself on the scarred wooden lid.

"The bey is not a patron of the arts, as is the padishah. My speaking in your favor would have hurt my own case."

"And where were you before that?"

Wolf ignored the question and instead gestured at the closed door. "Why didn't you follow him?"

"Degan?" I said. "Are you kidding? If he was going to be watching for one thing, it'd be me trying to tickle his shadow. He knows me too well, and is too good, to let that happen." I didn't mention that I also thought he deserved better from me, and that even if he didn't, I doubt I would have been able to make it five blocks in the condition I was in.

Wolf grunted, clearly not convinced. "In that case, you'll have to find him again. And persuade him."

"Weren't you listening? I tried to persuade him—he doesn't want to come back. Hell, he doesn't even want to get back into the Order; he's more worried about saving it from the outside."

"I heard," said Wolf. "Don't fool yourself. Bronze is a degan: In his heart, he burns to wear the sword again."

"Well, his heart and his head don't seem to be talking to each other right now."

"Then you will need to find what his head seeks, so that his heart may follow."

"Yeah, I'll get right on that." I began unbuttoning my doublet, hoping Wolf would take the hint. "Ivory and paper: no problem. I'm sure they're both very fucking rare in a city filled with artisans and poets."

"The ivory he seeks is."

I reached up and rubbed at my eyes with the heels of my palms. This wasn't going to end, was it? Fine: I'd play along, if only long enough to get Wolf out the door. I'd marshal and make the arguments about why it was hopeless later, when I was fully conscious.

"And what's so special about it?" I said.

"The ivory he seeks did not come from a beast or a great fish," said Wolf. "Nor is it something you'll find hidden away in a chest: Ivory was a degan back when the Order was begun, over two centuries ago. He was our first archivist, and one of the architects of our brotherhood."

"Wait," I said, sitting up straighter. "A degan? *Ivory* Degan?"

"You think we're only named after metals and their cousins?"

"Well, I—"

"You know nothing." He took a deep breath. "Ivory helped write the Degan's Oath, not to mention the Oath we exchange with our clients. He was the one who wrote the laws we follow, the one who shaped our initial pledge to the Empire, the one who kept our earliest records and traditions. He was, in many ways, the father of all who followed. And then he left."

"Left?" I said. "Why?"

"There was a falling-out: Ivory became disenchanted, even disgusted, with the Order over time—something to do with theology and souls." Wolf ran his hand over his silver-chased sword guard and shook his head. "What do we know of souls, eh? We're swordsmen: Our calling is to free souls from their bodies, not debate their nature and purpose."

I felt my ears perk up at this, despite my exhaustion. Souls were at the center of not only the Imperial Cult and the emperor's ability to continually reincarnate as Markino, Theodoi, and Lucien; they were also the secret behind the devastating power that was Imperial magic. Where other magicians relied on scraps of magical energy that slipped through from someplace called "The Nether" or, in the case of the most accomplished, established a direct tap to the power source, imperial Paragons somehow drew and focused that same magical energy using their souls. As I understood it, this was damn hard and damn dangerous—most Mouths considered it impossible—which only made Wolf's mention of the word all the more interesting.

In the empire, I'd been learning, "soul" was a loaded term on more than just the religious level.

"Still," said Wolf, "it was a different time. Whatever his reasons, Ivory came to believe not only that we degans couldn't be bound by the Oath—an Oath he himself had helped write and invest with power—but that we were unworthy to serve either the emperor or the empire.

"This change of heart did nothing to endear him to his brothers and sisters. They had sworn their lives and their swords to a cause he had created—one he now seemingly disdained. Dogs, some degans said, were more loyal than Ivory. Blood flowed in the Barracks Hall for the first time."

Wolf stopped. I thought I could almost see the chaos of that time reflected in his eyes; as if he could see it happening again in the present if he didn't succeed.

"So Ivory fled?" I said.

"No." Wolf shook his head and, mercifully, got up out of my bed. If I'd had the energy, I'd have leapt for joy. "No.

Ultimately, even Ivory saw what his presence was doing to the Order. He renounced his place among us and left."

"Then why is Degan looking for his papers?" I said.

"Because when Ivory left the Order—when he left the empire—he took the founding records of the degans with him: the old Oaths, the original formularies of ritual, the history of the degans up to that point. And, most important for my brother Bronze, Ivory took our first laws as well."

"Laws," I said. "As in, what it means to be a degan?" That made a kind of sense: If Degan wanted to help the Order, what better way than to find the documents could answer the question at the center of the split?

Wolf nodded. "And how a person can be restored to the Order, yes."

"But I told you," I said, "Degan . . . Bronze doesn't want back in."

"Perhaps not," said Wolf, "but for our purposes, it's the laws that matter. If we want to be able to get Bronze into the Barracks Hall, let alone give him a chance to speak, quoting from the old laws could prove helpful. Much of what the degans have now is based on memories and tradition written down after Ivory's departure. The first laws will take precedence, even when spoken by someone under the taint of killing one of his fellows."

"And you think those laws—Ivory's papers—are in el-Qaddice?"

Wolf stepped toward the door. "Bronze must, else why would he be here?"

I didn't feel quite up to pointing out the gaping holes in this logic, so I let it pass. Instead, I moved over to my bed and scratched my neck. The sweat that had been there much of the night had dried, leaving what felt like a thin, slimy film over my skin.

"And what if Degan refuses to recite those laws?" Never mind getting him to come back to Ildrecca in the first place. Or face the Order. Or even talk to me again, for that matter.

"Then I shall recite them for him."

"Are we talking about the same person here?" I said.

"Because I don't see Degan letting someone else do much of anything on his behalf if he doesn't want it done."

Wolf showed his teeth. "That will be my concern."

Now it was my turn to shiver. And I still didn't feel reassured.

Chapter Twenty-four

Despite being exhausted, or maybe because of it, I slept fitfully. Not because of the clatter and shouting of the rehearsal taking place in the courtyard—that kind of thing was second nature to me from years spent living near the night cart routes in the lower parts of Ildrecca; rather, it was the occasional silences, in which the squeak of a floorboard or a footstep in the hall could be heard, that caused me to crack my eyes and shift restlessly in bed.

At one point, I opened my eyes to see a dim figure moving about the room, and filled my hand with my knife before I was fully awake. But it was only Fowler, who gently pushed the blade aside and whispered something about locks and loaves. I tried to ask her who the hell picked locks with bread, but was already falling back to sleep before I could get the words out.

When next I opened my eyes, the sunlight pushing in through the window had a distinctly horizontal slant to it, telling me it was late in the day. I rolled to the edge of my bed, gasped at the pain the movement caused, and rolled back.

Cutters. Assassins. Fights in the dark. Right.

Maybe I'd just stay here for a bit.

I'd just settled back in and begun thinking about sending one of the innkeeper's sons out for some pilgrim's balm when Fowler said, "About time you woke up."

I nearly leapt out of my bed, then stopped as a fresh

wave of pain rolled through me. I groaned and looked off toward the other side of the room.

Fowler was seated on a stool, her back against the door, her arms folded across her chest. A ceramic teapot and an empty cup sat on the floor beside her, along with a partially eaten loaf of bread.

I didn't bother to ask how long she'd been there. I already knew.

"You didn't have to stay," I said as I slowly sat up.

"Yes, I did."

"It's not as if Wolf was going to come back."

"Who gives a fuck about him coming back?" Fowler nodded at the room in general. "I needed to figure out how the bastard got past me the first time, and this was the quietest place to think."

"Right." I swung my legs over the side of the bed and took a breath. This next bit was going to hurt. "So what did you figure out?"

"He had to have been here for hours—even before Degan arrived. My guess is he slipped in when I was busy setting up one of the Crows I recruited."

"Seriously? He got in while you were putting out more eyes?"

"Don't even start."

"But you have to admit—"

"I don't have to do anything, including not kill you."

I covered the fledgling smile on my face by taking a deep breath and letting it out. Then another. I stood up.

It was worse than I expected.

"Oh, Angels!" I gasped.

"Serves you right."

I didn't respond. We'd gone over the security lapse last night, as well as my encounter with Fat Chair's men. Any high ground I might have claimed about having found Wolf inside my room had been washed away by Fowler pointing out just how lucky I was to have made it back at all. It had been hard to argue with her, but I'd managed it nonetheless. We were good at nonetheless of late.

As for the *neyajin*, well, I'd left that part out. Given our encounter with the assassins in the tunnel, and given Fowler's propensity to hold a grudge, I didn't want to tell her about their newfound interest in me. She'd clearly suspected something—we both knew I wasn't good enough to fight my way past four Cutters with nothing more to show for it than a collection of fresh bruises and a bad disposition—but for once fatigue had won out over stubbornness and I'd finally been able to beg off any further argument for the time being.

I tilted my head, felt my neck pop, and then dipped my fingers into the pouch around my neck. It took all the willpower I could summon, but I made myself chafe the *ahrami* seed between my palms rather than immediately slip it into my mouth. My sweat would help open up the flavor, and if I was going to feel this lousy, I at least wanted to be able to enjoy one tiny part of the day.

"So how do you think Wolf got in?" I said.

"Short of climbing in through a window that's too small for him? I have no idea. I had Crows working the roof and the yard, and an Oak sitting in the common room with an eye on the stairs all night."

"Back rooms?" I said. I rolled the seed to the tip of my fingers and set it in my mouth. A faint shudder went through me, and my shoulders started to relax. Not pilgrim's balm, but it would do. "Maybe the kitchen?"

"The innkeeper and his people say no, but I'm looking into it." Fowler ran her hand along the back of her neck. "What I don't understand," she said, "is why Wolf didn't just step out into the hall when Degan was here. If he was listening in, then why not simply end the hunt? It's not like there'll be a better time for him to have a face-to-face with Degan."

"He thinks there will be," I said. "He said this wasn't the right time to approach Degan, what with Ivory Degan's papers suddenly being in play."

"And you believed him?"

"Hell, no. I think Wolf knew about the papers all along, or at least suspected. Degan said himself that Wolf is the expert on this. I think Wolf wants the laws and Degan together, and doesn't want to jeopardize his chances of getting both by playing his hand too early."

"Which means Wolf could be playing any number of games."

I nodded. "It's even possible he wants to find Degan for the reasons he said, although I doubt that's the full story. Short answer? I don't know. All I do know is that I stand a better chance of figuring out Wolf's plan and helping Degan if I stay in the game instead of outside it. And that means continuing to dance to Wolf's tune, at least for the moment."

"Even though Degan doesn't want your help?"

"Even then." Because, whether he liked it or not, I wasn't going to leave him hanging, not again.

I peeled off my shirt and looked down at the bruises on my chest and arms. There weren't enough visible to justify how sore I felt, which meant the rest were deep and likely wouldn't surface for a day or two yet. I grimaced at the thought.

Fowler shifted on the stool and cleared her throat. "I don't suppose there's any chance of talking him into helping us?"

"Degan made his position clear last night," I said, tossing my shirt on the bed. I walked over to my travel chest and swung it open. "Asking now would only push him further away when I need to bring him closer."

"And keeping silent is supposed to help with that?"

"The last time he asked me to do something, I did the opposite," I said. "I can't imagine repeating that course of action will win me any further love."

"But if you told him about the *Zakur* and the—"

Fowler was interrupted by a loud knocking on my door. Given how fast she sprang out of her seat, I guessed it had sounded right next to her ear.

I smiled. Good. Served her right.

I was opening my mouth to tell them to go away when the door latch rattled against the lock. Then the knock came again, along with a voice.

"Drothe?" It was Ezak. "You need to come downstairs. Now."

I looked at Fowler. She raised an eyebrow and shook her head. No ideas.

I let my gaze drift over to the washstand. Water and soap and a washrag sat, waiting. Tempting.

Damn actors.

"Tell Tobin that I haven't even—"

"It's not Tobin," said Ezak. "Nor is it the troupe."

"Then what is it?"

A longer pause than I'd like. Then, "Just come. Now."

There were two of them waiting downstairs, not counting Ezak: a cove that could have doubled as a sandstone pillar in his spare time, and an old woman. Except for them, the inn's common room was empty. Not even the owner was visible behind the bar.

No witnesses. Bad sign, that.

I stepped gingerly down off the last step. I hadn't been able to find any spare lacings in my trunk, and so had simply slipped my feet into the laceless shoes and clomped my way down the stairs. I'd briefly considered trying to shove my swollen, aching feet into my traveling boots, but one look at the dirt-covered, sweat-stiffened footwear had convinced me it wasn't worth the agony I would have experienced pulling them on. Now, seeing the situation in the common room, I was starting to wonder if something that allowed me the option of running wouldn't have been a better choice, pain be damned.

The woman was seated off to one side, a stemmed earthenware goblet before her on the table, its sides damp with condensation. She wore a simple veil, drawn down below her chin, along with a beige head wrap over silvery hair and an off-white kaftan. The only color on her was a single ring on her left hand, gold set with a sky-blue sapphire the size of my front tooth. As for her right hand, it sat in her lap—lame, if I had to guess, given the subtle slackness in her shoulder and the right side of her face.

I faced the woman and salaamed. It seemed like the smart thing to do. She gave nothing away as she inclined her head in turn.

Fowler, though, wasn't feeling quite so diplomatic.

"Where the hell are my people?" she demanded, pushing past me. "And who the hell are you, anyhow?"

The woman turned a cool eye toward Fowler. "You mean the ones watching the inn? They left."

"Why?"

"Because I told them to. Do you understand what this means?"

"Yeah, it means I'm going to—"

I grabbed Fowler and pulled her back. "We understand," I said. I turned to Ezak. "Your people are all right?" The yard, I'd noticed, was empty as well.

"They're in the stables," he said. He looked over at the woman. "I should go to them." She inclined her head again, and he left.

"Dammit, Drothe," said Fowler as she twisted her arm free of my grip, "if you think I'm going to stand by and let some old—"

"What you're going to do," I said, stepping close and dropping my voice, "is shut the hell up and go out to the stables with Ezak. Now."

"The fuck I—"

"No," I snapped. "No arguments. Not this time. Not if you want the people you just recruited to keep breathing. Think: She cleared three blocks' worth of Crows and Oaks with a word. What the hell will happen if you take one more step toward her?"

Fowler ducked her head and glowered at the room in general. I kept my hands loose and open.

"Fowler . . . ?" I said.

A heel to the floor. Hard. "Dammit!" Then she was out the door and stalking across the yard.

I didn't envy Tobin if he even so much as thought about opening his mouth.

I faced the woman and her human statue.

"She has fire," she said, tracking the Oak Mistress's progress through a window. "She'll either burn up the world or burn herself out. I like her." She turned back to me. "We need to speak, you and I. Come here."

I clomped-stepped over to her and took a seat. She leaned slowly to the side and looked under the table.

"You seem to be having trouble with your shoes," she said.

"Really? I hadn't noticed. Given how everything else has been going lately, they feel fine by comparison."

The left side of her mouth twitched momentarily. "You know who I am?"

"I know you're *Zakur*, if that's what you mean. And that you're high up in the organization. No one else could hush my people and clear out a place like this with just one Arm at her back."

"'Arm'?" She looked back over her shoulder. "What do you think of that, Ubayd?"

The pillar rumbled.

"Well, I like it. You're now my Arm." She glanced down at her lap, then back up at me. "Seems especially poetic in my case, don't you think?"

"I—"

"Be quiet. It was a rhetorical question." She raised her glass, causing ice to clink against the side as she sipped at whatever was inside. The inn didn't normally stock ice. "We need to figure out what to do about you."

I sat quietly and waited.

"Well?" she said after a moment.

"Oh, I'm sorry. I thought you'd already figured it out and were just waiting for me to say something so you could tell me to shut up."

Her left eye narrowed to a slit. Her right tried to keep up but fell behind. I focused on the narrower of the two.

"No one likes a cocky Imperial."

"I find they're not fond of belligerent old Djanese women, either." I leaned forward and placed my elbows on the table. "Look, I haven't had my coffee—or any of my other vices—yet, so I'll be brief. You carry a lot of water around here. I get that, even without the walking obelisk behind you. And you wouldn't have come to see me if you didn't know the kind of pull I have when I'm at home. So what say we stop pretending to be hard and get down to business?"

The man behind her grunted and settled a fist that

looked to be almost half the size of my head on his belt, putting it within easy reach of my face.

The woman didn't seem to notice. Instead, she stared at me for a long moment before finally shaking her head. Ubayd's hand uncurled but didn't fall away.

"My name is Jaida bint Iyab Bakr al-Modussa al-Hirim," she said, "although most people on the street call me Mama Left Hand. You're called Drothe?"

"I am."

A pause. "That's all?"

"Most days it's all I need."

She sniffed and took another icy sip of her drink.

I'd heard her name as I'd worked the Old City, but only in passing. Mama Left Hand was so far above the street, she was viewed as more of a presence than a person. As the matriarch of the Hirim clan, she was said to hold considerable sway not only among the more shadowy parts of her clan, but even within the overall tribe itself. Even her nephew, Hamzah, the titular head of the Hirim, was said to defer to her on most matters.

Unfortunately for me, that meant she was also some sort of great-aunt a couple of times removed from Fat Chair. Not strong as blood ties went normally, but then, there was nothing normal about having someone like Mama Left Hand sitting across from me less than a day after her nephew had sent a gang of Cutters after me, either.

I eyed the *Zakur* crime boss, then the slab of Arm behind her, as I flexed my wrist and thought about the knife up my sleeve. Only if I wanted to die quickly.

"Very well, Drothe One Name," she said. "Let's get down to business. I'm here for a simple reason: I want to know what you're going to do about Fat Chair."

I'd been letting myself slump down in my chair. Now I straightened. "Me?" I said. "What the hell do you expect me to do, other than stay alive? He's your family."

"Yes, but I'm not the one who killed his favorite cousin."

"His . . . ?"

"The one with the sword and small shield you met in the street."

"You mean the one he sent at the head of three other Cutters to *kill* me?"

"That would have been Sa'd, yes."

"And your grand-nephew is upset because I walked away? What was I supposed to do, let him dust me?"

"Family knows it would have made my life easier."

"Well, I'm sorry to fucking inconvenience you, but I—"

Her hand flashed up and the Arm's flashed out. I was out of my chair and on my back in an instant.

"Mind your language," said the *Zakur* matron. "I'll not tolerate filth. You'll not be warned again."

I raised my head and looked between my legs back toward the table. It was a good six feet away. That had been a *warning*?

I climbed to my feet, wiped at the blood seeping into my beard, and clomped back over to the table. Her city, I reminded myself as I righted my chair and sat down. Her army.

Still, I didn't hesitate to take up her goblet and drain the contents into my mouth. Winter wine—light and sweet and, thankfully, cold. I swished it around and spit out a red-pink stream.

My right ear was ringing. The side of my face sang a counterpoint of pain. I ignored them both.

"Okay," I said. "I'm clearly missing something here. What's your problem with Fat Chair, and how does it involve me?"

"The specifics of the problem are my business, and therefore none of yours. Suffice it to say Fat Chair is an ass—but a clever ass nonetheless. He's locked up the Imperial Quarter tighter than even I thought possible. And while that's helped some others in the clan, it's gotten in the way of my interests. He's like a stone in my sandal, and I'd have that annoying stone gone."

"And dusting me would have gotten rid of said stone?"

"It would have had repercussions," she said. "Killing a Gray Prince means something, even here in Djan. No, don't swell up at the notion: It's not what you think. I doubt anyone would have avenged you. But your death would have

made him look shortsighted and dangerous. I need Fat
Chair to lose face before I try to remove him: Your death
would have been the breeze that preceded the storm." She
paused to purse her lips. It wasn't a pleasant sight. "But then
you had to go and kill Sa'd and give the fat fool a proper
reason to come after you."

"Vendetta," I said.

"If that's the same as a blood price, then yes. He's put a
price on your head. A high one. And even I can't counter-
mand that: It has roots too deep in tribal honor for me to
touch."

"What if I lie low?" I didn't care for the idea, but I didn't
have the time or resources to go after this cove. "Stay out of
his way?"

"He won't let you."

"And if I dust him instead?"

"I'd prefer you didn't. Fool or no, he's still family. If he's
to die, I'd rather it be from a *Zakur* blade."

"What if it can't be helped?"

"He has many cousins. Not many like him, but there are
enough honorable ones that I expect you wouldn't make it
out of Djan alive."

"So I'm dead if I try to defend myself, and likely just as
dead if I don't." I turned my head and spit out more blood.
"How the hell do you people do business, anyhow? I'm surprised you're not all lying in the gutter from one another's
knives."

Mama smiled. It was a grim thing, but I couldn't help
noticing a hint of longing at the edges, too. "There have
been times . . . ," she said. She sighed. "But there are rules
and precedence, not to mention hierarchy, at play among
the *Zakur*. We have our twisting ways of avoiding slaughter.
None of which apply to you." She met my eyes. "Is it really
so different among your Kin?"

I opened my mouth to say it was, then stopped myself.
The excuses and lines of loyalty might be different, but we
had our share of butchery. Maybe even more, since we
tended to rely on ties woven from fear and money rather
than blood and family. Oh, there were traces of honor and

obligation mixed in as well, but it was a rare man among the Kin who could inspire people that didn't even like him to take up the blade in his memory.

None of which mattered just now since, except for Fowler, I was alone in a foreign land.

"So what do you propose?" I said.

She gave a lopsided shrug. "Disgrace him. Make him look the fool. Take part of the Imperial Quarter away from him." She picked up her goblet and drained it. "In short, do whatever you were planning to do when you arrived in el-Qaddice, before all this happened. Only do it quicker."

"Do whatever . . . ?" I said. "What I was planning to do was find someone and get out."

Her eyes didn't leave the bar. "Yes, of course you were."

"Dammit, woman, I'm telling you—"

Her hand came up. Ubayd tensed. I froze. She spoke.

"Don't take me for a fool. You don't do what you did back in your Empire and then just happen to come to el-Qaddice. The story about the mercenary may play on the street, but I know too much about how things work to fall for that." She lowered her hand. "If you want to try to take over the Imperial end of the route, I won't get in your way. In fact, I might even be able to help. I can smooth things over with the clan on this end, get the price off your head, and present you as the best alternative to Crook Eye. I may even be able to make sure the shipments keep coming without interruption." Her eyes came back to me. "Assuming, of course, you deal with my nephew for me."

I started to open my mouth to say . . . I don't know what. I knew I needed to answer her somehow: to agree or make a counteroffer or negotiate terms—anything to cover over my surprise over what she'd just said, over the implications she'd just made. To respond to the idea that I'd dusted Crook Eye back in Barrab so I could take over his connections in el-Qaddice. To make it seem as if I'd known about the dead Gray Prince's arrangement with the *Zakur* and Fat Chair. To hide the fact that, yes, it had just been dumb luck that brought me down here and landed my ass in her clan's business, as opposed to some kind of princely power play on my part. Because if I didn't, my value, not to mention my credibility, with the woman before me would drop into the "expendable" range almost immediately.

Damn me for being too much the Nose and not enough the prince, anyhow.

"Well?" said the *Zakur* matron.

I drew the pouch out from around my neck and spilled two seeds into my palm. When I offered the bag to Mama, she declined.

"I'm not excited about the idea of getting involved in clan politics," I said as I rolled the seeds between my palms. "But I get the feeling I don't seem to have much of a choice in the matter."

"You don't. And don't worry—you're far from what I'd consider 'involved.' You're a tool at best, an annoyance at worst."

"Well, as long as you put it nicely . . ."

Mama Left Hand gestured, and Ubayd pulled her chair away from the table with barely a sound. When she rose, she did so slowly, but also without taking the Arm's offered hand. It was clear it hurt for her to move; it was also clear she didn't give a damn.

"We'll discuss specifics once you've delivered on your end of the deal," she wheezed. "In the meantime, I'll start priming the clan for Fat Chair's downfall."

"About that." I stood—slowly, to keep Ubayd happy—and put the seeds into my mouth. "I'm going to need more to go on than just 'make him look like a fool.' Some ideas or suggestions. Details."

Mama shook her head. "If my hand is seen in this, it could ruin any rewards I may otherwise reap. Having this meeting is risk enough; if I give you any hints, their origins might be traced back to the *Zakur*, and thus to me. The deed is on you alone, Imperial."

She turned away. Ubayd handed her a stout cane, which she used to begin hobbling toward the door. In this, she let the Arm help her.

It was a setup—even I could see that. If I somehow succeeded, she'd come out ahead without having lifted a finger;

and if I failed she wouldn't have risked a thing. Either way, I'd be at her mercy when payment time came around. She could just as easily laugh in my face as honor her word, and there wouldn't be a damn thing I could do about it.

I needed something more, not only to save face, but to feel that I wasn't letting her walk all over me—even if I was. I needed to get something out of this as well.

"That's not good enough," I said to her retreating back.

"It will have to be."

"And if I were to go to your nephew instead?" I said. "To cut my own deal with him?"

She stopped. Craned her head over her shoulder until she was regarding me with her drooping eye. "Even you're not that stupid."

"I'm a marked Imperial in Djan: What have I got to lose?"

"Besides the obvious?"

I didn't answer.

Mama screwed up her face in a way that made me think of lemons. "What do you want?"

"I need help on the street."

"I told you, my hand can't be seen—"

"Not with Fat Chair," I said. "With something else—something that's my business alone. Something that won't make a bit of difference to you or Fat Chair or the rest of the *Zakur*."

"What?"

I put on what I hoped was a winning smile. "I need help finding some old books," I said.

Chapter Twenty-five

The sun was smearing orange and purple across the clouds on the eastern horizon when I left the Angel's Shadow the next evening and headed out of the Imperial Quarter.

My step wasn't as light as I might have hoped, nor as quick. I'd spent most of the previous night and much of this morning working the streets in the company of one of Mama Left Hand's men: a cove named Dirar who had a penchant for rashari leaf and a nose for artifacts. We'd haunted scribal shops and secondhand booksellers, talking our way into private libraries and out of tense encounters with rare document smugglers. We spoke with mercenaries in taverns, priests in temples, historians in gardens, and thieves in back alleys. Everywhere, people knew Dirar, and everywhere they had the same answer: no word, no idea, no hints — but they'd watch and listen and look, to be sure.

I'd finally left him close to midday, with assurances on his part that we'd made a good beginning. I'd had a hard time sharing his enthusiasm, but had nodded and smiled and crawled up to my bed with instruction not to be disturbed. Less than six hours later, I'd woken up to Fowler kicking my bed, telling me it was time to get my ass up and go meet Heron.

I'd thought about arguing, about telling her to go to hell, but we needed the stipend he held, not to mention however many days he'd managed to bargain out of the wazir on our behalf. Part of me wanted to tell her to go in my stead, but I decided I'd rather drink the mug of coffee she'd brought me than wear it.

I made a quick stop in the stables before leaving to check on Degan's sword. It was still there, and after a slight hesitation, I slipped it over my shoulder. It was probably just as safe sitting in the rafters as riding my back—hell, safer, given the last several days I'd been having—but after finding Wolf in my room, not to mention Mama Left Hand in the inn, I didn't like the idea of it being out of my sight anymore. Too many people were taking too close of an interest in me, and Degan's sword would make a handy bit of leverage if they found it. Better I know where it was than be surprised again, as I had been with Crook Eye.

Besides, it felt good to have it on my back again.

This time around, I avoided the main entrance to the padishah's palace and made directly for the Dog Gate instead. The same guard was there, keeping counsel with the yapping of the hounds in the falling night.

I smiled at him through the iron bars of the gate as I came up. His eyes grew wide, then narrowed quickly. I noticed that he'd invested in a new sash. Smart. I didn't want to think about what it would have taken to clean the old one after I'd finished with it.

"He's expecting me," I said. "Again."

The guard's fingers shifted on his spear. I saw his eyes flick back and forth, looking to see if anyone else was near, if anyone else would see or hear what came next. His jaw clenched in anticipation.

I sighed. He wasn't really considering trying to kill me, was he?

"If you thought it was going to be hard to explain why you had my money and *ahrami* in your pocket last time," I said, slipping my last seed into my mouth, "what do you think will happen when someone finds my body lying out here, stabbed by a spear and mauled by dogs?"

His fingers fidgeted some more. He licked his lips.

"Or are you hoping you can leave your post long enough to dispose of my body and not be missed?" I said. "Because, let me tell you, it's a lot harder than you think to drag this much deadweight someplace people won't find it. Especially if there are dogs barking and yapping and getting in the way."

I watched as he looked into the square behind me, considering the shadows and the hounds and where he might be able to dump me.

Fucking amateur. If you want to kill someone, kill him; thinking about it only gives you time to second-guess yourself.

I rattled the iron. "Just open the damn gate."

He paused a moment longer, then transferred his spear to his left hand and pulled out a set of keys with his right. The gate opened with a mild squeal. I stepped inside, pretending not to see the sheepish look on his face as he refused to meet my eye.

I considered telling Heron about this gap in the padishah's defenses, then thought better of it. You never know when a weak link will come in handy.

The guard stepped back over to his post house and rang a hand bell. After a short delay, a boy dressed in enough silk and silver to make a courtesan spit with envy came running up, torch in hand. He bowed to me and looked at the guard.

"For His Excellency, the Secretary to the Wazir of the Gardens of the Muse," muttered the guard. He didn't look at me as I left.

On the day we'd been escorted off the padishah's estate, the troupe and I had followed a wide, paved road from the artist's enclave to the main gate. Between the guards and the trees lining the road, I'd only managed glimpses of the grounds: a serene pool here, a carefully cultivated glade there, a stone-walled pavilion roofed in silk, complete with the sound of giggling maidens inside, up on a hill. It had been impressive, but hard to appreciate.

Now, though, I found myself walking through the midst of the garden's glory. Manicured lawns rolled away on either side in the torchlight and polished marble stepping stones marked out the path beneath our feet. We passed through a stand of trees planted to resemble what I could

only guess were supposed to be the jungles of Bakshar to
the south, and then, farther along, another grove that reminded me of the tall pine forests of the empire's Western
Client Kingdoms. A stream crossed our path, thick with lazy
fish, spanned by an arched bridge done in cedar and copper.
The flowing water fed into a small pond, its edges staked
with weeds and willows. I watched as small ripples appeared
and vanished on its surface, the fat fish growing fatter off
the night bugs that skated there.

The torch was spoiling my night vision, but its light allowed me to just make out buildings set off from the path.
Some were large enough to be residences or stables, others
smaller, their shapes and locations suggesting more private
purposes: tea pavilions and artists' workshops and quiet
rooms perfect for assignations ... or assassinations. Most
were dark, but a few showed faint flickers of light. Soft music wafted from one, while low, fast moans came from another. Occasionally, our path crossed other people's—court
functionaries, servants, men and women walking the
grounds—but never any guards or patrols.

I asked my guide about this.

"These are the padishah's grounds," he said. "You don't
come here unless you're invited. It is known."

"But why?" I said.

He looked at me, as if not quite understanding the question. "It is known," he said simply.

I let the subject drop. I was certain there were stories of
guards and glimmer and the padishah and his father making gruesome examples of people who hopped the wall, but
this clearly wasn't the time to hear them. Not that I didn't
think this boy was overflowing with tales—what boys and
servants aren't?—but he'd clearly learned not to share servants' gossip to visiting strangers, especially if those strangers were being taken to see someone who could have him
beaten for talking out of turn.

Smart kid.

Two curving sweeps of the path later, we turned onto a
wooden walkway and approached a low timber building set
beside a hill. In a city that favored stone and brick and tile,

this place stood out for its dark earthiness. Lights flickered in narrow glass windows, and I could smell, if not see, smoke coming from a chimney somewhere. The boy placed his torch in an iron holder a short distance from the building, then led me to the door and knocked.

A large man with a shining pate and an oiled mustache and beard opened the door. After relieving me of my rapier and Degan's sword, not to mention the dagger on my belt, he closed the door in the boy's face and led me into the house.

The inside was much like the out: simple, elegant, and mildly out of place. Thick rugs that would have made a desert sheikh wilt with envy ran over plain wooden floors. The walls were imperial in their feel—painted plaster, interspersed with the occasional mosaic done in cut stone and glass and marble, all depicting Angels and history (but not the emperor, I noticed)—while the ceilings were distinctly Djanese, their crossbeams made of heavy carved and painted timber. Silver lamps burned in holders on the wall, their smoke rising to brush over and around copper disks set above the flames: soot catchers, for making lampblack and ink. Heron, it seemed, was a clerk to the bone.

We walked along one hallway, turned down another, and then passed through a set of double doors already standing open. I crossed the threshold and stopped, awestruck.

Wall to wall, floor to ceiling, there were shelves. Shelves filled with books, with folios, with scrolls, with *stone tablets*, for Angels' sake. Papers seemed to drip from them, hanging out here, where a binding had split; there, where a scroll draped a teasing, curling corner across its neighbor; and off to the side, where a sheaf of documents bulged out, restrained only by the twine that held them together. The place smelled dry and dusty and full of secrets.

I licked my lips. To hell with Baldezar—*I* wanted to work out an exchange with Heron, to browse and thumb and read my way through even a fraction of a single wall.

"Ah," said, Heron. "On time. How pleasant. Tea?"

He was standing at a large, plain reading table near the far end of the room. The surface was immaculate, polished

by years of leather covers and sheepskins rather than wax.
A small iron tea service sat at one end, an elaborate cande-
labra at the other. Behind him, a blank section of wall—the
only one in the entire room—held a single antique long
sword, a jade vase full of dried flowers, and a large silk fan
draped in black gauze. The fan, I knew, would be covered
with intricately inked scenes—scenes that would start with
a wedding and end with a funeral pyre or a corpse, depending on which sect Heron followed. Once, when it had been
plainer, it had belonged to Heron's wife; now it was his widower's fan.

Hints of figures and gold leaf taunted me through the
gauze. I looked away before my eyes tried to make out too
many details of their life together, done small.

"Thanks, no," I said, coming the rest of the way into the
room. I took out an *ahrami* seed instead. Heron noted it
and nodded.

"I've not forgotten I owe you more," he said, pouring
himself a cup of pale green liquid.

"Nor have I."

We both smiled thinly at that. I noticed that there was
only one chair in the room. Heron took it, regarding me
over his steaming cup.

"And how is el-Qaddice agreeing with you?" he said,
running his eyes over my battered countenance. I could
only imagine how I appeared, since I'd specifically avoided
the offer by Tobin to see "how wonderfully horrendous" I
looked in his brass mirror. Ezak had stopped me on the way
out to study my bruises for purposes of stage makeup.

"The city and I are still getting a feel for each other," I
said.

"I can see that. And our actors? How are things pro-
gressing with them?"

"They're working their asses off."

He took a small sip, watching me through the steam.
"Will they be ready in time?"

"You know they won't," I said.

Another sip. "I do."

"Did you get us more time?" I said.

Sip.

"Did you?"

His eyes flicked away. "One day."

"What?" It came out louder than I'd intended, sounding out of place in such a hushed room. I didn't care. "One day? What the hell help is that?"

Heron's eyes came back to me. They were hard now. "It gives you one more day than you had."

"One day's nothing!" Not for Tobin's people, and especially not for me.

"One day is more than I'd hoped for: Accept it for the gift it is and make the best of it."

"You mean make our peace with being kicked out of the Old City."

Heron shrugged. "It was never a question of your audition succeeding; it was merely one of how long you'd be allowed to stay before being forced to leave."

"The Old City?"

"Djan."

That brought me up short. I took a step forward, resting my hands on the table, and stared down at the clerk. Heron met my gaze and sipped his tea, unperturbed.

"Why the hell would anyone want to force us out of the Despotate?" I said.

"Because you embarrassed someone."

"What?" I said. "Who?"

Heron sighed. "Think. Your troupe arrives in el-Qaddice. It moves up the queue for first auditions without anyone raising an objection. Then, having barely performed a scene, your people are granted conditional patronage and brought into the Old City to perform for the padishah. Clearly, someone was exerting influence on your behalf; and just as clearly, your success makes the person in charge of vetting new artists look like an ineffective fool."

"You mean the wazir?" I said.

"I mean the wazir," said Heron. "Who, I might add, only gave you the extra day because it turns out to have the least propitious omens for the month."

"Wait," I said, straightening up. "Are you saying the only

reason we got any extra time at all is because your boss thinks it will make things go even worse for us?"

Heron blew over his cup. "It seems the astrologer made an error in his initial calculations."

I almost wanted to laugh. Instead, I stalked away from the table.

Court politics? No wonder we'd been given a new script and barely any time to rehearse: We were meant to fail. And not just fail, but fail spectacularly—to do something so bad, so insulting, that the padishah would feel compelled to banish us from the Despotate.

Just what the hell was in that play, anyhow?

I could almost hear Christiana laughing from here. She would have seen this coming a league away, but me? No, not if it involved court politics, and especially not in Djan.

One extra day. Hell.

I turned and walked back over to stand beside Heron. I leaned back against the table and stared at his wall.

"What are our options?" I said. The dried flowers, I noted, were marjoram and larkspur, in imperial purple and deep indigo. Had he brought them with him, or harvested and dried them here? Had his wife picked the bouquet at one point?

Things I didn't need to know but was used to wondering.

"Options?" he said. "I'd suggest leaving early."

"That bad?"

"It could get that way." Heron shifted in his seat. "Mind, if you stay, I'd suggest you get an alternative translation of the play; not that I think it will make much of a difference."

"Banned?"

"Years ago. By the despot himself."

I nodded. It wasn't the most elegant setup, but it didn't have to be—not against a bunch of Imperial players. The cards were already stacked against us, and no one had even spoken a line yet.

That pissed me off.

"I'll get the troupe out," I said. Like it or not, I was still their patron, and still responsible for them.

"But not you?"

I let my eyes slide over to the sword. It was old but well cared for, the worn leather of the scabbard rich with oil. "I have unfinished business."

"It's not the actors who've earned my master's ire," noted Heron. "You're the patron, so yours is the name that was whispered in the proper ears. Once the wazir finds out you're not with the troupe, he'll send people to find you. And he will find you."

"That'll still give me a couple of extra days," I said as I stared at the long sword. The handle looked to be chain-wrapped bone, but the cross guard was another matter. Curved slightly forward toward the tip, the two bars of the guard had had piercings filed into the metal so that they formed three interlinked circles per side. As for the pommel, it had been chiseled into the shape of a tulip, its three petals folded shut.

The sword clearly had imperial roots. I wondered whether it had been Heron's at one point, or if it had come down during one of the earlier wars and been left behind.

"To do what?" said Heron.

"A lot of things," I said, stepping forward. I raised my hand, almost unconsciously, to run my fingers along the cross guard.

"What kind of things?" said Heron, his tone becoming exasperated. "And please keep your hands to yourself."

"To find a friend," I said, my hand stopping but not moving away. "And to see about getting back something I gave awa—" I froze, my eyes going from the guard back to the handle. It was too smooth to be bone, I realized; too fine. And the patterning in the material was all wrong. This looked more like . . .

"Holy shit," I said, my voice barely above a whisper.

"What?" said Heron. He was still behind me, but I could tell by his voice that he was standing now.

What I'd taken for piercings in the cross guard weren't. The white that stood out against the steel wasn't the plaster showing through from behind; they were carefully shaved and shaped pieces of material that had been set deep in the steel. I could almost imagine how, with the right light behind them, they would shine with a milky translucence. Like ivory.

"What?" said Heron again.

I looked from the ivory pieces to the long ivory handle, then reached out and gave the scabbard a quick tug. The pins under the cross guard kept the sword in place, allowing the leather to slide down and reveal the watery gray and white pattern of the steel. And a single etched teardrop.

"Here, now—!"

I spun away from the hand Heron tried to lay on my shoulder and let my wrist blade fall into my palm. I took a quick step back, both to let him see my steel and to keep him from laying hands on me.

"Explain to me," I said, "what the hell you're doing with a degan's sword that's over two centuries old. And believe me when I say, you want this explanation to be good."

Heron stared at me for a moment. Then his eyebrows went up. "You know of the degans?" he said.

"That wasn't the question," I said.

Heron looked from me to my blade and then to the sword on the wall. He scratched his jaw.

"I . . . collect things degan," he said at last.

It was my turn to raise an eyebrow. "Collect?"

"Acquire. Find. Study. Call it what you will. Ever since I heard about the Order of the Degans, I've been fascinated by it. By them." He gestured at the sword. "I found that, of all places, at the Grand Souk. It's a market held twice a year outside the city, when the despot opens and closes his summer court in el-Qaddice. Nine days after he arrives from the winter palace in Sajun, and nine days again before he and his court return, half the city and what seems like a sixth of the Despotate converge on the Plains of Akra to trade and dicker and gamble and race horses and . . . well, you get the idea."

"And you found *that* there?" I said.

Heron walked over to the sword and carefully slid the scabbard back in place. "Hard to believe, isn't it?"

Damn impossible, I thought. But instead, I said, "How'd you know it was genuine?"

"I think you've already answered that question yourself."

"The teardrop etched near the guard," I said.

"You mean the drop of blood."

I looked from the sword to Heron. "It's supposed to be
blood?"

Heron shrugged. "Some say a tear, some say sweat, some
say holy water. I've always preferred blood, mostly for aes-
thetic reasons. It seems to fit better with the Order, don't
you think? I've never had a chance to ask a degan directly,
to confirm it, though." He looked at me sidelong. "Have
you?"

I slid my knife back home up my sleeve. "It never came
up," I said.

"Pity."

We looked at the sword—Ivory Degan's sword—in silence for a bit.

"So, you . . . know a degan?" said Heron at last.

"Used to. How'd you find out about the Order?"

"They're not exactly a secret: People do hire them from
time to time in the empire, you know."

"I know," I said. "But, well . . ." I gestured at the sword,
giving him the opening to talk about his hobby. He took the
bait.

"How did I get so interested in them?"

"Yes."

Heron swept the room with a gesture. "A book, of
course."

I made sure I took a breath, so as not to rush my response. "A book? What kind of book?"

"A history."

"Of the degans?"

"Not at first, no." Heron walked over to a shelf. After a
moment, he pulled down a thin volume. "*The Commentaries of Simonis*," he said. "She was a historian during the
reigns of Lucien, and then Theodoi, over two centuries ago.
This isn't her main work, but it's the one where she talks
about the origins of the Order." He started to open the
book, then stopped himself and put it back on the shelf in-

stead. "She was a remarkable historian. It's thanks to her I first became interested in the idea of the degans."

I looked around the room—at the walls of books and papers, at Ivory's sword—and remembered Wolf's words, and Degan's. About the papers and laws Ivory had taken with him when he left the Order of the Degans.

It was too much to hope for—wasn't it?

"So, then what?" I said, stepping away from the sword and over to another shelf. "You started collecting more on the degans?"

"And history in general, yes, but at the back of my mind, there were always the degans."

I pulled out a book at random and opened to the frontispiece. It was an elaborate woodcut of a sea battle: galleys and waves, bodies and blood, with a bald man in a short cape holding the forecastle of the nearest ship against an onslaught of raiders. In the distance, behind the ships, there was a castle on a crag. Admiral Niphinos Byzezes at the Battle of Quetanos: not the best day for the empire, considering Byzezes surrendered and then led the raiders to the hidden harbor at Argnossi. It took the empire over a decade to rebuild the portion of the fleet that was lost in those two battles alone. As for Argnossi, we'd never reclaimed it: The raiders who had taken it were now a treaty city that specialized in piracy for hire.

"That's the naval section," said Heron.

I closed the book and put it back. "I got that." I looked around the room. "You have an impressive collection."

Heron surrendered a smile and preened. "It's been a long time in the building. A good portion of what you see is, if not unique, then quite rare."

I moved farther along the wall until I came to four stone tablets, each set into a special partition on a shelf. "Unique?" I said.

"Very. Are you familiar with Hout Yo?"

"No."

"Oh." Heron sniffed. "Well, they probably won't mean much to you, then."

"Likely not." I pulled out another *ahrami* seed and

rolled it slowly between my palms. If there was a "naval section," it seemed likely there would be a "degan section," too. The most likely choice was where Heron had pulled out Simonis's volume, but that was no guarantee: Merely mentioning them might not be enough.

I've known—and robbed—a few bibliophiles in my time and if there's one thing I've learned, it's that none of them sort or classify their collections the same way. One might shelve, say, Dossanius's *Five Views on the Engraver's Art* (a folio that traditionally fetches a good price among Ildrecca's Queer Hatchers, since most coin forgers won't let their competitors see it once they get their hands on a copy) with books on crafts, another with metallurgy, a third with discourses of money policy, and a fourth under history. Back when I'd still been drawing the latch, I'd spent half the night searching the walls and cubbies of a bookbinder's back room, hunting for a copy of Synod's *Poems and Polemics* I'd been paid to lift. Finally, with dawn creeping in and the sound of his apprentices rattling about their room in the attic, I'd found it bracketed between two books on mathematics. I still haven't figured that one out.

I slipped the seed into my mouth and continued my circuit of the room, making a point not to spend too much time looking at any one title or section, so as to avoid raising suspicion. I made appreciative noises as I went.

I was just coming up to Heron when he cleared his throat.

"You said you knew a degan," he said, trying to sound casual. "Do you mind if I ask which one?"

It wasn't a hard choice to make: I wasn't about to reveal Bronze Degan's presence in el-Qaddice, and I didn't expect mentioning Silver's name would win me any points with the Azaari. Not that I particularly cared one way or the other what Silver, in his guise as Wolf, liked at this point, but I didn't want to jeopardize anything by revealing his presence to a secretary of the despot's court.

I went with a safe choice: the dead one.

"Iron Degan," I said.

"I see." A slight pause as Heron drew out his case and

slipped his own *ahrami* seed into his mouth. "I don't suppose he's in el-Qaddice? I'd love to actually meet a—"

"He's dead."

The seed cracked in Heron's mouth. "Oh." He paused to chew and swallow. "Do you know when? Or how?"

"Four months ago," I said. "As to how . . ." I stepped around Heron and finished my circuit, ending in front of the small display again. It was time to throw him a bone, something to pique his interest and get him off his guard at the same time. "I'm not sure. Rumor has it it was another degan."

"What?" he said, his voice rising a fraction in disbelief. "A degan killing another degan? That hasn't happened since, well . . ."

"Him?" I said, pointing at Ivory's sword.

Heron's eyebrows dropped into a scowl. "You seem to know a great deal about the degans for a . . ." He paused.

"What?" I said. "The patron of an acting troupe?"

"No," said Heron. "A Gray Prince."

If he'd been expecting surprise, I disappointed him. Instead, I hooked my thumbs in my sword belt and smiled. "Who's in your pocket in the inn?" I said. "The innkeeper?"

"His wife. And the eldest son. You think it's chance I put you there?"

I shook my head. "No. I half expected it. Besides, it's not like I've exactly made a secret of who I am." Much to my recent chagrin.

"No, you haven't," said Heron, his tone telling me word had likely leaked into the padishah's court as well. "But that still doesn't explain your knowledge of the Order."

"I told you," I said. "I used to run with a degan."

"Iron."

"Right."

"And he told you about Ivory Degan?"

I shrugged and let a smile play about my lips. "Someone did."

Heron sighed in exasperation. "If you're going to—"

"How'd you learn about him?" I said.

"What?"

"How'd you find out about Ivory Degan?" I said. I waved at the overflowing shelves. "Don't get me wrong, all of this is ... nice, but you're not going to find information about the Order, let alone someone like Ivory, in Zacres or Nessian the Younger or any of the usual histories; they wouldn't know the first thing about it. This is something you need to get from the source." I smiled and tapped the side of my nose and leered my best Nose's "I know something you don't" leer. "You know: from a degan."

Heron glared at me from across the room. "I have it from a degan," he said coldly.

I arched a mocking eyebrow. "Oh, really?" I said. "What, are you telling me you have a degan in your pocket? I thought you've never met one. Or is that a line of shit, too, just like what you've been feeding me about the auditions?" I snorted. "Hell, I'd put money down that you didn't know what you had in that sword until some visiting imperial nobleman noticed it over tea. Is that what it's for, to impress the visitors from back home? To make them feel just a bit smaller, and you a bit bigger, so you can feel good about walking out on the empire?"

He moved fast for a scribe. Heron was across the room and in my face before I had time to react. I suspect it was only force of diplomatic habit that kept his hands from my throat.

"You have no inkling of why I left the empire, *thief*," he snapped. I could almost taste the indignation coming off him. "And you'll keep your tongue silent on the matter, or you'll come to regret it. As for that sword, the man who owned it was the historian of his Order. He helped found the degans, helped organize them, helped give a group of mercenaries a purpose. And if that were all I knew of him, it would be enough for me to put that sword on my wall, no matter what anyone may or may not think."

"But you know more than that, right?"

"More than you can imagine," he seethed.

Here it was: Heron was at the edge, ready to fall. To spill.

All he needed was the right push. I wet my lips and said the word, gave the nudge, making it an accusation as much as a question.

"How?" I said. "If you've never met a degan, how do you know so damn much?"

I almost got him. Heron opened his mouth, ready to speak, ready to show me just how little I knew; then he caught himself. I watched, poised for the kill, as he took a step back and followed it up with a slow breath.

So close.

"I've been studying the Order of the Degans for longer than you've been alive," he said softly. "If I say I know something about the Order, or its history, then I know it. I don't need to prove it to you."

I looked around the room, and then back at him. "You have them, don't you?"

"What?"

"Ivory Degan's records."

I'll give him this: His eyes barely flickered. But flicker they did, off toward a wall to my left. I pretended not to notice.

"Your acting company has an extra day," said Heron, his voice turning as brittle as early winter ice. He stepped back over to the table and poured himself a fresh cup of tea. "I would suggest you spend it packing up your scenery and preparing to depart. As for your allowance, the sum has been adjusted. You'll find the remainder of it—and the *ah-rami* I promised you—near the door on your way out."

I nodded and turned away.

"I don't want to see or hear from you until the day of your audition," he said as I left. "Am I understood?"

"You're understood," I said, not bothering to look back. The same servant met me in the hallway, led me to the door, and handed me my blades, along with a purse and a satchel. The satchel held a box.

Then I was outside, the door to Heron's house closing behind me. The boy was still waiting, a torch now in hand against the darkness.

I followed him along the boardwalk and onto the

grounds. He was chatty now, trying to pry gossip and secrets of the meeting from me; I wondered idly whether he was on someone's payroll, or if he simply sold what he gathered to the first person who paid.

Either way, I didn't say much. I was too busy trying to figure out how the hell I was going to break back into this place so I could raid Heron's library.

Chapter Twenty-six

I took to the streets after that.

I admit it wasn't the smartest move on my part—wandering a strange city with a price on your head will rarely get you labeled as clever—but given most *Zakur* didn't know me by sight, and most Kin stayed in the Imperial Quarter, I figured the odds were in my favor, for the moment. In a few days, though? Who knew?

Smart or stupid, though, I needed to wear down some shoe leather if I wanted to come up the beginnings of a plan to crack Heron's ken. Once, I might have sat down with Degan over a meal or a drink, to let his wry wit cut through the tangles in my head like a blade through cheese. But those days were gone. Now my knots and distractions were my own to deal with, and I'd discovered that in my friend's absence, the only solution was miles. Miles and movement and the ability to lose myself in the streets.

I went away from the padishah's grounds, seeking out the back ways and darker corners of the city that I knew would exist even within the second ring. I passed through midnight scroungers' markets and around poets arguing on street corners; waved off gap-toothed beggars and declined the services of eager linksmen. I hunted darkness and solitude, sought out the familiar smells of old garbage and fresh crime.

It was all coming down to time: begged time, borrowed time, even stolen time—all of it tight. Even without the wazir and Heron wanting me gone, balancing Wolf's impatience and the task Mama Left Hand had laid at my feet would have been a hell of a trick, but with only two days to do it? Maybe if I'd been in Ildrecca I could have pulled something off, but that required resources I didn't have access to in Djan. Here, being a Gray Prince had me more a target than a threat, had brought more peril than prestige. I'd foolishly thought to brandish my title like a sword, to cow the Kin and impress the *Zakur* with my rare status; instead, I should have taken a tip from the other princes and used it like a shield.

When you operate without an organization at your back, you can only rely on yourself and your reputation. I knew that—had operated on the premise for more years than I could count, both as a Draw Latch and then later as a Nose. Even when I'd had Nicco's reputation to lean on, I'd never let my own fall too far behind. Having an Upright Man's name in your pocket helps, but unless he or his Cutters are standing there with you, there's always the chance that the cove you're pushing will decide he'd rather push back than give in.

I'd forgotten that; or, at the least, I'd let it drift away over the last several months. Instead of worrying about being Drothe, I'd focused on being The Prince. And in Ildrecca, I'd been able to get away with it: I still had a name on the street, and the tale of my rise was fresh enough, that any stumbles or gaps were been easily ignored. Up until Crook Eye had called my bluff, I'd been able to pretend that the title was enough, that the dodge would take care of itself, as long as I moved fast and didn't let the other princes look too close.

But not here. Here, I was just another Imperial, a member of the Kin who brought a bit more to the table, but not enough to make a difference, not when it mattered. Gray Prince or Wide Nose, I was all but alone. And when you were alone, the best thing to do was not stand up and wave your arms as I had done, but to stick to the shadows, to keep your voice low and your eyes open, to play to your strengths.

To be what you were, and not what you were pretending to be.

I redoubled my pace, suddenly eager to get farther into the night. To get back to Fowler. To figure out how the hell I was going to get out of this, because while I didn't know what I was going to do, I knew how I needed to go about it.

I needed to be a Nose.

Not for the first time, I missed the bells of Ildrecca. The old temple ringer down in the Square Hills cordon, calling the monks of Corvous to prayers with its monster of a clapper; the somber wind-bells over at the Sisters of Despair's chapter house in Cold Street; the lyrical clapping of the brass hand bells up on Osprey's Crag that had been rung every night for the last hundred years, though no one ever knew by whom. All had helped me mark the night, letting me know how far from dawn or dusk or an appointment I might be, and all had kept me company. Their absence was something I'd felt ever since I'd gotten here.

Still, el-Qaddice had its fair share of night rituals as well. I'd already come to expect the deep, rolling chant that welled up from the Temples of the Horned Horse that stood in every circle of the city. The slight difference in each temple's timing made the prayer sound more like a wandering echo of itself, and the sound had caused me to stop, entranced, the first night I'd heard it. Later, sometime past midnight, I knew the mystics of the Old City would spin their cleansing chimes, filling the air with a thin, tinkling music that was meant, I was told, to keep two rival bands of djinni from resuming an ages-old war in the skies over the city. I hadn't been able to make full sense of it, but the ancient grudge supposedly had something to do with a silver thread and a peach and a thimbleful of dust. All I knew was that I'd yet to meet any guard patrols, let alone djinn, when the chimes were sounding, which was fine by me.

Those chimes sounded now, bringing an eerie sense of foreboding to the streets. I felt the hairs rise along my arms and neck, only to fall back down as the ringing faded. In the silence that followed, I became aware of the soft tread of slippered feet at my side.

I looked over, saw the ghost of a shadow in my night vision, and grimaced.

"How long have you been following me?" I said.

"Long enough to know you for a fool to walk the streets of el-Qaddice alone," said Aribah, her voice a near-disembodied thing in the darkness.

"Not alone as I first thought, it seems."

"Which only makes your actions that much more reck-less." I could practically hear her shaking her head. "To think that the Family would give one such as you the gift of dark seeing . . ."

"The Family had nothing to do with it," I said. "I got my night vision from my stepfather."

"And he received it how?"

That was a good question. I'd always wondered where my stepfather, Sebastian, had gotten his night vision: who had performed the ritual for him, and how he'd learned to use it and pass it along to me. Those first few nights, I'd lain awake studying the still house with my freshly magicked eyes, spinning tales in my head about Sebastian and the kinds of adventures he must have gone through to receive the gift that was now mine. I'd always known he'd traveled before settling down with us in the Balsturan—with the tales he told of Sadaz and Un'Naang and Cyprios, it was no secret he'd ranged far and wide in his youth—but after that night in the forest, those wanderings had taken on fresh meaning in my imagination, complete with demons and djinn and hoar-goblins. How else to explain the solemn rit-ual he had performed, the magic that had passed from his eyes to mine? A ritual he had never had a chance to teach me, because he was dead three days later.

After Sebastian's murder, my imaginings had taken a darker turn: Clever bargains with inscrutable wizards had turned into desperate deals with demons in my head. I'd known better, of course, but I'd been young, and with no better answers I made up something that seemed to fit with the sole fact I had: Sebastian had been cut down by assas-sins in our doorway, and I'd never known why.

I looked at a flicker of amber that was the young assassin next to me. No, it hadn't been the *neyajin*. Sebastian's killers hadn't been Djanese. And even if they had, the killing had been done in daylight. That didn't seem like a *neyajin* practice.

I turned my eyes forward. "I don't know how he got it," I said.

The sound of shoes stopping suddenly in the street. "Truly?"

"Truly. I have no idea who gave it to Sebastian, nor how he passed it on."

"Then we share an interest in your eyes."

"For different reasons, but yes, I suppose so."

Another pause, and then the slippers began walking, although this time at a more contemplative pace. I fell in beside them as best I could, given I wasn't sure where precisely Aribah was in the darkness. I noted that we both naturally drifted away from the few lights we found spilling out of windows or doorways, invariably favoring the darker path when presented a choice.

"So why the shadow?" I said.

"My grandfather still thinks you're too valuable to risk losing."

"And you?" I said. "What do you think?"

"I do as I'm asked."

"Asked," I said, "or told?"

Aribah's voice grew prickly. "I'm here to make sure you don't fall prey to the hazards of el-Qaddice."

"You mean to make sure my eyes don't fall hazard. I can't imagine that my overall health is of much concern to your grandfather."

"The two are one and the same. To lose you is to lose the potential of your gift."

"I thought your grandfather decided my gift wasn't the same thing as what the despot handed out, that what I have can't help your school."

"Not being able to possess something does not make it any less dear."

Meaning things weren't as cut-and-dried as the old man had made out in the tunnels. Interesting. And worrisome.

I glanced over at the amber-tinted smudge beside me.

"How do you do that?" I said.

"What?"

"Hide from my ni—from the dark sight."

A snort in the night. "You think I'd reveal our secrets to an Imperial?"

"Just as you thought I'd reveal mine to a Djanese?"

I watched the blur that was Aribah as she kept pace with me. Finally, "It's a special dye," she said. "Painted on in the form of runes, over and over, and then pounded into the cloth until the power is bound to the fibers themselves."

"And your faces and hands and blades?" I said.

"A similar procedure." Then after a moment, she added, "Only with less pounding."

I grinned at the unexpected comment. "Humor?" I said. "I didn't think that was allowed among the *neyajin.*"

"It is not only allowed, it's encouraged. I thought you, being of your people's *Zakur,* would understand."

I thought for a moment, trying to translate her meaning. "You mean gallows humor?" I said at last.

"If by that you mean using laughter to defeat the dreams that come to you in the night—and the regrets that haunt you during the day—then yes, that's what I mean."

"In that case, yes, I understand, and I apologize for my surprise."

We went a handful of paces farther along before I heard a rustle of cloth beside me. Looking over, I was startled to see Aribah drawing the tail of her turban away from her face.

It wasn't only her eyes that were stunning: The fine arch of her eyebrows was echoed in the sharp lines of her cheek and the downward turn of her mouth. The swath of dye only accentuated the reveal, making it seem as if the upper part of her face was hidden by a mask, or the night.

She didn't look at me as she walked, and I made a point not to stare. I understood the gift she'd just given me.

"My grandfather says that to be able to laugh in the face of what you've done, and what you will do again, is one of the most important skills we can learn," she said softly. "It's why we tell tales not only of success, but also of failure, not just to learn from them, but to learn to laugh at death."

"I'd think failure in your line of work would carry too high a cost to be laughed at."

"Sometimes, yes, but there are more . . . nonlethal close calls than you might think." She looked over, and I looked away so as to not fall into her eyes. "Is it the same for you?"

"Similar," I said. "Although I don't make a habit of . . . well, I don't belong to a school like you do, so I have to be a bit more selective about who I share my failures with." I tapped my nose. "Reputation, you know."

"It must be hard to be on your own," she said. "With the school, as long as people fear one *neyajin*, they fear us all."

"Oh, it's supposed to work that way with the position I have, too."

"But it doesn't?"

I hesitated. "Not exactly, no."

"Then you're doing it wrong."

"Excuse me?"

"If the others like you are feared, and you aren't, then you're not one of them; if you were, it would be the same for you."

"It's not that simple. We—"

"It is *precisely* that simple." She stopped and began refastening her face cloth. I stopped as well. This close, my night vision could make out her eyes between blinks. "If the other members of your school are feared, but you are not, then you're not only failing yourself—you're failing them. To leave an opening for doubt, to give your victims reason to hope they might live when you come for them, is to walk the path of weakness. Weakness not only for you, but for all those who share your status." She poked a finger against my chest. "Whether you respect them or not—whether you even like them or not—you're doing your fellows no favor by undermining them."

"And if they're the ones doing the undermining?" I said, maybe a bit too defensively.

"Then they're fools as well. Harming your reputation only harms their own. If people see you as being weak enough to fall, how long before they start to see the same weakness in those who caused your fall?"

I shook my head. "That's a good theory for a school of assassins, but it doesn't quite work the same for a group of crime lords. We have every reason to want to see the others fail; their fall only helps us rise higher."

"But at your own expense," said Aribah, her eyes gleaming so bright in the night I expect anyone could have seen them just then. "Even among the *neyajin*, we know to keep our disputes hidden. If our school was known to be fractured, none would come to us; worse, a rival, or even the agents of the despot, might see it and know us to be ripe for the breaking."

"So in other words, you're saying it's better that the door appears whole even if it's rotting from within, so no one knows they can kick it down?"

"That's not how I'd put it, but yes."

I studied the rooftops around us as I considered what she'd said. I'd long known the value of appearances—or lack thereof—on the street and in criminal organizations; as a Nose, I'd spent a good deal of time either shoring up or slowly dismantling them, one piece at a time. What Aribah was saying was nothing new, but the way she was saying it, the way she was talking about the illusion of unity keeping the despot at bay . . . I'd never considered that that kind of an approach could be applied on a broader, and higher, level.

"My thanks to your grandfather," I said, turning back to her. "He taught you well."

Aribah bowed, albeit a bit stiffly. "I will convey your praise to him." The words didn't come out exactly supple, either.

"As for you . . ." I gave her a formal salaam, smiling when I saw her eyes widen at how deeply I bowed. As my junior, she had every right to expect much less than I gave. "Thank you for the lesson," I said, straightening up. "I will take it to heart."

It was hard to tell under the cloth and the dye, but I could have sworn I caught the faintest hint of a blush on her cheek as she began another bow, caught herself, and then turned and hurried off into the night.

I stood smiling as I watched her—or what I thought was her—go, then turned and headed toward the Imperial Quarter. I hummed as I walked.

It was still dark—but only just—when I came limping up to the gate to the Imperial Quarter. It felt as if I'd covered half the Old City in one night, and I was starting to wonder if I might not have been far off. Given the looks the guards on each side gave me, it was clear I was wearing my fatigue all too openly. The brief lift I'd gotten from my conversation with Aribah had fled; now all I wanted was a long day in a soft bed, followed by a hot meal. There was nothing at this point, I'd decided—not even the promise of Heron's library—so important that it couldn't wait a few hours.

Then I reached the Angel's Shadow, and the chaos its courtyard contained, and knew that food, let alone sleep, was going to be a while coming yet.

The yard before the inn was awash in activity. Torches burned, wagons creaked, and bodies moved to and fro, casting shadows about like owls from a spendthrift's hands. Tobin stood on the deck of the nearest wagon, shouting orders to the actors as they scrambled about, clearly ignoring him. I knew from the trip down that the troupe could load and unload these carriages in their sleep; his performance was as much to distract the locals from noticing anything of value "accidentally" being loaded onto the wagons as it was to keep him out of their way. I wondered just how many of the finer items in the inn would be discovered missing in the days to come.

I also wondered why the hell they were packing up, let alone at this hour.

"Tobin!" I yelled, stalking as quickly as I could across the yard. "Tobin!"

The troupe leader waved a hand in my direction but didn't turn around. "Not now, if you please," he boomed across the yard. "I've people to shepherd and props to pack!"

I came up beside the wagon. "What the hell is going on?"

"Departure, sir!" he projected, his voice bouncing effortlessly around the yard. "Always a trying time, to be sure." Then, more softly, and out of the corner of his mouth, "Fade, would you? The innkeeper keeps sticking his head out, and there's an exceptional chair and two bags of flour Yekeb's waiting to get loaded. You'll throw off our timing."

"But why now?" I said.

"Because they're so busy trying to make the breakfast I requested for us all, they won't—"

"No, I mean why pack up and leave now, you idiot?"

"Why, the note, of course."

"What note?"

Tobin glanced around the courtyard, then waved quickly off to his right. Yekeb dashed from the barn to the second wagon, a large, rolled-up carpet in his arms.

"Isn't that the rug from—?"

"Yes. And I'm busy. Speak to Ezak." Tobin turned away and made a point of directing his—and any watcher's—attention to the other side of the courtyard. "Marianna, dear, be careful! You think buttons like that grow on trees? Now we have to fix the front of your frock, girl!"

I turned away from Marianna and her escaping cleavage and walked over to Ezak. He stood to one side, quietly watching people move to and fro, all the while making small marks on a wax tablet.

"What is all this?" I said. "And why the hell wasn't I consulted?"

"Last to first," he said, "you weren't here. And 'all this' is in response to this." He reached into his shirtsleeve and pulled out a folded piece of paper. "I don't know what you did, but whatever it was, it was well done."

I took the letter and opened it. The top half of the note was an elegantly flowing Djanese script that looked more like smoke than writing; the lower half was a translation into imperial cephta. That calligraphy was impressive as well, with the symbols having a precise, yet free, feel to them. A simple seal, consisting of a blob of wax and a silk ribbon, hung at the bottom.

It was from Heron. It advised the company that, while the wazir's patronage had not been rescinded, it would likely be best for all parties if the company managed to find its way out of the city. Matters being what they were between the empire and the Despotate, there was concern he could no longer guarantee the safety, let alone the financial support, that the company would require to remain safely within el-Qaddice. Regrets and please come back and all the rest of the usual crap.

"Dammit," I said. Heron was moving faster than I'd expected.

"It's true?" said Ezak.

"The facts aren't, but the sentiment behind them is."

"So the wazir wants us gone."

"Not the wazir," I said. "His secretary."

Ezak turned back to his tablet. "Isn't it the same thing?"

I didn't answer, and instead read the letter again. Nothing was specifically in the wazir's name—Heron knew better than to try that—but the phrasing had been set down in such a way that, unless you read closely, it was easy to miss that it was the secretary offering the warnings and suggestions, and not his master.

But why do that? If anything, it seemed likely that the wazir would want us to stay. Vengeance, after all, is that much sweeter if you can watch it meted out; what better seat than at the padishah's side when the prince became enraged at the troupe's audacity and poor performance?

No, by hustling us out of el-Qaddice, Heron likely risked incurring the wazir's *dis*pleasure, rather than the other way around.

So why the hurry?

It had to be something I'd said. Something that had changed the game—so much so that Heron wanted me out of the city as soon as possible, the consequences be damned.

Something about the degans.

Now I definitely wanted to get into that library of his.

I folded the paper back up and slid it into my own sleeve. Ezak didn't bat an eye.

"How long do you think this will take?" I said.

"Assuming Tobin doesn't set his cap on stealing the roof tiles? A few more hours at most."

"Let me know when you're getting close to ready," I said, touching the pouch Heron had given me. "I have some traveling money."

For the first time since I'd come up beside him, Ezak lowered his tablet. "You mean you're going to let us leave? Just like that?"

"It's for the best."

Ezak gave me a long look. "I won't argue with you, if that's what you're looking for," he said. "Between the letter and the schedule that's been forced upon us, I doubt you'll find many of us anxious to stay."

"But?"

"But I have to admit . . ." He glanced out at the street, then up toward the city's spires and domes. "To perform in Djan? To audition for the despot's son? To, maybe, play the court of the enemy himself? It had its appeal." He grinned. "Not many other troupes can lay claim to those particular feathers."

"And Tobin? How does he feel about it?"

"He won't show it, but my cousin would have given his left hand to walk a stage of that scale even once. So would some of the others."

"Which is why he won't show it."

Ezak nodded. "Someone has to remain untouched, if only for the rest."

I looked back at the troupe's leader perched on the wagon, shouting and pointing and getting on with things, up there for everyone to see.

A true showman.

"Remind me to write you a letter," I said. "I know a baroness back in Ildrecca who might be willing to take a look at you, even if the recommendation does come from me."

Ezak tipped his head in thanks. "One question," he said as I turned away.

"What?"

"Why?"

"Bring you here? I thought that was obvious."

"No. That I understand. But considering everything you went through to get us here, everything you spent, everything we've done since we arrived in el-Qaddice, I have to wonder: Why let yourself be pushed out without a fight?"

I grimaced. "Who said I'm leaving? You're the ones who're taking to the road."

Ezak's eyes widened. "But you're—"

"Trouble," I said, walking away. "And not the kind you people need right now, especially not in Djan." I patted my pouch again. "Find me before you leave."

I reached the inn's main door and went in, stepping from chaos into near silence. Except for a single candle guttering on a table in the common room, the place was black, and except for Fowler Jess and Bronze Degan at the table, their heads bent together over said same candle and pair of cups, it was empty.

My Oak Mistress and my estranged best friend, sharing a drink in a dark tavern, waiting for me to return: What could be bad?

Chapter Twenty-seven

I closed the door and limped my way across the room toward the bar. I heard a small gasp as I did so, didn't realize why until I remembered that I had Degan's sword across my back, until I remembered he hadn't known it was here until now.

Well, that made it one surprise for each of us, then, didn't it?

"You two are getting as thick as thieves," I said as I settled gingerly on one of the stools. "Pardon the saying."

"Given the present company," said Degan, "I'll take it as a compliment."

"Take it however the hell you like." I undid the sack holding Heron's box from around my waist and set it on the bar. Back in the depths of the inn, I could hear the clatter and bang of the kitchen working on the company's breakfast. "I thought you had other business," I said to Degan. "That you didn't want to be here, near us, because it would be . . . how did you put it? Oh, yes, it would be 'too hard.'"

"Drothe," said Fowler quickly. "He didn't come here. I went and—"

Degan held up a hand. "No, it's all right," he said. "No one made me come, Jess, and I wasn't exactly charitable toward Drothe last time I was here. He has the right of it."

I sniffed and pulled the box out of the sack. It was a little smaller than a man's head and made of polished mahogany, the beaten copped bands that held it closed complementing the red of the wood nicely. Leave it to someone at court to spend more on a box than on what it held.

"Do you mind if I ask how you came by my . . . by the sword?" he said as I swung the lid back on the box.

"Took it off a Gray Prince," I said. "He's dead now. Long story."

"They usually are with you."

"Don't suppose I can convince you to take it off me?" I said.

Degan shook his head. "We went over that the other night. It's not mine to carry anymore."

"I'll hold on to it, then."

"Sentimental value?"

"Something like that."

There were six cloth bags inside the box. I picked one, drew out a seed, and put it in my mouth. After the night I'd had, the *ahrami* should have been ambrosia; instead, it just sat under my tongue, tasting bitter.

I turned my attention to Fowler. "How'd you know where to find him?" I asked.

"Followed him. The night he came to see you."

I raised an eyebrow at Degan. He shrugged. "I was watching for you. She keeps a different line."

Fowler sat up a bit in her chair, clearly pleased with herself.

"Fowler says you're having some problems with the *Zakur*," said Degan.

"Nothing I can't handle." Fowler snorted. I ignored her. "Me, I'd rather talk about your brother—"

"Former brother."

"*Former* brother, then. Silver."

Degan picked up his cup, swirled the contents about, and took a sip. "I told you, he has an overly high opinion of himself."

"He also seems to have a fairly high opinion of Ivory Degan as well."

Degan looked up sharply. "You told him?"

"No, you did. Silver was sitting in my room when we spoke the other night in the hallway. He heard everything."

Degan gave Fowler a sharp look, which she ignored. Good for her.

"And you knew this?" he said to me.

"Hell, no. If I had, I would've dragged him out, or you in, and finished this damn thing there and then."

"And what did my former brother have to say?"

"Turns out you're not the only one interested in Ivory's papers."

"He told you he wants them as well?"

"Yes."

"To use as leverage against me?"

"That's his story."

"And you believe him?"

I shrugged. "I believe he has plans for you, and now for the papers as well. I don't know if your coming down here was an excuse or a happy accident, but he definitely sees you as a means to laying hands on them."

Degan frowned. "That doesn't make sense. Why would he assume I'd be able to find them?"

"Maybe he didn't," said Fowler.

We both looked at her.

"Maybe he didn't expect a former degan to find them," she said. She turned to me. "Maybe he expected a former Nose to do it instead."

"Me?" I said. "Why the hell would he think I could come down here and find anything, let alone that?"

"No," said Degan, giving Fowler an approving look. "Maybe she's right. Silver's not stupid: If he knew I was looking for something, and he knew he could get you to help by having you come after me, then it makes sense."

"But how would he know what you were looking for? I didn't even know until I got down here and talked to you. Hell, he didn't know you were in Djan until I told him."

Degan cleared his throat. "He, ah, might have heard something through other circles."

I sat up on my stool. "What other circles?"

Degan looked off into the darkness. "You weren't the first person I told what I was looking for."

I was about to say it didn't matter who he'd asked in el-

Qaddice when I realized he wasn't talking about that. That
he was talking about Ildrecca, back before he'd vanished.

Oh, hell. "You asked other degans about Ivory, didn't
you?" I said.

"One or two."

"And they told Silver?"

"Possibly. More likely, he figured it out without them
knowing they were telling him. Like I said, he's not stupid."

I reached up and rubbed my temples. It didn't help. "Remind me: Weren't you supposed to be, I don't know, on the
run from them? Something about the Order wanting your
head because you dusted another degan and threw your
sword away?"

"It's complicated," said Degan.

"I'll just bet it is." I folded my arms and leaned back
against the bar. "Talk. And don't even try to tell me it's
some sort of degan-only secret: You're out of the Order, and
I'm in this up to my neck."

Degan blew out his cheeks and sat back in his chair.
"Let's just say there's what the Order is supposed to do, and
there's what some of the members choose to do. I chose to
talk to two of my fellows, and they chose not to kill me. It
was just after Iron's death, and things were still uncertain.
Besides, it wasn't as if I could walk in and check the records
in the Barracks Hall after what had happened."

"And your two brothers were all right with this?"

"A brother and a sister, actually," said Degan. "Jade and
Brass. They didn't approve of what I did, but they understood how it happened. More important, they sympathized
with what I want to do." He took a last gulp from his cup
and set it aside. A sad smile spread across his face. "They
were weeks sneaking records in and out for me, with Brass
and me going over them for any hint of what might have
happened to Ivory Degan after he left Ildrecca."

"But not Jade?" I said.

"He drew the line at helping me look. He said he could
bring the information out and back, but he couldn't countenance taking a more direct hand in something he felt could
just as easily break the Order as mend it."

"Was he right?"

"Everyone has to follow where their conscience leads; who am I to say he was right or wrong to stop where he did?"

"But you still found something that pointed you down here."

"Brass did," said Degan. "She came across a reference in one of the old journals—the members still kept journals as a rule back then—about Bone Degan saying she'd thought she caught a glimpse of Ivory in el-Qaddice. This was almost three decades after he'd left the Order, but Bone didn't go after him to find out for certain."

"Why not?" said Fowler.

"Something about her being busy holding off five of the despot's men while her charge made an escape out a palace window, I suspect."

"Ah," said Fowler. She glared at me.

"What?" I said.

"Just noticing the similarities."

"I haven't had to jump out of a window since we got here. Not even a palace's." I slipped another seed into my mouth, then added, "Yet."

"Yet?" said Degan and Fowler together.

I shrugged. "There's a library that's showing some promise on the Ivory front."

"'The Ivory front'?" said Degan. He sat up in his seat. "I thought I told you I didn't want your help."

"Tell it to the degan who has my people over a barrel. What you want isn't necessarily what you're going to get."

"I could say the same for you."

I shifted my weight on the stool, wincing slightly in the process. "Is that a threat?"

"A threat?" Degan rocked his head back in disbelief. "Drothe, you have one *Zakur* crime lord putting a price on your head even as another is trying to blackmail you into killing the first. Me threatening you at this point would be like kicking a dying horse: It might hasten things along, but it sure as hell wouldn't make a difference in the end."

I got up and walked over to their table. Outside, I could

hear Tobin raising his voice, yelling at someone to be careful with a crate. Probably covering for Yekeb and the flour.

"So does that mean you're here to help?" I asked, stopping before Degan.

He shook his head. "I can't risk drawing attention to myself."

"Then why come?"

"Because I wanted to say good-bye."

"You going someplace?"

Degan glanced past me, toward the door and the yard beyond. "You are."

"That's where you're wrong."

"Excuse me?" This from Fowler.

"They may be leaving," I said, jerking a thumb over my shoulder, "but I still have things to do here." I looked at Degan. "Just like you."

"No, not like me," said Degan. "I'm here because of a promise I made long ago—a promise I have to try to keep, even if it means failure. You don't have that burden. You can walk away."

"The hell I can. I came down here to preserve my organization and protect my people. If I try to walk away—"

"If you walk away," snapped Degan, "you end up back where you started: in Ildrecca, with people at your back and a problem to solve. Do you realize how lucky you are? How fortunate that is? You can walk out of el-Qaddice and not have to worry about what you're leaving undone behind you. Silver threatened you? So what? Threaten him back, or better yet, make it so he can't hurt you."

"He's a degan, dammit. I can't just tell him to go fuck himself."

"Why not? You did it to me. You did it to a pair of Gray Princes, and killed one of them when he back came after you. Hell, you even sidestepped the emperor. So don't tell me you can't get a single swordsman off your back if you want to."

"I came down here because it *was* the best way to get him off my back."

"Bullshit." The word was heavy with venom as it left Fowler's lips.

My eyes snapped over to meet hers. "What?"

"You heard me. The organization was just an excuse, and you know it. You're not here for your people back in Ildrecca or your position as a Gray Prince. Hell, you're not even here for him." Fowler jerked a thumb at Degan. "You're here for you."

"For me?" I said. "In case you haven't noticed, it hasn't exactly been a string of festival days since we arrived. If I wanted to do something for myself, it sure as hell wouldn't involve coming to Djan so I could get pissed on by the Despotate and the *Zakur*."

"Get pissed on?" Fowler was out of her chair and in my face in an instant. "You've been eating this up! You came to Djan so you wouldn't have to play the Gray Prince anymore. By chasing after him, you got to leave everything else behind: the planning, juggling the Uprights and Rufflers and Princes, having to weigh politics and build connections. All you have to do here is be a Nose and run the streets, which is exactly what you want to do."

"Well, let me tell you something: It doesn't work that way. You can't leave it behind. You're not just a Nose anymore—not even down here. I know that. Fat Chair knows that. Mama Left Hand knows that. Hell, even Tobin and his people know that. The only one who doesn't seem to understand it is you. And maybe him." She jerked her chin at Degan, who lifted an eyebrow in response. "But here's the thing: I'm done watching you play at being the Nose. Denying it is just going to get you dusted, and I didn't come back to watch you talk yourself into a winding sheet. Like it or not, you're a Gray Prince of the Kin—start fucking acting like one."

I was still opening my mouth the reply when Fowler pushed past me and stormed up the stairs. I watched her go without moving.

"It's good to see she hasn't changed," said Degan.

"Fuck you."

"She does have a point, though."

I looked over at him. "Not you, too?"

Degan regarded me for a long moment. "Let me ask you something: Would Kells have come down here if he'd found himself in your position? Would Solitude? Shadow?"

"It's not the same. They have, or had, stable organizations."

"That's not the point."

"Then what is?"

"If Fowler's right, then it won't matter whether I return with you or not, because the problem will still be there." He pushed himself away from the table and stood. "You might end up feeling better about yourself, but it won't solve the dilemma that drove you here in the first place."

"And if she's wrong?" I said. "If I really did come down here because of you?"

"Then you're going to be a very disappointed man, because I'm not going back to Ildrecca."

"But I think I found a lead. There's this secretary named—"

"I've already said no twice, Drothe. Don't make me say it a third time."

He began to turn away. I reached out to stop him.

"Dammit, Degan, I'm trying to tell you that if I can—"

I'm still not sure if my fingers made it to his sleeve or not—all I know is that one moment I was reaching for him, and the next I was bent over the table, its edge forcing the air from my gut, my face pressed against the stained top. Fowler's empty mug wobbled inches from my nose.

"Go home, Drothe," said Degan from the other end of the arm bar. His voice was tight, but also tired. "Walk away from me and the Despotate and the *Zakur*. Go home before you get hurt."

He held me like that a moment more, then let go. By the time I was able to suck in enough air to roll over and look for him, the common room was empty.

I collapsed into Degan's chair and took a deep, shaky breath. My shoulder hurt.

Well, that had gone well.

Was Fowler right? Had I told myself I was trying to save my organization, trying to help Degan, just so I could get back on the street? Had I walked away from Ildrecca not because it was the best option, but because it was the easiest one? The one I wanted most?

I shook my head. I hadn't asked for this, that was true enough. Hadn't asked for Crook Eye or Rambles, for Wolf or Fat Chair. For actors and organizations and Kin to be looking at me for answers. Hadn't asked to be made a Gray Prince, let alone sought it out.

And yet here I was: a street-level Kin standing at the top of the criminal heap. King of my own little hill, worried about all the other coves planning to push me off. Afraid the fall might be harder than the climb, which, when you thought about it, was a given. Fighting to keep something I hadn't even wanted in the first place.

But that was the nature of being a member of the Kin, wasn't it? To want what wasn't yours—to want it so badly that you took it from someone else. Power, money, luxury, smoke, glimmer, the thing itself didn't matter so much as the getting of it. And the keeping, of course. There was no worse, more vengeful, more spiteful victim of theft than the professional thief. Oh, we might happily lose a month's worth of gains in a single night at bones, but that was on our terms. Woe indeed to the cove who was caught cutting another Cutter's purse.

And that's what I was doing now: holding tight to my swag, lest anyone else take it from me. Clutching my princedom as if it were something I'd gotten after months of planning and slouching and spying, as if I'd cracked a ken and stolen it away by the skin of my teeth. I was acting as if I'd gotten my status on the dark and dirty rather than admitting the truth, which was that it had all but fallen in my lap. I wasn't about to let anyone take my bit of glitter, dammit.

Only . . . why the hell not?

I was still turning that question over in my head when a shadow fell across the inn's door. I looked up, hoping against hope to see Degan; instead, I saw Raaz slipping inside.

"Ah, Master Drothe," he said, his arms wide as he came across the floor. "I'm pleased to find you still here."

I grunted and picked up the mug in front of me, not remembering until it was too late that it was empty. I set it back down in disgust.

"Let me guess," I said. "You heard about the troupe packing up and wanted to make sure you caught me before they—and I—left with your precious package."

"You've found me out," he said, lowering himself into the chair across from me with enviable ease. He was clean, trimmed, and had probably gotten a full night's sleep recently. I hated him. "And while we hate to see you go, we'd hate it even more if you took the other half of Jelem's pages with you when you left."

"I'll just bet you would," I said. "But there's no need to worry on either count. I'm not going anywhere for a while."

"Oh?" Raaz glanced back toward the door. "I'd assumed you'd be heading out with your . . . people." He spared a forlorn look at the empty bar, then turned back to me. "Would it be forward of me to ask who will be acting as your patron once the padishah rescinds his favor?"

It was a question I'd been kicking around in my own head ever since walking into the courtyard. A question I'd only been able to come up with one answer to so far.

"About that . . . ," I began.

"Oh no," said Raaz, quickly reading my intentions. "Absolutely not. We can't act as your patrons."

I leaned forward. "Need I remind you that you still owe me?" I said, wiggling the fingers of my left hand meaningfully. "You and your master both?"

"I haven't forgotten what you did," said Raaz. "Nor has he. But neither are we in a position to offer patronage to . . . someone such as yourself."

"You mean a member of the Kin?"

"I mean an Imperial. My *tal* already stands in disgrace. If we were to openly take responsibility for you and your actions . . . ?" He shook his head. "We mean to honor our agreement, my friend, but I'm afraid in this matter what you ask is beyond our grasp. We can't act as your patron."

It was an answer I'd more than half expected but had been hoping not to hear. Without a token of patronage, I was a marked man on the streets—and that was even before considering the price Fat Chair was offering for me, let alone the likely consequences of failing to keep my bargain with Mama Left Hand. Between the three, the thought of trying to find Ivory's papers and bring Degan around, let alone simply function in el-Qaddice, went from daunting to nearly impossible.

"Then I guess I'll have to do it the hard way," I said. "But that isn't your problem, is it?" I stood up and took off my doublet. "You're here for your delivery, and I can't rightly hold it back any longer, especially considering what the next several days might be like."

I pulled out my boot knife and began working at the relevant seams.

Raaz's eyes went wide. "You . . . you mean you've been carrying it on you this whole time?"

"I'm an Imperial living in an inn with a bunch of actors in the middle of Djan—where the hell else would you hide it to keep it safe?"

"I had just thought . . ." Raaz shook his head and chuckled. "No, never mind what I thought. You're right: It's best you hand it over now, especially if you're going to be without a token. Not having a patron is bad enough, but if you were caught with those papers? Even a merchant sheikh wouldn't be able to worm his way out of that."

"Yeah, well, I'm no merchant sheikh. Hell, I'm barely a criminal one back home, let alone down here. I don't even want to think about what would happen if . . ." I stopped midcut, my knife poised, and looked up at Raaz. I grinned.

He inched back slightly in his chair. "What?"

I set my blade down and turned toward the stairs. "Fowler!"

Raaz started. "If I could ask—"

"*Fowler!*"

"Is there anything—?"

"*What the fuck do you want?*" Fowler's voice came flying down the stairs, followed hotly by the woman herself.

I pointed at the courtyard. "Get out there and tell Tobin and his people to stop packing. In fact, get them to start unpacking. Now."

"*Un*packing?" said Fowler. "Why?"

"Because they have an audition to practice for."

"I thought the audition was fixed."

"There's fixed," I said, "and then there's fixed."

"What the hell is that supposed to mean?"

"Just get out there and stop them. I'll explain later."

Fowler glared and grumbled, but she headed out the door.

Raaz cleared his throat. "This is all very dramatic," he said, leaning forward ever so slightly, his hand reaching for my doublet, "but if I could just get Jelem's papers . . . ?"

I ripped open the rest of the seam and pulled out the remainder of the packet. "You said even a merchant sheikh couldn't shake these off if the despot's people found them on him, right?"

"Ye-es."

"So, then, what do you think would happen if they found them on a prince of the *Zakur*?"

Raaz's eyes filled with understanding, followed quickly by dread.

"No," he said, standing "No, I can't—"

"Sit," I said, doing the same myself. "Calm yourself. And let me tell you a little story about an ambush and a group of *neyajin* and a conversation in the dark. . . ."

Chapter Twenty-eight

"Stop fussing," I said.

"Go screw yourself."

I dropped my hands and stepped away from Fowler. "Fine, have it your way. But it's not going to work."

"The hell it isn't." Fowler adjusted the sheathed knife so it sat farther along the small of her back. "There, how's that?"

I looked at her, at what little there was of her costume, at the brass handle of the weapon peeking out, glaringly obvious from at least three different directions. I shook my head.

"Dammit!" The knife hit the wooden floor with a solid, angry clatter.

"*Hsst!*" whispered Ezak, standing a few feet away. He gestured out toward the stage and gave us a stern look. Fowler offered a gesture of her own. Ezak rolled his eyes and returned his attention to the performance.

We were standing in the wings of one of the padishah's amphitheaters in the second ring of el-Qaddice. I'd been told that the son of the despot had constructed several theaters around the city over the years for the various troupes and performers he sponsored. Each was designed to lend itself to different kinds of presentations, with such things as acoustics, lighting, floodable versus hollow stages, and even movable topiary being taken into consideration. Even though we were performing a Djanese play, the troupe had been booked in a theater constructed in the imperial style: high walls, open roof, with a wooden stage that extended out into the open area, or "pit," where the more common members of the audience stood and watched the show. Those with the ready, or the social standing, or both, occupied the higher tiers and balconies, the better to look down upon the rest of us.

Despite what Ezak had said in the yard about Tobin wanting to play Djan, I hadn't been sure he'd be willing to stay, especially considering Heron's letter. But he hadn't hesitated a heartbeat when I'd broached the subject.

"Done," he'd said, turning to direct his people.

"Just like that?" I'd said.

"We're players, sir. You are our patron. You've told me there will be a place to play and an audience to watch. What better reason do I need than that?"

"I can think of half a dozen, easy."

He had smiled. "As can I. But what good will they do me, hey? I'm a boardsman, sir. An actor. I'd rather earn my banishment through my tongue and my trod than sulk away like a kicked dog. As would, I think, the rest. No, keep your reasons and your plots and your schemes to yourself. That you are willing to stand between us and the wazir is enough for me to walk the boards." He'd paused to beam. "To walk them in Djan, no less!"

And now he was.

"And what of me?" cried Tobin from the stage, playing the part of Abu Ahzred—the future first despot—with more relish and zest than I'd ever seen in the rehearsals. *"Am I to simply stand aside and look the fool this night?"*

"Why should this night be different from all other nights?" Marianne, the troupe's female lead, stage-whispered to the audience, pantomiming a pair of cuckold horns behind Tobin's back. Tonight she was the djinn Efferra, draped in silks and beads and tiny cymbals that gave off an audible shimmer whenever she moved.

Laughter and a few shouts from the crowd. Even though we were performing in Imperial, there was enough broad humor—and enough translators scattered through the crowd, all at the padishah's expense—to make the play work.

I picked up the knife, touched Fowler on the elbow, and drew her farther into the wings. Even here, back among the props and the clutter, light from the magical globes hovering over the stage cast weak shadows across the boards.

"Listen," I said. "You know how this has to happen. I barely got Fat Chair to agree to meet me here in the first place. If that bastard sees people prancing around with half-concealed steel, he's going to stroll. Or worse."

"I won't even be near you," said Fowler. "How the hell is that a threat?"

"How will it do me any good?"

Fowler set her jaw and turned away. When Tobin had initially asked her to play the spirit, Sekketheh, who came to haunt the despot-to-be with visions of eroticism and cruelty, she'd barely been able to say "yes" fast enough. But now that I'd come up with a plan that involved meeting with Fat Chair during the performance, she was itching to put her actor's drapes aside and haunt my blinders. The only problem was, the play couldn't go on without her down here—and I needed it to go on. Without the performance and the finale I had planned, I wouldn't be able to set up Fat Chair, let alone make it out of the theater and across town to Heron's alive.

It was going to be a near thing. Nearer than I liked, and nearer than I'd let on to Fowler. Which was the other reason I wanted her down here. I didn't care for the idea of putting my people in any more danger than I had to. Not here, not tonight.

I put a hand on Fowler's shoulder. She didn't rip it off at the wrist. Good sign, that.

"I need you down here," I said. "Need you to keep your Oak Mistress's eye on things. If anything goes wrong, I want to have someone I trust ready to read the signal and come to the rescue."

"If anything goes wrong," she said, "it won't matter how fast I see the sign: I won't be able to make it to you in time."

"Then I'd best not let anything go wrong, had I?" It

sounded weak even as I said it, felt worse as she turned and set worried eyes on me.

"Let me come with," she said. "I can keep out of sight, shadow you."

"Dressed like that?"

"You know what I mean."

I reached out and took a strand of her sun-gold hair between my fingers. I shook my head. "Not in this crowd, Fowler. Not even dirtied up and in your street clothes." I let her go and forced my voice to take on a more businesslike tone. "You made sure everything is where it's supposed to be?"

Fowler nodded. "I've got my street drapes and Degan's sword stashed near here. Once it's done, I'll gather them up and wait for you at the Black Ken."

"Good." I didn't like the idea of leaving Degan's sword behind, but I liked the idea of trying to crack the padishah's ken with it on my back even less. Added bulk aside, the thought of it ending up in some guard's hands if things went wrong and never having the chance to make it back to Degan didn't sit right with me. Better Fowler keep it for now.

"Be careful on your way out," I said.

"You, too. And keep an eye on Wolf. He may have agreed to help with this, but I don't trust that bastard any farther than I can kick him."

"That makes two of us."

I turned away and headed toward the tiring room and the small door beyond that to the main theater.

"Hey," said Fowler.

I stopped, looked back. "What?"

"You realize that when I told you to start acting like a Gray Prince, I didn't mean for you to try to emulate the dead ones, right?"

"Sure, now you tell me."

I smiled. Fowler smiled back, neither of us quite believing the faces we were putting on. Then I left.

"Please explain to me," said Fat Chair as he looked up, "why I shouldn't have you killed right now."

We were in a balcony roughly halfway up the left side of
the theater. Screens carved to look like interwoven grape
vines separated us from the boxes to either side, and a low
wall with a spiral-turned railing kept us from accidentally
strolling off into space. Fat Chair was seated before me on
a long low couch that had clearly been brought in just for
him, taking up what had once been enough space for five
chairs. Now it was a challenge to fit him and me and the two
coves he'd brought with into the balcony and not have
someone fall out.

Not that I wasn't starting to think that might be the
idea. . . .

"Aside from the fact that we both agreed there'd be no
bloodshed," I said, "there's always them." I pointed past the
crime lord and out into the theater, to the large, canopy-
draped box that sat two-thirds of the way up the gallery,
center theater. It was within easy shouting distance. "I don't
think the padishah's guards would appreciate a murder
happening this close to their charge, even if it was just us.
They seem to be picky that way."

Fat Chair glanced over his shoulder at the box and the
two-deep array of green-jacketed guardsmen surrounding
it on three sides. Within, several more soldiers stood to
hand, as did a small host of functionaries, servants, and
councilors. In the center, resting on a deep cushion, sat a
thin-faced man with uneven cheeks and pursed lips, studying the play. He was dressed in silks that shone even from
here, and wore a turban so elaborate that it looked as if it
might require structural support on a bad day. Rings and
jewels clung to him like rainwater after a storm, and I
couldn't help thinking that a deft filcher with quick hands
could lift a lifetime's worth of profit in just a few moments
up there. But then again, given how the padishah's eyes
seemed to take in everything—not just the play, but the pit,
the audience in the seats, the movement and shift of both
the light and the shadows cast by the breeze-blown fabrics
around him—I couldn't imagine many thieves making it out
of that box alive, no matter how good they were.

And that was ignoring everyone else who was standing

around him—including, I was pleased to see, both Heron and the wazir.

Fat Chair let out a small snort and turned back to me. The effort had caused a sheen of moisture to appear on his upper lip. He wiped at the sweat mustache and said, "You think my man can't kill you silently?"

"You think I can't make a lot of noise if he tries?"

The crime lord's gaze flicked past my shoulder. I resisted the urge to turn around, to shift my eyes, to tense my back. The man was the closer of the two behind me and had had cold eyes. The woman, at least, had nodded when I came in, but she was also the one who had taken the sole dagger I had on me—I'd been relieved of the rest of my steel even before I'd been allowed to climb the stairs to the gallery. Two on one, both behind me. Bad odds.

"Very well," said Fat Chair. "Never let it be said that I don't keep my word." He leaned back on his couch and picked up a small square of paper from the table beside it and held it up. "Any requests?"

"How about a letter of patronage?"

He made a crease and chuckled. "Or maybe just a token instead? No, I don't think so. Not that I'm not that good . . . I am . . . but no."

"Not even for some other pieces of folded paper in exchange?"

He paused. "What kind of papers?"

"The kind that you aren't going to want to turn into birds and apes and Angels know what else to leave lying around for the despot's people to find."

He looked up at me. "So I was right, you are here to smuggle magic."

"I'm here to do a lot of things, but crossing the *Zakur* isn't one of them." I reached into my doublet—slowly, so as not to startle the coves and their knives behind me—and pulled out the paper animal I'd bought on the way over. I set the figure on the edge of the couch, its bared teeth toward him, its bushy paper tail pointed at me. "I should have known better than to challenge the wolf in his own den. That was a mistake, and I apologize for it."

He picked up the folded wolf and turned it in his hands. It was made of crisp, bone-white paper, the creases knife-sharp. Pigments had been carefully applied and then gently washed away in spots, making it look as if the creature were ready to breathe, ready to leap, ready to howl, if only the right words were spoken.

Fat Chair held it to the light shining up from the stage. "Exquisite."

It damn well should be, I thought—I paid enough for it.

He turned it some more. "But you still lied to me."

"After getting nipped by a couple of Cutters and escorted to your chair? Damn straight I lied." I stepped forward, leaned in. I could see the stage beyond him, Tobin upon it, the hired *yazani* controlling the magical effects from a roped-off area just below. "But I wasn't lying when I said I was here looking for someone, and that I have other reasons for wanting to stick around."

"You mean Crook Eye?"

"I mean his routes," I lied. "I didn't stab him in the eye on accident, and I didn't come to el-Qaddice on a whim. I'm still pulling the pieces of his organization together and bringing his people in line, but it's only a matter of time until I do. And when that happens, I want to be ready to start moving glimmer. That's why I'm here, and that's why I initially told you to go to hell: I thought I could put things in place on my own with the Kin in the Imperial Quarter."

"But now you know differently."

"Now I know differently," I agreed.

Fat Chair glanced down at the stage and the players upon it. "And them?"

"They got me into the city," I said. "But no matter how well they do tonight, they're going to be escorted out tomorrow morning. The fix is in."

"The padishah?"

"His wazir."

Fat Chair nodded as if that made perfect sense. "And you don't want to leave when they go."

"Like I said, I have other things to do."

"Such as try to strike a deal with me."

"That, too."

The crime lord set the wolf aside and laced his fingers together across the expanse that was his waist. "I assume you have an offer in mind?"

I smiled. "Business as usual."

Fat Chair blinked. "Which means?"

"Just what it sounds like: You keep sending magic north, I keep sending money south."

Fat Chair ran his fingers along his knuckles once, twice. "And?" he said at last.

"And what?"

"And what about the Imperial Quarter?"

"What about it?" I said. "Crook Eye didn't have anyone in the Quarter." At least as far as I'd been able to find out.

"Exactly," said Fat Chair. "He never extended his fingers beyond the border provinces. But you? You come to Djan with magic in your pocket; come all the way to el-Qaddice posing as the patron of an acting troupe, just to avoid suspicion. Why is that?"

I ran a nervous tongue across my lips. "I just—"

"I'll tell you why," said Fat Chair. He shifted on the couch, pushing himself into a sitting position so he could swing his mastlike legs over the side. "You don't just want to bring our magic north, you want to send yours south. To your people. To your organization in el-Qaddice." He placed his hands on his knees. "You want to put yourself in a position to challenge the *Zakur* in the Imperial Quarter. And the first step is to show that you can get magic to your Kin in there."

"What?" I said. "Do you know how far we are from the Empire? Why the hell would I want to do that? There's no way I could win."

"I agree," said Fat Chair. He took a slow breath, then levered himself to his feet. I took an involuntary step back to give him room . . .

And walked right into the arms of one of his Cutters.

Dammit.

"But," said Fat Chair, as his man tightened his grip on my arms, "if you had the backing of a *tal*, perhaps? One

that has fallen far enough from favor that it would be willing to help the Kin in exchange for an agreement to supply
you with magical baubles once we cut you off? If you
could gather enough money and men, not to mention
magic, it's possible you could make it too costly for the
Zakur to dislodge you. You could force us to have to deal
with you—at least for a time." He bent over and picked up
the paper wolf, held it before my face. "Your own tiny den
in the center of our hunting grounds. It's an audacious
plan, and quite exquisite." He admired the figure a moment longer, then let it drop to the floor. "Too bad it will
never happen."

I jerked forward against the Cutter's grasp, trying to
loosen his grip, to push myself past, or at least beside, Fat
Chair. To get a view of the stage, so that I might be seen—so
that I could give the signal.

No luck. The Cutter didn't budge.

I looked up at Fat Chair. He had a bright line across his
upper lip again. It nearly matched the gleam in his eye. "Listen," I said, "I dusted Crook Eye, sure, but—"

Fat Chair looked past me and nodded. I was taking a
deep breath to scream my head off—for the stage, for the
padishah's men, hell even for Wolf—when I heard a low
voice mutter something behind me. A soft weight settled
across the back of my neck, and suddenly my muscles decided to stop paying attention to me. My deep breath leaked
out in a wheeze.

"Thank you, Nazin," said Fat Chair. He looked back at
me and smiled. "Oh, that's right—as an Imperial, you're
probably not used to having magicians at your beck and
call, are you? It's a shame, really—they come in so handy."
To the man behind me: "Since he came to negotiate, he
probably has the package on him. Check."

The hands let go of my wrists and began to go over me,
patting sleeves, undoing buttons, checking inside and out.
When they came across the long, triangular assassin's needle I'd threaded up along the seam of my doublet's sleeve,
their owner whistled in appreciation.

"Clever bastard," he said as he drew out the eight inches

of tapered steel and set it atop his boss's papers. He resumed his search more carefully after that.

For her part, the *yazani* stepped around to my side and adjusted the glimmered scarf she'd laid across my neck, tying it off and tucking it in, all the while making sure it never stopped touching my skin. She smelled of tobacco and mint and hummed as she worked.

And all the while, I stood there, breathing (just) and blinking (rarely), staring at Fat Chair because I didn't have any other choice. He stared back.

"If it were simply business," he said to me, "I might have let you leave the city, less a finger or four. It was a brilliant plan, after all, and I have no desire to stir up your people in the Quarter. But you killed S'ad, and I can't let that pass. He was a distant cousin, but he was still blood, and he was close to me." He shook his head, almost sadly. "I don't look forward to what my fellows will say after I've killed you, but clan comes first."

It was a good thing I was unable to react; otherwise, I might have laughed in his face. He was doing exactly what Mama Left Hand had wanted him to do in the first place, and didn't even realize it was the wrong choice. She was right: He was a fool.

Still, I would have given anything just then to be able to talk, to be able to tell him that I didn't have people in el-Qaddice, that I wasn't half as clever as he was giving me credit for, that I really had come down here just to find one man and do a *yazani* a favor. But instead, all I did was stand there, listening to my heart hammer in my ears and wondering whether or not I'd choke on my own vomit if I threw up like this.

The Cutter found Jelem's package shortly after that—I'd been planning to hand it over anyhow, so it wasn't as if I'd hidden it well—and handed the small bundle off to the *yazani*. After she chanted a few words and rubbed a silvery brown powder over them, the wax seals let off a small puff of smoke and dropped away from the paper.

"Well?" said Fat Chair as the woman unfolded the papers and looked them over.

I saw her eyes widen out of the corner of my own, watched as she whispered into Fat Chair's ear, causing much the same reaction. He snatched the pages from her, stared at them, and then turned his eyes to me.

More than just his upper lip was sweating now.

"What . . . ?" he began, but his voice trailed off. He waved the paper at me as if I could answer him.

I blinked.

"I take it back," he said, his voice little more than a whisper. "You're not brilliant. You're mad. Mad, and doomed." He turned to the Cutter. "Take him down to the third ring and leave him in the first alley you find. Make sure no one can tell who he was when you're finished." He refolded Jelem's papers and stuffed them into his sash. "I don't want anyone to know he lost these for as long as possible."

The Cutter reached up and touched the back of the scarf along my neck. "Turn around," he said, "and walk."

Much to my disappointment, I did so. Smoothly.

He guided me out of the box and along the hall to the narrow steps that led down to the next level. I could hear shouts and applause through the walls, feel the stomping of the audience through the soles of my shoes. For good or ill, the play was clearly having an impact. I just wished I could enjoy the knowledge more.

We went down the stairs. At the bottom, we found another one of Fat Chair's men. I'd passed him coming up and left my weapons in his care. He didn't bother to look up as we approached. Instead, he sat in his chair, feet crossed at the ankles, his head tilted forward in boredom or sleep.

It wasn't until we were almost even with him that the Cutter behind me realized his comrade was neither bored nor sleeping, but dead. But by then, it was too late.

Wolf stepped out of the gallery entry we'd agreed he should linger in the day before and silenced the Cutter with a single, clean thrust over my shoulder. I heard the blade pierce skin, smelled its oiled steel, felt the breeze of its passing, followed by the spray of blood across my back. And still I kept walking.

"Well, that was . . . here, now, where are you going?" said Wolf. He stepped in front of me. I walked into him. He took a step back and held me at bay with one hand.

"What kind of game are you . . . Ah." He frowned. "Just like the Djanese to use magic when a good gag and a bit of rope will do. Damn show-offs." He shoved my shoulder, causing me to pivot to one side. Then he kicked my legs out from under me.

I fell like a tree.

It must hurt to be a tree.

I heard Wolf wipe his blade clean and then slide it home in its scabbard. He knelt down before me. My legs were still moving.

"Apologies for your nose," he said. My nose? What about my nose? "So, magic." Wolf studied me. "I'm presuming the one I killed wasn't the shaman, which means he'd need something to control you. And that means . . ." The degan cleared his knife, flashed it near my throat, and had it away again, all between one heartbeat and the next. A moment later, the scarf fell from my neck and my muscles returned to me.

I gasped. I groaned. I curled up on my side. And yes, I reached up and touched my nose.

Not broken, and it all seemed to be there. Just bloody. That was something.

"All went well with the fat one?" said Wolf, standing. He grabbed the dead Cutter by his ankles and dragged him into a space behind the stairs.

"He took the bait, if that's what you mean," I said as I sat up. "Although I wasn't sure I was going to live long enough to see things through, to be honest."

"Which is why you should have simply killed him, as I suggested."

"I told you why that wasn't an option."

"Then you should have killed the old woman as well." Wolf gave the body one last shove and came back out. It wasn't a perfect fit, but you'd have to look to see the Cutter in this light.

"Mama Left Hand isn't someone you just . . ." I stopped,

shook my head. Who the hell was I to argue with Wolf about dusting a crime lord? We'd both done it, for Angels' sake. Besides, we'd already gone over this when I'd pitched the plan to him and—reluctantly, but what could I do, I was shorthanded—asked for his help two days back. Despite his concerns about there not being enough bodies on the ground at the end of everything, he'd agreed. "The point is," I said, "Fat Chair has the packet. Now all I need to do is give the signal."

"Then we'd best get to it. We've wasted enough time as it is dealing with your distractions."

"Distractions," I said. "Right. Because anyone can simply ignore a price on his head, never mind half a criminal organization threatening to come down on him."

Wolf extended his hand and helped me up. "If it doesn't involve finding Bronze and getting him back, it's a distraction."

"Must be nice to have your life so simply defined."

"Don't confuse simple goals for a simple man."

"I'll keep that in mind." I brushed off my pants, then poked cautiously at the severed scarf on the floor. My body stayed my own, so I picked it up and used it to wipe the back of my head. There wasn't as much of the Cutter's blood there as I thought. I wiped at my nose as well. "Besides, it's like I told you: What happens here tonight isn't just about the *Zakur*. If things play out like I hope, I may have some good news for you come morning."

I retrieved my rapier and knives from where the Cutter had set them and started walking. Wolf joined me. "I'd rather I come with and find out tonight," he said.

I shook my head. "I go alone. That, or you get to find your leads on your own."

We'd been over this as well. He hadn't liked the idea of me heading off alone, but I liked the idea of him knowing about Heron, let alone the sword hanging on his wall, even less. No matter how many times I played the scene of he and I walking into the library together, it never ended well.

Wolf scowled. "Very well. But I want to hear from you first thing if you find anything."

"Not to worry," I said.

He grunted, but otherwise didn't respond. When we reached the bottom of the next set of stairs, we turned and followed an archway that led out to the pit. I stopped just short of the three steps leading down into the mob and looked across at the stage.

They were deep into the second act. Tobin was offstage just now. Instead, Ezak, in his role as the Caliph Hesad, was striding about, making excuses for Tobin/Abu Ahzred to his councilors. Surely, he argued, the rumors about such a trusted and valued adviser had to be false! He would not honor them with the gift of belief! And so on and so forth....

I knew this part well. Within the next few minutes, Abu Ahzred would finalize his deal with the djinn and move to throw down the Caliphate. Bodies would fall onstage, magical mock fire would burn, and the origins of the Despotate would be portrayed in the darkest light that had been seen in a generation. We were, in essence, on the cusp of banishment.

I turned to the audience. To a person, they were held rapt. I could see their eyes devouring every detail, their ears soaking up every word and nuance. Smiles and frowns, laughter and disgust: The reactions were scattered across the audience like shells on a beach. There was no telling which way the crowd would go when it happened, no way of knowing how they would react when the padishah's men began to move. And move, I knew, they would.

I dabbed at my nose again and looked up at the padishah's box. From here, I could only make out the top of his turban, but the men around and behind him were readily visible. There were keen eyes up there studying the play, I knew, along with practiced lips smoothly translating the lines. No one on the balcony could have any doubt about where this performance was going, what it was saying about the origins and nature of the Despotate.

And yet there was no serious stirring among the guards and attendants, no angry dip to the royal turban, no hasty gesture of command or dismay. It seemed, in fact, quiet.

What the hell was he thinking up there?

No, never mind. If he didn't want to shut things down, we were prepared for that as well. It wouldn't be quite as chaotic as I'd planned, but there'd still be enough distractions to go around. Starting now.

I turned back to the stage but didn't lift my eyes to it. Instead, I focused on the small knot of sweating, murmuring, gesticulating men and women standing in front of it. There were five of them there, all Mouths, all brought in at Tobin's request to light the stage and see to the pyrotechnics that the palace and sea battles would require. All of the *yazani* had been paid for by the padishah, but two of them, for tonight, belonged to me.

I waited until the shorter of the two—the one missing most of his right hand—looked over and met my eye. And I nodded.

Then I turned to go.

Wolf blinked. He'd been staring up at the padishah's box, but now he turned his eyes to me. "That was it?" he said.

"It will be," I said.

"But wha—?"

Wolf was interrupted by a bright pulse of red-tinted light, followed by what sounded like the report of muted thunder. Only, I knew, the thunder came from a balcony two floors up, where a crime lord and his pet Mouth now sat in stunned silence as magic that had been triggered from the pit below writhed and sparked from the paper I'd left in their possession. Magic that, even from half a theater away or more, any competent magus would be able to identify as Imperial in nature. Magic that, for all visible intents and purposes, seemed to be summoning a djinni, or something damn near like it, disturbingly close to the padishah's person.

Magic that Raaz and his master had cast upon the papers, just so they could set it off. Because, as much as they had wanted Jelem's notes, they'd wanted Fat Chair even more after I'd told them he was responsible for the *neyajin* who'd come after them in the cellar.

Thankfully, revenge isn't limited to criminals and the court.

I cast one final glance over my shoulder just before the

Chapter Twenty-nine

Tempting as it was to use the main thoroughfares to save time, I stuck to the back streets on my way to the padishah's estate. Part of that was habit, but much more came from the simple fact that I had no idea how big or bad things would get at the theater. The magic had been designed more for show than anything—to get the attention of the padishah and his magi, and maybe give Raaz and his master a chance to swoop in and save the day by capturing the *Zakur* crime lord who'd been foolish enough to try and smuggle magic from the Empire into the city, let alone use it so close to the despot's son. Clearly, such a combination could not have been meant for anything other than the darkest treachery?

I didn't know if Fat Chair would walk out of there alive or not, but that wasn't my problem. Mama Left hand had only stipulated that she wanted him embarrassed, and that I wasn't supposed to dust him. Done and done as far as I was concerned, and good riddance. All I knew is that, no matter what else happened, the padishah and his people—including Heron—would have their hands full for the next several hours or more dealing with the threat and the confusion and the chaos. Maybe even all night, if I was lucky.

And, from what I'd seen of what lay ahead of me, luck was something I was going to need.

While Tobin and his people had been practicing for the performance, I'd spent my time casing the padishah's estate.

What I'd found hadn't made me happy: tall, smooth walls with a broad swath of open ground at their outer base. Neither building nor tree was allowed near the wall, meaning that the idea of covering the gap with a leap from a similar height was out. Likewise, while the idea of a hemp stroll was a possibility, I wasn't a good enough rope walker to risk running from a roof to the distant wall without risking either a spill or a sighting. As for climbing over: Well, aside from the iron spikes that graced the top of the barrier, I'd also been informed about a glass-lined channel that ran around the top of the wall—a channel that reportedly contained a string of quicksilver beads. It was said that each bead bore a small symbol on its surface, inscribed by a magi with a ruby stylus. How a person could make a lasting mark in a dot of quicksilver was beyond me, but I'd heard enough accounts on the streets of the Old City about would-be thieves bursting into flame atop the wall to decide that going over the top wasn't an option.

As for under, well, let's just say that the tales of the gates and guards and sewer spirits had made the wall seem a charming diversion by comparison.

Which left only one viable route into the grounds. Fortunately for me, it was one I'd become familiar with during my short time in el-Qaddice.

The hounds roaming the plaza outside the Dog Gate snarled and snapped and raised their hackles as I passed, but nevertheless kept their distance. Beat a dog enough—even a feral one—and they'll shrink from any man with a bit of iron in his step. I don't know who'd been taking a rod to the poor beasts in the courtyard, but I could make some guesses about the one behind the gate. The only question was whether the dog I was coming to see had had enough of his own master's rod for my purposes.

"Open up," I said crisply as I came up to the iron-barred archway that was the Dog Gate. I kept my eyes off to one side, both to seem unconcerned as well as to save them from the lamplight shining out from his post house. The dogs inside, I noticed, were quiet.

"Fuck off," said a voice from the other side. There was

much more relish in the guard's tone than I'd heard in my previous visits.

My eyes snapped up, meeting his. "Don't push me," I said, taking a step closer to the bars. "You know where this can go." He didn't move back; instead, he came a pace closer. That wasn't a good sign.

"You're not to be admitted," he said, his hand shifting along the haft of his short spear. "In fact, you're to be turned away." His other hand gripped lower on the wood, and the steel tip began to dip down in my direction. "Even by force, if necessary. And I think that's necessary."

Heron. He must have put the order in the other day, after I'd left him feeling less than warm toward me. I should have guessed.

Theoretically, it's possible for a man with a rapier to take a man with a short spear. Degan had done it in the past, and even discussed the premise behind the practice one night. But there's a long walk between talking about something and doing it in a fight, and I knew better than to even set foot on that path. There was no way I was going to challenge a man holding a spear, especially when he was on the other side of a locked gate, and especially when I'd used his sash to wipe dog shit off my boots.

I took a step back and held up my hands to show him I respected the threat. He didn't seem impressed.

Think fast, Drothe.

"When did those orders come down?" I said.

"What does it matter?" he said, bringing the tip of the spear in line with me. "The point is, you're not getting in. And if you try . . . well, it's my word against a corpse's, now, isn't it?"

I nodded. "Yes, but then you'd be in the awkward position of having to explain why you just killed one of the padishah's newest dependents."

That got a blink. "What?"

I jerked a thumb back over my shoulder. "Play. Tonight. He liked us, offered us patronage. I'm his now."

"Ha!" He spit, just in case I missed the disdain in his laugh. "My master take you on? I don't think so."

"Think whatever you want, just open up so I can deliver my message."

"What message?"

I sighed and lowered my hands. "The one the secretary gave me, of course."

The spear tip wavered for a moment, but then became firm again. "There's no message," he said, sounding more certain than I liked. "And you're not a dependent. If you were, you'd have one of my master's tokens on, instead of the wazir's."

I looked down as if I'd forgotten the small bronze lozenge that hung against my chest. "Like I told you, he just took us as . . . oh, never mind. Here. . . ." I reached into my doublet. The guard tensed and jerked his spear forward. I froze.

"Don't!" he cried.

Well, I'd certainly done a number on this one, hadn't I? I didn't know whether to be pleased or irritated with myself on the matter.

"Easy," I said. "Easy. I just wanted to show you the message." I slowly drew a pale, nonstained corner of the Mouth's scarf I'd stuck in my doublet on the way over, hoping it could pass for paper in the gloom. I stepped forward. "Here, take a look." Another step.

The guard came forward. So did his spear. "Far enough," he said. "Put it on the blade and I'll draw it to me."

Crap. I'd been wanting to get him into knife range, or closer. Even if I did have something that could pass for paper, sticking it on the tip of his spear wouldn't get me there.

I pushed the "message" back into my doublet, took half a step closer. "And let you read it?" I said. Could I grab the haft of the spear, maybe use it to pull him into the bars? "Or destroy it and say I never showed it to you?" Would that give me time to close before he scrambled away? I shook my head. "I don't think so."

His scowl deepened. I was losing him with my story. Hell, I was losing me, it was so bad.

"I don't—" he began, but then stopped as a surprised look came over his face. That seemed reasonable, considering the tufted end of a dart that had just appeared above his collar, the thin steel of the needle lodged into his neck.

He raised his hand, fingers brushing at the fine hairs on the end of the weapon, and gasped out the first half syllable of something. Then he fell over.

I was already spinning and crouching when a voice behind me said, "What kind of fool tries to talk his way into the padishah's estate?" It came from a piece of night that was walking toward me, complete with sultry eyes and a mocking voice; a piece of night that also happened to be tucking a short blow tube back up her sleeve.

"One who's already done it twice before," I said, straightening as Aribah joined me. "What are you doing here?"

She shrugged. "As I said before: I'm supposed to keep you from killing yourself. Since you seemed intent on doing just that . . ."

"I don't need you on my blinders." Not here. Not now.

"You can wish the stars to fall from the sky and become diamonds at your feet for all I care. Until I decide otherwise, you're going to have two shadows lingering at your heels tonight: your own and me." She folded her arms and arched an elegant eyebrow. "Now, do you wish to stand here until someone comes to investigate, or are we going through the gate?"

I took half a step back. "You're not going to try to stop me?"

"Why would I do that?"

"You know . . ." I gestured over my shoulder at the estate. "Not getting myself killed?"

"I'm here to keep you alive, not to prevent you from being stupid. Not that I think the latter's even possible."

"Right," I said. "Great." I turned back to the gate. The guard had fallen close enough that it was only a moment's work to grab his leg, drag him the rest of the way over, and search his clothing for the keys.

I unlocked the gate. The sound of the rusty hinges swinging open caused the dogs in the kennels to start barking, which in turn got the ones in the piazza to join in as well.

"Here," I said. "Help me." We dragged the guard out into

the square and then off into one of the side alleys. While the guardhouse was a closer stash, the alley was a better choice, since a missing guard tends to generate less immediate fuss than a dead one.

The dogs were already at work on the body before we made it back through the gate. I closed the iron behind us and we headed into the deeper darkness of the padishah's grounds.

It was closer to the middle of the night than the beginning by now, but that didn't mean the grounds were deserted. The occasional servant or functionary still walked the paths, torch in hand, running errands, delivering missives, or lighting the way for lavishly dressed nobles or high officers of the court. Patrols of the padishah's guards roamed the grounds, too, but they were few, and made enough noise that even I could hear them coming, let alone Aribah. And, of course, there were the pavilions and open sitting circles—both lit and dark—dotting the landscape, providing cover from, and distractions for, any eyes that might have otherwise spotted us.

In a sense, it was an ideal situation for any kind of Prigger: open spaces, plenty of cover, with enough Lighters wandering about to make things like guard dogs and other night hazards impractical. I couldn't believe this place didn't get rolled every week: Once you were past the walls, it was a thief's delight. I mentioned as much to Aribah when we paused in the shadows of a small grove of pistachio trees I'd recognized from my last visit.

"The grounds aren't the palace," said Aribah, her gaze sweeping the lawn before us, her head cocking back and forth like a songbird's as she listened to the night. Even with the dye rubbed across her exposed skin, I found I could make out enough of her face to determine not only where she was, but what she was doing, but it took work. "There's a difference," she said, "between gaining access to those who serve the prince and reaching the prince himself."

"What kind of difference?"

The smudge in the night regarded me. "Do all Imperials talk this much when they work?"

"Only the good ones."

"Then I look forward to your impending silence."

It was my turn to snort. I looked out over the grounds. A small troop of guards were walking across the turf downslope from us, their cresset lantern sending up flame and smoke from the end of its chain. They were far enough out that the light only caused me to tear up. I blinked and rubbed at my eyes. The patrol was crossing between our trees and a rise that I remembered being near Heron's lodge. We settled in to let them pass.

"So, who watches over the padishah besides them?" I said, pointing at the moving light.

"The Opal Guard, for one," said Aribah.

"And they're not the Opal Guard?"

"Hardly. If they were Opal, we'd be moving away, believe me."

"That good?"

"That good."

I shifted on the ground, moving a fallen limb out from under my thigh. "You said 'for one,'" I said. "Who else stands Oak around her?"

". . . stands Oak?"

"Watches. Guards. Keeps a lookout."

Aribah muttered something under her breath about Imperials and insanity. Aloud, she said, "Sometimes the Lions of Arat. And djinn."

"Djinn?"

She nodded. "Chained with silver shackles, forged and inscribed anew by magi every day so the spirits can be enslaved again every night. So my grandfather says."

"He's seen them?"

Aribah turned a dark, contemptuous gaze my way. "My grandsire is one of three assassins to have ever—*ever*—entered the despotic abode and returned to tell his tale. He is a Black Cord: His word is not questioned."

I looked back out at the guards, saw the lantern bob and dip. A small spot of fire took life on the ground. Someone had stumbled and spilled some of the burning pitch. Laughter and jeers drifted up to us.

Even here, it seemed, Rags were Rags.

"Imperial?" she said to me after a moment.

"Yes?"

She paused to lick her lips. When she spoke, there was just the slightest bit of a tremor to her voice. "What's it like?"

I didn't need to ask, but I did anyhow. "You mean the night vision?"

"Yes."

It wasn't something I talked about much, but then, it wasn't something most people knew about, either. Habit made me want to brush the question off, to play it down or simply lie. But she'd told me about the glyphs and the dyes in her robes: The least I could do was tell her about the thing she was putting her life on the line for.

"I've had the night vision so long now," I said, "I'm not sure how to describe it. In some ways, it's just another part of the night for me, like the stars or the moon or the stink of an alley. How do you describe what it feels like to walk or smell or taste? It's like that, only different. But I suppose that's an excuse, not an answer, isn't it?" I paused, staring out into the night as she sat beside me, silent. Waiting. "It's red," I said at last.

"Red?"

"Red." I nodded. "Red and gold, and it sticks to everything I see. Everything is touched with hints of amber, almost as if it were dusted with light only I can pick out." I gestured out at the grounds. Aribah followed the motion, as if trying to see what I saw, as if will alone could give her the vision. "Have you ever seen an artist at work, when he's sketching out the lines for a painting? My . . . I know a baroness who patronizes one. I don't know if they do it here, but in Ildrecca there's a cadre—some say a cabal—of painters who are moving away from the old iconic style of art. They sketch everything out in careful detail first, using charcoal and chalk: textures, distance, shadows. Then they paint it. And it looks real; not real like you can tell it's a man on a horse, but real in that it looks almost exactly like a specific man on a specific horse. You don't have to guess—you'd know him on the street after you saw the painting.

"Night vision is like the charcoal sketches they do, only instead of blacks and grays and whites, you have ambers and reds and golds. It's hints and details and gaps, all in one: a picture you see as much by what isn't there as what is."

"Like dark fighting," she said. "You listen for the silences and fill them in, using the sounds as limits as much as guide-posts." She shook her head. "A-ya, but if I had your gift— the blood-red path I would cut. The Lions would weep for their losses, and my grandfather . . ."

"Your grandfather would what?" I said.

Her hand reached up and pulled gently at the cloth covering the lower part of her face, drawing it tighter. I caught hints of her sharp nose, her straight jaw clenched tight against words that wanted to come out.

I stayed silent, holding my words close. If Nosing had taught me anything, it was that most people wanted to talk, even when they thought they didn't. A good Nose—and maybe even a good Gray Prince—left the silence there for others to fill.

Aribah stared out over the grounds, her eyes focused not on the darkness without, but rather the shadows within.

"My grandfather," she said at last, the words heavy and solemn as granite, "might finally see me as myself, and not my mother's pale shadow. See me as *neyajin*, and not as a disappointment." She sniffed, staring out into the night. I watched as her thumb played with the battered silver ring on her finger.

"She was astonishing," said Aribah. "The best assassin our school has produced in generations. A natural, both as a killer and a leader. Grandfather says she could walk up to a Sentinel on a moonlit night, count the hairs in his beard at her leisure, and then cut a line across his throat, all without him knowing she was there. Salihah Shiham: Salihah the Arrow. She made her first kill at thirteen years, became *ka-lat* at seventeen, and took over as *amma* of our school at twenty-six."

"What happened to her?" I said.

"She died."

I let the silence stretch, watched her worry the ring some more, but this time she didn't respond.

"On a dodge?" I said, then caught myself at her look. "A job," I amended.

"And this is your business how?"

"It isn't," I admitted. "I just . . ." I shrugged.

Aribah turned back to the night. "She went to slay the Imam General of the Sentinels."

"And did she?"

"Yes, but not, it turns out, the demon he rode. The djinni was able to escape the saddle and slay my mother. I know because of this." She held up her hand, showing me the ring. "Three months to the day after she left, I heard a knocking at our door during a dust storm. It was my mother's special knock, but when I threw the door wide, all I found was her ring hanging on a braided cord of hair and . . . other things, spiked to the door."

I looked away. Thoughts jostled up against one another in my head, demanding attention: of my own mother wasting away in bed, of Sebastian being cut down before my eyes in front of our cabin, of my trying to provide for Christiana and failing on the streets of the Barren. I pushed them away, back down into the darkness of the past.

All of a sudden, I wanted a ring of my own to worry.

"I'm sorry," I said.

"There's nothing for you to be sorry for."

"Still, I can sympathize."

Dark eyes turned my way. "Yes, I believe you can." A pause. "Why are you here?"

"You mean why am I breaking into the padishah's grounds?"

"You can start there, yes."

"For a friend," I said. "I broke my word, and now I'm trying to . . . well, I'm hoping to make amends in some small way."

"And will what you do here be enough to mend what you broke?"

"I doubt it," I said. "But that's not the point: The point is that I need to try. Even if this isn't enough, at least it's something—it's an effort. And that's all I can give him right now."

Aribah stared off into the night. "It won't be enough," she said softly. "Once something is broken—be it your word, your friendship, your family—you can never do enough to repair it. A broken thing mended is still weaker than when it was whole. No matter how hard you work at it, no matter how much you bleed, no matter how much you cry, the flaw will always be there, beneath the surface."

"Maybe," I said, "but that doesn't mean you shouldn't try."

"One should always try," said Aribah. "But trying isn't the same as succeeding." She gave the ring one last rub, and then looked down the hill. "The patrol's gone. Go."

"You're not coming with?"

Her eyes smiled. "Your amends are yours to make. Who am I to tell you how to repair your word?"

I smiled back, but instead of rising to leave, I looked over at her hand.

"Tell me something," I said. "When you found your mother's ring, you said the cord that held it had been spiked to the door."

"Yes."

"What did the djinn use as a spike?"

A long, long pause. Then, softly, "Her dagger."

"Uh-huh." I reached down into my boot and drew out Aribah's, once Salihah Shiham's, shadow-edged dagger and placed it beside her on the turf. "In that case, I apologize. I never should have taken this from you in the first place. And your grandfather should never have made you give it back."

"You had no way of knowing—"

"No, but he did."

I watched as she reached out and took up the blade. A soft hiccup of a laugh, a gentle stroke along the handle. She lowered her scarf and gently kissed the weapon, then slipped it into the darkness of her robes.

"Don't take this the wrong way," I said, "but your grandfather's an asshole."

A soft sigh. She kept the scarf down. "A truth is a truth: as such, it can never be taken wrong."

"Is that your grandfather talking?"

"The holy books."

"Oh." I looked back out over the grass. I should be up and going; should be cracking Heron's ken before it got too late. I didn't move. "What do those books say about changing a truth?"

"What do you mean? Lies?"

"No, not lies. The opposite of a truth doesn't have to be a lie."

Aribah narrowed her eyes, curious and dubious at once. "But then . . . what?"

"Another truth," I said. "A different one. One that you make for yourself." Instead of, I thought, letting your grandfather do it.

"I don't . . ." She shook her head. "How does one 'make truth'? Something is either true or it isn't."

"Not when it comes to you. When it comes to you, you can decide on the truth about yourself." I glanced out into the night, considered my circumstances and what had brought me here. "Well, up to a point, anyhow."

Aribah stared at me for a long moment. "You mean my grandfather, don't you?" she said, her voice turning brittle, along with the rest of her. "You mean I should tell him I'm not my mother. He knows that, believe me. I'm reminded of the fact every day."

"No," I said. "I mean you should tell him to go to hell and walk away."

"What?" She had the presence of mind to keep the outburst to a whisper—barely—but still, I flinched. "Leave him? Leave my school? He's my blood, my *clan*. I'm *neyajin*—we don't walk away."

"Then maybe you should start."

She was on her feet in an instant, a dark smudge against the night. "You know nothing about what it means to be *neyajin*, nothing about what it means to serve your people, to be part of something larger than—"

"Than what?" I said. "You said yourself he's the last of your blood. You belong to a clan of two, Aribah, and half of that clan treats you like dirt." I sat up on the grass. "You think I don't know what it's like to belong to something bigger than yourself? I *am* something bigger than myself: I have people cheating and lying and dying for me right now, hundreds of miles away—coves I don't even know. Coves I don't want to have under me. But they all look to me for direction and answers anyhow, because *their* truths say I have those answers. Well, here's the answer: I don't have one. And neither do you. And neither does your grandfather. We're all just making our truths up as we go."

"No." She shook her head. "No. It's not that simple for me. Maybe for you, maybe in your Empire, bonds are broken and truths are molded to your liking, but not here. Not in Djan. Here, you are nothing without your clan, without your family. And yes, he may be the only blood I have, but there is also the school. They are mine and I am theirs."

"But they aren't your blood," I said. "They aren't your clan, right?"

"They . . ." She sighed and sat down and looked at the ring on her hand. "No, they're not clan—not my clan. They come from other tribes, other traditions. They're here because of Grandfather, because of his Black Cord."

"And when he's gone?"

Aribah shook her head. "The school will become mine, but . . . will they stay? I don't know."

"You know," I said.

"It's complicated."

"No, it's not. It's as simple as you want it to be."

She stayed silent.

"You want to know a truth?" I said. "Here's mine: I'm a street-level sneak trying to pass himself off as some sort of criminal genius. I didn't choose that truth, but it's the one I'm stuck with. But before that, I made my own truth: I worked the streets and sifted secrets and carved out my own path. It wasn't until I stepped away from the truth I'd made that someone else started to define it for me."

"And now? What is your truth now?"

"It's . . . complicated."

She smiled. "Only if you let it be."

I smiled back. "Maybe so, but we're not talking about me."

The smile flickered on her face, vanished. "It's not easy."

"To think about?"

"To do."

"So you *have* thought about it?"

She nodded. Of course she had. Who wouldn't?

I let the silence sit there between us, waiting for her words.

"It's frightening," she said at last. "And exciting. The thought of leaving? Of being my own person, responsible only to myself? It both pulls and pushes me, feeling like bravery and cowardice at once. But I don't know which one is true, don't know which one is right. They keep changing."

"They'll do that."

She looked up, meeting my eyes in the moonlight. "How do you leave everything you've ever known?"

I thought back to the day Christiana and I had left Balsturan Forest, when I'd been half a decade younger than the woman before me now; thought back to when I had in turn walked away from my sister and any hope of repairing the damage between us; back, closer, to turning my back first on Degan, then on what I thought it meant to be part of the Kin. It hadn't been a noble or glorious path, and Angels knew there'd been more than a fair amount of pain and heartbreak along the way, but at least it had been my path. I had chosen the truth of it.

"You start by taking one step," I said, "followed by another and another, until you realize the road you're following is your own and not someone else's."

"You make it sound easy."

"It's the hardest thing you'll ever do. But the best part?" I reached out and tapped the worn ring on her finger. "She can come with you. Inside."

A relieved laugh. "That sounds good."

"It is."

Aribah was just opening her mouth to reply when a grim, harsh voice spoke from the darkness behind us. "It may sound good," said the voice. "But it will never happen. My granddaughter isn't leaving el-Qaddice. And she certainly isn't leaving with you."

Chapter Thirty

We both leapt to our feet and spun around in one motion. A darker patch of midnight was just visible among the trees.

"Grandfather!" began Aribah. "I didn't mean—"

"Enough," snapped the shadow. "No excuses. I heard what you said. I know what you meant."

I took a step off to the side. My wrist knife was already in my left hand. My right was hovering out at my side, ready to reach for either my rapier or my dagger, depending on what he did.

"What the hell are you doing here?" I said.

"He followed you," said Aribah, answering before her grandfather could. "Followed us. He didn't trust me to keep you safe, and didn't trust you not to leave."

"Leave?" I said.

"El-Qaddice," said the elder assassin. "Although I didn't expect you to try to take Aribah with you." I heard him hawk, saw the flicker of his spit in my night vision. "Didn't expect her to be so quick to turn away from her family, either, for that matter."

Aribah snapped up straight. "No one's trying to take anyone anywhe—"

"Silence, girl. You've already done enough damage to your mother's memory for one night, let alone my honor. Don't drive the blade in any further."

Aribah seemed to shrink at that—to retreat into herself,

the fire I'd seen moments ago dimming in the process. She shuffled back half a pace.

I turned my eyes back to the dark smudge before us. *You old bastard.*

"This isn't about her," I said, stepping to my left, trying to put the silhouette of one of the trees behind me. "It's about you and your legacy." Another step. Hand on my sword handle. "About using her, and my night vision, as a way to let your name live on after you die."

He let out a soft chuckle. "Is that what you think, Imperial? That I'm so vain I can't stand the thought of being forgotten? That I'd risk her life by having her watch over you, just so I could craft a legacy for myself?" His head shifted, turning, I assumed, to Aribah. "And you? Is this what you think, also?"

"I don't know what to think right now," she whispered.

"Then you're a fool." He shifted, facing me fully. Ignoring her. "I'm a Black Cord, Imperial—what use do I have for fame? Fame brings attention and death. My only wish is to preserve my family and revive my clan. To restore the status of my school and the *neyajin*. To make sure they're strong."

"Sounds very noble," I said, drawing my rapier from its scabbard. The scrape of steel against leather and brass sounded loud in the night. "But you have to admit, being known as the one assassin who discovered the secret of dark sight after all these years? To be the Black Cord who single-handedly turns the fortunes of your school and tribe around?" I shook my head. "Heady stuff."

"I won't deny it has its appeal, but it's not my primary motive."

"If you say so."

He moved now, and I caught the amber-touched glint of steel in one hand. Small sword, if I had to guess. There was something in the other, but I couldn't make it out. Fine. I dropped my wrist blade and pulled my dagger, the better to parry and slash with.

"It won't work, you know," I said. "I already told you: I don't know how to pass it on. Kill me, and the secret goes

away; capture me, and all you get is someone who can't tell
you what you want to know."

"So I thought, too," he said, "but then I remembered:
This is el-Qaddice, seat of prophets and scholars . . . and
magi—not all of whom are afraid to step into the shadows
now and then. Especially if the incentive is right. And as a
Black Cord, I have both the pockets and the presence to
command their attention." He took his own step back, slipping into the dappled, moonlit shadow of a tree. "There are
learned men in this city, Imperial—men who know not only
how to consult tomes and histories, but also creatures far
wiser in the ways of magic than ourselves. Creatures who
have long memories and carry great grudges."

"Grandfather, no!" Aribah's rune-dyed hands came up
to her mouth, making the flesh of her jaw look mottled in
my eyes. "Not the djinn. Don't tell me you consulted with
them."

"If we want the secrets this one possesses, we need to
walk the paths that were closed to us before now. We
needed to make a choice,"

Her voice was tiny by now—the voice of a child in the
night. "What have you done?"

"What I must."

It wasn't until after he'd spoken that I realized his voice
had moved—was moving. That he was nowhere near where
he'd been a moment ago.

Crap.

I crouched down out of habit, sword high, dagger low.
An instant later, I heard a soft hiss, followed by the *tck* of
something small sticking into the tree behind and above me.
Dart? Knife? Throwing crescent?

Did it really matter?

I tucked my shoulder and rolled, knowing that even as I
did so I was telling the old assassin what I was doing, where
I was going. But there was no way I could stay put: not with
his knives flying and him creeping closer. I had to move.

I came to my feet and kept going, ducking behind trees,
staying close to their trunks in the hopes that an exposed
root might serve to slow the *neyajin* down.

Another hiss, another *tck*, this time just in front of me. I jerked back and changed course.

This was *not* how I was used to fighting in the dark.

I ducked around another tree, putting it between me and where I'd thought the last attack had come from. I tried to slow my breathing, tried to will my heart to stop pounding in my ears, but to no avail.

If I waited until I could hear him coming, I'd end up trussed and gagged before I knew what was happening. No, I needed to get close—to put myself in a position where I at least had a chance of seeing the attacks coming. And that meant rushing a man who could track me by the sound of my approach.

Great.

"Aribah?" I called.

No answer.

"Aribah!"

"Don't answer him," called out her grandfather. "He's just trying to use your voice to distract me."

"I know what he's doing!" she said.

"Then be silent."

He sounded closer—off to the right. I peered into the darkness, my night vision turning the shadows of the trees blood red against the amber of the grass.

"Not for this," said Aribah. "Not like this."

"Dammit, child—"

"We're *neyajin*," she said. Nearly cried. "You taught me what that means. Taught Mother. Told us that to be feared, to be effective, we have to stand apart. That we can't let ourselves be known to those we would hunt. 'By being the darkness, we become the fear that haunts the darkness.'"

"And we will be," he said. He was on the move again, still on my right. "Once we have the dark vision, the *neyajin* will again be synonymous with justice and death."

I strained my eyes until they burned. There. Had that been the back of an arm? Maybe his whole back?

"Magi and djinn will cower at the mention of our name, and we will once more sit in the shadows on the right hand of the despot."

As he spoke, I slipped out from behind my cover, moving low and fast. The leaves murmured in the breeze, shifting the moonlight and shadows around on the ground. Ahead, I could make out slippery, amber-etched movement, just in the lee of a trunk. I squeezed the grip of my rapier, then let my fingers relax once more. *A double handful of strides, Drothe. Don't tense up.*

"You said something about a choice," she said. I glanced over, saw the flash of her exposed jaw and mouth as she moved among the trees now, too. "What was it?"

I wanted to tell her to stop moving, to keep talking, to get the hell back, but did none of them. It was too late for that. The slick amber of warded cloth was before me now, her grandfather lurking in the shadows of a pistachio tree. Six paces away. Five.

I raised my rapier, extended my arm slightly.

Keep moving, Aribah. Let him hear you instead of me.

Four. I shifted my weight, bringing it forward.

"What did you agree to?" she called.

Three.

Enough.

I lunged, my arm leading the way, my sword pulling the rest of me forward as its tip sought out the shadow before me. I let my left foot pass forward as my right landed, driving me forward, pushing my sword into the cloth-draped shadow and through it, dagger following after, in and out and in and out, working hard at turning a man into a corpse.

Only no blood spilled and no corpse fell. Instead, I found myself gutting a *neyajin*-tinted coat and a column of smoke that rose away, giggling, on the wind.

"I agreed to sell something," said Aribah's grandfather from behind me. "For a bit of help."

I was still spinning, still lashing out with my dagger, when the fire wrapped itself around me. Or, at least, that's what it felt like. All I knew is that my weapons dropped from my hands, my feet left the ground, and I tilted my head back and screamed. Or tried to.

"Ah, ah, little thief," said a voice that seemed to burn itself across my mind. "No need for that. We don't want to be summoning any of my chained kindred, now, do we?"

My scream died in my throat, coming out as nothing more than a strained gasp. Still, I huffed and choked on the agony, until finally the pain eased back a tiny fraction and I was able to draw a shaky breath. It felt like bliss.

"Th-thief?" I gasped, my head still back, my eyes tight shut. I could feel the heat enveloping me, could sense the tickle of flames held just at bay against my body. No way I was getting an eye full of fire. "I . . . haven't stolen . . . from . . . you." I think I would have remembered lightening someone who could do something like this.

"No?" burned the voice. "Then how do you explain this?"

Suddenly my eyes were open and I was looking down into the grove from twice my normal height. Everything glowed with a brilliant amber-gold light, brighter and sharper than any version of night vision I'd ever experienced before. Not only every leaf, but every vein of every leaf, every fold of bark and blade of grass, shone under my gaze, cut with details so sharp I feared they might slice my eyes.

Below me stood Aribah's grandfather, the sharpness of his smile cutting through his veil like a razor. I got the feeling it would have been hard for me to make him out in his robes even now, save for the fact that he had a rope of fire rising from his hand. The fire came from a small vial he held in his palm and snaked up and around me, wrapping me from toes to throat in bands of pain. As I watched, smoke rose off the burning rope and coalesced in the air to form a thin, vaguely man-shaped cloud. It would have been tempting to write that last bit off as a coincidence, save for the burning eyes in its head. Eyes that made a point of staring at me.

"*You see with the eyes of the djinn,*" said the cloud, its words scribing themselves in fire between me and the assassin. Like the rope, they didn't seem to bother my night vision. "*Eyes stolen from one of my kind.*"

"Wha . . . what?" I said through the pain. Eyes *stolen*

from a djinni? *Just what the hell had you done, Sebastian?* "I don't—"

"Your dark sight," said Aribah's grandfather, reading the fading flames. "It didn't sound right, your gift never going away. Even the Lions lose their sight after a day and a night. So I began to ask around, to seek out the old sufis and the mystics who claimed to be able to speak with the darker spirits." He lifted the vial, causing the rope to sway, me to drift, the djinni to waver. "Imagine my surprise when I learned that not only were there tales about a lord of the djinn being tricked out of his sight, but of that spirit still thirsting for revenge."

"But I didn't steal its sight," I gasped.

"Maybe not," said the elder assassin, "but from what I can tell, djinn have a different way of looking at these things." *We will dine on your soul.* "They don't so much care that you took it as that you have it now."

"And your price?" I asked, already guessing the answer.

The old assassin smiled. "They teach us the secret of the dark sight, of course."

"No!" The word exploded from Aribah's throat as she stepped into the glow of the djinni's rope. No, not stepped—stalked—her mother's dagger in her hand and a hard set to her jaw. Streaks of skin were just visible beneath her eyes, the dye washed thin by the tears rolling down her cheeks.

I'd never been so happy to see an assassin in my life.

"No," she repeated. "We are *neyajin*. We don't make deals with the things we hunt. We don't bargain with the things we kill. We don't accept rewards from . . ." She gestured at the cloud. "*Them*. We are *neyajin*."

"We are *shadows*," snapped the old man. "Shadows of what we used to be, and pale reflections of what we might become. Think, Aribah. Think what this will mean for our clan, for our school. For us. One small bargain, on small infraction, and we begin our climb back into the light."

"But you yourself said we belong to the shadows, not the light."

He made an impatient gesture. "You know what I mean, girl."

Aribah looked at her grandfather, looked at the rope, looked at the cloud with its burning, merry eyes. The only one she didn't look at was me, but I wasn't part of the equation at this point anyhow—not really. She bit her lip.

"It's not *neyajin*," she said at last.

"Enough! You forget your place. *I* determine what is and is not *neyajin*, what serves the school and the clan, not you. After we have the dark sight, after we are respected and feared as in the days of old, you have my permission to come to me and argue about what is or is not *neyajin*, but until then, your place is to obey. And you *will* obey."

Aribah's head snapped back as if she'd been struck. She took a breath, squared her shoulders, and stepped forward.

Fiery laughter sounded in my head.

"That's not my truth," she said.

"What?" Her grandfather peered at her in the night. "'Your truth'? What does that mean? What do you know about truth?"

"I know that it doesn't involve working with djinn. Or . . ." She rubbed her thumb over her mother's ring. "Or obeying you. Not when it comes to this. Not anymore."

His eyebrows crawled so far up his head, I expected them to come squirming out the back of his kaffiyeh. "You disobey me? Again?"

"I . . . disagree with you."

I more than half-expected him to hit her right then. Instead, he made a fist with his free hand and turned away.

"Go," he said. "Leave me. I disown you and all you do. You are *neyajin* no more."

Aribah's eyes went wide. She raised a hand and took a step toward him, then stopped. "Grandfather," she said. "Listen to me. Please. These things you bargain with, that you accept payment from—they're the same spirits we've been fighting for generations. The leopard doesn't allow the fox to buy its freedom, and we don't spare the djinn. Do you think the creature that killed your daughter offered her the chance to buy her life? That it asked my mother if she would like to make a bargain? No. It killed her and stuck her—"

The old man spun around. "You think I don't know that?" he cried. "That I didn't consider it? That I didn't sit up nights, wondering and weighing?" He reached up and wiped at his face with the back of his sword hand. "The djinn took her, yes. But we need what this one has to offer, to make the *neyajin* strong again. To be proud again."

"But at what cost? The cost of her memory? Of her honor?"

"She would have understood!"

Aribah's head came up, the rest of her straightening with it, until she was staring her grandfather in the eye. "No," she said. "No, she wouldn't. She would have told you you were wrong."

The elder *neyajin* considered her for a long, cold moment. When he spoke, his words were ice in the middle of the desert. "Leave her ring and her dagger, leave your robes and your name. You don't deserve to carry any trace of what you once were." He showed her his back again. Then, almost under his breath, he added, "And you don't deserve to have been born her daughter."

It was the wrong thing to say.

When she struck, it wasn't with a yell of rage or a scream of defiance: It was with cold and silent efficiency. One step, two, and then she was in the air, her dagger raised, its edge trailing smoke or shadows or whatever the hell they were behind her.

Still, her grandfather hadn't earned his Black Cord for nothing. He was already dodging, already spinning and raising his sword to counterthrust when she landed where he'd been standing.

Only, that wasn't where Aribah had been aiming. Instead, she landed a good three feet away, gathered herself on the turf, and sprang into the air again, her dagger overhead.

When she slashed through the burning rope, three things happened at once. First, the djinni screamed. Second, her grandfather cursed. And third, I started to cheer, but was interrupted by my falling out of the air.

By the time I recovered from my awkward landing and had rolled onto my back, the flames were gone and the cloud that had been the djinni was already dissipating. I thought I caught the final hints of some smoky mutterings on the wind, but couldn't be sure because of the sounds of combat that were now filling the grove. I scrambled to my knees and then into a crouch, only remembering at the last moment that my sword and dagger were lying somewhere on the ground.

I scanned the darkness, thanking the Angels that my night vision seemed to be back to normal again. No more polished gold and brilliant rubies glinting in the night for me—now it was all blacks and blood and dirty brass. Which was just fine.

The only problem was, I was looking for two people who were all but invisible to me. The sound told me roughly where they were, but—ah, there: a flash of uncovered chin, a hint of oily red cloak, a dulled gold glimmer of steel. Not a clear picture of the fight, let alone the combatants by any means, but I at least had a better fix on them.

Now, what the hell was I going to do about it?

I reached down into my boot and drew the long knife I kept there. Then I moved forward, listening as much as looking for my prey.

Grunting and grasping. The dull thump of feet on grass, of flesh on flesh. They'd moved past blade work, into the realm of punches and holds and trips. Not surprising, really: There was so much anger there, so much fury, that I don't think mere steel could have sufficed. It was down to raw things now: blood and bone, teeth and sweat.

Love had fallen off the knife's edge, leaving hate's well-honed blade unimpeded.

Then I saw them a dozen steps away. A mass of half-seen shadows, shifting and straining, both against each other and in and out of my vision. Someone had someone else down, holding fast while the other bucked against them.

I rushed forward. Either the old man was on top, which gave me his back, or he was on the ground, which meant I had time to angle for the kill. I just hoped I'd have time to tell who was who before the question became moot.

I was maybe five feet away when the figure on top jerked up, rammed what I guessed to be a hand down onto the other assassin's exposed, stain-free and visible throat, and then tumbled away and into the darkness. That gave me a good idea of who had been who. It was confirmed when I found Aribah lying on the ground, half-conscious and gagging for breath.

"Easy," I whispered, crouching down beside her. "I think—*urk!*"

The old man had moved fast. Where I thought he might have moved off to regroup, or was just putting some distance between himself and two opponents, he'd circled around and come up behind me—all in the space of a handful of breaths. Now he drew the garrote tighter about my neck.

I gagged. My boot knife fell away in the surprise of his attack. Instead, I clawed with my fingers at the cord, at his arms, at the ground, trying to establish some sort of hold, some sort of grip on the world around me. All I succeeded in doing was getting dirt under my nails.

He jerked back on the garrote, pulling me away from Aribah. I staggered a pace or two, then fell to one knee. He stayed with me the entire time.

"Not to worry," he hissed in my ear. "I still need you alive, Imperial. You're just going to sleep for a bit, is all." Another tug on the line. "Can't be having you interfering in family business."

I would have said it was like having a line of fire across my throat, but I knew from firsthand experience what that felt like now. This wasn't that. This was sheer pain and panic—a sensation that there was something wedged in my throat, and if only I could get it out, I could breathe again. A desperate need, not to end the pain, but to simply pull air into my lungs.

The garrote was too tight to get a finger under, let alone a hand. I reached back and over, feeling his cloth and skin and stubble behind me. I raked and pulled with my nails, came away with his kaffiyeh, threw it aside, tried again. He drew his head back, held me at arm's length, and leaned a knee into my back.

I looked frantically at Aribah. The moonlight was shining down through the leaves, painting her in the amber of my sight, shimmering on her face even as it cast a bloodred shadow beneath her. She was on her side now, hands at her throat, drawing a ragged, desperate breath.

Her eyes met mine, and we both knew: She wouldn't recover in time. Not even close. Her grandfather would strangle me into unconsciousness, possibly kill her, and then cart me off to whatever cellar best suited him to renegotiate his deal with the djinni.

And yet Aribah shifted. She moved on the ground, reaching out, clawing at the dirt—no, clawing *in* the dirt, for something. For, I saw as she lifted it and tossed it my way, a shadow-edged blade.

I didn't catch it, didn't even come close, but I did manage to jerk my body enough that I was able to fall over, the nearly deadweight that was me pulling the old assassin after. I flung my arm out, feeling for what I couldn't see.

A ring of black had formed at the edge of my vision and was working its way in. All I could make out was the grass before me, the tops of tree roots just cresting the surface of the ground. I blinked, but the circle only got bigger. Sparks fired in my vision. My head felt ready to fall off. My lungs were filled with the fire of need.

I don't remember finding the blade so much as feeling it in my hand—one moment, nothing, the next, a hard, smooth thing in my quickly weakening grasp. I gripped it tight, hefted it. It was heavy, so much so that I was amazed I could get it off the ground.

I didn't swing for him. Even then, I knew better than to try; knew that the angle was wrong, that I wouldn't be able to generate enough power to do anything meaningful. No, instead I swung at the ground—at the blotch of bloody blackness that was our combined moon-cast shadow, praying that what had happened in the cellar, what I had seen Aribah do to the magi's shadow with her mother's blade, would work on her grandfather now. That the Angels or the Family or whoever was watching would let me cleave into his shadow. That I would kill either him or me, or both of us. Because I'd be damned if I'd die the way he wanted.

The blade bit. The assassin screamed. So, for that matter, did I.

"Get up!"

"Wh . . . " I paused to cough, rubbed at my neck. "What?"

Aribah tugged hard on my arm, pulling me to a sitting position. "You have to go," she said. "*We* have to go. We made too much noise. Someone will be coming."

Her voice was throaty and rough, and I noticed that she was pausing to swallow between each sentence. Blood trailed down her jaw from the vicinity of her ear, and the left side of her mouth was already starting to swell. Her turban was gone, revealing a tightly braided nest of raven-black hair set with brass pins. I wondered if the pins had steel tips to them, then decided it didn't much matter at this point.

She looked about as shaky as I felt. But her eyes were hard and her grip was solid, so I didn't argue. I knew all about the value of staying quiet, let alone of becoming a memory when that failed to work out.

I moved to put my legs under me, felt resistance. I looked down and found her grandfather lying across my right foot. He didn't have to worry about being quiet anymore.

"Yes," she hissed. "He's dead. Now come on. It does me no good if I get him out of here and leave you lying about for the guards to find. Get up!"

I did as she said, wincing at a sharp pain along my right biceps. I looked down to see a clean slice in both the fabric and the skin below.

I grimaced. Only I could manage to cut myself with a knife on the same arm that was wielding it. Fucking shadows.

Then I stood fully and nearly fell over again. I gasped at the roaring pain in my head.

"Here." Aribah stuck a small bottle in my hand, then stepped into the darkness. "Drink it."

I did as ordered, nearly choking from the bitterness as it seeped over my tongue and forced its way past what felt like a permanent dent in my throat.

"Angels, what is that?" I gasped as she came back. She had my rapier and dagger and boot knife in her hands.

"Herbs, brewed *ahrami*, spices, a bit of kaffa—we use it to keep alert and dull pain."

I traded the empty bottle for my weapons, spitting all the while. The flavor stayed with you. Still, I could already feel the storm in my head beginning to ease.

Aribah took my face between her hands and studied me in the moonlight, turning my head this way and that. She slapped me once, twice, then tilted my head back. "How many moons do you see?"

"Two?" I said. "One and a half?"

"Good enough." She let go and bent down. When she straightened, she had her grandfather's kaffiyeh in her hand, her mother's knife at her belt. "Do you think you can make it to where you were headed?" she said as she draped and then tied the cloth around her head.

I took a step aside and looked out over the expanse of ground between us and the next hill. It looked farther away than before, but was still empty. For the moment.

"If there are no surprises, yeah." I turned back to find her no more than a whisper in my vision.

"Good. Then do so." I blinked, realizing that the shadow before me had been just that. Aribah was already kneeling beside her grandfather, adjusting his clothes and using her own turban to bind and cover him in darkness. "I can get Grandfather and me past the guards if I hurry."

I considered her, considered the body. "Are you sure?"

"I must be."

"I could—"

"No," she said, her voice both brittle and sharp at once. "You can't. Not with this. He's mine to bear. Alone."

There was no room left for argument in her voice, and I didn't try to make any. Instead, I stalked over to where we'd been first talking and looked through the shadows until I found my wrist knife. When I turned back, she had pulled the body into a sitting position and was arranging him across her shoulders. She stood with a grunt, staggered a bit, then found her footing. I was just able to make out her eyes in the darkness.

"I . . . I'm sorry," I said, not finding any other words just then.

"No more than I." I watched her eyes blink wetly once, twice. Then, "Good luck finding your truth, Imperial." And she turned away. I watched, but after a moment, she was little more than a blur. Two steps farther on, and she was gone.

I stood there for a moment, watching the darkness. Thinking.

The eyes of a djinni?

Damn you. Damn you twice over for being dead, Sebastian.

I turned and headed off down the slope. Like it or not, there was still more to do.

Chapter Thirty-one

I hadn't had a chance to case Heron's ken on my prior visit, and there wasn't time for it now. A quick circuit showed a building designed as much for security as aesthetics: There were plenty of windows, but all of the accessible ones were narrow, more reminiscent of glass-filled loopholes meant for archers than for letting in light or air. Higher up, the few wider windows and balcony doors were fitted with elaborate gates of iron scrollwork, and those sat over equally ornate carved wooden screens. As for the doors at ground level, all were beautifully and solidly built, with locks that looked to be a study in intricacy, if their delicately acid-etched casings were any indication.

I didn't relish the notion of trying a new lock on the spur of the moment, especially with my head still pounding and my breath coming in gasps. While every lock may be ultimately pickable, that doesn't mean every lock maker goes about his business in the same way. Just as each lock master has a personality, so do his locks; back in Ildrecca, I could have told you that the mechanism from the Iron Hand shop always turned in a clockwise direction, while a Dorynian lock used a double-turn system, and that Kettlemaker often as not installed a false pin that, if stroked incorrectly, could freeze up the rest of the mechanism. But here, in el-Qaddice, on the padishah's grounds? I had no idea how simple or elaborate any given lock might be, let alone the particular traits of the device or its maker. And while I could likely feel and analyze my way through all but the worst of the tumbles I'd find here, the thought of being spotted by a member of the Opal Guard—or worse—while working my spiders didn't exactly excite me.

So instead, I decided to go with a tried-and-true method from my youth: I knocked on the front door.

Despite everything I'd gone through tonight, it still wasn't as late as I might have liked. That meant the steward wasn't yawning and rubbing his eyes when he answered the door, but he still opened it readily enough. We were on a royal estate, surrounded by walls and guards and Angels knew what else—who would expect a gig rush here? Certainly not him.

The pommel of my dagger caught him in the temple the moment the door had swung to, sending his woven skullcap flying.

He staggered, and I followed up with another strike, this time to the back of his head. At the same time, I reached out with my free hand and directed his fall; I couldn't have him blocking the doorway, after all. He hit the floor at the same time as his cap.

It wasn't the most elegant of entries, I admit, but the most effective methods sometimes aren't. Far more Kin make a quick hawk with an expertly applied bludgeon or fist than those who take the time to slide a lock or cut a purse. As much as some Lighters may like to see us as smiling, capable rogues, the truth is most Kin are little better than back-alley thugs at heart. And even though I like to see myself as standing above the rest of my cousins, I have to admit to having washed my fair share of blood off coins before spending them over the years. Sometimes it's just more expedient to spill a bit of claret.

I pulled the steward the rest of the way into the entry and closed the door behind me. Then I crouched there, listening, running my hands over him even as he groggily tried to push them away. A ring of keys came off his belt, and a small whistle from around his neck. The belt itself I removed and cinched around his wrists, making them fast behind his back. Then I sat him up in the shadows beside the door and gave his face a few light slaps to get his attention.

I held up my dagger. "How many besides you?" I said.

He looked at the blade vaguely, clearly still having trouble focusing. "None," he slurred.

"If you stick with that answer and I find anyone else, they die."

"Two."

I nodded. "Where?"

"Upstairs."

I unwound his sash, tied a knot in one end, and stuffed it in his mouth. The rest went around his head twice and became a gag. "Stay," I said. It would have been nice if he'd passed out completely, but I wasn't about to beat him until he lost consciousness; there are lines and there are lines, and not all of them need to be crossed simply for the sake of convenience.

I retraced the steps from my previous meeting, first finding the library and then finding the key to it on the steward's ring. The house was clearly settled in for the night, with only a handful of tapers burning against the master's eventual return. A rhythmic creaking from the floor above told me what the other two servants were up to. I returned to the front door to retrieve the steward.

He was trying to regain his feet but having a hard time of it, given his sallow complexion and sweating brow.

"Easy," I said, steadying him. "I wouldn't recommend vomiting when you have a gag in your mouth. Good way to choke to death."

He thought about it and nodded weakly. I led him back down to the library, veering only to retrieve a taper on the way. Once inside, I set him in the middle of the floor and then locked the oak doors behind us.

"Your life depends on your silence," I said, turning around. "No kicking, no knocking things over, no noise of any sort, and you get to live. Make a sound, though, and I guarantee that, even if they break the doors down, they'll only find one man breathing. Understand?"

The steward glared and nodded.

I straightened and looked at the shelves.

"I don't suppose you know where your master keeps his books on degans, do you?" I said.

This time, all I got was the glare.

"I thought not."

I began in the section Heron had pulled Simonis Chionates from, finding the work itself without much effort. A quick leafing through the pages showed both a well-marked and well-used text, with marginalia in at least two hands. More interestingly, beside it I found what appeared to be an earlier, draft version of the text, all in the same hand as the later work. The original notes and the finished work? One hell of a scholarly coup, but given that neither of them seemed to relate to Ivory Degan or the original practices of the Order, they didn't do me much good. I moved on.

The surrounding books were a mixture of general imperial histories, diaries of people who had done business with degans, two folios filled with fading letters, a handful of fighting manuals—including Gambogi, which I remembered Degan disparaging once—a dog-eared copy of Usserius's opus *On the Nature of Imperial Divinity*, and what could only be described as a hodgepodge of fanciful tales and lays bound in one volume. The last was titled *The Adventures, Heroic Deeds, and Perilous Dangers faced by the Most Noble Order of the Degans* and attributed solely to "A. Gentleman," which, glancing at the text, seemed to be an insult to any gentleman worthy of the title.

It was far less than I'd hoped for and, after spending a good hour paging through the pile, clearly not Heron's only sources on the Order. For someone who'd proclaimed a lifetime's interest in collecting, let alone his fascination with a specific topic, the books before me constituted more of an embarrassment than a reason to crow. Maybe I'd been spoiled by the tomes that passed through Baldezar's hands, or even the ones that came out of his workshop back in Ildrecca, but Heron had spoken too knowingly about the degans for me to think this was the extent of his knowledge. From what I could see, Ivory was barely mentioned, let alone the early Order.

No, there had to be more, and not just because I wanted there to be.

I glanced over at the steward. He'd drifted off into unconsciousness, brought on no doubt in part by the drubbing I'd given him. Even if he were awake, though, I knew better than to expect help from that quarter.

Instead, I began searching the surrounding shelves and cases, paging through volumes, looking for any other tomes or folios that might pertain to my quest. Just because Simonis was in one area didn't mean Heron couldn't have degan-related material in another spot; like locks, libraries have their own personalities.

As good as that theory was, though, it didn't result in my finding any more books on the degans, obvious or otherwise. Sooner than I'd like, I was back before the shelf with Simonis and "A. Gentleman."

I looked around the room, wondering briefly if Heron was the kind to keep a written catalog of all his books. Probably not: He was just arrogant enough to carry it around in his head. And while getting in here had been easier than I'd hoped, I didn't have any illusions about being able to lay hands on the secretary, let alone persuading him to tell me where he kept his materials on the degans. He didn't seem the kind to break very easily.

Still, appearances can be deceiving, and it wasn't as if I had a lot of other options. I couldn't see myself being invited back for coffee and a bite anytime soon. As for repeating tonight's performance—well, a smart Draw Latch doesn't crack the same ken twice, especially when that ken lies inside the domain of a royal prince. People like that tend to have enough resources to make a second attempt fatal.

Which meant I got to wait. I wasn't in the mood to wait.

I entertained myself by searching the research table for hidden drawers and compartments, just in case I was wrong about Heron's arrogance. I wasn't. From there, I poked about the back of the shelves that held the degan folios, then the more likely bits of molding and joints along the walls. Nothing.

If there was something hidden in Heron's library, I decided, both Christiana and I had something to learn from the man.

After checking to make sure the steward was still breathing, I found myself before Heron's "memory" wall, staring at the flowers and the fan and the sword. On a whim, I pulled a chair over, climbed up, and gently lifted the fan off its mounting pins.

It was big, even for a funerary fan, and required both hands to lift. This close, I could see an impressive amount of gold leaf and even a few precious stones through the dark gauze that covered the body of the fan. The ribs were polished ebony, held open by a rod extending across the back.

The wall behind the fan was smooth and blank: no keys, no careful catalog of books, no conveniently hidden compartment containing centuries-old papers. Just plain white plaster and the trailing wisps of freshly broken cobwebs.

Well, it had been a long shot anyhow.

It was while I was shifting the fan back into place that the mourning cloth slipped off, raising a small cloud of dust even as it drifted to the floor. I turned my head and sneezed, both out of respect for the fan, and because I didn't want to send myself toppling backward from my perch. The chair still teetered a bit, and the fan wobbled treacherously in my hands, but neither of us ended up falling. Relieved, I turned back to finish the remounting, and gasped.

Exquisite didn't even begin to describe what I saw before me. The calligraphy alone was a work of art, with each symbol, each accent, a study in technique: effortless and stylistically perfect at once. The painted cephta seemed to shimmer, the finely powdered pearl that had been mixed with the pigments catching and reflecting the lantern light behind me, making the writing come alive on the silk. It was as if the story of the woman before me wanted to step off the fan and dance its way across my eyes, rather than simply be read.

The artwork was just as stunning: each figure, each mountain, each vista crafted with the fewest possible brushstrokes, but each clearly visible for what it was. As was tra-

ditional, the predominant color was black, but here and
there, small hints of color had been added to underscore
particular memories and moments: the blue-green edge of
the sea, the pink of an almond tree in bloom, the sandy
brown of a peregrine falcon's belly in flight.

It was a life laid out not just to be remembered and
mourned, but to be glorified. To be reveled in. To be loved.

But as stunning as the calligraphy and the art and the
devotion apparent in the fan were, they weren't what had
caused me to catch my breath; that had been caused by the
name written in fine golden symbols across the top of the
fan: Simonis Chionates. The same name that had belonged
to the woman who'd penned the two-hundred-year-old history on the shelf behind me. The woman who had inspired
a secretary's interest in the degans.

And the woman who, scanning the details of the life
stretched out before me, had been married to a man named
Heronestes Karkappadolis. A man who was depicted on the
fan wielding an ivory-handled sword, and who stood with a
whole host of other men and women with metal-chased
weapons.

A man who was recognizable to me, even in two hundred year old drapes, even in miniature.

A man who was a degan. Ivory Degan.

Heron.

The library doors swung open to admit Heron, trailed by
a pair of men in iridescent white-enameled armor. The two
had their swords out—shining, curving things that, pretty
as they might be, were nonetheless clearly designed to see
use.

Opal Guardsmen, if I had to guess.

All three paused when they spotted me sitting in the
chair directly below the fan, the steward trussed up at my
feet, the sword from the wall lying unsheathed across my
lap. I held Simonis's book open in my hand.

Heron took in the scene at a glance and held up his hand
before the guardsmen could take another step.

"Leave us," he said.

The guardsmen hesitated, exchanging a doubtful look behind his back.

"With respect, master, we—"

"There's been a misunderstanding," said Heron, his eyes meeting mine. "This man and I had an appointment. I forgot."

Another shared look. "I'm no expert on etiquette, but that doesn't explain the binding and gagging of your man there. Are you sure you don't—"

"Take my man with you," said Heron. "Untie him. And if he says anything to you . . ." Here the secretary dropped his gaze to meet that of his steward's. " . . . anything *at all*, kill him. Am I understood?"

Both the guardsmen and the steward nodded. A minute later the door closed behind them, and Heron and I were alone.

He'd clearly had a long night, and was none the happier for it. Hair disheveled, face drawn, ash and sweat and someone's blood smeared into his robes. He looked as if he'd come off a small battlefield, or out of one big damn tavern brawl.

"I expect you have questions," he said.

"I've got a hell of a lot more than that."

"Yes, well." He stepped farther into the room. "Can I at least ask you to put my sword down?"

"Don't tell me you're worried I'll use it."

"Let's just say I find the image of you holding it . . . aesthetically displeasing."

"And if I refuse?"

Heron sighed. "Do you really want me to take it away from you?"

I leaned the sword against the chair. "Better?"

"And now the book, if you please."

"Which one? The original draft, in your wife's hand, with your suggestions in the margins," I said, reaching behind me and pulling out the earlier edition, fronted by thin laurel wood boards and leather bindings, "or the finished version"—I raised the one I'd been holding when he walked in—"with her handwritten dedication to you below the frontispiece?"

I'd spent enough time around Baldezar back in Ildrecca to develop a basic appreciation of the forger's art: evaluating the age of a document, distinguishing between real signs of wear and the tricks a Jarkman can use to prematurely age a piece, recognizing the natural flow of a person's hand versus the hesitancy of a forger's later additions. Simonis's hand was identical in both books—a tight, efficient script, favoring a rigidity of form. Classical, if you will. The other hand, by comparison, was relaxed and flowing, favoring the abbreviations and blurring of figures favored by scribes, or secretaries. And, in this case, identical to the writing on some of Heron's other papers I'd found among the shelves.

Heron's gaze went from the books to the fan over my head, then returned to me. There was a carefully banked fire in his eyes now. "You will put both of them down."

I closed the volumes and settled them in my lap. "Ivory Degan?" I said.

He bowed at the waist. "I used to be, yes."

"The same one who founded the Order of the Degans?"

"Once; now I'm simply Heron."

Even though I'd been half expecting the answer, I still wasn't sure what to make of it; wasn't even sure if I fully believed it. What do you say to someone who's managed to pull off what even the emperor hasn't been able to do?

I decided to start with "How is that possible?"

"I resigned from the Order and surrendered my name."

"You know what I mean."

"Yes, I do."

We stared at each other for a long moment. I wondered, belatedly, if I was going to be allowed to walk out of here, given what I knew.

"Are you like him?" I said.

"Who?"

"The emperor."

"You mean have I been reincarnated?" Heron chuckled and shook his head. "No. Nothing so simple."

"Then tell me how," I said. "Explain to me how a man—how a degan—can live for over two hundred years, while Stephen Dorminikos, with the resources of the empire and a troop of Paragons at his disposal, had to fragment his soul and turn himself into three recurring people."

"Easy," said Ivory, folding his hands before himself. "Dorminikos wanted to keep his soul; I was willing to give mine up."

"Give up your . . ." I shook my head. "That doesn't make sense."

"Oh? Why not?"

"Because . . . it's your *soul*," I said. "Paragons need one to cast Imperial magic; the emperors need parts of one to be reincarnated; people need one—"

"So the Angels can weigh your life?" he said.

"Well, yes," I said. "Or, at least, so people think they will. I'm not so sure anymore." Ever since I'd found out that the emperor had lied about the Angels choosing him to be the perpetual ruler of the Dorminikan Empire, and that they in turn hadn't seen fit to exact any kind of retribution, my use for the Angels had dropped even lower—not that it had been all that high to begin with.

"And you think a man can't live without a soul?" said Ivory.

It sounded too much like a question that could lead someplace I wouldn't like, so instead of answering, I said, "I think you're spouting theology instead of answers."

A tired smile played across Ivory's face. "It's all one and the same in some ways, isn't it? But you're not interested in that: You want to know how I can be here, two hundred and eleven years after I helped create the Order of the Degans."

"It's a good place to start."

"The answer's simple enough: the Oath."

"Which one?" I said.

I admit it: I smiled when Ivory took an unconscious step back in surprise. "What do you mean?" he said, too late to cover for his error.

I stood. "I mean," I said, stepping forward, "which Oath? The original one you crafted for the Order, or the Oath the degans used to use for their clients before you walked away. Or did you make a different promise? To the emperor, maybe, or a Paragon somewhere? Some Oath of service in exchange for a couple centuries' worth of life?" I was half-way across the library now, Ivory standing straight and stern at the other end. Even from here, I could make out the uncertainty dancing in the corners of his eyes. He hid it well—after spending two hundred years as an Imperial living in Djan, I'd expect no less—but they were still there if you knew how to look. And looking had been, and still was, part of my job.

"I'm told you got disenchanted with things," I said, running with the theories now, putting the few pieces I had together to make up new pictures, new accusations. All to push him. Four lifetimes was a long time to sit on something, after all. "But was that even it? Maybe it wasn't theology; maybe it was politics. Maybe your Order was too much of a threat to the emperor . . ." A thought occurred. "Or to his White Sashes. They're sworn to protect the emperor, too, after all." I stopped two paces before Ivory, the better to be able to look up into his eyes. "Did they complain about you? Did your new club step over some kind of line?"

"Don't be ridiculous. You have no idea—"

"I know people," I said. "And I especially know people with power: how they don't like to have up-and-comers threaten their tidy little arrangements. You don't put as much effort into building something like the degans as you did and then simply walk away; you don't swear to protect someone like the emperor and then abandon him. Something pushed you out."

"Put the books down and leave."

"Was it the emperor or his Sashes?" I said, ignoring the offer. "The Paragons maybe? We're talking souls here, after all. Did they promise you a long life, or did they threaten you with something worse?"

Ivory's eyes flicked away from my face, to the wall behind me, and then back.

I jerked a thumb over my shoulder, pointing at the fan. "Or did they threaten her?"

He was a degan, all right: I didn't even see him move before his fist connected with my face. The punch sent me sprawling on the floor, my limbs splayed, the books skidding away on the wooden floor. An instant later, he was bent over me, a fistful of my doublet in one hand, pulling me up.

"You dare!" he hissed through clenched teeth, his other arm drawing back for another blow.

"I dare," I said, laying the steel of my wrist knife across the artery on the inside of his thigh. "More than you know." I'd used my reaction to his punch as an excuse to flick the blade down into my palm and keep it there.

Ivory froze, brow knit, fist raised. "You think I can't kill you before your cut is finished?"

"I know you can," I said. "But now I also know you can die; otherwise, you wouldn't have stopped for my steel."

Ivory grunted and lowered his arm. "Maybe I just don't want to ruin these pants."

I admit, I've had my life saved by less over the years. Still, out loud I said, "Either way, I think it's time we stopped dancing and started talking." And I withdrew my knife.

To my relief, Ivory didn't kill me; instead, he hoisted me to my feet and then approached the chair. Carefully, he retrieved the books and replaced them on the shelves: Simonis's book among the other degan materials, and the wooden-fronted draft with the old codexes on imperial philosophy, where it blended in nicely. It wasn't until I'd seen the fan and put all the pieces together that I knew a book entitled *Promises Through Time* might have been more than it appeared.

"You're here with someone from the Order, aren't you?" said Ivory, still facing the bookcase. "They hired you to track me down so I wouldn't see them coming."

"I wasn't hired," I said. "And I'm not so much here with someone as for someone." When Ivory glanced over his shoulder and raised an eyebrow, I added, "It's complicated."

"But a degan?"

"I'd say yes; he'd say otherwise."

Now Ivory did turn all the way around. "The one who killed Iron?"

I hesitated, not wanting to talk out of turn, not sure how

Degan would feel about me spilling his deeds to . . . what? A living legend? A fallen exemplar? How would he consider Ivory, anyhow?

"If there's anyone who can commiserate with your friend," said Ivory, "it's me. I felled five brothers and sisters before I was done. I won't judge his actions."

He had a point. And it wasn't as if they wouldn't be seeing each other before long, if I had any say in it. The man before me was more than Degan could have hoped for when it came to information about the laws and purposes of his Order.

"Bronze Degan," I said.

Ivory's eyes widened for a fraction of an instant; then his face was passive again. He turned back to the bookshelf. "I assume he had his reasons."

"That's not for me to say."

"No, it isn't. Good for you." Ivory pulled a codex from high up on the wall—higher than I was likely to reach without climbing shelves or using a library stool—and began flipping absently through the pages. I could hear the dry creak of the vellum and the whisper of his fingers on the pages from here. "And he wants to see me why?"

"Same answer."

"But it has something to do with his killing Iron and leaving the Order, yes?"

Instead of answering, I wandered back over to the chair and looked down at Ivory's long sword. Despite all the elegance of the chiseled cross guard, it was a straightforward thing: a tapered, double-edged blade meant to be used with one or two hands, a sword equally as elegant in its use as my own, but from an earlier era. A weapon more for the battlefield than the street.

I reached down to run my finger along the ridges of the tulip's leaves.

"Don't," said Ivory, not turning around.

I withdrew my hand and instead moved around to place them against the back of the chair. "How does a degan become a clerk?" I said.

"A better question would be, how does a clerk become a

degan?" He shrugged. "I was educated in both the pen and the sword when I was young, along with any number of other things. I've lived by most of them at one point or another."

"You've certainly had the time." I said. "Remind me how that's possible again?"

Ivory let out a slow breath. He kept his eyes on the page before him rather than looking at me. "You asked earlier why the emperor didn't follow the path I have," he said. "The answer's simple: The option wasn't available. When Dorminikos was trying to become immortal, reincarnation was the best his Paragons could manage. But that didn't mean they stopped examining magic and the soul; didn't stop trying to push the boundaries of what you call Imperial magic. A little over two centuries ago, a couple of them figured out a way to . . . well, I won't say a way to become immortal: rather, a way to not die easily."

"And it involves removing your soul?" I said.

"It involved many things, most of which His Divinity, the emperor, chose not to do, out of either faith or fear. Questions of theology aside, no one was sure how that kind of magic would effect someone whose soul had already been shattered, let alone reborn as many times as his. Given what the man had already done to himself to rule forever, he decided it wasn't worth the risk."

"But you did."

"Eventually, yes."

"Why?"

"Because, at that point, I was sworn to serve him with my life and my soul. It seemed an easy choice at the time."

My life and my soul: I'd heard that expression before. I felt my eyes go wide. "A White Sash?" I said, straightening up. "Are you telling me you used to be a Sash?"

Ivory's head snapped up, a genuine look of shock on his face. "What? No, of course not!"

"Good," I said, letting myself lean back down on the chair. "Because if—"

"I wasn't a White," said Ivory haughtily. "I was a Paragon."

Chapter Thirty-two

An hour later, I stepped out of Ivory's house and back into the darkness of the padishah's grounds.

A thin crescent of the moon shone overhead. It felt as if it should be later, as if the sun should be rising, as if the world outside should somehow have changed since I'd crossed the threshold and had the world inside me shift. Again.

This shit was getting old.

I moved farther into the shadows at the end of the walkway and waited for my night vision to awaken. As the world sketched itself in amber, I reached over and ran the back of my hand against the folded piece of paper in my opposite sleeve. No more dusting guards for me: The paper was my pardon, as well as my pass in and out of the estate.

Ivory had agreed to see Degan. It hadn't been an easy argument to make: Ivory had been avoiding his former brothers and sisters for ages, and wasn't inclined to make an exception. He'd still refused to tell me his side of why he'd left the Order, but he hadn't been as shy about discussing the founding of the Order itself. Once I'd explained to him what Degan was looking for and why I felt obliged to help him, the former degan had warmed considerably. He remembered not only what it was like to walk away with his brothers' blood on his hands, he'd said, but also how it felt to break his word to them as well.

"The biggest mistake I made, though," Ivory had said, a

cup of tea steaming in his hand as we sat at his study table, his sword remounted on the wall behind him, "was turning to the imperial elites for initial membership in the Order in the first place."

"Why's that?" I said. I sipped at my own brew and tried not to make a face. There was a reason I preferred coffee over tea, and this particular batch of tepid, sour, soggy leaf-water was an excellent example of why that was. Still, it's best to be polite when you're trying to pump a two-hundred–year-old sword master and former imperial magician for information. I added another dollop of honey.

"Because Emperor Lucien created the Order of the Degans to stand separate from the Black Sashes of the imperial military and Gold Sashes of the house guards," he said. "If you're going to do that, you probably shouldn't recruit a bunch of Sashes into the Order. Or, at least, you'd think that, but neither I nor the emperor knew where else to turn. He wanted people he could trust with not just his life, but the empire's well-being. That makes for a small pool of candidates."

"Wait," I said, setting my cup aside. "You created the degans at the behest of the *emperors*? They know about this?"

"I was a Paragon; who else do you think would, or could, tell me to surrender my soul?"

"Well, I—"

"And it wasn't the whole of the Eternal Triumvirate who did this: We were Lucien's project, and his alone. He'd been growing distrustful of the Gold Sashes for a while. Ever since the Coup of the Unborn that forced Theodoi the Sixth into exile, each incarnation has been trying to build a faction loyal to himself among the guard. By my time, the politics had started to get ugly, and Lucien saw it. He decided to step outside the Imperial structure and create the degans."

"By recruiting among the White Sashes?" I said. "But the Whites were put together specifically to take on Isidore and the Kin. They didn't become personal bodyguards to the emperor until later, I thought."

"Yes and no," said Ivory. "Like so many things with the emperor, there are multiple facets to the single gem that is his genius. Your so-called Dark King came along at an excellent time and served as a convenient excuse for creating a new cadre of swords within the palace. The White Sashes were created to hunt the Kin and guard the emperor, yes, but they were also formed to provide a recruiting ground for the Order of the Degans."

I sat up. "Are you telling me that wiping out Isidore's organization two hundred years ago—along with more than half of the Kin—was a distraction for the benefit of imperial politics?"

Ivory arched an eyebrow. "Why wouldn't it be?" He took a slow sip of tea. "Believe me, the emperor, and the empire, have done far worse over the ages, often for less commendable reasons. The blockade and resulting famine in Phykopolis, for example, can be traced to—"

"Your 'distraction' resulted in thousands of Kin being hung from rooftops or staked out in the streets," I said. "And not just Kin: The Sashes butchered anyone who knew them—neighbors and friends and family. There was open warfare in the streets of Ildrecca for almost a year."

"Yes," said Ivory. "There was. And most of the people who died were either criminals or those who consorted with them." He set his cup down with a solid *clink*. "Now compare that to the tens of thousands who died in Phykopolis simply because an anonymous clerk discovered an unlicensed trade monopoly, and that the easiest way to cover it up was to devastate the city it was based in. As things go, the slaughtering of a comparative handful of Kin and their friends is high moral ground for the Court."

"That doesn't justify it."

"You should know by now that the Imperial Court feels no need to justify itself to the likes of us." Ivory sniffed, made the slightest hint of a sour face. "Still, good results can sometimes come from ill actions."

"You mean the degans?" I said.

"I mean the ideals we tried to incorporate within the Order and the Oath: the idea that a person is answerable for whatever events he puts in motion; that to receive service is to owe it in return; that a person's promise, no matter who he is, is something he should be held to."

"I've found that ideals don't carry a lot of weight in the real world," I said. "At least, not with most people."

"If I was concerned with 'most people,' I would have remained a Paragon instead of becoming a degan."

I almost asked how those ideals fit with him cutting down his own brothers and sisters a couple of hundred years back, but that didn't seem like the most constructive path to take just now. Instead, I folded my hands on the table before me and said, "So you're telling me none of the other incarnations of the emperor have caught on about the degans? That, because he formed you, only Lucien knows you exist?" It didn't seem likely, but then again, if anyone knew how to pull the cloth over the imperial eyes, who better than the emperor himself?

"I haven't exactly been keeping in touch," said Ivory, "but my guess is no; otherwise, the Order would have been wiped out by now."

"What about the other Paragons?" I said. "You couldn't have done this alone."

"Of course not."

"Then why didn't they tell—?"

"There was a purging."

"Ah," I said. Stephen Dorminikos had done the same thing when he first had his soul shattered. The imperial policy seemed to be that it was easier to kill the casters than ask for their silence. I wondered if the current Paragons in Markino's service knew about the fate of their predecessors. It seemed unlikely. "That seems to be an occupational hazard with imperial magicians."

Ivory took a sip of tea. "Get close enough to the emperor, and everyone becomes expendable."

I grunted agreement. It certainly seemed to be a recurring pattern.

"So why did you get to be the one who gave up his soul?" I said.

Ivory stared into his cup, took a last swallow. I got the

feeling he was wishing for something stronger right about now. "I told you," he said, pulling the iron teapot over to himself. "I was a Paragon: Someone had to cast the incantations and make the bindings. Someone had to speak the first Oath and bind the Order and the members to its purpose. When you're talking about the empire and a divinely selected emperor, not to mention a secret sect of swordsmen, words often aren't enough; you need magic."

I chose to ignore commenting on how the emperor had founded his cult based on nothing more than a carefully planned lie, and instead said, "And your soul locked the deal?"

"Among other things, yes." Ivory lifted the pot and poured. He frowned when only a tiny trickle of liquid, along with the dregs of the tea leaves, came out. "If it helps your understanding, I made the sacrifice—of my soul and my magic—willingly." He set the pot back down. "I'm not sure I would do the same today. But that's the curse of time, isn't it? We get to look back and pick apart our actions, criticize our younger selves without the benefit of that self being able to offer a defense—only a justification."

I played with my own cup on the tabletop.

I had to ask.

"So, what's it like living without a soul?" I said.

"That's none of your business, Kin," he snapped. Then he blinked and seemed to shake off his mood, as well as his memories. When he turned his eyes on me again, they held the false cheer of a man trying to put a good face on a crappy situation.

"So," he said, "Bronze wants the old laws, does he?"

"He seems to think finding your papers could somehow help preserve the Order."

"He's hoping to find something," said Ivory. "A line or a page that will put a sword through the heart of this argument once and for all. But it isn't there. If it were, I would have used it when the dispute, and the Order, was young."

"No one's seen the laws for two hundred years," I said. "That's a lot of time to operate on hearsay and passed-down memories. Who's to say how this crop of degans will react to the original documents?"

"I think I can make a fairly accurate guess. Besides, old papers and old men rarely change minds."

I perked up at that. "Old men?" I said. "Does that mean you'd be willing to come back to Ildrecca to make the argument?"

A melancholy smile. "Perhaps. It's been a long time. I wouldn't mind seeing the paths Simonis and I used to walk again, if only for the memories." Then a harder look. "But I'm not going to agree just on sentiment: It all depends on how Bronze makes his case. If you're right, there's too much idealism in his plan for my taste, but the least I can do is hear him out."

I could barely keep a smile from creasing my face. Between Ivory and his papers, not only did my odds of getting Degan back to Ildrecca suddenly look up; so did my chances of, if not making things right between him and me, then at least putting him in touch with the founder of his Order. A founder that, by all rights, should be dead.

That sure as hell had to count for something.

Ivory had penned my gate pass after that, signing it in his guise as Heron. To his credit, he'd only paused momentarily when I mentioned I needed it to get me off the hook for a certain incident at the Dog Gate as well. With a quick, elegant hand, he'd added a passage about the good of the state and the undesirability of my being delayed, and sent me on my way.

I passed back through the grove, just out of curiosity. It was empty, both of guards and assassins. I was glad for the former, sad for that latter. It would have been nice to see her one final time.

I took one last look around to make sure I wasn't overlooking any *neyajin*-shaped shadows, and then slipped off into the night.

"Well?" said Fowler as I sat down across from her. "Find anything?"

We were in an all-night tea shop, just outside the Imperial Quarter and just within spitting distance of the gate to the fourth ring. The place catered to mild chiba addicts and severe music aficionados. The man seated on the small stage was said to be one of the best oud players in the central Despotate, brought in from his village in the Venatti hills for the month. All I knew was that the music helped cover our conversation. The air was thick with smoke.

"One or two things," I said. I picked up the pot on the table, filled the extra cup before me, and drank. Cardamom. "Turns out Heron is Ivory Degan."

"*What?*"

Even the oud player stopped playing to stare at Fowler's outburst. I smiled into my tea, then held up my hands and apologized to the room in Djanese while she glared at me. General laughter all around. The music resumed.

"Ivory Degan?" she hissed once attention had shifted back to, variously, the music and the water pipes. "As in the one who started the Order of the Degans?"

"One and the same."

"How is that even possible?"

"Long story."

"No shit."

I lifted my eyes until they met hers. "Longer than we have time for right now."

"Humph."

I poured more cardamom tea, added two strips of candied lemon from a dish on the serving tray, and stirred. "What happened at the theater?"

"You mean after you caused all hell to break loose?"

"That was the general idea, if you recall."

"Well, then your idea worked. The performance was cut short, the Rags cleared the seats, and the pit nearly rioted until the padishah had handfuls of dharms thrown into the crowd." Fowler held up a small handful. "I clipped a couple coves coming out."

I rolled my eyes. "And Fat Chair?"

"Led off in chains."

"Any word from Mama Left Hand about that?"

"Were you expecting any?"

"Not really." Her mention of coming to some sort of agreement about Crook Eye's old routes had sounded

good, but I'd suspected it had been meant to string me
along rather than make any real kind of offer. Like as not,
she had other routes into the empire for her glimmer.

"Just as well, then," said Fowler, "because her people
wouldn't be able to get word to us anyhow. The padishah
had the troupe escorted back to the Angel's Shadow under
guard. Half of the Rags are still there."

I nodded. We'd expected something along those lines,
Fowler and Tobin and I. You don't unleash forbidden Dorminikan magic—even if it is just a lot of noise and show—and not
have the Imperials in the room rounded up. Which was why
we'd made certain there was nothing to connect them to what
happened with Fat Chair. Not that that was a guarantee—the
despot was called a despot for a reason: He could do whatev-
ever the hell he wanted when it came to us.

"Any word on them?"

Fowler shook her head. "Haven't been back yet. I was
planning to go after we get done here."

"And the wazir?"

"Nearly eating his own arm off, I expect."

"I expect." I sipped my tea. The lemon hadn't helped.
"You can get back into the inn all right?"

Fowler held up a small, gauzy bundle. "I've got my stage
drapes right here. Figure I can change back and say I got
lost in the mayhem."

"And the sword?"

I felt something hard bump up against my knee under
the table and Fowler shoved it over.

"Good." I took a last drink and reached under the table,
my hand closing on the now-familiar scabbard and baldric.
"Let's get going, then. I've a degan to find."

I found Degan a scant three blocks from his rooms, standing
under a lantern in the street, picking at a sad pile of greens
and charred meat, all sitting atop a soggy piece of flatbread.

"What the hell is that?" I said as I sidled up beside Degan.

He looked down at me and cocked an eyebrow in question.

"Fowler followed you, remember?" I said. "It wasn't hard to find you once I knew where to look." I nodded at the food in his hand. "I repeat, what the hell is it?"

He sighed and dropped it on the ground. "A mistake."

"Good. I'm hungry. Let's go get something worth eating."

Ten minutes later saw us standing at a small window set in a dingy wall. Across and just down the street, the sounds of music and people talking spilled out of a curtained doorway. Here, there was little light and less sound, but the smells coming from the window more than made up for it. Onions frying in butter, coriander seeds toasting in a pan, cheese charring over a fire. Mint and peppers and the thick, sour smell of shredded meat simmering in a spiced yogurt sauce. And the bread—the smell of the crust browning and cracking as it warmed over a heated stone.

I passed coins through the window, got two short loaves in return, their tops split and scooped out, the innards filled with onions and fried cheese and stringy strands of goat, all topped off with a salad of parsley and mint and lemon juice tossed.

"How do you find these places?" said Degan after his fourth bite.

I jerked my head toward the lively doorway. Three men were just staggering out. "I worked that ken a while back, looking for word of you. No success, but everyone in there ends up coming here for late-night tuck."

Sure enough, as if to prove me right, the three men began to make their way up the street, their hands already reaching into sashes and sleeves for money.

Degan shook his head and took another bite. I led him away from the window and deeper into the night.

I glanced at the man beside me as we walked and ate. It almost felt like old times, but I knew better. There was a tension between us, an unease that rode beneath the silence that had once been easy. Part of it, I knew, came from the presence of his sword—a tangible, visible indictment of my failures and his choices, riding my back a handful of feet away from his hand. I'd known bringing the blade wouldn't make things easier, but I didn't trust leaving it behind, didn't know if I'd be able to get back to it again even if I did.

The sword was only part of it, though: The rest came from the uncertainty that lingered between us. Even back when we'd first met—when he'd almost killed me and I'd nearly poisoned him—there hadn't been this kind of hesitant unease. He hadn't trusted me and I hadn't trusted him, but it had been an honest distrust, born of unfamiliarity and simple street caution. This was different. This was born of regret and betrayal, of memories and might-have-beens.

It was a silence that seemed both too heavy to lift and too fragile to leave in place. A thing that threatened to either smother us with its presence or cut us to the bone with its breaking.

As usual, Degan was the first one to step into the breach.

"So," he said as he finished the last fragment of his bread and swallowed, "I take it you're heading back to Ildrecca?"

I looked him a question, then did my sums. "You heard about the audition, I take it."

"Heard about it? I was there."

"You were there?"

"Not a lot of imperial theater in this city, have to take what you can get." He paused to cough up a couple of crumbs. "I thought Fowler was good."

I smiled. "Who knew she could act?"

"Didn't see you, though."

"That was the idea."

"Too bad. I think you would have made a good Babba."

I snorted. Babba was the despot's talking mule in the play. It was one of several Djanese tropes that hadn't made sense to me. "Walking the boards isn't my style."

"True, you seem to prefer offstage productions. Mind if I ask the purpose behind all the theatrics?"

"I needed a distraction."

Degan glanced and me and raised an eyebrow. "You needed that much chaos to set up one criminal?"

"That was only part of it."

"And the other part?"

"Ivory Degan."

"Ivory?" said Degan, grabbing my arm. "You mean you found his papers?"

"More than that, I found him. The man himself."

"What do you mean?"

I took a last bite of my own loaf and tossed the rest away. "I mean he's alive," I said, swallowing. "Breathing. Talking, even." I smiled up at Degan. "How's that for finding—*oop!*"

Before I knew what was happening, Degan had dragged me up a short flight of steps, into the shadow of a vine-covered archway. Behind us, I could smell the soft perfume of a garden asleep in the night. It was almost enough to mask the sudden scent of sweat coming from the swordsman beside me.

"Degan?" I said, pulling my arm away. I put hand to my own sword. "What the hell is going on?"

"You saw him?" he said, his eyes scanning the street, searching the shadows. "Does he know you figured out who he is?"

"Does he . . . wait." I took a step back to better glare at him. "Are you telling me you *knew* Ivory was alive?"

Degan didn't take his eyes off the street. "Let's say I suspected."

"You suspected?" I said. "How the hell do you 'suspect' someone might be alive two hundred years after he should have died?"

"You hear things."

"Things? What things? And why the hell didn't you tell me you thought there might be a two-hundred-year-old degan walking around el-Qaddice?"

"I was hoping I was wrong." Then, after a pause, "I also was hoping you'd leave."

"Congratulations: You were wrong on both counts."

"So I see. How did you find him?"

"Turns out he's the secretary to the wazir of Garden of the Muse. I've been reporting to him on the progress of our troupe ever since we got into the Old City."

"He's the . . . ?" Degan shook his head. "Amazing. And he told you who he was, just like that?"

"Of course not. I figured it out."

"How?"

"Well, for one thing, I saw his sword—"

Degan's eyes flew to the blade across my back. "He still has his sword?"

"On the wall of his study. Apparently, not everyone resigns the Order by leaving their blade lying in a burning warehouse."

Degan gritted his teeth. I admit the comment wasn't kind on my part, but I was still smarting from not being told about Ivory. I figure it evened out.

"I suppose finding that would have done it," grated Degan.

"If I'd known he was still alive, it might have, yes. But I had no reason to suspect Ivory would be anything more than a heap of moldering bones by now. It wasn't until I broke back in tonight, raided his library, and held his steward at sword's point that he told me who he was."

"So you did talk to him."

"At length."

"And?"

"He wants to see you."

Degan chuckled and turned his attention back to the street. "I'll just bet he does."

"It's not like that, Degan."

"No? Ivory Degan cut down half a dozen of his brothers and sisters before he left the Order. And when he did, he made it very clear that he'd do the same to anyone who came after him. I doubt that sentiment's changed, even after all this time."

I thought back on the scholar with warrior's reflexes. Both faces of the man had struck me as tired, maybe even a bit resigned. Any fires that burned in him about his past, I guessed, had been banked long ago. "Two centuries is a long time."

"Not as long as you think."

"He said he might be willing to come back to Ildrecca."

Degan actually eased up on his grip on his sword. "Back to the empire?"

I swallowed. "Maybe." This was now every bit as delicate

a negotiation as the conversation I'd had with Ivory. I wasn't sure what Degan's plans had been in coming to el-Qaddice, but it clearly hadn't included having a sit-down with the founder of his Order. Except that was exactly what I needed him to do, for all our sakes—but mostly for his. "I told him about what happened with you and Iron. About—"

"You *what*? You had no right—"

"I have every right," I said, cutting him off. "I helped cause this mess, helped put you in a position where you had to make that choice. If it hadn't been for me, you wouldn't be down here."

"Don't flatter yourself. The problems in the Order were building long before you crossed paths with Shadow and Solitude. Or me, for that matter. I made the choices that got me here, not you."

"I'm not saying you didn't. But I played a part in it, just as I'm playing a part in this now." I gestured up in the general vicinity of the second ring. "Ivory's had a lot longer time to think about his choices, but at the core you and he made the same call: You both drew blood and walked away from the Order. No one—not me, not Silver, not any of the other degans—knows what that's like. Except for Ivory. And he's willing to talk."

Degan sighed, took off his hat, and ran his fingers through sweat-damp hair until it stood up in uneven spikes. "You have to understand something," he said. "I didn't come down here looking for absolution. Or redemption. I came here to try and save something I cared enough to kill for, even though that killing meant I could no longer lay claim to that thing anymore. I came to protect my former brothers and sisters from having to do what I did, to keep others from having to walk the path I'm on. I'm not worried about restoring my name or reclaiming my place in the Barracks Hall; I expect I'll never see the walls of Niceria again. No, I'm here because while I may no longer be a degan, I can still serve the Order."

"I know," I said. "That's more or less what I told Ivory."

Degan blinked. Then he smiled. "Did you, now?"

"Maybe not so eloquently, but I got the idea across."

"And how did Ivory take it?"

"He says he doesn't think he has the answers you want, but he's willing to go over the old laws and discuss possibilities."

Degan rose out of the half-conscious fighting stance he'd been maintaining and took a deep breath. When he let it out, most of the tension he'd been holding seemed to leave with it.

I let out a breath of my own as well. I had him.

Degan took another breath, then chuckled. He put on his hat. "Ivory in the despot's court. Who would have guessed?" he said as he tugged down on the brim. "Angels know it's the last place I would've looked."

"You and me both," I said. "Although I suppose I should have thought of it."

"How so?"

Degan stepped out into the street. I joined him. We began walking.

"When we first arrived, Wolf headed over to el-Beyad to look for you. He said he figured if a person was used to serving others, even with an Oath, then he'd go looking for—eh?"

Degan had put his hand on my arm again, although this time it was to turn me to face him. "Wolf?" he said, a strange expression on his face.

"Sorry: Silver Degan. I first met him as Wolf, and to be honest, that's the name that I've hung on him in my head. It fits."

Degan nodded slowly. "It does." He stepped closer. "Tell me about Silver."

"Tell you what?"

"Tell me about his scar."

My stomach twitched. "What scar?"

"The one that runs from just above his right eyebrow down to his jaw," he said, tracing the line across his own face. "The one that made him blind in one eye."

My stomach began tying itself in something that felt like a tutorial for sailors' knots.

Degan read my face. "Your Silver isn't blind in one eye, is he?" he said.

"No." My hands were shaking so hard I could barely form them into fists. That son of a bitch had played me again. "No, he isn't."

"Then he isn't Silver Degan."

Chapter Thirty-three

"Son of a bitch!" I yelled. *Twice* that bastard had conned me. *Twice.* "That lying, scheming son of a—"

"Does Wolf have his sword?" said Degan.

"What?"

"Silver's sword," he said, looking down at me impatiently. "Does Wolf have it?"

I thought of the silver-chased blade I'd become so used to seeing at Wolf's side. "If you mean a silver-worked scimitar, then yes, he does."

Degan's mouth became a thin, tight line. "That's Silver's."

I almost asked how I'd been fooled, but I already knew. I'd seen the sword, seen Wolf's skill, heard him talk, and had simply followed my assumptions. After all, who the hell pretended to be a degan?

More to the point, though, Wolf had had the air about him, had carried himself like a degan. And part of me, I was sure, had missed that.

"Is he even a degan?" I said.

"Oh, he's a degan, all right," said Degan, making me feel only slightly better. We began walking again. "We even called him Wolf sometimes because, as you say, it fits—all too well. But within the Order, he's Steel."

"Steel Degan," I said, trying out the name. It fit him better than Silver. "So if he has Silver's sword, that means—"

"It means I'm not the only one who's shed blood within

the Order recently," said Degan. He shook his head. "Angels, what have we become?"

I didn't have an answer to offer on that one, and so kept my peace.

"Does Ivory know about Steel?"

"The only reason Ivory knows you're here is because I told him," I said. "Wolf . . . that is, Steel, never came up."

"That's something, then. If Ivory knew there were two of us here, and that one was Steel, I expect it would take another two centuries to track him down again."

"Steel's that dangerous?" I said.

Degan nodded. "He's one of the best of us when it comes to the blade—maybe the best."

"But it's been two centuries," I said. "Ivory has no way of knowing anything about this Steel. The Steel Degan he knew died ages ago." Every degan took the name of one of the founding degans when he or she joined the Order—the Bronze Degan beside me was the seventh degan to bear that name.

"Don't kid yourself," said Degan. "Ivory may have hidden himself away in Djan, but you can bet he has agents in the empire. He may not know all the doings of the Order, but he's not as ignorant as he likely led on. You don't create something like the degans and then forget about it, no matter where you go."

We walked on in silence for maybe half a block. Degan was setting a quick pace, and between my still-sore muscles and the night's exertions, I was having a hard time keeping up. He didn't seem in the mood to slow down, though, so I poured some *ahrami* into my palm. I'd meant for two, but five seeds fell out of the bag instead. To hell with it: I tossed them all into my mouth.

"Degan?" I said around the seeds.

"What?"

"What the hell is going on?"

"At a guess? Steel wants Ivory's sword."

"Why?"

"Because that sword is the key to our Order."

"How?"

Degan stayed silent for a moment, then said, "What did I do after I killed Iron?"

I thought back to that day in the A'Riif Bazaar, when, after a long, wandering fight, Degan had dusted Iron with one single, perfect thrust. "You took his sword."

"Yes. And when the Order came asking after Iron—after they found his sword, thanks to you—what did they ask you about me?"

"They wanted to know where you were, of course."

"And?"

"And . . ." Oh. I'd been so focused on getting them to believe my version of the story, I hadn't separated the two questions until now. "They wanted to know what had happened to your sword."

"Exactly. There's a reason we swear our Oaths on our swords, and it isn't just for the symbolism: Each blade records not only the Oaths of the degan who wields it, but also the Oath of each person we've pledged ourselves to. It's the walking record not only of our service, but of our debts, and the debts owed to the Order."

I reached up, my hand going for the weapon lying across my back. This time, I stopped just short of touching it. "You mean my Oath to you is in your sword?"

"Along with its status, yes."

I bit down on the seeds in my mouth and swallowed. They didn't go down easy. I was suddenly grateful I'd never let Wolf handle Degan's blade. "And any degan who picks up your sword can, what, read that from it?"

"It's not quite that simple, but given some time and a bit of quiet, yes, they could. That's how the Order keeps track of what promises have been kept and which ones are still owed when a degan passes."

"Which explains why you took Iron's sword," I said. "You were going to return it to the Order."

"Given what I'd just done, it seemed the least I could do. I owed it to Iron as well as the rest of my brothers and sisters."

A thought occurred. "Did Iron still have any debts due?"

"I didn't have it in my hands long enough to find out,"

said Degan pointedly. I looked away. "But," he continued, in milder tones, "given he was in the process of trying to deliver you to Solitude when we crossed blades, I'd wager there's still a balance due on her part, if that's what you're asking."

It was. It also meant that Solitude was still on the Order's leash, either now or in the future. That was both good to know, as well as worrying. If Wolf had been playing me, who was to say another degan wouldn't be pushing Solitude as well?

Because, Angels knew, I needed another thing to worry about. . . .

"I understand about your sword, and Iron's, and maybe even Silver's," I said, "since whoever Silver had in his debt is probably now in Wolf's pocket. But how do Ivory's Oaths play into all of this? Those debts are two hundred years old."

"Did Ivory tell you about the founding of the Order?" said Degan. We were coming up to the gate to the second ring. A pair of guards stood to either side, just outside the circle of light cast by a torch set in the wall. I slowed and looked away from the burn of the light.

"A bit," I said.

"And?"

"And he told me the degans were founded to serve as a foil against the other sashes at the time."

"On whose order?"

"Lucian's, of course. Who else could order a Paragon to bind his soul to a sword and then have him craft an Oath that would bind a bunch of swordsmen to hi . . ." I trailed off as the implications of what I was saying sank in. Oath. Degans. Emperor.

Oh, hell.

"Are you saying," I said, my voice dropping despite itself, "that the *emperor* swore the Oath on Ivory's blade? That Lucien is in debt to the Order of the Degans?"

"The Order had to be bound to him," said Degan. "And the strongest promises run both ways. What better binding—and what better show of faith—than for the emperor to take the Oath that was to become to core of our Order?"

"And he swore that Oath on Ivory's sword?"

"All the degans did."

"Which meant all the original degans were bound to that sword, too."

"Yes."

I whistled. "But that was Lucien. Markino's emperor now, with Theodoi coming next. Lucien's next incarnation isn't going to sit the imperial throne for at least another thirty or forty years. What good will the Oath do Wolf?"

"The Oath was taken on Ivory's blade, which holds Ivory's soul," said Degan. "And Ivory was a Paragon before he was a degan. That makes things . . . different."

"How different?"

"The Order can hold any incarnation of the emperor to the Oath," he said. "Including our current one."

I stopped, pulling Degan to a halt with me. "Are you telling me that if Wolf gets his hands on Ivory's sword, he can call in Lucien's Oath through Markino?"

Degan nodded grimly. "That's what I'm telling you."

"But how? Markino's not even the same . . . well, not person, but incarnation."

"How should I know? It's soul magic; all I know is what Ivory told me." Degan gestured toward the gate. The guards were starting to eye us. "We should keep moving."

I followed his advice.

"All right," I said, measuring my pace as the guards watched. "Let's say you're right. But even with it being soul magic, you'd think that Wolf would need to, I don't know, have part of . . . wait." I looked up at Degan. "Wait. What *Ivory* told you? When the hell did you talk to Ivory?"

Degan's eyes went wide for an instant, and then quickly narrowed. When he spoke again, his voice was all iron and ice. "Now isn't the time, Drothe."

"The hell it's not. Now is *exactly* the time. When did you talk to Ivory?"

"I didn't."

"Bullshit. You wouldn't know about the sword unless he told you." A thought occurred. I didn't like it. "Have you been playing me to keep Wolf at bay? Lying about not knowing where Ivory was because you were afraid I might tell Wolf?"

"What? No, of course not."

"Then how do you know?"

Degan paced on in silence.

"Dammit, Degan, I didn't come down here for my health. I came to help."

"You came because Wolf has you over a barrel."

"Fuck Wolf and fuck his barrel. I came because of you. Because you deserve better than what you got from me. All Wolf did was show me there was a path; I'm the one who walked it.

"Look, I'm not going to pretend that anything I do will make up for breaking my Oath—I know better. But that doesn't mean I can't try. And I'm going to, no matter if it involves saving the degans, or hiding you from them, or forcing them to take you back—I don't care. That's up to you. All I know is that I need to understand what's going on if I'm going to help you. And I am going to help you."

Degan gave me a long, hard look. Then he studied his sword on my back. Then me again. Finally, he nodded.

"Fine," he said. "I know because I was there."

"Where?"

"There when Ivory put his soul in his sword," said Degan. "And again when Lucien made his vow. There when the rest of the Order swore to serve the empire, and through it, the emperor." Degan gave a half-melancholy, half-rueful smile. "I was there when we all became degans."

"What?" I said, almost falling over my own feet as I stumbled to a halt. "But that would mean that you . . . that you're . . ."

"Two hundred and forty-two," said Degan, doing the sums for me.

"What?"

"Will you stop yelling?" he said, tilting his head toward the gate. "We're attracting enough attention as it is."

I didn't resist as he led me past frowning guards and into the second ring of the Old City.

"Two hundred and forty-two *years*?" I said once we were away from the gate.

"Give or take. It all depends on which calendar you follow. I was born under the old Wystrian calendar, which has six fewer days per year than the imperial. By that reckoning, I'm—"

"*Two hundred and forty-two*? But how the hell can you be—?"

"The same way Ivory is as old as he is," said Degan, his voice growing tight. "And Silver. And Copper. And Jade. The same way I knew Iron for over two centuries before I killed him. We all took the Oath with one hand on Ivory's blade and the other on our own, binding our lives to service and steel." He looked away. "Binding our souls."

"Your . . . ?" Of a sudden, the weight of his sword didn't feel quite so comforting. "You mean your soul is in your blade?"

Degan didn't answer, but then he didn't need to. The look on his face said enough.

"And the rest of your Order?"

"The same."

I shifted my shoulders, and in doing so, shifted the vessel that rode across my back. My stomach suddenly felt queasy. I jerked my thumb at the handle jutting up over my shoulder. "I don't suppose . . . ?"

"I told you before: I don't want it. It's not mine to wield anymore."

"But it's your *soul*."

"It was given in service to the Order. I'm no longer of the Order. That means it's no longer mine to claim."

My guts, which had been going cold, flared back to life.

"Don't be a fucking idiot," I said.

"Excuse me?"

I stripped off his sword, held it out to him. "Promise or not, this is yours. Hell, I can't think of anything that would be more *yours* than this blade. It's everything that you are, everything you've been, for two hundred years. You can't just throw it away because of one mistake."

Degan took a step back, a step away. "It wasn't a mistake,

it was a choice. A choice that opened the door for the Order to fall in upon itself. I knew what I was doing even before I took your Oath. I knew the risks, and I chose to take them. My price for that choice is setting aside what I was."

"Like hell," I said. "Now you're just feeling sorry for yourself. Even Steel says the Order's ready to turn on itself over the emperor, that it's only a matter of time before the blood starts flowing again."

"If you're going to believe Steel, then—"

"I'm not finished." I stepped forward, Degan retreating from his old blade as if it might burn him. "Yes, you killed Iron, but you did it because you thought it would save the empire you swore to protect. Hell, maybe even part of you thought it would help the Order—I don't know. The point is, you don't have to give up your soul over it. Ivory still has his blade, and he dusted more degans than you; I'll bet Steel is still carrying his around as well." I took another step. Degan shifted, almost skittish, but decided to hold his ground. "You don't have to surrender who you were just because you can't be that person anymore. You don't have to give up *this*"—rattling the sword—"just because you can't be a degan."

Degan stared down at me, at his sword. Somewhere over the city, I heard what I thought was a desert owl call.

"It's not that easy," he said.

"It's never that easy," I said. "I ought to know." And I pushed his sword up against his chest.

Degan stiffened. I saw his pupils grow even wider in the darkness, felt his breath quicken under the pressure of the blade. Sweat appeared on his upper lip. His hands remained poised in the air, hovering to either side of his sword, trembling. I pushed harder. He gasped.

Then, suddenly, he stepped away. "No," he said, letting his hands drop. "I can't."

"Why not?"

"Because I can't help the Order if I'm a degan."

"What the hell is that supposed to mean?"

"It means I can't take that sword from you. Now let's go."

"That's not an answer," I said as he resumed walking.

"Imagine that."

Muttering, I returned Degan's sword to my back. I didn't quite cringe as the weight settled on me, but I didn't exactly relish the sensation, either. There's something about having another person's immortal soul riding across your kidneys that distracts you in ways you never thought possible.

The square before the Dog Gate felt strange when Degan and I arrived a short while later. Oh, it still stank like shit, and a few mongrels wandered about the edges, but the roving packs were missing, as were the yips and barks and snarls of their challenges and submission.

"Problem?" said Degan as I stopped short of entering the small piazza.

"Maybe."

I'd been stopped at the gate by a *cheri-bashi* and the four guardsmen he commanded when I'd left the grounds earlier. The man who was supposed to be watching the gate, the sergeant had informed me as he read Heron's letter (twice), had gone missing, and there were rumors of some sort of disturbance on the grounds. No sign had been found of either the man or the reported problem, but they'd strengthened the guard on all the gates nonetheless. Since I had Heron's pass, I hadn't worried about getting back in; but now, squinting out at the empty square and the circle of torchlight near the unmanned gate, I had a sneaking suspicion that gaining access to the grounds wasn't going to be our main worry.

That suspicion became a certainty when I saw a low, crouched figure come slouching up on the other side of the gate. It pushed on the iron with its snout, opening wide a gap I hadn't noticed until now, and trotted out into the piazza. It was one of the alley dogs, and it had a bloody, bootless foot in its mouth.

"No, make that definitely," I said as the dog vanished down a side street. "We definitely have a problem."

Chapter Thirty-four

There were four of them. It was hard to tell because of the work the hounds had done on the guards' bodies, but it looked as if they had all died from a bare handful of sword strokes. Quick, efficient work. Degan barely paused to glance down before he was moving out of the circle of torchlight. After a quick glance inside the guardroom to make sure it was still empty, I followed.

The hounds snarled and showed red teeth as we passed, but otherwise ignored us.

I didn't bother asking who had carved up the guards; we both knew the answer to that one.

Dawn was three hours away, if that.

"How did Steel know to come here?" said Degan as we moved deeper into the darkness.

"I don't know," I said. "The last time I saw him was . . ." Oh. Of course. That explained it.

"Was what?"

"Was at the play," I said.

"I don't see how—"

"I caught him staring up at the padishah's box at one point. Ivory was on the balcony near him."

Degan grimaced. "That would do it. Steel would only need a glimpse of Ivory, even at a distance, to mark him. Then it would just be a matter of following him back from the amphitheater and biding his time."

"And given the events at the play, Ivory would have been

too distracted to notice he was being shadowed," I muttered. Thanks to me.

Degan started walking faster.

I steered us off the patchwork trail of marble stepping-stones and took us overland. It was similar to the path Aribah and I had taken to Ivory's residence, but not identical.

I led Degan around a large reflecting pool, then up over a small rise, and halted. I was half-surprised and half-pleased to see the side of Ivory's house below us. There was light coming through two of the lower windows toward the back of the house. The rest was dark.

"That's it?" said Degan.

"That's it."

Degan started down the slope.

"One thing," I said.

Degan paused but didn't look back. "Yes?"

"There were five guards at the gate when I left earlier tonight."

"And only four when we returned," said Degan. "Meaning Steel may have forced the fifth to act as a guide."

"That'd be my guess."

Degan drew his sword and continued down. I did the same.

Sure enough, we found the fifth guard lying on the walkway outside Ivory's front door. The door itself stood ajar. There was a smear of blood along the lower edge.

Degan didn't hesitate: He pushed the door open and stepped in, head tilted to the side, sword angled up and out to catch any cuts someone might throw from hiding. I came after, my own blade low, so as not to stab him should he need to retreat. We both had to step over the body of the steward lying just inside the doorway. The left third of his face had been sheared away by a blow that had continued down and into his neck and chest. His blood made the rug squelch underneath our boots.

"Where?" said Degan, his voice tight as he peered into the darkness. Compared to the starlit expanse of the grounds, the hallway seemed oppressive, even to me.

"My guess is the study," I said. "Near the back of the house." Where we'd seen the lights.

Degan was moving down the hallway before I'd finished speaking, his footfalls alternately muted by the rugs and amplified by the bare floor between. I swore and hustled after, the mosaics on the walls to either side little more than a blur of amber and shadows in my night vision.

"Right!" I called as Degan reached the intersection ahead of me. Any semblance of secrecy was gone anyhow. "Then your first left."

Degan made the turn, guiding himself as much by instinct as half shadows at this point, I guessed. I followed an instant later, and immediately averted my eyes. Already, there was a glow coming from around the next corner. I slowed my pace out of habit, heard Degan pushing on ahead.

To hell with it.

I redoubled my step, keeping my gaze to whatever shadowy corners and crevices I could find in the corridor. I'd hoped to creep up on Wolf, to catch him unawares, to maybe be able to fucking *see* before crossing blades with him, but Degan clearly had other ideas. Not that I expected to be much use once the two of them cleared steel, but there was always something I could do: maybe bleed on Wolf excessively, say, or get my ribs stuck around his sword.

I took the second corner fast. Ahead, I could see light spilling out of Ivory's study, forming a brilliant golden red pool in my night vision. Eyes burning, I put my head down and ran.

No sounds of steel on steel came to me as I covered the last few feet and ran through the doors. Instead, I was met by a profound silence—a silence broken only by my own shoes skidding on the floor as I tried to avoid running into Degan from behind. He had stopped just inside the room and stood, staring.

Even with blurring, watering eyes, I could see that the place was a mess. Books and papers had been knocked from the shelves, and the large reading table at the far end of the room was tipped over. Three spent candles lay in pools of hardened wax on the floor; two more stood, burning feebly, on an empty shelf. The smell of burning wick and freshly raised dust filled the space—so much so that it took me a moment to notice the darker, earthier scent that ran underneath.

But I didn't need to smell the blood to know it was there: I could see the smeared trail that led from a spot near Degan's feet, across the floor and over papers, to the form that sat slouched beneath the now-empty space on the display wall between the widower's fan and the vase of dried flowers.

Ivory was here, but both his sword and the man who had used us to find him were gone.

Degan was across the room in an instant. I moved more warily, as if Wolf might somehow slip out from between the spines of a book or rise from the crackling vellum and paper scattered underfoot. The bastard had been two steps ahead of me from the start and I wasn't about to lower my guard just because the room was empty.

There wasn't much doubt as to Ivory's condition. Between the missing right hand, the gash in his head deep enough to let notched bone show through, and the pool of thick, dark blood that had gathered in his lap, not only did I know he was dead; I also knew there was no way the old man could have made it to his current position on his own. Wolf had dragged the body over and propped him against the wall for us to find. A message left for me and Degan.

"How long ago, do you think—"

"He's alive," said Degan as he knelt down beside Ivory.

"He's *what?*" I said, now hurrying across the room as well. "How?"

"Degans are hard to kill."

I moved closer. Sure enough, I saw Ivory's lids flicker briefly. Degan wiped gently at Ivory's eyes with the cuff of his shirt, smearing the worst of the blood away. With the red gone, Ivory's eyes opened more fully. When they landed on Degan, he smiled, causing a fresh well of blood to run from his mouth.

It was then that I realized Wolf had cut out his tongue.

Bastard.

"Sorry I'm late," said Degan softly.

Ivory lifted his good hand and laid it on Degan's arm. He opened his mouth, as if to speak, only to have it turn into a choking gurgle. Degan quickly leaned the wounded man to the side and held his head while he vomited up the blood that had been draining down his throat. It was dark and thick.

"Why his tongue?" I asked as Ivory coughed.

"I don't know," whispered Degan. "To keep him from speaking healing spells? I don't know."

When Ivory was done, Degan gently righted his friend again. The older degan's color made some of the centuries-old parchment on the floor seem rich and luminous by comparison. His eyes were closed now.

"Ivory," said Degan, gently.

Ivory's lids fluttered but didn't truly open. I was close enough now to hear the bubbling hiss that came with each breath of the dying man, telling me that at least one lung had been punctured.

How the hell was this old bastard still alive?

Degan cleared his throat. Despite that, his voice was still thick as he said, "I'm sorry, but I have to ask: Your sword. Does Steel have it?"

The old degan went rigid, and I couldn't help thinking he'd decided to die rather than to admit to the loss. But then a slow breath escaped his lips, and he nodded.

Degan's jaw clenched. He looked up at me, and I saw despair there: deep and dark. Despair over not just the sword, or even Ivory, but over what had become of his Order, and what was to become of it. What he was afraid he had started when he killed Iron, and had finished when he'd led Steel to Ivory.

Only it hadn't been Degan, or not wholly him. I'd played more than my fair part in this as well, hunting after my own form of redemption, wanting it so badly that I'd let myself get played by Wolf, and then falling in line with his plans with hardly any resistance. Wanting to play the clever Nose one last time, to show that I could still scheme and con my way out from under a setup. Wanting to go to Djan so I could pretend I wasn't a Gray Prince, only to have the title follow me here.

To be as much a cause of Ivory's death as anything else.

I turned my eyes away from the dying degan and instead looked over the room again. At the empty and disheveled shelves, at the books and documents strewn about, at the trail of blood that marred the otherwise pristine carpet of paper and parchment and vellum on the floor. Most had been pushed aside as Wolf dragged Ivory to the wall, but a few pages had fallen back after Ivory's passage. Their edges were now heavy with red, the old rust-colored ink fading into the background as the paper drank its fill.

I wondered whether the pages could be saved, whether trying to clean them off would help, or only cause more damage. Baldezar would know, but the old scribe wasn't here. Then again, if he were, I expect the dry bone of a man would already be cataloging and sorting, cooing to himself and the books, ecstatic at not only the wealth scattered at his feet, but also the fact that most of them had somehow avoided getting damaged in the melee that had taken place. Looking at the clean pages and intact bindings, it was almost as if . . .

I turned back around. "What about the laws?" I said.

Degan blinked. Ivory didn't stir.

"What do you mean?" said Degan.

"The laws of your Order," I said, stepping closer. "The rites and rituals and whatever the hell else Ivory took with him when he left. Did Steel get those?"

Degan stared at me. "He has Ivory's sword, Drothe. I'm not worried about finding a damn clause that might—"

"Neither am I." I knelt down on the other side of Ivory and took the old degan's jaw gingerly in my hands. I turned his face to me.

"Ivory," I said. *"Ivory."* A faint gurgle and a wavering of one lid. Not good enough.

Degan bristled. "Drothe, what the hell—?"

"Look at this room," I said. "These books and scrolls and papers didn't get knocked down during the fight—they were pulled down afterward. After Wolf already had the sword. Which means he was looking for something else."

"But if he has the sword, he already has the Oath," said Degan.

"Then maybe he wanted something more. Maybe there's a law or ritual that lets him use the Oath differently, or extend it, or something. I don't know. All I know is that I can't think of any other reason for him to tear this place apart, let alone remove Ivory's writing hand and carve out his tongue."

"Remove his . . ." Degan looked down at Ivory, then out over the disaster that was the library. As I watched, I could see worry creep into his eyes.

He looked back down at Ivory. "Ask," he said.

I leaned in closer to the dying degan, tilting his head to put my mouth near his ear. "Ivory," I said. "What about your laws?"

Ivory's eyes snapped open, so sharp that I almost recoiled under their gaze. Suddenly, he was all here, and I could only guess what it was costing him.

"The laws," I said. "Did Wol—did Steel get them, too?"

The skin around Ivory's eyes crinkled in a dark grin. I felt his head shake weakly in my hand.

"Are they still here?"

The slightest pressure of his chin in my palm. The ghost of a nod.

"Where?"

His eyes slipped off me and up, to the left.

Ivory turned his gaze up to his widower's fan. "Himomif." It came out of his ruined mouth sounding more like a wet croak than a word, but I knew what he meant.

"Simonis?" I said, saying his wife's name for him. "Does she have the laws?"

Ivory smiled.

I looked at Degan. "It's hidden in her history," I said, already turning toward the shelf that had held her books. "Likely written in—"

Ivory's left hand grabbed at my ankle, stopping me. I looked down to find him glaring from me to the wall and back. I followed his gaze.

"The fan?" I said, staring up at the large, crepe-covered arc. I'd taken a close look at it the night I'd figured out Ivory's secret, but seen nothing concerning any laws, or even the Order itself.

Still, who was I to argue?

I righted Ivory's reading chair, stood on it, and drew the covering away from the fan. The details were both fine and intricate, so much so that I found myself leaning forward, afraid I might overbalance the chair.

And still, even with that, I almost missed it.

It was a small thing, in the second to the last depiction of Simonis. She was more outline than image in that: the dark curve of a woman's form, highlighted by a mirroring slash of white for her gown, bent over a kneeling desk in her study. Three lines of red for the ribbon in her hair, echoed by three dots of carmine for the cephta on the page before her, a pale line of gold leaf for a reed pen. A scribe at work, deep in the throes of her knowledge and craft: an image that clearly held a special place in Ivory's heart if it was one of the last ones he'd had depicted of her. An image that centered on his wife, with each detail becoming less defined as the eye drew away from her—save for the pale row of tiny books on the wall behind her.

I leaned in even closer, placing one hand against the wall to keep from toppling over. I couldn't be sure without an enlarging lens, but I would have sworn that the cephta on the bindings was legible, even at that size.

I looked down at Ivory. He was reclining now, his head crooked in Degan's elbow, eyes regarding me from beneath heavy lids.

I wasn't a White. I was a Paragon.

The sly old bastard.

"It's not a clue, is it?" I said. "The laws are here, in her study." I pointed at the figure. "You somehow glimmered the books into the fan, didn't you?"

A relieved—or was it tired?—smile split his face. More blood trickled out.

"Eh," he gasped. Yes.

"So how do we get them out?"

Ivory's hand was still trying to lift itself off the floor when Degan spoke for him. "The sword," he said, without looking up. "His sword holds his soul, which means it also holds the key to his magic. And to the laws."

I stepped down off the chair. "His . . . ?" Of course. Ivory had been a Paragon before becoming a degan, and Paragons focused their power through their souls. Just because Ivory didn't have his soul in his body anymore, it didn't have to mean he'd lost his ability to—

"Oh, shit," I said. "Does that mean Steel can use Ivory's glimmer?"

"I wouldn't think so. It's Ivory's soul after all, not Steel's. Just having the sword doesn't give him control over it, let alone the knowledge of how to use that magic."

"But you don't know."

Degan looked back down at Ivory. The old degan's eyes were closed again. His chest seemed to be barely moving.

"I'll try to find out," said Degan. "In the meantime, you should gather up Fowler and get out. We can meet up in the Lower City and see about picking up Steel's trail there. There can't be that many Azaari tribesmen leaving el-Qaddice; we shouldn't have a hard time finding someone who saw him leave."

"Assuming he didn't dust all the witnesses," I muttered.

"Then we'll follow the vengeful mob on his tail instead."

"I'm less worried about losing Steel than I am in getting out of here," I said. I jerked a thumb back the way we'd come. "In case you forgot, it's almost light out there. Between that and the pile of bodies at the gate, just getting off the grounds is going to be tricky."

"Which is why I told you to leave now."

"What about you?"

"I'll go when Ivory's gone."

"That'll be too late."

"When he's gone."

I thought about arguing, didn't. Degan had already been too late to save Ivory; it wasn't right to try and talk him into walking away before he'd said his good-byes.

But I wasn't ready to leave just yet.

"Degan," I said. "Why does Wolf want the laws so badly?"

"I'm not sure."

"But you have a suspicion."

The briefest pause. Then, "Yes."

I waited. The wheezing, bubbling sound of Ivory's breathing filled my ears.

When Degan spoke, he didn't look at me. "There's an old story," he said, "that when Ivory took our original Oaths, he bound them in such a way that we could be held to account. That we could be made to serve the holder of that Oath much the same way degans used to be able to compel those who swore to us. Not just by honor or threat, but by magical bonds."

"And let me guess: The holder of that Oath was the emperor."

"No," said Degan. "Most said it was Ivory."

"You mean he made you all . . . clients? Just like anyone who swore an Oath to you?"

"'Oath-bound' is the term we use, but yes, that's the idea." Degan wiped a fresh bubble of froth from Ivory's lips. "I have no idea if it's true, but I can see why he might have done it. We were new, trying something new, and had no idea if it would work, if it would last. And Ivory was a Paragon. It was his duty to watch over the emperor before all else. Who knew what a group of undying warriors would get up to in a hundred years? Better to have some way to rein us in."

"And no one confronted him about this?"

"Oh, some of us confronted him when the story came out, all right—especially Steel. He said he'd sworn himself to the emperor, not to Ivory, and that he wouldn't have a sword like that hanging over his head. Said it dishonored him."

"So what did Ivory do?"

"Do? Nothing. And neither did the rest of us."

"What?" I said. "Why?"

"Because we were young and still had too many fresh memories of being White Sashes to think about arguing. And because he was a Paragon. And because the Oaths were already sworn. Besides, it was only a rumor: true or not, there were other things to keep us busy back then."

"So you served?"

"We served," said Degan. "But from that point on, the debate over whether we were sworn to serve the empire, or an emperor who may have lied to us, began. It's been with us ever since."

"And the laws of the Order?"

Degan looked to the fan in my hands. "Some theorized Ivory wrote down a ritual on how to call in the Oath. Or to renew it. Or to destroy it. No one knows for certain. All I know is that while having the sword gives you sway over the emperor and the Order via the Oath, having the laws might give you complete control."

"And Wolf wants them both," I said.

"I don't know," said Degan. "Maybe. But my guess is that as long as Wolf has Ivory's sword, he can accomplish what he wants. After all, there was no way to know the laws had survived until now. Going after the sword would have been the more certain bet."

"You came for the laws," I observed.

"I came for whatever I could find, to do whatever I could to help my former sword kin. There's a difference."

I looked down at the dying man in Degan's lap, then at the ruins of the study. Pieces of the story were still missing.

"Why do you think Wolf left him alive?" I said.

Degan shook his head. "I don't know. But there's a reason. With Wolf, there's always a reason. And I plan to find out what it is."

I didn't argue. Instead, I got up and went back to where the fan had hung on the wall. I undid the two silk ribbons that had wrapped around the fan's supports, straightened them out, and used them to tie the fan closed.

When I turned back around, I found Degan hunched over his sword brother, his lips almost touching the other degan's ear, whispering. Ivory's own lips moved in silent time with Degan's, rhythm matching rhythm, pause matching pause.

I laid the fan at Degan's feet, along with Ivory's letter of passage, and left. Degan didn't look up as I went.

Chapter Thirty-five

The eastern horizon was showing hints of purple when I walked out Ivory's front door. An hour to sunup, maybe a hair more. Degan had best not dawdle.

I dragged the guard's body into the house—he was heavy—and closed the door. A few handfuls of sandy soil kicked across the boards didn't exactly cover up the trail of blood he'd left behind, but they kept it from being glaringly obvious.

I stayed off the paths and tried to act normal. A messenger on a mission; a functionary on an errand; a lover coming back from a late-night rendezvous with his mistress—anything other than what I was: a thief leaving his best friend and a dead body behind in the night.

There were a handful of servants and guards about, but their lanterns made them easy to avoid. Still, it wasn't until I came to the gate and found the dogs gnawing on the remains of the guards that I let myself breathe easier. That they were here meant no one had discovered the breach yet. We still had a chance, albeit a shrinking one.

The hounds had done their work well: The gate was a bloody mess, with bits of flesh and bone scattered across the paving stones. I'd had vague notions of trying to hide the bodies on my way out—maybe move them into the guardhouse, or at least deeper into the shadows—but between the puddles of gore and the bloody paw prints, not to mention the sullen glares of the feasting hounds, I knew it was hopeless. Damn Wolf for leaving the bodies out in the open in the first place, let alone keeping the gate open.

I skirted the hounds, creaked open the gate slightly, and slipped out into the piazza. Compared to the charnel house behind me, it smelled almost fresh out here. Almost.

I resheathed my blade and drew out the patronage token from around my neck. That was when I realized I had a problem, or rather, another problem. What had been a bright brass lozenge only hours ago was now a lump of blue-green verdigris—a *glowing* lump of verdigris.

Clearly, my patronage had been revoked.

It's not that I hadn't been expecting it—the events at the play had all but guaranteed it—I just hadn't realized the cancellation would be quite so . . . visible. Then again, this was Djan.

I held the lozenge up against the night. The light coming off it wasn't a radiant glare, but it was still bright enough to mark me, noticeable enough to make me an easy target in the dark, or even in a crowd. Enough to keep me off the main routes, which was exactly where I needed to be to make haste.

Hell.

I dropped the token down a drainage grate and headed for the nearest side street. As expected, it ran like a snake, twisting and turning until I wasn't sure which way I was headed. I ignored the looks I collected from shadowed doorways and windows, pretended not to be bothered by the whispers that ran in my wake. I moved quickly, but without haste, keeping my chest from easy view as much as possible to hide my lack of brass.

A stairway took me up to another street, which quickly turned into an arched alleyway. That in turn led to a small walkway that ran over the first street I'd come down. I paused, noting the reassuring lack of lurking shadows, then made the short leap onto a nearby roof. A dog woofed in the rooms below me, but I was on to the next building before the owner had time to yell at the beast. It ignored him and kept barking.

I smiled grimly as I left the noise in my wake. If the

hounds in the piazza beyond the Dog Gate had been any-thing like the one behind me, there was no way Degan and I could have gotten in to find Ivory, let alone out again. For that matter, Wolf would have had a harder time of it as well. Not that he'd seemed to care: Leaving a pile of dead men and an open gate wasn't exactly the height of subtlety.

I hopped a low wall and wove my way among a jungle of empty laundry lines. Ahead, I could see a gap coming up, indicating a broader street to cross. I looked left and right, spied what appeared to be a narrowing of the way a block or so on, and adjusted my course.

I wondered briefly how the meeting between Wolf and Ivory had played out. Had they begun with talking, or was it steel and blood from the start? I could see Wolf wanting to take his time, to taunt his former brother, maybe even offer Ivory a way out, all the while knowing it would come to blows. That seemed to be Wolf's style: He liked to show how clever he was, to let the mark know just how much he'd been played. Angels knew he'd enjoyed it enough with me. I couldn't seem him not pausing to twist the knife when it came to confronting Ivory—the temptation would have been too great to miss.

The rattle of stone on stone to my right brought me up short and put me in a crouch. I hadn't seen anyone else up here so far, but that didn't mean I was alone. A curse fol-lowed the rattle, and after a moment, a figure pulled herself up onto an adjacent building. She paused to dust her hands against her robes and scan her surroundings; then she was off, crossing the roofs at an easy lope.

I waited until she was out of sight and then continued on, my own pace frustratingly less certain by comparison.

My guess, if I had to make one, was that Ivory hadn't stood for any of Wolf's baiting. He was too practiced at pol-itics, had lived too long with an eye over his shoulder, to fall for the Azaari's bluff and bluster. I could almost hear the old degan telling Wolf to get on with it as he took his long sword off the wall; could practically see the glint in his eye as they crossed steel. As for how he handled himself once he'd lost, well, I didn't have any doubt that the old degan had told Wolf to go fuck himself when it came to the Order's laws.

I smiled at the thought. That would have been something to see: Wolf coming up short, his plans brought to an abrupt halt by one man's defiance. To watch as he realized there wasn't a damn thing he could do to make Ivory give him the laws.

Yeah, I would have paid for a seat to that performance.

I came to the edge of a gently sloping roof. It was a short jump down to an adjacent one, followed by what looked like a nice long run over closely set buildings. In the distance, I could make out the gray-black line of the wall that separated the second ring of the city from the third. Fowler would be in the shadow of that wall, in a basement tavern we'd picked as our Black Ken, waiting for me. From there, it would be a small matter of putting the proper bribes in the proper hands and joining the traffic leaving the Old City. True, the turned tokens might make things more expensive, but we'd been prepared for that possibility and laid down contingencies. Guards could always go blind for enough money.

No, the tricky part wouldn't be getting out; it would be catching Wolf and stopping him. I didn't relish trying to track him through the wilds, but at least we knew where he was headed. And besides, if worse came to worst, we could simply put on the miles and try to beat him to Ildrecca. After all, it wasn't as if we didn't know what he was planning. We had the laws; he had the sword: It wasn't as if his options were limitless.

I adjusted my footing, eyed the drop to the next roof, and . . . stood up.

No.

It didn't make sense. The path was too straight, too predictable. Too easy to see it laid out before me.

I looked over my shoulder, back toward the padishah's estate and the Dog Gate and the guards lying on the stones. Back to the papers on the floor and Ivory dying in his study. Back to Wolf's failure.

None of it made sense.

Why leave Ivory alive? If Wolf had shown anything, it was that he did everything for a reason. From killing Crook Eye to manipulating Nijjan to putting me on Degan's trail, every move had been made with one goal in mind: to get his hands on Ivory's sword and the Order's laws. As plans went, it was beautiful—he hadn't wasted a single motion, hadn't missed a single step. Every action, every conversation, had been a setup for the next phase, a prelude to the next step in the dance.

It was the kind of execution any Gray Prince would have been proud to call his own.

Had Wolf thought the old degan would bleed to death before anyone got to him? Or had he simply wanted to make sure that Ivory died a slow, lingering death—a kind of grim payback over their falling-out so many years before? Angels knew Wolf was vicious enough to do that.

But then why leave the guards lying out in the open? I didn't know whether he'd dusted them coming or going, but either way, Wolf must have known that even if the padishah's men didn't find them, Degan and I would. And that if we did, we'd . . .

Oh. Of course.

Shit.

I turned and began sprinting back the way I'd come.

Fool! We'd been meant to find them. And not just the guards—he'd wanted us to find Ivory, too. Alive. So we could talk to him. Comfort him.

Talk the dying degan into telling us where the laws were hidden.

Bastard.

Wolf had to be back there, had to be somewhere in or above the piazza, watching the Dog Gate even now, waiting for Degan to step through the gate. Just because I hadn't seen him didn't mean he wasn't hiding, wasn't waiting to spring once we were off the grounds and away from despotic interruptions. He'd gotten into my rooms under Fowler's nose: If anyone could place himself without being seen, even by my night vision, it was him.

And why let me go? Why let me stroll away from the ground unmolested? Because he was after bigger fish. Wolf wanted the Order's laws, and he knew that if anyone was going to have them, it would be Degan.

And that he'd have to kill him for them.

I flew back the way I'd come, scrambling and leaping where before I'd moved with a more cautious pace. The dog barked again, but this time when its owner shouted, it was because of the tiles I sent crashing to the street as I jumped down off his roof.

I ran back along the covered alley and practically tumbled down to the street in my haste. Amber-limned shapes drew back as I rushed past, shouting curses in my wake. I didn't care: didn't care about gathering attention, didn't care about my missing token, didn't care that I might be drawing ready blades after me. All I cared about was getting back to the damn gate before Degan stepped into whatever Wolf had planned for him.

I raced around the final turn and jerked to a halt, my feet skidding on the dusty stones beneath me. A lone figure stood where the street opened onto the piazza. The figure had a drawn sword in his hand and a smile on his face.

He was a degan, all right—just not the right one.

"I was wondering if you'd put the pieces together," said Wolf. He was dressed in the Djanese style, with loose pants and a short tunic, all under a flowing burnoose, all spattered in blood.

"It wasn't that hard," I lied.

Wolf raised a dubious eyebrow. "Oh?"

"No," I said. *Talk. Buy time. Let Degan walk out the gate and hear you, find you. Maybe take Wolf from behind.* "Remember what I used to do, why you brought me. I poke at things until they make sense, collect pieces until I can see the picture through the puzzle." I rested an easy hand on my sword. Wolf didn't react. "You broke your pattern."

"My pattern?"

"You left Ivory alive. That isn't like you."

"Ah. That." Wolf gestured at the wall beside him. There was a long sword leaning up against it. Ivory's long sword. "Perhaps I was feeling merciful? He was a friend once upon a time, after all."

"Friends don't cut out friend's tongues."

"You don't know some of the people I've called friend."

"Nor does a smart killer leave a pile of corpses to advertise his comings and goings."

"And if I said I was in a hurry?"

"I'd say you'd stop to cover your tracks on the way out of a burning house."

Wolf rested his saber's tip—his own blade, I guessed, given the raised steel chasing on the guard—on the ground and regarded me. "Yes," he said. "Very clever. I was right to pick you."

"And I was wrong to come."

"I gave you no other choice."

"There's always another choice."

"You mean stay in Ildrecca?" Wolf snorted. "You wouldn't have survived, not once I set the other Gray Princes against you."

"Maybe not," I said. "But I could have tried. I could have at least stuck around and backed my own organization, instead of walking away." Could have put something of myself on the line, rather than coming down here and putting everyone else on the line for me. For what I thought a Gray Prince could be.

"You could have," said Wolf, "but that's not your nature. You've worked alone too long to let others claim you. You're like a wolf who tries to run with a pack of hounds: As good as it may feel, you know you're meant for better things—broader fields, wider skies." He lifted his sword and let the spine of the blade rest against his shoulder. "Consider yourself fortunate to have figured it out now. It took me three lifetimes to realize an Oath isn't a cause, that a brotherhood isn't a tribe. For the others, it may be enough, but for me?" He shook his head. "I'm Azaari: I'm not meant to gather up promises and trade them for my honor. I gave my word to serve a purpose and for action, not to sit and wait and count."

"Then why not leave the Order?"

"An Azaari doesn't break his word."

I couldn't help it: I laughed.

Wolf took an ominous step forward. "You mock me?" he said. "Even now? Knowing who I am and what I can do?"

"I mock you," I said, ignoring the hole forming in my stomach, "precisely because I know who you are and what you can do. Sworn brothers dead at your hand? The founder of your Order dusted so you could steal his sword? That's not keeping your word, not even close."

Wolf straightened to his full height and glared down at me. "You know nothing." He picked up Ivory's sword with his left hand and began to turn away.

"I know plenty," I said to his back. "Why else carve your way to Ivory's door, if not to find out how to break free of the Order? Why go to all this trouble, unless you plan to call the emperor to heel and force him to release you from your Oath?"

That stopped him. "What do you say?"

"Markino," I said. "The emperor, and his other two incarnations, all indebted to the Order of the Degans. All bound by the Oath sworn on Ivory's sword when you founded your gang."

Wolf looked back over his shoulder. "Bronze told you this?"

"No, the emperor mentioned it over drinks before I left Ildrecca."

A thoughtful silence, then, "My sword brother must love you indeed, to share something the Order's kept secret for so long."

I wasn't sure how to respond to that, so I didn't.

"You're right that I came for the sword," he said. "But it's not what you think. I've no desire to be severed from my Oath. What I told you before is true: I wish to save the Order. But unlike Bronze and most of the others, I'm not deluded enough to think we can fix our problems with talk or laws. Only action can save us now."

"And what kind of action would that be?" I said. "Littering the streets with more bodies? Forcing the emperor to absolve you of all your sins? Or are you planning to put the question in Markino's hands? To force him to pick between having the Order serve him or the empire? Because if you are, I can tell you which way he'll jump, no guessing necessary." Anyone capable of creating a religion for the sole purpose of ensuring his perpetual rule wasn't about to let a tool like the degans slip through his fingers.

"You think me a fool?" said Wolf. "Of course I know what he'd choose: He'd say we were his, and the Order would be shattered for good. The fractures among us have grown too deep to be solved by a simple proclamation, even from the emperor. To declare for one interpretation is to drive the adherents of the other away.

"No, the only reason the Order has remained whole this long is that we haven't sought out a resolution, haven't given one another cause to back our views with steel. We've been careful to avoid repeating Ivory's sins. But now, with Iron and Silver and Ivory dead? With degan blood on degan blades? It's only a matter of time before someone draws in anger, or pride, or vengeance, and the Order collapses."

"But you helped cause that," I said. "You killed two to Degan's one, for Angels' sake!"

"Yes."

"You knew what would happen."

"Yes."

"Then why?"

Wolf regarded me for a moment, then looked up at the sky. It had gone from black to charcoal around us on the street, with the stars fading overhead. His eyes creased with the hint of a smile.

"You're trying to distract me," he said. "To give Bronze time to get away, or come upon me unawares. Very good. Useless, but very good." He turned and gestured toward the square. "Come, let's await my brother together."

I didn't budge.

What the hell was I missing? If the Order of the Degans was beyond repair as Wolf said, then why hasten its collapse? Why push them over the edge and destroy the truce they'd been holding for centuries? Even if he did get his hands on Ivory's laws, the odds of him being able to fix the Order once its members started killing one another seemed to rest somewhere between slim and none. If they—

No. Wait. Not fix. Wolf hadn't said "fix," he'd said "re-forge."

I looked up to find Wolf staring at me. Waiting.

"You *want* the members of the Order to clear steel," I said. "To start fighting and killing one another." To see that the Order was doomed, to see that there was no compromise. To see there was no hope. "You want to break the degans."

"Sometimes to repair something, you must break it first," said Wolf. "To forge something anew, you have to tear it asunder. My Order can't be saved as it stands, but if it were to be built again, from the ground up? Then. Then it would be saved."

"Betrayed isn't saved," said a voice behind Wolf. "Betrayed is just betrayed. Calling it anything else is a weak man's excuse."

Wolf spun about, his sword snapping to guard, while I slipped to the side and looked past him.

To see Degan standing in the square.

Chapter Thirty-six

Wolf tensed for a moment. Then, seeing Degan wasn't advancing, he laughed.

"You say this, Bronze?" he said. "You, who have Iron's blood on your blade? Who are you to speak of justifications? I don't see you putting yourself before the Order for your crimes, don't see you standing in the Barracks Hall awaiting judgment. How is your excuse for avoiding justice and coming after Ivory any better than mine?"

Degan was maybe fifteen feet from Wolf. He had his chain-hilted sword in one hand, Ivory's widower's fan in the other. I couldn't read the look on his face.

"I didn't come to kill Ivory," he said.

Wolf snorted. "Then more fool you."

"He didn't deserve—"

"He deserved everything I gave him and more," snapped Wolf. "Deserved a century's worth of agony for the lies he told us, for the lives he stole from us. That old man chained us with our honor and then walked away. Worse, he let us be set aside when he left. We, who were supposed to serve Lucien as his swords, instead spent our time trading promises like merchants doing business in the bazaar. Swords that were once meant to support an empire now settle private debts." Wolf spit into the square. "A blade rusts if it's not used, Bronze, and I've no intention of rusting anymore. It's time for our steel to shine again."

I eyed Wolf's back, then took a tentative step forward,

making sure to keep the Azaari between Degan and me. If he saw me, if he guessed what I was planning, I knew Degan would speak up rather than let me strike down Wolf from behind. Easy solution or not, he wouldn't allow that when it came to one of his sword brothers.

Which meant I just had to be careful as I moved in, is all.

"And what kind of shine would you have?" said Degan as I took another step. "The glisten of blood on steel? Listen to yourself! You talk about restoring the Order in one breath and destroying it in another. Setting us against one another isn't going to bring us together, Steel—we're too hardened to the slaughter for that. You might get a few to relent out of sympathy for the past, but once the blood starts flowing the rest won't stop. Gold and Jade, Pearl and Brass: They'll go to their graves before they give in."

"I know."

"Then why?" I could hear the desperation in Degan's voice, could imagine the look of frustration on his face. "Why make it so we cut one another down?"

"Because we need to realize how truly broken we are. For the last two hundred years, all we've done is argue about which path is the proper one, ignoring the fact that both roads lead nowhere. Serve the emperor? Serve the Empire? Both have forgotten us. Like fools dying of thirst, we sit in the desert remembering the taste of water instead of seeking it out on our own. If the Order of the Degans is to reclaim any kind of purpose, any kind of honor, we have to leave the dust of our past behind. We have to free ourselves of the old ways before we can create the new."

"Killing someone doesn't make them free," said Degan. Another step.

"It's not the dead I'm worried about," said Wolf. "Let the zealots and the true believers slaughter one another; let them paint the empire with blood. Once we start littering the streets with our dead and hanging fatherless swords in the Barracks Hall, the others will begin to waver. Those degans who remain will see the need."

"And what need is that?" said Degan.

"To be free of the Oath," said Wolf. "To serve the empire

as we see fit, without chains of words and magic holding us back. We have all of us seen and made history—we should be chieftains in our own right, sheikhs and sheikhas, leaders of men, not hired swords waiting on a summons that will never come. Ivory called us a brotherhood, but to be brothers and sisters there must also be a father. Well, I've outgrown my father the emperor, as I think the rest of us have. We are no longer a brotherhood; we are a tribe, joined together by the souls we surrendered and the blood we've shed. When this is done, we will stand together as tribesmen should: free and equal and bound to no one but one another."

"And what do you think 'father' will have to say about that idea?"

Wolf hefted Ivory's sword. "I don't think he'll have much of a choice once I remind him of his former incarnation's promise."

Degan's voice grew cool. "So you were planning on killing Ivory for the sword all along."

"Planning? No. I merely thought to find the blade. Ivory being alive was merely good fortune on my part, less so on his."

"And if you hadn't found it?"

Wolf shrugged. "There was always you."

"Me?" said Degan. "You can't think I would have come back to Ildrecca with you after I found out you killed Silver."

"Come back to . . . ? Ah, I see: The Gray Prince has been sharing his tales. Very good. But the truth is, I never planned to bring you back. Not that I don't think you could sway the Order if you put your mind to it—you could, which is the problem. You would bring balance when I need blood. No, I wouldn't have returned with you—I would have returned with the sword of the degan who killed not only Iron, but Silver and Ivory as well."

"You would have blamed it all on me?" I could hear the pain, the disbelief, in Degan's voice. "Why?"

"When an exemplar falls," said Wolf, "it can be almost as powerful as the thing he represents falling. You becoming a butcher, not to mention turning your back on the degans because you saw us as too flawed to continue, would have shaken the Order to its core. And while it may not have given me the war I wanted, you would have at least turned me into a savior. Not as effective as having access to the emperor's Oath, I admit, but there are other ways to steer things to a breaking point."

"And now that you have Ivory's sword?"

"Now?" I heard the smile in Wolf's voice. I was close now. Very close. "Now I call in your Oath."

"My Oath?" Degan chuckled. "You forget: I relinquished my sword. I walked away. That's why I'm here—of all of us, I'm the only one who can stop you."

I was maybe six paces away. I cocked my left arm to flick my wrist knife free, then thought better of it and let my right hand slip into my left sleeve instead. This close, I didn't want to risk even the tiny *click* the knife would make sliding free.

Damn, but I wished I'd thought to ask Aribah about borrowing some poison.

I took another step. Degan came into view just around Wolf's shoulder. He was too busy glaring at his sword brother to notice me.

"Walking away isn't the same as leaving the Order, Bronze," said Wolf. "Ivory could have told you that. Well, he would have if he'd still had a tongue, I suppose."

"You lie."

In answer, Wolf brandished Ivory's sword. "Bronze Degan. By the Oath sworn on this steel, I summon you to account. I call on you, in accordance with the laws of the Order of the Degans, to fulfill your Oath as a degan."

I saw Degan's eyes go wide at the words, his sword hand begin to tremble. Watched as what must have been the grip of a two-hundred-year-old promise begin to close around him.

Shit. Wolf wasn't bluffing.

"By blood and magic, by soul and steel, I call on you to—"

I moved.

Unfortunately, so did Wolf.

I knew better than to think he'd forgotten about me—Wolf wasn't that dumb. But to hope he'd lose track of me as he talked, to think he might have missed my padding up on him while he focused on Degan? That had seemed worth the risk.

Now it just seemed stupid.

Wolf spun as I lunged, bringing the long sword in his left hand around in a blurring arc. I felt the sword's handle hit my wrist, grunted as the knife slipped from my suddenly tingling fingers.

I kept moving forward, going for the close fight. Backing away would let Wolf bring his own sword to bear; but here, in tight, I had the advantage.

I thrust the heel of my left palm up toward his face even as my right foot stomped down toward the inside of his leg. Shin, instep, toes—I didn't give a damn where I landed at this point, as long as it hurt him. As long as it gave Degan enough time to close the distance and strike.

Wolf raised his shoulder and ducked his head, deflecting my palm. I felt my foot connect with something, but only sparingly. I was still shifting my weight, still trying to turn my palm thrust into a vicious elbow to his side, when Wolf brought the long sword guard back around and connected with the side of my head.

Pain and light exploded behind my eyes. The world wobbled. I reached out for support, felt something against my shoulder, and grabbed hold. Wolf cursed. For a moment I was upright; then my legs became entangled and I fell, taking the support with me.

I heard Wolf yell something at Degan, only to have it cut off by the sound of steel meeting steel.

I tried to push myself up, to roll myself over. That turned out to be a bad idea. The world spun some more, and what little food I had in me decided to come up and see what all the fuss was about. It spread itself across the street and the side of my face in roughly equal measure. I gagged some more.

Grunts and gasps; the sound of feet moving quickly over

pavement; sword meeting sword—all came to me through
the lingering sound of a bell echoing in my head. I couldn't
tell if the two degans were right on top of me or half a
square away.

I took one shaking breath, then another. The heaving in
my middle settled down to an uneasy quavering. I blinked,
saw street and bile and bits of what once had been food, all
with barely any hint of amber. Dawn was nearly here.

I lifted my head, moved my hands, and pushed against
the ground. Something scraped and shifted on the street
beneath me. I looked. Ivory's sword.

So that's what I'd grabbed hold of. Between the tangle of
my arms and it somehow getting caught between my legs, I
must have levered the sword out of Wolf's grip. Good.
Served the bastard right.

I started to laugh, felt the world tip a bit, and stopped
myself. *Gloat later, Drothe: Live now.*

I gathered my knees beneath me and turned my attention toward the sounds of fighting.

Degan and Wolf were standing just short of the square,
where the narrow street opened out into the filth-strewn
piazza. Degan was trying to hold his ground, using the superior reach and speed of his rapier to keep Wolf trapped
between the buildings, where the Azaari's curved blade had
less room to maneuver. As for Wolf, he was attempting to
push forward, using a dizzying array of cuts and off-line
thrusts to beat Degan's blade aside and force the other man
back.

Normally, I would have put odds on Degan when it came
to controlling the fight; but seeing how he was facing another degan, and seeing how Wolf looked to have just as
much, if not more, say in the matter, I wasn't willing to make
any predictions at the moment.

I watched, slack-jawed, as Wolf threw a downward cut,
slid his shamshir off Degan's parry, swept the blade around
for a cut from the other direction, turned that attack into a
thrust at the last moment, and then stepped forward and
pushed a third slice at Degan's head, all in one seamless
action.

Degan, for his part, avoided Wolf's steel, but was forced to take two quick steps back, then a third, and finally launch himself into a lunge just to interrupt Wolf's advance.

Blades met, bodies twisted, balance shifted, and both swordsmen sprang apart.

They were well and truly in the square now.

Wolf chuckled. "You still favor the Virocchi school, I see. I'd have thought you past that by now."

I began to push myself to my feet, using Ivory's sword as a third leg.

"Old habits," said Degan. He shifted the angle of his blade. "Besides, I seem to recall Piero Virocchi doing well enough when the two of you crossed steel."

Wolf took a step, widening his stance, then another, closing it again. "Pah. Exhibition bouts mean nothing."

"Losing is still losing."

"And dead is still dead." Wolf flicked the tip of his sword in dismissal. "That little Ibrian rabbit has been rotting in his grave for a hundred and a half years. His prancings failed him in the end."

"But not against you."

I watched as Wolf circled Degan, as Degan slipped his back foot forward while he turned to keep the Azaari in sight. The fan was still in Degan's left hand, though he now held it back and slightly canted at his side.

"As I said: If there's no blood, there's no meaning."

"That sounds like an excuse," said Degan, extending his sword. "I'd have thought you were past that by now."

Wolf opened his mouth as if to respond, then became a blur. His shamshir leapt out, sweeping Degan's blade aside as the Azaari pressed forward. For his part, Degan took a small step back, dropped the tip of his sword below Wolf's, and lowered his body and extended his sword into the on-coming rush.

It was a beautiful move: smart, concise, and deadly. And on anyone else, I expect it would have worked. But Wolf wasn't anyone else.

Degan's tip had barely settled into its new line before Wolf's own sword was moving back in the other direction, catching the rapier and edging it aside. Metal scraped on metal as Wolf slipped past Degan's point and brought his own tip to bear, all while moving down the other man's sword.

Degan sidestepped and raised his guard, but even I could see it wasn't going to be enough: Between Wolf's leverage and the curve of his blade, Degan wasn't going to be able to get out of the way in time. He was done.

Which is why I expect Wolf and I were both equally surprised when Degan stepped forward, pressed his guard into the saber's, and forced the sword—along with Wolf's arm—up and away. The move ended with the two men in dagger range, their arms extended, their swords crossed, their eyes locked.

For anyone else, there might have been a pause then: a fraction of an instant to register the surprise of an attack thwarted, the relief of a killing stroke foiled. But these were degans: Their guards had barely crashed together before Wolf was pulling his sword free and aiming a slice at the other man's body. As for Degan, he'd already begun pivoting in anticipation of the blow as he swung his sword guard at Wolf's head.

Still, he wasn't quite fast enough: At the last instant, Degan was forced to sweep Ivory's fan forward and down, to keep Wolf's at bay. The *crack* of steel striking laminated stays echoed off the surrounding buildings. Sadly, there was no answering crack of Degan's sword striking Wolf's jaw. The Azaari had ducked as he threw the cut.

The sound seemed to startle both men, and both took a hasty step back. Clearly, this hadn't been part of the chess match they were playing.

Degan looked down at the fan and swore. The final third of it was dangling at an odd angle.

Wolf regarded at the length of wood in Degan's hand. He tilted his head like his namesake. "Ivory's?"

Degan didn't answer. He merely resumed his guard.

Wolf grinned. "Of course. The laws. I should have known. The sly old bastard."

The two degans began circling one another again.

I was standing by then, albeit not steadily. The world had developed on a slight lean to the left, but as there didn't seem to be much I could do about it, I didn't complain.

I looked down at my right hand. My wrist was already swelling from the sword blow, and I was having trouble closing my fingers. I tried my rapier anyhow. Digits trembled and nerves screamed, but I was able to force my hand into the guard and pull the weapon free. Not that it stayed there long: I'd barely cleared the scabbard before my grip slipped. It it wasn't for the swept steel cage of the guard, my rapier sword would have clattered to the street.

Hopeless.

I looked back at the square.

The initial flourish had died down. Now, rathering than rushing forward to kill one another, each of the degans had taken a couple of paces back. They were still fighting— there was no question about that—but the two men men were being more thoughtful about it. I had no idea how long it had been since they'd faced one another, but it was clear that there was a lot of reevaluating going on out there.

Just as it was also clear that this lull wouldn't last

I switched my rapier to my left hand, gathered up Ivory's long sword as best I could with my right, adjusted Degan's blade across my back, and began to make my way toward the square.

Like hell I was going to leave this to chance.

I entered the square charting a careful course, eyeing the two degans all the while. I wasn't fool enough to think they didn't notice my arrival, but neither man so much as glanced in my direction. They, and I, knew who posed the real threat here.

It was hard to tell who was faring better at this point. Both men had been pressed hard by the other at least once, and each had managed set the other back on his heels. As skill with a blade went, I was in no position to judge, so far above me were they. But that didn't mean I couldn't have an opinion; and right now my opinion, I hated to say, favored Wolf. Not because his ability or technique or brutality looked to be vastly superior to Degan's—on that, I doubt I could have found a finger's worth of daylight between them. No, it was something much more basic that had me worried.

It was Wolf's sword.

Or, to be more precise, it was Degan's sword that had me concerned. Good steel though it might be, it wasn't a degan's blade by any measure. Between Wolf's cut-heavy style and the superiority of his Black Isle steel, I was already beginning to see a growing collection notches along the edge of Degan's sword. Sword blades were strongest along the edge and designed to take punishment there, but not to the extent I was seeing—and certainly not this fast.

I flexed the fingers of my right hand around Ivory's sheath, just to see how they were doing. Not good. The numbness was starting to fade, but it was being replaced by a throbbing ache that extended from my knuckles up through my hand and past my wrist. Even if I were to switch my rapier back to my sword hand, I doubted I could do much more than wave it about, and only then as long as no one connected with it. One good beat or parry and it would be out of my hand and on the ground in an instant.

No, if I wanted to help Degan, I was going to either have to come up with something that didn't involve a weapon, or wait for the exact right moment to strike.

I glanced over at the Dog Gate for the third time in twice as many steps. It was wide open again thanks to Degan's hasty exit, and the hounds had begun to skulk around the arch again. With the sun coming up and a fight sounding on the padishah's doorstep, I figured it was only a matter of time before the gate vomited forth a stream of men decked out in opal jackets and ostrich-plumed turbans. I had no idea whether they'd decide to overwhelm us with numbers or feather us with arrows, but either way, I didn't want to be here when the time for the decision finally came.

I turned my attention back to the fight.

The fight had taken the degans to the far side of the square. Steel rang on steel, the noise bouncing off the buildings until it sounded as if a regiment of ghosts was doing battle in the piazza.

Both men were showing signs of wear now. Degan, despite what looked like a bloody patch on his left leg, had resorted to a more upright stance, blade held near shoulder level, sword arm loosely extended, his left arm held at his side. Whenever Wolf threw a cut, Degan either moved his tip around the other man's blade or let the force of the blow carry his own blade around as he stepped in for the counter. It was smooth and efficient and had a decidedly calculating air to it.

But as ruthlessly cold as the tactic seemed, Degan's steel never managed to do more than threaten Wolf. The Azaari was a shifting, swaying reed, sliding forward and back on bent knees over a wide stance. Lean back to parry, lean forward to cut, with gathering and crossing steps to change the distance and line. There was a tear in his burnoose. Metal scales glinted beneath it in the growing light, telling me Wolf had come armored. I doubted Degan had a similar advantage.

Well, that did it, then. Offhanded or not, I couldn't hold off any longer. Between his Black Isle steel and the metal jack he looked to be wearing, Wolf had too many cards in his favor. I needed to disrupt the game.

I'd just started to move toward them when Degan advanced into one of Wolf's assaults and began to press the Azaari. What had been a fit of exchanges suddenly became one long, lopsided rush.

Degan, it seemed, had decided to push Wolf, and was now raining blows down on the other degan. Thrusts, cuts, reverse strikes, counterblows—the attacks flowed out of Degan like a river, crashing against Wolf's defenses and sending him reeling back step by relentless step. The Azaari, whose eyes had been narrow and cool before this, were now wide; his defense was verging on frantic.

I quickened my pace, sensing opportunity was at hand. And I was right. The only problem was, it wasn't the opportunity I'd been hoping for.

I was still half a dozen paces away when Degan brought

his sword down in a hammer blow, striking Wolf's blade so hard that the heavy rapier should have not only forced the shamshir aside, but continued down into Wolf's shoulder and chest. And it would have, too, save for the sudden, unmistakable *snap* of steel breaking against steel. Daylight shone, metal flashed, and I caught the briefest glimpse of the first two-thirds of Degan's sword as it sailed through the air and landed in the muck.

I froze, momentarily stunned. Wolf had no such problem. Without missing a beat, he reached out, grabbed Degan's extended sword arm, and yanked, lashing out with his sword guard at the same time. Degan staggered, took an awkward blow to the head, and was thrown to his knees.

In any other place, in any other circumstances, that would have been the end of it right there. But we were in the square off the Dog Gate, which meant that they weren't fighting on paving stones so much as a carpet of shit and muck. Muck that, when Degan landed, carried him a good three feet further along the ground than either of them had expected. This meant that while Wolf was prepared to slash his blade into the spot where he'd expected Degan to stop, he wasn't ready to see his former sword brother turn his slide into a roll and come up on his knees, facing him, broken sword held at the ready.

Wolf blinked. Degan winked. Then the shamshir was moving again.

The sound of Wolf's steel striking Degan's guard snapped me out of my stupor. I took a reflexive step forward, then stopped. No, I'd never make it in time. If I was going to save Degan, I'd have to get Wolf away from him, have to somehow make myself a more viable target than Degan and the fan . . .

No, not viable. Valuable.

I held up Ivory's sword.

"Hey, asshole!" I yelled. "Hey!"

To my relief, Wolf looked up.

I sheathed my rapier as I began to retreat back the way I'd come. "You need this, right?" I said, waving the sword over my head.. "Can't get anyone to do anything without it, right?"

Wolf's eyes narrowed. He took a step back from Degan. Degan, wisely, maintained his guard, though he cast a wary eye at me as well.

"Now, I don't know about you," I said as I paced backward, "but I'd feel like a right proper ass if I came all the way to Djan and ended up letting some Kin walk off with the sword I came looking for. I mean, that'd be pretty fucking embarrassing, especially for a degan, right?"

"You don't want to do this, Gray Prince," said Wolf. "You know what will happen when I find you. Put it down."

"You say 'when.' I say 'if.' I've spent my whole life on the dodge: If I know how to do one thing, it's fade."

"You won't be able to hide. Not from me."

"Who said anything about hiding?" I said as I glanced over my shoulder. Halfway there. "I used to smuggle artifacts, remember? I know people. People who know how to get things places. People who can call in special favors." I waved the sword again. "People who might be able to, say, get this to the monks at the Monastery of the Black Isle."

Wolf's eyes went wide. "You wouldn't."

"Wouldn't what?" I said, refusing to glance at the hint of movement I'd thought I saw in the Dog Gate—movement too large to be from a hound. "Hand it over to the monks? Why not? Way I hear it, they're the only ones who know how to melt one of these swords down. Might even be able to pray away the magic, for all I know. Figure it's worth a try, either way."

Wolf took a step toward me, and therefore away from Degan. I smiled.

"Not that I'd go personally, mind," I added. "You'd know to lie in wait for me. But how much coal goes into that place, I wonder? How many bushels of grain? How many pilgrims? It'd be Eriff's work to sneak a blade in."

The Azaari looked back at Degan, still kneeling in the muck, broken sword before him.

Degan nodded. "I'll draw it out long enough for him to get away, Steel," he said. "Even like this, you know I can."

"Best choose," I said, nodding at the Dog Gate. A small swarm of figures were gathering there now. "We're not going to be alone much longer, and I thought I saw a couple of bows being strung."

Wolf swore—a deep, lyrical Azaari curse that, had I been able to understand it, probably would have seared my ears off. Then, with one last look at Degan, he swept Ivory's fan up from the ground and started running toward me.

"There's my boy," I muttered as I turned and ducked down the street. "Let's see how well you can play the hunter when your quarry isn't running the path you laid out." Behind us, I heard Degan begin to call out, but his voice was covered over by the sudden sound of a horn. The padishah's men, it seemed, had decided it was time to sally forth from the grounds. I only hoped that by the time they got there, all they'd find were sullen hounds and foot-smeared shit.

Chapter Thirty-seven

As it turned out, Wolf fit his moniker far better than I would have liked. Not that I wanted to lose him right away. If I did that, it was possible he'd double-back so he could finish things with Degan—Degan who, I reminded myself, had no sword. No, I needed Wolf on my scent, if only until it felt safe to lose him. The problem was, it was quickly becoming apparent that I might not be able to shake him, whether I wanted to or not.

I ducked and wove as I went, slipping down alleys, taking sudden turns, using the height of the crowd around me to mask my passage. But I also made sure to leave signs he would catch: a tipped poultry cage here, an angry crockery seller there, a muddy footprint whenever chance permitted. Let him think he was following so that he didn't know he was being led.

It was an old street urchin trick: Get the mark used to looking for the bigger signs so he'd miss the smaller ones when it came time to fade. I'd done it plenty in the past, and while it tended to work better with a gang, or at least in a city where you knew the layout, it was still a solid dodge. The only problem was, I was beginning to suspect that Wolf knew it at least as well as I did, if not better.

I reached the next cross-street and heard a crash behind me as someone crushed a reed cage underfoot. People yelled, others screamed. Something fell to the ground and shattered.

Wolf was still behind me, and from the sound of it, he still had his sword out.

I turned down a narrow street, bounced off a man dressed in some sort of shimmering cloak, recovered, and ran up a set of stone steps. The man began yelling behind me as I ducked through an arched gate and found myself on a street that looked familiar but I knew wasn't.

I hesitated. It was nearly time to leave Wolf chewing my dust: but which way? The last thing I wanted was a path that ended in a blank wall.

I looked up, saw a shadow skimming a roof, watched as it made the short hop across an alley and vanish along the top of a building. If only . . .

Back in Ildrecca, there'd have been no heitations about which wall to hop, which roof to dance, which shop to run into so I could leave out the back. I'd know what painters were working where, whose scaffolding I could use, which plasterers would look the other way for a payment later. But here? Here I couldn't even tell if I'd stumbled down the same street by accident sometimes. In Ildrecca, I could choose to become invisible; in el-Qaddice, I was lucky if I wasn't conspicuous.

Wolf's voice came to me on the other side of the gate and down the stairs. He was yelling a question at the man who was busy yelling after me. Time to go.

I chose to go right.

I was feeling it now: the heat, the blow from the long sword, the day and the night without sleep. Fear was keeping me moving, but that didn't erase all my ills. My head, which had begun to feel clear in the square, was pounding again. My legs burned. A stitch like a knife wound pulled at my side. As for my mouth . . . well, I couldn't have managed to spit if you promised me the imperial throne just then. The mere idea of water seemed unattainable even as I dodged around a line at one of the public spigots set in a wall.

I followed the curve of the street as it emptied out into a wider lane, which in turn filled with people and pavilions and stalls, all covered over with a patchwork of canvas awnings. The morning street market was in full swing.

I dove in, moving with the flow of people whenever possible, swimming against their current when necessary. Flies buzzed and musicians played, one no less annoying than the other to my aching head, while butchers and herb sellers wielded their blades to trim down their wares. Dust and blood and exotic oils fought one another in the air, rolling over and past me, vanishing among the sea of scarves and sandals and curious looks I left in my wake.

I kept to myself, ducking and dodging, drawing the kaffiyeh across my face as I held the shit-smeared long sword close. A couple of private guards gave me a dark eye as I passed, but for the most part everyone was too busy with their own business to notice the small, filth-speckled Imperial weaving his way through the morass.

Ahead, I could see a break in the crowd. A fountain, by the look of it, with a street beyond. If I could get on the other side of that before Wolf managed to . . .

"Thief!" cried a voice I knew. He was behind me. "Stop! Thief!"

Years of practice kept me from altering my gait or drawing attention to myself as I glanced over my shoulder. Wolf was perhaps thirty paces behind me and closing. Shit. I knew he had a longer stride, but I hadn't expected the bastard to close the gap so fast.

It was the right thing to shout, especially in a market: Nothing got a faster reaction, or elicited more aid, than a call to stop a Palmer or a Purse Cutter. Thieves were the common enemy of both sellers and buyers, and that meant a call of warning just as often turned into a call to arms.

I studied the crowd. Most eyes were still turned toward the degan, but a few had already begun to scan the street—especially the guards'.

"Thief!" Wolf shouted again. Maybe twenty-five feet away now, with people starting to actively get out of his way.

One of the market guards was looking at me now, considering. I glanced away, my eyes busy. He didn't seem convinced, but I didn't much care. I wasn't playing to throw him off; I was searching for a convenient—

There. Thin, dirty, with quick eyes and a slightly bent stance, clearly ready to run. Her pale green dress hid her intentions well, but there was no mistaking the flex of her knee beneath the fabric, let alone the fresh sheen of sweat on her upper lip.

Thief. A Palmer, by the look of it, given the gap in the neat row of copper spice pots on the table before her. No one had noticed yet, but that didn't mean they wouldn't, especially with the cry being raised. She was scanning the crowd as well, but not for suspects: She was looking for a way out. Measuring the lines of traffic, the gaps between the stalls, the density of the the crowd.

Our gazes met, locked. Instantly, I knew she could tell. Never having met, we still knew each other across the dusty space.

Her eyes narrowed. I smiled. Then I pointed at her and screamed, "There! Thief! It's her. She took the spices!"

The guard who thought I hadn't noticed him moving up on me spun about. Others followed suit. Someone took up the cry.

The local thief favored me with a baleful glare and took off running. I turned in the opposite direction and did the same.

"No!" I heard Wolf bellow above the sudden din. "No, not her. It's him. The one with the—"

But I was already around the next stall and making for the narrow street that opened up behind it.

Shadows took me in. Garbage deepened underfoot, and rats and I did our best to avoid one another. Behind me, I heard the crash of wood and brass, the shouting of an angry merchant as his stall was bulled through.

I prayed to the Angels that it was a Djanese guardsman on my tail, and not Wolf. As usual, the Angels ignored me.

"Imperial!" The degan's shout echoed off the walls, making him sound even closer than I feared he was. He didn't sound happy.

I risked a look back, saw a grayish silhouette set against the light at the end of the street. I'd maybe doubled my lead, but Wolf already looked to be closing it.

I put my head down and ignored every sensation but the burn of my legs and the slap of my feet against the ground.

I wasn't going to make it. Not now. The street was too narrow, the options too limited. There were no roofs to take to, no switchbacks to try, no more crowds to blend in to.

Running wasn't going to work.

I spied a crossroads ahead, the pale light creeping down into the space where the streets met like some lost and lonely thing. And so what? It was just another turn, and an obvious one at that. Maybe if it were darker, and the cross-street was an alley, and I had my night vision, I might be able to use it to lose Wolf; but like this, with the light shining down and him closing on me? He'd be able to see precisely what I did, know exactly where I'd gone. At best, I'd maybe gain a handful of paces on him after I made the turn, and that would be because I could likely cut it closer than him. Once he'd lumbered around the corner and regained his stride, he'd . . .

Wait. That was it. The corner.

I pushed myself for a final burst of speed, then swung wide as I made my turn, making sure to cross the patch of daylight as I did so. Then I was down the new street and away.

For all of six paces before I skidded to a halt.

The stopping almost undid me, not because of the footing, but because my legs suddenly wanted to do nothing more than collapse. My breath was coming in ragged gasps, and it took every speck of willpower I had left to not lean over and vomit up the bile that was roiling about in my stomach. Instead, I forced myself to turn and take two staggering steps back towards the crossroads.

That was the easy part. The hard bit was not dropping Ivory's sword as I unsheathed it .

It came free without any resistance: a clean, oiled blade in a well-used scabbard, ready for the call to service. Double edged from tip to guard, it ran straight and true, with a gentle taper that made it look like a long, wicked tooth. I expected it looked even worse to the person on the business end.

It was lighter than I'd have thought: stouter than my rapier, but not so much that it seemed as if I was holding something completely unfamiliar. The balance was good as well, even with one hand. The sword felt as if it wanted to be swung, to whistle and cut the air—a silver arc of death eager to be put to the test. A man who knew what he was doing could carve his way through a host with this sword; that, or perhaps make short work of an angry degan.

Only I didn't know what I was doing when it came to a long sword. Other than swinging it like a metal club, I was short on not only technique, but also on options. With one hand looking and feeling like an overstuffed sausage, and enough time for a single desperate move, I needed something that had a better than average chance of stopping a charging degan. Nothing fancy, nothing complicated, nothing requiring any kind finesse. I just needed to kill the bastard, preferably as quickly as possible.

Which is why I decided to use Ivory's long sword like a spear and set for the charge.

I'd had the presence of mind to turn left when I took the corner, meaning that when Wolf followed me around, his sword would be on the opposite side of his body to me. That made parrying on his part hard, and a counterblow even harder. Add to that I'd be thrusting instead of cutting, and his time to react would be down to almost nothing.

It was that "almost" part that had me worried.

I took a half step back, putting my shoulders as close to the wall behind me as I dared, the long sword held across my body, its point directed the space where I expected Wolf to appear, ready to step and thrust at the first sign of the degan. My breath was coming in wheezing gasps, and I could hear my heart raging in my ears like a drum. I tried to slow both, to silence my body, for fear that I'd miss hearing him coming.

I shouldn't have worried. I caught the soft slap of slippers as he approached, heard the skid of leather on filth-covered stone as he slowed in preparation for the turn.

I shifted my weight back and waited.

He appeared in an instant. One moment, the street before me was empty; the next, Wolf was barreling around the turn, his shamshir out, his teeth bared in exertion.

I thrust hard then, my arms and my body pushing the long sword forward as I stepped into the attack, its point aimed at the spot where Wolf's neck met his body.

Wolf's eyes went wide. His foot skidded on the street as he tried to stop. His right hand moved to bring his sword across his body for the parry. Too far. Too slow.

I had him.

Almost.

Against anyone else, it would have worked. The sword would have gone forward, the point would have found his neck, the fight would have been over. But this was Wolf. And more importantly, it was Wolf with a fan in his left hand.

As the long sword thrust forward and Wolf tried to turn his body out of the way, his nearer hand swept up, bringing Ivory's widower's fan along with it. The tapered steel tip that had been heading unerringly for his throat was suddenly caught by the closed laminated stays and pushed off course.

It wasn't a strong parry, and it wasn't a perfect one; but it was enough to redirect the sword from Wolf's neck to his shoulder. Still, the point bit hard enough for me to feel along the blade; struck hard enough for the tip to push cloth and metal aside as it slid through a gap or forced a weak spot in whatever Wolf was wearing and found the flesh beneath.

The degan screamed. He also kept moving, turning away from the blow so that I couldn't drive it home or pin him down. Sweeping his sword around in a vicious arc so that I was forced to draw Ivory's sword back in my own desperate parry, lest I lose my head.

I caught the first blow, missed the second. Wolf, being Wolf, had thrown a combination, likely without thinking about it. Two-hundred-plus years of training meant that as soon his high-line strike encountered resistance, he'd immediately followed with a low-line attack. And hit me.

Fucking degans.

I was still trying to change momentum and redouble into his first attack when I felt the second blow hit and draw a line of fire across my leg, just above the knee. I gasped and staggered back, holding Ivory's sword before me both to defend against another blow as well as discourage Wolf from following. The degan retreated as well, cursing all the while.

I tried to put weight on my bloody leg. It complained and screamed and argued against the idea, but held nonetheless, although not steadily. No running away for me, then.

As for Wolf, his left arm was now hanging limp at his side, a dark blossom of blood already forming at the shoulder. He raised his sword hand toward the wound, then stopped halfway and instead extended the blade toward me.

"You bastard," he said, forcing the words through clenched teeth. Spittle flew out with every breath, flecking his dark beard. "I was going to take the blade, maybe make you pay for running. But now?" His shamshir cut the air, making a whistle that sounded like the air crying out in pain. "Now I show you what the Azaar do to their enemies when they have the time and hatred to spare."

Of a sudden, drawing Wolf away so that Degan couldn't follow didn't seem like such a good idea.

I thought about switching Ivory's sword to my left hand so I could draw my rapier with my right. Even with tingling fingers, a sword I knew how to use had to be better than one I didn't—except I knew I'd be dead before my hand reached the handle. Instead, I centered Ivory's sword and tried to close off as many opportunities as possible.

Wolf advanced on me.

Anyone will tell you that it becomes harder to hit someone when he decides to do nothing but defend himself. Without having to worry about trying to strike the other person, the defensive fighter can concentrate solely on not getting hit. It's not the most practical tactic in the long run—odds are good that an attack will get through eventually; plus, if you're not attacking, you're giving all the momentum of the fight to the other person—but for buying time, it's a wonder.

That is, unless you're fighting a furious degan—then all bets are out the window.

The blows from Wolf's sword fell down like rain. Cuts, thrusts, back-edge slashes, expulsions—it was like trying to ward off a thunderstorm with a tattered cloak: You might manage to catch the early drops, but sooner or later you knew you'd end up soaked to the bone.

The one thing that saved me was Ivory's sword. Its balance, combined with the pure efficiency of its design, allowed me to defy Wolf's attacks with a startling amount of power and speed. Having two hands—well, one and a half—on the handle gave me the strength to stop his hardest cuts, while the long cross guard and straight blade allowed me to push aside the more subtle thrust, if only barely.

Still, I knew it was a losing proposition in the long run. My only hope was to hold out long enough for either a troop of the local watch to wander by, or for Degan to come stumbling across us by sheerest luck. Beyond that, it was down to me waiting for Wolf to make some sort of fatal mistake that allowed me to finish him off.

Yeah, I wasn't holding out for that one either.

When it finally happened, I didn't even see it coming. One moment I was sweeping his blade aside with Ivory's sword like I'd done so many times before, the next Wolf had turned his wrist and used the shamshir's curve to slide around my block and stab me in the shoulder.

Now it was my turn to yell as my right hand dropped away from the long sword's handle. I fought to maintain my grip with the left, but that failed too when Wolf rotated his steel free and then punched me in the face with the cross guard of his sword.

I dropped to the street.

I watched, disturbingly detached, as a filth-covered slipper kicked Ivory's sword away. My left hand pawed distractedly after it, was kicked away in turn. I barely felt it.

Fresh pain sloshed around inside my brain, carving new channels of agony with every motion. I fought it, pushed it, cajoled it—anything to get it to go off and wait its turn with the rest of the miseries vying for my attention. Things to do here, dammit; lives to save. Or, at least, death to greet with some dignity.

The pain must have been paying attention, because it pulled back enough for me to realize someone was speaking through the buzz in my ears. I concentrated. Words formed.

". . . piece of Imperial shit," said Wolf. I was looking up at him without remembering having lifted my head. How had that happened? It wasn't until he shook me by the hair that I figured out he was using it to hold my head up off the ground.

One less mystery in the world, then.

"Good," said Wolf. "I want you to be awake for this." He shoved my head back down to the street—as if I cared at this point—and reached across my back. A moment later, I felt tugging, heard the muffled sigh of steel clearing leather as he drew Degan's sword from the scabbard on my back. Then he stood and took a step back so I could see.

He held Degan's sword loosely in his hand. Casually.

I surprised myself by speaking. "I suppose after using so many other degans' swords," I croaked, "holding one more doesn't feel awkward anymore."

Wolf grimaced. "You've made work for me, Gray Prince. Now I'll have to hunt Bronze down before he returns to the empire. Ah well." He shrugged. "One more step on the road. No matter—it will reach its end soon enough." He slipped a foot under me and rolled me onto my back, extended Degan's sword so that the point hovered over my chest. "I thought it fitting to kill you with his blade, considering . . . everything."

"Why, so you can taunt him with my blood at the end?"

Wolf's face took on a horrified expression. "What? No. Bronze is my sword brother: why would I—?" But whatever he was going to say was interrupted by a puff of yellow powder appearing around his head.

Wolf spun about and dropped into a crouch, Degan's sword lashing out at shadows. The blade cut nothing but air, and the swordsman gasped and coughed inside the quickly settling cloud.

A grayish figure separated itself from a patch of darkness farther down the street, a long, slender tube in her
hands. Wolf wiped at his eyes, snarled, and took a step forward. Aribah, standing ten paces away, didn't move.

My guts lurched inside me, and not just from the blow to
the head. *No,* I thought. *Don't just stand there. He's a degan.
Get the hell away!*

By his third step, Wolf was shaking his head as if trying
to clear it; by the sixth, he was gasping for air. When he
made his ninth, the degan was staggering. But still he came
on. Aribah's eyes grew wide, and she took a hasty step back
of her own.

Degans are hard to kill. Fuck.

Wolf growled. He brought Degan's rapier up, the blade
looking more like mottled mist than steel in the faint light.
For her part, Aribah drew forth a familiar dagger. Shadows
dripped from the shorter weapon's edge.

I tried to push against the ground, tried to get my feet
and hands underneath me. It worked, but not well. I was
barely to my hands and knees when Wolf launched himself
at the *neyajin*.

And died almost instantly.

I expect the poison had a lot to do with it, but still, when
Aribah sidestepped his blow and ran her blade first across
his throat, and then back through his shadow as he fell, it
was nothing short of physical poetry. When Wolf hit the
street, he didn't move, didn't gasp, didn't shudder. He just
lay there, dead.

I was still staring at his body when Aribah knelt by my
side.

"He was a fool," she said as she helped me into a sitting
position up against the wall. Once it was clear I wasn't going
to fall over, she turned her attention to my leg. "You should
never waste time speaking to your target. Once it's time to
kill them, kill them. Delay only makes you vulnerable." She
peeled down the top of my boot, lifted up the edge of my
slops. I winced, surprised that the pain suddenly mattered.
"Fool," she muttered again.

I sat staring as she bent over my leg. Her veil was hanging loose, still untucked from when she'd used the blow tube, showing her in shadowy profile. It suited her.

"Aribah . . ."

"You're fortunate," she said, talking over me. "It doesn't look like he did any serious damage to the knee. The cut's dirty, though. You'll need to get it properly cleaned and sewn once we're done here. In the meantime, I can use some of the dead one's robes to—"

"What are you doing here?"

"I'm *neyajin*." As if that answered everything.

"I know what you are," I said, "but that doesn't answer my question."

"It answers it perfectly." She leaned in, inspecting my shoulder. "You can see in the dark. I can't. If I wish to learn, I need to keep you alive."

"But I already told you . . ."

"Doesn't matter." She produced a knife and began cutting away the buttons that held my doublet closed. "The *neyajin* didn't know how to hide from the djinn in the beginning, but we learned. We figured it out. Just because you don't know how your sight works right now doesn't mean you won't figure it out later." She peeled back the cloth from my shoulder and I gasped at the pain. There was plenty of blood.

"I thought you weren't going to stay in el-Qaddice," I said, trying to distract myself. "That you were going to leave your school behind."

Coolly: "That was before I inherited it."

I winced, and not from her ministrations. "I'm not going to apologize for that," I said.

"Did I ask you to? I was the one who attacked my grandfather first. He was my blood, but what he was doing, what he had planned . . ." She shook her head. "His intentions may have been on the right path, but his actions? I couldn't allow him to take our clan down that road. If you hadn't killed him, it would have been me. There was no other way."

I watched as she walked over to Wolf's body and cut a length of cloth from his robes, then came back. "So you're head of the *neyajin* in el-Qaddice now?" I said as she knelt beside me and began to fold up the fabric.

Her mouth became a tight, thin line. "Not quite. I may be the last of my blood, but I don't have the rank or reputation my grandfather did. I expect some will leave. One or two others may challenge me for leadership of the school."

"Can you take them?"

"One of them? Yes. The other, probably not. But it doesn't matter. I won't be staying."

"But I thought you said—" The rest of my words were cut off by a hiss of pain as Aribah pressed the pad of fabric against my shoulder and closed the doublet back over it.

"What I said I was that I am *neyajin* and that I had inherited my grandfather's school. This is true. But if I stay, the school will fracture and die. Better I take it with me and begin anew somewhere else."

The pain I felt was joined by a sinking feeling inside me. "What 'somewhere else'?" I said.

A self-satisfied smile. "Why, wherever you and your dark sight go, of couse."

"You mean Ildrecca?"

"Is that where you're headed? Then yes, Ildrecca."

"But you can't just—"

Her bloody finger came up, laid itself over my lips. "You've lost a lot of blood and nearly lost your life this night, so I'll be as plain as I can. I need you. I need you alive. Because as long as you're alive, I have a chance of not only redeeming my family's line, but of restoring the *neyajin* through your sight. As I said, my grandfather was right—it's only his method that was wrong. So if that means following you to Ildrecca, then that is where I will go. Not only for my family, but also for me: I still owe you."

I shook my head. "We're even."

"In terms of deaths, yes, but in terms of saving lives? No. You did far more to save mine than simply kill someone, and I will not forget that."

I considered the notion of walking into Ildrecca, a string of Djanese assassins in my wake. Or even just one. Yeah, that would go over well. . . .

But it could be handy.

"Come," said Aríbah. "We've lingered long enough. I need to get you to your people so they can look after you."

"I need the swords," I said, indicating Wolf's body. "And the fan."

Aribah scowled. "Surely you're not in need of money so badly that—"

"No," I said. "It's not like that. I have debts to people, too, and I need those to pay them."

Aribah considered the small collection of swag for a moment, then sighed. As she gathered them up and formed a rough sling from Wolf's sash and robe, I pulled my doublet closed as best I could and forced myself to my feet. My leg burned and my head felt light, but I knew we wouldn't be able to make it if I couldn't walk. Better I get it over with now.

I fumbled two *ahrami* from the pouch around my neck and slipped them into my mouth, ignoring the coppery taste of my own blood that mixed with the smoke of the seeds.

When Aribah came back over, the swords wrapped and slung across her back, the fan in her hand, I was looking up at the pearl-colored sky through the buildings. Dawn was a thing well in progress.

"Any idea how we're going to get across town, let alone through a couple of gates, in this condition?" I said as she slipped her shoulder under mine and her free arm across my back.

"Of course." She smiled. "I am *neyajin*, after all, am I not?"

Chapter Thirty-eight

The door swung back on rusty hinges, sending a high-pitched squeal reverberating through the empty hall and up into the rafters. The noise unsettled the birds nesting there, and I saw several pigeons and what might have been an owl make their exit through the large hole that had claimed a good third of the roof, along with part of an upper wall.

I looked around the dusty, empty space and resisted the urge to sneeze.

"*This* is the Barracks Hall?" I said to Degan.

"What?" he said, pushing the other half of the double doors wide. "Oh, no—this is far older." He stepped back and brushed his hand against his pants, staring past the drifting feathers and slanting morning light, into the past. "This is where the Order of the Degans began."

We were three weeks out of el-Qaddice and somewhere between two and five days east of Ildrecca. I couldn't be certain of the latter because we'd left the coast road days ago, cutting across farmland and pastures and up into the stony hills beyond. We were between the port town of Niceria and the capital city, but if you'd asked me to point to our location on a map, the best I'd be able to do is indicate one of the many spurs of the Aeonian hills that ran beside the sea. What I did know was that this ruin of a fortress likely hadn't been marked on any map for at least two hundred years, and maybe more.

Fowler had continued on to Ildrecca at my instructions. She hadn't been happy about it, but I needed someone to evaluate just how far things had deteriorated in my absence and have a report ready when I returned. Besides, I knew that Degan wanted as few people tagging along to his meeting with the Order as possible. Ideally he would have gone alone, but I still had his sword—he'd refused to take it back even now—although I'd started keeping it in my bedroll rather than wearing it in his presence. There's only so much salt some wounds can take. Even then, I suspect he would have left me behind, but for the fact that I was the one who'd retrieved both Steel's and Ivory's swords, not to mention the laws. Well, "retrieved" if you counted Aribah carrying them, and in the end, me, to the courtyard of the Angel's Shadow before vanishing into the night. I hadn't heard from her since then, but that didn't surprise me: She was *neyajin*, after all.

As for Tobin and his people, they were taking the long, potentially profitable route back. While the play they'd performed might have gotten them expelled from el-Qaddice, that hadn't stopped several rural sheikhs, and even a provincial Beg, from offering to put up the troupe and pay their way in exchange for a series of private performances. As it turned out, there was a not-so-secret audience for banned plays in hinterland, well away from the despotic court. And that it was a bunch of Imperials performing the forbidden art? Well, that made it all the more intriguing. Mama Left Hand had made all the arrangements, for what I was told was only a mildly rapacious cut. I'd been told to expect the troupe back in the Imperial capital come next spring— probably.

All of which meant it had been a pleasantly quiet, and speedy, trip back. Until now.

"I thought you said Lucien created you?" I said as I took a hesitant step into the space. Bare red and gray stone walls rose almost three stories to a peaked ceiling, with high, narrow windows that had long ago lost any hints of glazing marching in narrow formation to either side. Two massive fireplaces stood opposite each other midway along. The one on the right showed signs of recent usage, although the fire that it had held must have been dwarfed by the potential of the space. Bandits using the hall for shelter, maybe, or more likely a lone shepherd. A few sticks of furniture were scattered about, along with the scarred remains of a long trestle table. None looked to have been original to the place. "I'd think the emperor would favor a more . . . resplendent locale. Or at least more convenient."

"You don't create a secret society of warriors in the courtyard of the Lesser Moon Palace," said Degan as he picked up a chair and set it aright. One leg was broken off short, causing it to wobble. "That defeats the whole point of it being secret. Especially if all of the members of said society are known, or at least recognized, around the palace. Better to do it away from the Imperial City, where no one is in the habit of spying or prying."

"So why here?"

"Why not?" Degan shrugged, adjusting the wrapped bundle of swords he carried over his right shoulder. "No one thought to ask, I suppose. We were told to come, and we came. That's what we did back then."

"Unlike now," I said, limping slightly as I entered the hall. Even after a week on my back in the Lower City and regular visits from physickers and Mouths sent by Mama, the wound Wolf had given me still tended to be stiff come morning. I hoped getting home and off the trail would help, but I was beginning to have my doubts on the matter.

"Oh, the Order still listens," said Degan. He patted the bundle. "When the call is loud enough, or the stakes high enough."

"Which they are now, I expect," said a voice from the far end of the room.

Both Degan and I reacted: me by dropping into a crouch, hand on my sword; Degan by turning around and then smiling.

"I was wondering if you'd come early," said Degan.

"Why should I change my habits now?"

A broad, solid woman with wiry hair, dark skin and an easy smile was standing in a small archway off to one side of the hall. She was dressed for the road, but it clearly wasn't

the same road we'd been traveling: not in a beaded and embroidered tunic, kid-lined riding pants, and a travel coat
that looked to be either of finest linen or roughest silk. She
seemed suited more for the estate than the wilderness. The
only thing on her that did look as if it belonged here was the
battered, faded hat she had pushed back on her head, and
even that had been a fine specimen once upon a time. Now
it just looked like an old friend.

"Good to see you again, Bronze," she said as she strode
across the room, her coat flowing along almost as easily as
she did. I spied a tapering triangle of a sword at her side, the
forte of the blade a good six or more fingers wide where it
met the guard. The handle was simple—black wood, with a
rounded pommel—and had a forward-sweeping crescent of
a guard done in deep, honey-yellow metal.

"Brass," said Degan. He turned to face her but didn't
advance. She picked up on this and stopped farther away
than I think she would've liked. Her smile crumbled a bit at
the edges.

"That uncertain, are you?" she said.

"That careful."

Brass regard him. "Probably just as well, for your sake."
She looked at me. "And you are?"

I wanted to say something like, "In over my head," but
instead went with, "Drothe."

Brass cocked an eyebrow. "The Gray Prince?"

I turned to look at Degan. Degan was smirking. "What
can I say?" he said. "You're famous."

Brass laughed. It was an easy, silken thing. "Or infamous.
Copper's had a few choice words to say about you over the
past few months, I can tell you."

Oh.

Degan's voice grew serious. "He's under my protection."

"Fine," said Brass, "but whose protection are you going
to be under? That's the real question." She held up a folded
piece of paper—one of the messages Degan had sent out to
his fellows the moment we'd crossed the border. "This is all
well and good, but you know it'll carry about as much
weight as what it's written on for some of our fellows."

"I know," said Degan. "But I didn't have a choice."

"There's always a choice, Bronze."

Something passed between them in that moment that I couldn't catch, couldn't hope to understand. Something that spoke to two hundred years of fighting and feuding and family. Something I suspected you had to be a degan to understand.

After a moment, Degan nodded and looked away. Brass sighed. Then she pointed at the bundle.

"So you actually got it? Ivory's sword?"

"And the laws."

"And the . . . ?" Brass took a stunned step closer. Her jaw hung slack. "You didn't say anything about the laws, Bronze."

Degan smiled. "Well, I've got to hold something back for the big surprise, don't I?"

"Can I . . . ?"

"Of course." Degan set down the canvas, untied the leather laces, and rolled it open. Brass stared down at the three swords and the broken fan and whispered a prayer.

"Silver and Steel's, too?" she said after a moment.

"Steel's is a long story."

"And Silver's?"

Degan shook his head. I could still see him coming to my room, two nights after I'd woken up in the Lower City, Silver's sword clutched in one hand, other men's blood spattered across his clothing. He hadn't been willing to tell me how he'd tracked down the sword Wolf had worn when I first met him, just that he had.

"I'd rather tell it all at once," he said.

"I understand." Brass knelt down before the weapons and reached out toward Ivory's sword.

"Getting a bit ahead of yourselves, aren't you?" said a voice from the main doorway. We looked up to find three degans standing between the open doors. One I recognized from months ago when I'd been questioned about Degan's disappearance. That was Gold Degan. The second I didn't know.

The third was Copper.

She grinned a dark grin at me. I pretended not to notice.

"There's no harm in looking," said Brass. Still, she stood without laying hands on any of the weapons.

"There's every harm if you let Bronze's offerings to the Order sway you," said Gold as he came forward. He was a trim, compact man who nonetheless seemed to own the room just by stepping into it. Silver-haired, slate-eyed, with a measured way about him, I got the feeling that the last place you'd want to be was across a gaming board from this man. "Don't forget why we're here, sister: Iron and Silver are dead, Steel is missing, and now Ivory's sword conveniently shows up in our fallen brother's hands? You don't gather up that much Oath-bound steel without shedding blood and taking lives." He stopped and looked at Degan. "Do you, brother?"

"I'm not your brother anymore," said Degan, his head dropping low as he stared at Gold from under his eyebrows. "I cast away my sword."

"How convenient for you, then, that we can't examine it. And where might it be?"

I forced myself to continue watching Gold, to not glance past him toward the doors and courtyard and my mule beyond. If he noticed the effort, he didn't show it.

"Safe," said Degan.

"Yes, I'm sure it is." Gold deigned to turn his eyes to me. "Who's the rapier?"

"Drothe," said Copper, stepping up beside him. "You remember: the one who lied to us about Iron?"

"Ah, yes. I didn't recognize him. What are you doing here, thief?"

"He's here at my request," said Degan, stepping in front of me before I could respond. "If it weren't for Drothe, we wouldn't have any of the swords, let alone the laws. He's the one who got them from Steel."

Gold looked truly surprised for the first time. "Him? Are you saying that Steel's dead as well, and that this one killed him?"

"He's here, isn't he?"

"And Steel isn't. Another convenience for you, brother."

Brass took a step forward as well. "Back off, Gold. The tribunal hasn't started yet. We're still waiting on the rest."

"Hm, yes." Gold looked over his shoulder at his two companions, then back at us. "Although I have to wonder if it wouldn't be easier on everyone if we just had the adjudication now? Call it a field court, if you will, and settle things quickly. Save us all some time." He smiled. "A show of hands, perhaps?"

"Or of steel," said Brass, putting her hand on her sword hilt.

The degan beside Copper grinned. "Oh, I don't think you'd want to choose that option, sister," he said, putting his own hand on his weapon. There were white dots set in the ribbon steel that made up the guard, but I couldn't tell what it was. Pearl? Bone? White opals?

"No, you wouldn't," rumbled a voice behind them. "Because once steel comes out in this company, you never know who's going to walk away."

A tower of a man stepped into the hall, tall and wide enough to make the entryway look small. He was dark, with broad features that gave nothing away, and a great sword propped up against his shoulder. He wore a simple brown-and-green-striped tunic and bloused pants, with a head scarf whose pattern looked disturbingly familiar. The sword's cross guard and ring looked to be of plain metal, with chips of something gray in it I couldn't quite make out.

I leaned over to Degan. "Who's the tree?" I whispered.

"Stone," he said. "Steel's brother."

"His . . . ?" I suddenly found it hard to swallow.

"I know what you mean," said Degan. "I've always found him intimidating as well."

"Oh, good. That puts me at ease."

Gold looked from us to Stone, and then smiled. "A fair point, brother. I stand admonished." He gave a brief bow to Stone, then turned to his two companions. "Let's take our ease while we wait for the rest, shall we?"

The three went off to a corner, their heads together.

"I take it that's the opposition," I said.

"Something like that," said Brass. "Gold's been sensitive about degan blood ever since we lost Bone."

"Bone?" I said.

"They were together," said Degan. "Gold took his death hard. He promised to see any degan punished who followed in Ivory's footsteps."

"Meaning you."

"Meaning me now, yes." Degan let out a long sigh. "You should go," he said.

"Like hell."

"You have no standing here. No voice. Better you go before the rest arrive."

"I didn't come all this way just to turn around and leave. I came here—"

"I know why you came," said Degan. "And I appreciate it. But if you stay, the least that will happen is that you get thrown out."

"'The least'?" said Brass. "Come, now, Bronze, I don't think—"

"But I do," snapped Degan. He took my by the arm and pulled me off to the side, away from everyone else. "Go." It was almost a plea.

"Why?"

Degan's eyes raced around the room. He leaned in closer. "Because no one outside the Order is supposed to know what you know. They won't stand for anyone who's not a degan being privy to our internal disagreements, let alone the emperor and the true nature of our service. If Gold or any of the rest realize how much you've found out . . ."

"Are you saying they'll kill me because I know too much?" I said. "That's not exactly a new development for me, you know."

"Maybe, but not like this. Not with them. There won't be any haggling or chatting or debating—they'll just cut you down. It's what we do. The time to go is now, when no one knows where you stand. Get out before things start, so the question remains unanswered."

"And your sword?" I said. "What do I do about that?"

"Take it with you."

"What? But I thought—"

"If they get my sword," hissed Degan, "they can find out you're still beholden to the Order. After everything else, I'd have you free of that—free of them. I took the Oath with you because of who you were, because of who you are, to me. They won't understand that. To them, you'll just be another tool to use, and I won't have that. Take my sword and go."

I looked up at Degan and smiled. It was good to hear what I'd been hoping to hear. Worth all the miles to hear.

Then I shook my head. "I can't do that."

Degan's jaw clenched. "I can't let you stay."

"You can't make me leave."

"Oh?" Degan turned, called to Stone. "Sergeant?"

Stone turned his massive head. "Aye?"

"This man isn't a degan," said Degan. "Escort him out, please."

I jerked my arm away from Degan's grasp. "Like hell," I said.

"Come, now," said Stone. His voice, I noticed, while normal for any other man, sounded small in his mouth. "Don't make me work. The others can tell you I get ornery when I have to work."

I thought about dodging, about running, about trying to stave off the inevitable—but it was a room full of degans, with more on the way. What the hell was I going to do, fight them off?

I sighed and let my shoulders droop. "You're a son of a bitch," I said to Degan.

"And you're welcome," he said as I headed toward the doors, Stone at my back.

Stone escorted me from the hall, down the long passage beyond, out to the entry to the keep. I stopped at the top of the stairs that led down to the main courtyard, blinking in the morning light. Stone stopped beside me.

When he spoke, it was without preamble. "Gold tells me you killed Steel."

I froze.

"Is that true?" he said.

"I . . ."

"Don't lie, boy. I'll know."

Had I? Technically, no: Aribah had performed the final deed, but it hadn't been for lack of trying on my part. If it were up to me, he'd have died on Ivory's sword and not a *neyajin*'s blade. But did it matter? And more important, was I going to quibble now, in the face of Wolf's brother?

"I had a hand in his dying," I said.

"Credit to you for telling the truth, then." Stone grunted and cleared his throat. "I just want you to know, before things begin, that I don't hold grudges when it comes to Wolf. Not anymore."

"If it matters, I didn't—"

"It doesn't." He cleared his throat again. "As much as he tried, I don't think Wolf ever managed to place the Oath before himself. For that reason alone, he stopped being my brother a long time ago." The degan looked down, showing me an uneven set of teeth. "I just thought you should know that."

"Thank you?" I said.

"You're welcome. Now, leave this place before I'm forced to kill you."

Chapter Thirty-nine

I didn't leave, of course—not really. Oh, I climbed aboard my mule and rode away from the fortress, but only until I was certain I was being neither followed nor watched. Then, being careful to avoid any degans that were still arriving, I put on Degan's sword and circled around through the hills until I was able to come at the place from a different direction.

It wasn't easy. The fortress was situated on a bluff overlooking a narrow pass. It had been placed wonderfully in terms of defense, and there was no way I would have been able to approach it with an army even now and stand a chance of taking it against even a dozen degans. But there's a difference between an army and a man on a mule, and besides, no one had been clearing brush or worrying about keeping sight lines open or the place defensible for a long time. It took a while, but I was able to find my mule and me—and then just me—enough goat paths and dried-up washes to make my way up to the wall and then through a gap, well away from the gate and the main courtyard.

I'd been harboring a vague hope of somehow gaining the empty windows or some hole in the hall's wall or roof to gain a view of the goings-on inside, but reality quickly put an end to those dreams. Without climbing gear, there was no way I could get to either, and even then I'd have risked being seen by Stone or another degan in the courtyard. Instead, I spent precious time scouting and skulking about the perimeter of the main building, trying to find a way either through or in. As luck would have it, every door seemed either to be locked or to open on a room or passage that led away from where I wanted to be.

Finally, as I was passing through what might have once been a garden but was now an overgrown tangle, eyeing the side of a crumbling tower that stood almost close enough to the hall for a foolhardy jump, I heard them: voices. Just a trace, mind you, and lost on the wind as quickly as they'd been found, but I had the scent. After a bit of searching and listening, I found the source: a crack the width of my hand in the hall's outer wall, put in place by a seed that had taken root in some fault in the masonry and become a Djanese maple over the years.

The fault didn't run straight, and it narrowed as it went in, but that didn't matter. What I couldn't see I could hear, and that was enough for the moment. I settled in against the rough, reddish brown trunk of the tree and put my ear to the gap.

They were shouting. About what, I couldn't tell, but there were enough voices to make it sound like a hollow buzz through the crack. Eventually, the buzz lessened and I heard Gold's voice rise over the others, forcing them down by its sheer weight of authority.

"While I don't deny the importance of them," said Gold, "I want to remind everyone why we're here today. It isn't to ooh and aah over Ivory's blade and the laws Bronze has brought back to us. That's a noble gesture and an impressive feat to be sure, but their presence doesn't change the fact that we have three swords on the table before us without owners, and one more hanging on the wall back in the Barracks House. If anything, those blades underscore the reason for this tribunal: four deaths in less than twice as many months, and all of them hovering around Bronze. That is why we're here, brothers and sisters. Don't forget that."

"The reason we're here," said Degan, his voice cutting through the air like the arc of a sword, "is because of the chasm that exists within the order. Everything else—the deaths, our lost laws, Ivory's sword and what it holds—can

all be traced back to that. Until we deal with the issue of our
Oaths and how they relate to the emperor and the empire,
what I did or didn't do is minor by comparison."

"How convenient for you," said Gold.

"Convenient or not," said Degan, "it's true."

"Why should we even believe you?" Another voice, one
I didn't recognize. "Why are you even here, if not to buy our
favor and bribe your way back into the fold?"

"Because he's come here to put himself at our mercy, is
why." Brass's silky, easy tones were instantly recognizable.
"Bronze brought back the swords *and* the laws. Who of us
have tried to do one in the last century, let alone both? Who
of us have done anything other than ignore the question
that has plagued us since our founding? Who has settled for
the status quo?"

"I don't dispute that Bronze brought the swords and the
laws home," said Gold, "but at what price? Where is Ivory?
Where is Steel? Without them here, we have nothing but
the word of the man on trial for their deaths."

"You have no cause to lay their deaths at Bronze's feet."
This from a voice that sounded familiar but I couldn't place.
Someone who'd questioned me in Ildrecca about Iron? In
any case, other voices rose in agreement. Still more rose
against.

"I have their steel before me," shouted Gold, his words
smothering the rest like a blanket. "What else do I need?
Which of us would willingly give up their steel and still live?
Oh, excuse me—which of us, save for Bronze?" A few
laughs, but not many. "Are we to believe these swords didn't
come with a cost?"

"Of course they did," answered Brass. "But you can't
simply assume Bronze killed them because he's alive. If so,
why should he even bother to come back? Why not keep
running? Or, if he's the killer you say, why not keep hunting
us? Why call the Order together and stand before us when
he has so many other options?"

"Fear." The word fell from Gold's lips like a weight, and
the hall grew silent. "Fear of being hunted. Fear of being
found. Fear of being judged by the sword rather than by his

deeds. Fear, at last, of infamy. Our brother Bronze returned because he'd found more than he bargained for, more than he knew what to do with. Even an Oath-breaker and a killer can have his limits, and Ivory's blade was Bronze's, I think. When he held the whole of the Order in his hands, it was too much even for him: too much to act on, and too much to risk." A pause. I could almost see Gold turning dramatically to face Degan as he said, "Am I right, brother? Was it fear that brought you back?"

"Yes."

Even out here, I could hear the collective gasp within the hall.

"You're right," continued Degan. "I came back because of fear. But not because I was afraid of being hunted or found or defamed. Not because I feared you or what Ivory's sword represented. I came back because I was afraid for you, for the Order. I did what I did because, after I saw Iron lying on the ground, I knew that the Order was broken and that something needed to change."

"And you would be that change?" said Gold.

"I would be part of it."

"And what kind of change would you bring, brother Bronze? A tide of blood and steel, as you say Steel would have wrought? Or would it come on the edge of Ivory's sword, with the bindings it holds? How would you save us?"

"Neither of those."

"Then what?"

There was a long pause. Finally, when Degan spoke, I had to press my ear to the stone, straining to hear.

"Steel wasn't wrong, at least in part," he began. "I didn't realize that at first, but as I spent time on the road coming back, looking through some of the other books I took from Ivory's library, I began to see his point. And Ivory's."

A murmur through the crack that I couldn't gauge. After a moment, it faded and Degan's voice slid through again.

"When you start something," said Degan, "you have a picture in your head of how it will be. You build that image in your mind and you hold on to it, hard, because that's your guide. But once that thing starts to become a reality, once you actually start to bring it into being, you realize it will never be that thing you saw in your dreams. You begin to see the flaws and the failures, the shortcomings and the mistakes; and try as you might, you can't reconcile it all. Try as you might, the reality never shines as bright as its potential. It becomes disheartening. This perfect thing, you suddenly realize, will never be—can never be. Not as you dreamed it when you first began.

"I think that's what happened to Ivory, and to a lesser extent, to Steel. It's what I think has haunted this Order from the beginning. We aren't what we dreamed, and emperor or not, we never will be. But that doesn't mean the dream has to go away. The thing we made is still here, waiting.

"There are flaws in this Order, yes. They've been here since the beginning. In that sense, Steel was right—we need to start anew. But not with blood, and not with death. He would have torn us down past the foundations, started from scratch—but that ignores everything we've done up to now. Everything we've done right.

"The main question for the Order is what to do about our Oath to preserve the empire. Wolf would have used the Oaths in Ivory's sword to bind the emperor to us, to force him to redefine our service and our purpose. To make us what we were before the Oath. But we are all of us more than the White Sashes we once were." Sounds of agreement.

"Wolf's mistake," said Degan, "was thinking he could force us onto what he saw as the honorable path. But you can't force someone to be honorable, just as you can't buy it with a promise."

"And so what would you have us do?" This from Gold, not quite mocking, but not quite conciliatory, either. "Would you call on the emperor to decide? Would you use Ivory's sword and the laws to push us one way or the other? Be our arbiter and guide on whichever road you choose to redemption?"

"No. I'd choose a third path."

"And what is that?"

Silence. Even the wind in the maple above me seemed to pause, waiting for the answer.

"I don't know," Degan finally said. "But I—" But his words were drowned out by the shouting that erupted within the hall.

It didn't sound like the answer they were hoping for.

After more yelling and what sounded like someone pounding on a table with the pommel of a sword, the room was called back into a semblance of order.

"Well, this is enthralling," said Gold after things had settled, "but it still doesn't get us any closer to a solution for the matter at hand."

"And neither do your questions," said Brass, nearly shouting. Her voice had the taint of desperation now, making me wonder what the mood was in the room. As used as I was to eavesdropping from my years as a Nose, it still didn't help with the frustration I was feeling right now. Damn this crack for not being a window, anyhow. "Do you merely plan to cast aspersions on everything Bronze says?" said Brass. "Is that your plan? To color his every deed with doubt? Because if so, I'd remind everyone here that this is Bronze Degan we're talking about. This is the man who—"

"We all know what he's done," said Gold sourly. "And yes, since you ask, it is my intention to doubt everything about him precisely for the reasons you say: This is Bronze Degan. And because of that, we can offer him no quarter. He'd expect no less, am I right?" A majority of the room seemed to agree. "Our respect and admiration isn't sufficient reason to pardon him, let alone welcome him back with open arms."

"Then what would you have him do?" said Brass, her patience clearly gone. "Would you have him summon up Steel or Silver and ask them how he came by their swords? Would you ask Ivory what Bronze did to get his hands on the sword and the laws? Because if it's a village shaman you want, Gold, I can be back with one in two hours' time."

Scattered laughter, but not enough. Not near enough. Brass and Degan were losing.

"I appreciate the offer," said Gold, "but I think I have an easier way."

"And what's that?" said Degan.

"I would have you answer a simple question," said Gold. "One that cuts straight to the heart of the matter, and that speaks to everything that comes after. Nothing about Steel or the laws of Ivory—just one simple question."

"Again, what's that?" said Degan.

"Did you kill Iron Degan?"

Crap.

I was away from the tree and running in an instant. I didn't need to have my ear to the crack to know what Degan's answer would be, didn't have to be paying attention to hear the roar that came tumbling out the hall's windows as I raced through the garden and around toward the main doors, Degan's blade slapping against my back.

Of course Degan had answered honestly. Of course he said yes, because that's who he was.

And, damn Gold, of course he'd phrased the question in a way that didn't allow Degan to explain the circumstances, or the fact that by fighting Iron he'd actually been keeping his Oath to me and, he thought, to the emperor. All the roomful of degans in there knew was that Bronze Degan had just admitted to killing one of their own. And, like him or not, there was only one response for that.

Unless I could get in there and somehow make them listen to me. Or at least get Degan his sword, so he might have a chance. Either way, I wasn't going to sit by and let everything come crashing down on his head.

I sprinted through the courtyard, my wounded leg complaining every other stride, and took the steps two at a time. Through the doors, down the passageway, and then around the turn to the entrance to the main hall.

Where Stone Degan stood, his sword in his hand.

I skidded to a halt maybe six paces from the degan. Fortunately for me, he hadn't lowered the point of his weapon, otherwise I'd have been hanging off it like a piece of meat ready for the grilling.

As it was, the degan widened his stance slightly and gripped his blade at the half-sword, one hand midway up the blade, the other still on the handle, ready for the close fight.

"You're supposed to be gone," he said.

"I need to get in there."

Stone glanced over his shoulder. The doors hadn't been shut all the way. Whether this was because they couldn't be, or simply because he'd wanted to listen, I didn't know—all I did know was that I could hear shouting still coming from the other side.

"No," he said.

"They're going to kill him."

Stone nodded. "Probably."

"I can't let that happen."

"And I can't let you in."

I opened my fists, closed them. Stone stood waiting, doing a good imitation of his namesake.

Beyond him, I head the shouting subside, caught Degan's voice rising above the din. "By my Oath," he began, but was drowned out by Gold.

"By your Oath?"shouted the other degan. "By *your Oath*? You mean the thing you broke when you drew steel on Iron? When you killed him? The thing you threw away when you tossed your soul and your sword in the dust? And now you want us to hear you swear on your Oath?"

I reached up over my shoulder and drew Degan's sword. Stone lowered his stance and growled.

"No!" I said, quickly switching it so I held the blade at the forte, below the guard. "Look. I need to get in there. To bring this to him."

Stone's eyes went wide, but his stance stayed deep. "Where did you get that?"

Gold was still going at it on the other side of the door. "You threw away this Order when you threw away your blade," he said. "You cast away your honor with your steel."

There were ominous grumbles and shouts of agreement.

"Where the hell do you think I got it?" I said, trying to peer around the degan. "He gave it to me."

"Bronze?"

"No, the fucking emperor. Of course Bronze!"

I could hear Brass trying to say something, trying to come across as calm. No one seemed to be having any of it.

Stone lowered his sword a bit. "Why? Why give it to you instead of bringing it before the rest of us? It could only help him in there."

I thought about what Degan had told me, about what it would mean if his fellows found out I was under Oath to him, let alone what I knew about the Order of the Degans. About how there might not even be time to say, "Wait" before the sword fell.

I thought about it all, and then threw it away.

"He gave it to me because it holds my Oath to him, dammit, and because I know all about your Order's dance over the emperor." I swallowed and held the sword out farther. "He gave it to me because he didn't want the rest of you to know I was yours for the asking."

Stone blinked.

I could hear Gold clearly now, addressing the room as only a man can when he knows he owns it, body and soul. "Can we trust the word of any man—even Bronze Degan— when he's willing to cast so much and so many aside? When he's already stained his honor so?"

I held my breath as Stone reached out and ran a finger lightly along the flat of Degan's blade. As he looked up and met my eyes.

"It doesn't matter if he killed Silver or not," said Gold. "Or if Steel did the things he claims. I don't care if Ivory gave Bronze his sword with a smile on his face and a song in his heart. None of those things matter.

"What matters is that Bronze killed Iron. Not for the Order, not for Ivory, not even to rescue the laws—but for the simple fact that Iron stood with the empire, and Bronze stood with the emperor. Everything else came later. In the end, he killed Iron because—"

"Because," I said as I pushed open the doors and strode into the hall, Degan's sword held above my head and Stone Degan at my back, "he was under Oath to me, and the only way for him to keep that Oath was to fight Iron." I walked across the room and up to Gold and stared straight into his cold gray eyes. "Bronze fought Iron because it was the best and only way for him not just to honor his agreement with me, but to protect the empire as he saw it. He did it to honor his Oath, not betray it. And I repaid him by clicking him from behind and taking Iron's sword. So if you want to talk to anyone about breaking their Oath, you should be talking to me, because Bronze has done nothing but honor his from start to finish—including letting you walk all over him so I wouldn't have to face you." I lowered my arm and shoved Degan's blade and scabbard up against Gold's chest. "Now give the man back his fucking sword and let's you and me settle our business." I was sitting outside on the steps to the courtyard, nursing the fresh bruise along my jaw, when Gold Degan came storming out of the keep. He stopped long enough to glare at me, then took a turn staring at Stone and Crystal Degan, who were standing guard over me. They stared back.

Everyone having gotten their share of eye contact in, Gold stalked off down the steps, Opal Degan close on his heels. Copper was nowhere in sight.

Well, so much for my making any new friends today.

I took that as a good sign.

I turned my attention back to my jaw and watched the entrance for any more signs of life.

The tribunal had gone to hell after Gold's fist had connected with my jaw. Voices had been raised, hands had slapped hilts, and Degan had stepped forward, ready to both defend me and to try and clarify the twists I'd put in my story about him and his Oath. He never got the chance to do either. Before I knew it, Brass and a degan I later came to know as Lead had pulled me and Degan's sword aside and put their heads together over the blade, while Stone had made it clear that anyone who came after Degan *or* me would have him to answer to. After a bit more muttering and steel touching in the corner, it was announced to the assembly that yes, indeed, I was under Oath, and no, it had not yet been honored.

A situation that was quickly put to right, at least to a small degree, by my ass being sat down in a rickety chair and me being compelled via Oath to tell the assembled—what? Onslaught? Revenge? I still didn't know what to call a gathering of them—degans what had happened with Iron, and then later with Wolf and Ivory.

The story hadn't pleased anyone. In fact, there seemed to be bits for almost everyone to dislike, but that hadn't stopped the assembled swordsmen and -women from deciding that while they still needed to sit in judgment of Degan, they now had to do it in a different light. Another round of questions later I was thanked, dismissed, and escorted once more out to the courtyard, where I was amazed to find the sun not even halfway down toward the western horizon. This time, though, they made sure to keep a guard on me at all times while the Order conducted their business.

Now I sat and watched as degans dribbled out in pairs and groups. All told, I guessed there was less than two score of them, although Stone had told me that at least four hadn't shown up. In the past the assumption was that they either were too far away to make it back in time or had Oath-related business to tend to, but with the rash of bodies of late, I got the impression that some members were being reminded of what it was like to truly worry about a brother's or a sister's absence. Degans, as Ivory had said, were hard to kill, but the difference between "hard" and "impossible" was being served up as a hard reminder.

Finally, Degan stepped out into the light, his sword hanging at his side. Brass was with him. When she saw me stand to meet them, she grinned and let out a chuckle.

"I'll say this: You sure know how to make an entrance, Kin."

"I've been spending more time than I like to admit around actors lately," I said. "You pick things up."

"Well, you picked them up well." Brass turned to Degan. "I'm sorry I wasn't more help in there."

"You stood your ground like a degan," he said, "and against Gold's onslaught, too. That's no small feat. I couldn't have asked more of anyone."

Brass tilted her head to the side and put a hand on Degan's cheek. "Ah, that's sweet of you to say so, but we both know you're full of shit. I needed a Kin to kick down the door and save your ass when I couldn't do it. That's a failure in my book."

"Maybe," said Degan, "but I still consider us even for Yrenstone."

"Oh, hell yes," said Brass. "I'm not about to let you hold that over me any longer. Seventy years is long enough." She turned to me. "It's been a pleasure, Rapier. I look forward to our paths crossing again."

She turned and glided away down the steps, her feet touching but not quite seeming to land on the ground. Stone gave me a wink as well and lumbered away. Crystal simply turned and left.

"So," I said, turning back to Degan and eyeing his sword, "I take it you're back in?"

"In a manner of speaking."

"What is that supposed to mean?"

"It means that while the Order decided I violated my Oath when I fought and killed Iron, they also realize that, with the actual laws before them for the first time in two-hundred-plus years, there might be extenuating circumstances they've forgotten about up to now."

"Meaning?"

"Meaning they're going to hold off closing the tribunal until they've had a chance to study what I . . . what we brought back."

"In other words," I said, "they may never get around to deciding to hold you to account."

"Oh, they'll decide," said Degan. "I'll make sure of that. I won't let Iron's death linger over me or the Order. He deserves better than that."

Just like Degan to not take the easy out. Still, what did I expect?

I sat back down on the steps. Degan joined me. More degans were coming out of the keep now, some talking in small groups, others heading for the stables. A few were clearly lingering off to one side or another, waiting on Degan. He nodded to them but didn't seem in a hurry to go catch up. I noted and appreciated that.

"And in the meantime?" I said.

"In the meantime, we've decided we need to figure out what to do with Ivory's sword and the laws. When he first left, no one much worried about the Oaths we'd all sworn on it; then later, it seemed as if he and the blade had both vanished. But now, with it back, we need to decide just how we want to deal with the bindings it contains. In the right hands, that blade could bring the entire Order to its knees, at least for the short term."

"Can you break the Oaths that were sworn on it? Make them, I don't know, go away?"

"I don't know," said Degan. "Nor am I sure if we'd want to."

"What? Why the hell not?"

"Because we're used to being bound," said Degan. "Think: We've been swearing Oaths since our founding, attaching ourselves to people and causes, one after the other. I don't think we want to stop that—it's too much a part of who we are."

"And the emperor's Oath?" I said.

Degan leaned forward and picked up a few pieces of loose gravel, began tossing them down the steps. "That's going to be harder. We're still split over what our Oath means, but having the sword and the laws at least gives us the opportunity to try and settle the question—or maybe recast it."

"You have a plan?"

"I'm sure several people have plans, or at least the beginnings of them, at this point."

"Meaning Gold?" I said.

"Probably Gold, but others, too."

"You worried?"

"Right now I'm too busy enjoying breathing to worry. Ask me again in a week."

I chuckled. So did Degan.

"But you do have a plan?" I said after a moment.

Degan sighed and eyed me sidelong. Finally, he relented.

"I wasn't joking when I said Steel was right," he said. "We need to rethink what and who we serve, and how we do it. All of us being bound to one person, be it the emperor or a sheikh of the degans, isn't the answer. The last two centuries have shown us that. We're just not sure where to go yet. Me, I'm going to give some more thought to Steel's idea of us treating one another more like a tribe or a clan, and less like a sworn brotherhood. There's a, I don't know, pomposity to what we have right now that makes it easy to keep one another at arm's distance. After two hundred years, you'd think we'd be able to be frank with one another, but it happens less than you think."

I chuckled and shook my head.

"What?" said Degan.

"Only you would think a bunch of immortal swordsmen being more open with one another is a good idea."

"We're not immortal," said Degan, "just long-lived."

"Oh, well, that makes all the difference, then."

He smiled and cast more gravel at the ground. "Maybe you're right. But we have to try something different than what we've been doing."

"At least you don't have to worry about growing old while you debate the topic."

"There is that." Degan brushed his hands together. "Thank you, by the way."

"For what?"

"For not listening to me, for one thing."

"Oh, that. I've had a lot of practice at it. Not a problem."

"And for coming back and taking the risk."

"You risked far more for me than I could ever hope to do in return," I said. "It's the least I could do."

Degan rubbed at his bottom lip. "So what about you?"

"What about me?"

"Well, assuming it's still standing, you've saved your organization, not to mention put yourself in a position to start taking shipments of glimmer from el-Qaddice. Seems to me like you're in a sweet spot, wet-behind-the-ears Gray Prince or not. What's next?"

It was my turn to pick up a handful of small stones and throw them at nothing in particular. "I've been thinking about that as well," I said. "Both on the road and while I was waiting just now."

"And?"

"And I think I'm done."

"With what?"

"Being a Gray Prince."

"What?"

"If going to Djan taught me anything, it's that I'm a crap prince. I don't think like one, don't plan like one, and certainly don't act like one. I'm street, down to the bone. It's what I do." It was stupid that it had taken nearly getting dusted in a foreign city to realize it: I was a better Nose than I was a Gray Prince. I always would be. No matter how many years I spent at it, I knew deep down that my first instinct would be to scrounge the whispers and mumbles, not make them. I could direct Ears and spread rumors now and then, but to coordinate dodges and manipulate gangs, not just in Ildrecca but eventually across the empire? That wasn't me—not on the scale I needed it to be. "Nosing is what I do and where I belong."

It felt good to say it. Free.

"What about your people?" said Degan. "Your organization?"

"What organization?" I said. "I have a bunch of Noses, some Cutters, and a few smugglers right now, along with an Upright Man who doesn't know better, Angels bless him. They'd all of them be better off under someone who knew how to watch out for them—Kells, say, if he wants the title. Or Solitude. That, or they can head out on their own. I've been nothing but a target on people's backs since I got handed the title."

"And Fowler?"

"Hell, she might just break down and kiss me, it'd make her job so much easier."

"I think you underestimate her."

"Habitually."

Degan pushed his hat back on his head and ran a palm across his brow. "Drothe, you can't just walk away from being a Gray Prince."

"Sure I can," I said, sounding leagues more confident than I felt. "I walked into it, I'll walk back out. Oh, it'll take some planning and a few deals and rumors, but I've been a prince for such a short time, I expect everyone will have forgotten me within six months. The trick will just be staying alive and out of sight until them."

Could I do it? Would it be possible, let alone that simple? I wasn't sure—certainly, no one had done it before that I was aware of. Then again, no one had made the jump from street operator to prince like I had, either. A big step up can mean a big fall down, but if you were planning the fall? If you turned it into just as big a step as the one you'd made on the way up?

Angels knew it was better to try than to wait for more coves to pile up in the street because of my bad decisions.

"That's not what I mean," said Degan, his voice becoming tight. "You can't quit. It's—"

"Dangerous, I know," I said. "But if I plan it out and think it through; if I make sure the other princes have no reason to—"

"Stop," said Degan. "You're not listening."

I shifted to face him. "Fine. I'm listening. Tell me why I can't quit, O wise degan."

Degan met my eyes, then looked away. "Because I won't let you."

I smiled. "This isn't a room full of degans. You can't just—"

"And the Order won't let you, either."

"The Order? What the hell do they care . . . ?" I let the sentence trail off as a cold, hard ball of premonition began to form in my stomach.

"We've already started talking about what we want to accomplish," said Degan. "How we want to serve the Empire. You have to understand that we've built up an impressive collection of debts and favors over the years. Some, like yours, are recent, but there are others that go back a century or more and are still waiting to be called in. Banks, merchants, guilds, families—it's a tapestry of Oaths, all woven together, with the Order at its center."

The ball had solidified now and was beginning to work its way up toward my mouth. I tried to swallow it back down, to banish the dread it was bringing with it, but I couldn't—just as I couldn't take my eyes off Degan even as he refused to meet mine.

"Before today, we were saving those promises for the day we needed them to serve the emperor. But now, with us looking at alternatives? With us beginning to think about breaking that first bond? Well, we're going to need those debts, those Oaths, among the bankers and guild masters and high and low families."

No . . .

"And among the Kin."

"No." The ball had finally reached my tongue, had pushed itself up and out past my lips, into the world. "You can't be telling me this. Not now. Not after all this. Not after what we just went through, after what we just did."

Degan turned his face back to mine, met my burning eyes with his ravaged blue ones. "I'm a degan again, Drothe," he said. "You helped see to that."

"You can't. Not after all this, damn you. You can't."

Degan stood up slowly—almost as slowly as you'd expect a two-hundred-and-forty-two-year-old man to stand—and looked down at me. "Drothepholous Pasikrates, I call in your Oath. I, and my Order, would have you remain a Gray Prince." Degan paused a moment, then added, "And help us preserve the empire."

Son of a bitch.

Epilogue

The door swung open and hit the wall behind it with a satisfying *thunk*. On the other side of the room, a tall man with a gray beard and a shock of white hair looked up from his desk and cleared a dagger in one smooth motion. The man who'd been sitting in front of him did even better. The door hadn't even bounced off the wall before he was out of his seat, blade in his hand, eyes on the doorway.

He was good. But then, that's what bodyguards were for.

Me, I just stood in the entry and smiled.

"Hello, Longreach," I said.

"Alley Walker," he said. "I'd heard you were back. Didn't think you were that dumb."

"Please," I said, stepping into the room. "It's just Drothe. I don't go in for the street names."

The bodyguard looked at his boss, who in turn looked at me. Longreach then looked toward the doorway.

"They're fine," I said.

"Who?"

"The guards you're wondering about."

My fellow Gray Prince gave his man a nod. The man moved toward me.

"You hire that Djanese Mouth again, is that it?" said Longreach, inching around his desk. "Have him glimmer my people down?" He shook his head. "Not a good idea, Alley . . . Drothe. From what I hear, you haven't been back in Ildrecca long enough to take a shit, let alone collect your people. Bad time to risk a war"

"I've been back three weeks," I said. "Even on a straight diet of cheese and wheat, I don't take that long."

Longreach smiled. "Funny. But you're not in a position to be making jokes."

"Neither are you." I nodded, and a bit of the shadows stepped forward and laid a blade across the Gray Prince's throat.

"Breathe too heavily," said Aribah in Djanese, "and I'll take the wind from your lungs."

"She says she thinks there's a draft in here," I said.

The bodyguard spun around, then turned back to me.

"Tricky one, isn't it?" I said. "Who to stab first? Let's see if this helps you make up your mind."

The bodyguard's eyes went wide as I moved to the side and Brass and Garnet and Degan stepped through the doorway. When his sword dropped to the floor a moment later, I wasn't sure if it was due to choice or shock.

I strolled into the room. "Good choice."

"So they were right," said Longreach, his voice tight as he tried to watch me and talk without actually moving. "Crook Eye was just the first move: you're trying to cut us all down." He spit. "Fucking street trash."

"And proud of it." I stopped before the bodyguard and looked up at him. He quickly sidled out of the way. I sat down in his chair. "But that's not why I'm here."

"Oh? Well, if it's not to start a war, then you better kill me, because that's what you've got the moment you walk out of here."

"It's to get your attention," I said. I scooted the chair forward until it was close enough for my feet to reach the desk, then sat back and set my heels on his papers. "As you may know, I did a bit of traveling of late. See the world, expand your horizons. All that crap. But aside from a few interesting new friends I picked up on the way . . ." I paused to nod to Aribah, who sniffed in turn. "I did manage to learn a few things."

"Who thought something like you could learn anything?"

"Imagine my surprise as well. Try to keep a djinn from burning out your insides, and you end up becoming a better person. Who knew? But the point is, I found out something very interesting about people and survival and respect. Turns out if you have people who are similar to one another, how they treat each other is how others eventually treat them as well. Take cordwainers: If you have three cordwainers living on the same street and they all spend half their time making shoes and the other half berating their fellows, not only do you end up with fewer shoes, but you have fewer people willing to buy the shoes because all they hear is how terrible each man's work is. By attempting to build themselves up at the expense of the other—"

"Is this a fucking *joke*?" gasped Longreach. "You're talking about trade guilds, you idiot. It's what they use to keep the fucking cordwainers and cobblers and whatever else you want to name from fucking over the whole industry. They've been around for centuries—it's not a fucking revelation."

"Ah, good: You've heard of them. That saves us time."

"What?"

"What I'm thinking of," I said, leaning back slightly in the chair, "is something like that for us. The Gray Princes. Only not so involved, and not so . . . structured. More of a council." I looked past him to the *neyajin*. "A tribal council, if you will."

Her eyes smiled back.

"What?" said Longreach again. "You want to . . . what?"

I sighed and looked back at Degan. He shrugged, as if to say, "I told you so."

And here we'd thought Longreach would be the easiest one to persuade.

I turned back around.

"All right," I said, "let's try this: What do you know about Djanese assassin schools . . . ?"

ALSO AVAILABLE FROM

Douglas Hulick

AMONG THIEVES
A Tale of the Kin

Drothe has been a member of the Kin for years, rubbing
elbows with thieves and murderers in the employ of a
crime lord while smuggling relics on the side. But when
an ancient book falls into his hands, Drothe finds
himself in possession of a relic capable of bringing
down emperors—a relic everyone in the underworld
would kill to obtain.

"A mind-blowingly good read."
—Fantasy Fiction

Available wherever books are sold or at
penguin.com

facebook.com/acerocbooks